PRAISE FOR SAM CARRINGTON

'Sam Carrington has done it again. *One Little Lie* is a twisty, gripping read. I loved it.'
Cass Green, bestselling author of *In a Cottage In a Wood*

'Expertly written . . . with plentiful twists and unforgettable characters. An insightful and unnerving read.'
Caroline Mitchell, bestselling author of *Silent Victim*

'A kick-ass page turner . . . I was knocked senseless by the awesome twist.'
John Marrs, #1 bestselling author of *The One*

'I LOVED *Bad Sister*. Tense, convincing and complex, it kept me guessing (wrongly!)'
Caz Frear, bestselling author of *Sweet Little Lies*

'This book is not only gripping, but it explores the mother/daughter relationship perfectly, and ends with a gasp-out-loud twist'
Closer

'I devoured this story in one sitting!'
Louise Jensen, bestselling author of *The Sister*

'How do you support victims of crime when you live with unresolved mysteries of your own? Psychologist Connie Summers is a fascinatingly flesh-and-blood guide through this twisty thriller.'
Louise Candlish, *Sunday Times* bestselling

'Keeps you guessing right to the end'
Sue Fortin, author of *Schoolgirl Missing*

'I read *One Little Lie* in one greedy gulp. A compelling thriller about the dark side of maternal instinct and love – I couldn't put it down!'
Isabel Ashdown, author of *Beautiful Liars*

'A gripping read which moved at a head-spinning pace . . . I simply couldn't put this book down until I reached the dramatic and devastating conclusion'
Claire Allan, *USA Today* bestselling author of
Her Name Was Rose

'I was fascinated by the cleverly written threads linking the psychologist, police, criminal and victim. Utterly original and thought provoking . . . This cries out to be made into a TV series.'
Amanda Robson, *Sunday Times* bestselling author of *Guilt*

'Engrossing psychological suspense about the effect of a murder on the mother of a teenage killer. Sam Carrington had me hooked!'
Emma Curtis, bestselling author of *One Little Mistake*

Sam Carrington lives in Devon with her husband and three children. She worked for the NHS for 15 years, during which time she qualified as a nurse. Following the completion of a psychology degree she went to work for the prison service as an Offending Behaviour Programme Facilitator. Her experiences within this field inspired her writing. She left the service to spend time with her family and to follow her dream of being a novelist.

Readers can find out more at http://www.samcarrington. blogspot.co.uk and can follow Sam on Twitter @sam_carrington1

I DARE YOU

SAM CARRINGTON

avon.

Published by AVON
A division of HarperCollins*Publishers* Ltd
1 London Bridge Street
London SE1 9GF

www.harpercollins.co.uk

A Paperback Original 2019

First published in Great Britain by HarperCollins*Publishers* 2019

A catalogue copy of this book is available from the British Library.

ISBN: 978-0-00-833137-5

Typeset in Minion by Palimpsest Book Production Limited, Falkirk, Stirlingshire

Printed and bound in UK by CPI Group (UK) Ltd, Croydon CR0 4YY

For Doug
Chill out. You'll live longer.

Ginger, Ginger broke a winder
Hit the winder – crack!
The baker came out to give 'im a clout
And landed on his back

— 19th-century British nursery rhyme which is believed
to have given rise to the childhood prank game
Knock, Knock, Ginger (also known as *Knock Down,*
Ginger and other regional variations)

Prologue

1989

'Go on, Bella – do it now!' the girl hissed. She slapped both hands over her mouth to prevent her near-hysterical laughter carrying across the man's garden and alerting him to their presence.

Bella whipped her head around, her golden hair sweeping across her back like a closing curtain, and looked at her friend. 'I don't *want* to.' Her voice was a broken whisper as tears threatened.

'Don't be a baby all your life. It's just a silly game. He can't even see you, I promise.' The girl dared to edge out slightly from her hiding place behind the metal dustbin at the front of the garden, out of direct eye-line of the kitchen window.

The one *he* was at.

Bella followed her friend's gaze. The man, his upper body filling the frame, stared out – his eyes like black slits, lost beneath bushy eyebrows.

The girl shrank down lower still. Bella knew her friend didn't want to be the one caught out. She'd done her dare yesterday and succeeded. It was Bella's turn now.

'This is a stupid game,' Bella said, moving forwards, her shoulders slumped, until she reached the bungalow. She pushed herself flat against the wall; the hard-stippled surface dug into the backs of her bare legs. She stood stock-still – only her eyes moved as she sought out her friend. She glared at her, silently begging to be let off the dare.

'*Creepy Cawley, Creepy Cawley,*' the other girl chanted, her tone hushed but loud enough to send chills down Bella's spine; her legs began to shake, her fear visible. She wished she'd worn her corduroy trousers now, not the stupid cotton shorts again. *It's just a game, no need to be scared.* But, despite trying to calm herself, her mum's words of warning rang in her ears: *You must never go near Mr Cawley. Ever. Do you understand?* She'd said the police had been called lots of times because of kids trespassing on his property, annoying him. *Terrorising him.* Those were the words her mum had used. Bella closed her eyes tight, remembering how her mum had put one hand on her hip, holding the finger of her other hand out, wagging it like a metronome as she spoke in a stern voice: 'It's important you listen, Bella. To every word I say.'

Her mum said that one day someone would get hurt.

Bella didn't want that day to be today, or for her to be the someone getting hurt.

'You're almost there! Go on!'

'*But it's not nice.*' Bella's voice susurrated through her gritted teeth.

'Don't be a chicken. I won't play with you anymore if you don't do it.'

Bella's eyes, glassy with tears, travelled to the door. It was only a few feet away. But it seemed like the longest journey she would ever make.

Taking a deep breath, she lunged and ran, crashing against the door accidentally as her legs turned to jelly. In her fright, she almost bolted without completing the dare, but with her friend's high-pitched screech hurtling across the garden, shouting, 'Knock on the door, idiot!' Bella did as she was told.

2

Two hard knocks later, her knuckles stinging, she was done.

The two girls ran – squealing with a mixture of exhilaration and terror – out of Creepy Cawley's garden, out of the cul-de-sac and into the road leading back to their street.

Billy Cawley smiled as he watched their retreat.

They'd be back.

And next time he'd be ready.

Next time, he'd live up to his nickname and give them a real reason to scream.

Chapter One

2019

Anna

Friday 12th July

Anna replaced the receiver, forcibly tucked her hair behind her ears, and walked out of the secretary's office without conversation. It wasn't the first time her mother had phoned her at work, but it was one of the more worrying calls. She was determined not to pander to her, though – she'd responded to Muriel's demands to leave right away by pointing out she had a responsibility for the children and it was only another hour until the bell. Then she would begin the journey down to Mapledon.

To the house where she grew up.

The one she'd longed to leave way before she had the means to do so.

'Mrs Denver, Charlie is throwing the papier-mâché gloop everywhere!'

The shrill whine of the child brought Anna out of her thoughts.

'He is going to have to clear up the mess he's made, then, isn't he?' She placed her hand on the seven-year-old's shoulders and guided her back to the classroom. Leaving her class unattended, even for a matter of minutes, was never a good idea

– and especially on the final day of the term when all the children were hyped up ready for the summer break. 'A spirited bunch' was how the head teacher described them. Anna, whilst agreeing, also thought a few of them were just plain naughty. She'd never have allowed Carrie to act up like that – she expected more from her daughter – whether as a result of teaching other people's children and witnessing their sometimes unruly behaviour, or as a result of her own strict upbringing, she couldn't ascertain. It was a case of the chicken or the egg.

Having finally paired all the children with their respective adults, Anna flitted around the classroom clearing away the activities, tutting at the globs of slushy, sticky newspaper remnants now clinging to the tables like shit to a blanket. As she picked at some of the hardened paper, Muriel's words played out in her head.

Something's wrong, Anna. Something is very wrong.

Anna had sighed at her mother's words, wondering what melodrama was about to unfold. But her gut had twisted as Muriel carried on with her story.

Now, washing and drying her hands with the small, rough towel, Anna decided she'd have to ring James and get him to have Carrie for the night despite it not being his turn. The journey to Mapledon would only take two hours or so from Bristol, but she didn't want to take Carrie there – didn't want her dragged into whatever was going on. If anything. Her mother *could* be over-reacting. When Anna was growing up that'd been her MO – even before Anna's father had left and then more so when old-age shenanigans took over. But just in case, it would be better to go alone.

Grabbing her bag, she shouted goodbye to the remaining teachers, swept out of the building and climbed into her car. Her blue Escort spluttered into life and she drove out of the school gate. With a sick feeling in the pit of her stomach, she turned right, joining the traffic that would take her to the M5.

Her mother's words continued to repeat themselves inside her mind as she drove:

There was such a racket at the front of the house, it scared me half to death. When I mustered the courage to go out there, I found it.

Found what, Mum?

The doll's head. Hammered to my front door.

Chapter Two

2019

Lizzie

The envelope, its corner peeping out from within the clump of mail she'd shoved behind the purple key pot – the one neither of them actually used for their keys, preferring instead to spend stressful minutes searching for the last place they'd flung them – glared at her like an accusation. Lizzie snatched it up, then slammed it down on the counter, taking a step back as though it were a dangerous object about to inflict harm.

Something told her it *would* do her harm. Its content, anyway. Mentally, not physically. She knew physical pain, had endured years of it growing up in various care homes. She could cope with that; was hardened to it. Her mental well-being had never caught up, though. That was still fragile, like butterfly wings – delicate, prone to breaking. She had to guard herself from outside factors.

Guard herself from the words the envelope held within.

She'd ignored it for as long as possible. Hidden it from Dom. Tried to forget about it. She should've ripped it up and binned it. Why hadn't she? Sleep had been impossible, her thoughts, her imagination, keeping her awake hour after hour. She knew this had to be done.

Taking the envelope once again, she stared at the postmark. At the logo. It was definitely from the solicitor.

It'd happened thirty years ago. Lizzie had only been eight years old, but some memories never faded. Some intensified with age. There was much she *didn't* remember – but those gaps had often been filled in for her by the people in the children's home. Carers, teachers, the other kids – they'd all had something to say about it.

A sour taste filled Lizzie's mouth as saliva flooded it.

She had to face this.

Tearing open the envelope before she could change her mind again, she pulled the crisp, white, headed paper from it.

Dear Mrs Brenfield,
As per your request, I write to inform you that Mr William Cawley is to be released from HMP Baymead, Devon, on the 9th July 2019.

Lizzie's vision blurred, her grip loosened. Before she could read on, the paper fell to the ground.

Creepy Cawley had been released from his thirty-year sentence three days ago.

He was a free man.

Chapter Three

1989

Bovey Police Station,
outskirts of Mapledon

Friday 21st July – 36 hours after the incident

Shock covered her face with a white mask. She didn't remember how she'd come to be there, standing alongside her mother, whose long, thin arm formed a tight band around her shoulders. Protective, yet angry at the same time.

'I'd told her. Told *them*. Warned them.' Her mother's voice was clipped, spoken in such a way as to make her seem out of breath. Maybe she was in shock, too.

'I'm sure you did what you could,' police officer Vern said. 'As a parent myself, I know how difficult it is to keep your eyes on your children all the time. You have to give them some freedom, and as you say, it's a small village – you don't expect something like this to happen.'

'No. No, you don't,' she agreed, her head shaking from side to side.

'I'm sorry to have to keep you, I know you'd like to get your daughter back home, but I do need to speak with her. Try to get a fuller picture – a timeframe of events. It's crucial we don't waste any *more* time . . . You understand, don't you?'

Her mother looked down at her as the officer spoke. A tingling feeling spread through her, reaching her fingertips, making them feel as though they were on fire. There was something in the tone of the policeman's voice – a hidden meaning she couldn't grasp. But by the look on her mother's face, she knew it was bad. It was all bad. And now she'd have to tell them what had happened. What she'd *caused* to happen.

It was all her fault. She'd get the blame for it all.

Chapter Four

2019

Anna

The sign, greying with age and rusted at the edges, came into view and Anna's hands gripped the steering wheel tighter, her knuckles blanching.

MAPLEDON.

Even before she turned off the main road she could feel her world shrinking. The village had been all-consuming when she'd lived there – everyone had known everyone else, everyone attended the same events, frequented the same – and only – pub; all her friends' parents lived in each other's pockets, socialising together, some even working together. There were no secrets in Mapledon. No chances to mess up without someone knowing. No opportunities to play outside the rules.

She didn't suppose it'd got any better in her absence.

As she took the right turn at the old tollhouse, the road narrowed. Anna tugged the steering wheel, pulling the car over abruptly. The light was fading more quickly now, the sun dipping behind the dark granite rock of Haytor on nearby Dartmoor. It was still warm, or maybe it was Anna's anxiety heating her blood. She wound the window down, breathing in slowly and

12

deeply. It even smelled the same. That couldn't be possible, she knew – but it transported her back to her childhood. Back to the memories Mapledon held; the ghosts she'd left behind. With a deep sigh, Anna shook off the feeling and tried to gain control. She should get to her mother's house before dark – before the ghosts came.

Shifting the gear into first, she set off again, heeding the twenty-mile-an-hour speed limit through the village. That was something new, at least. Second right, next left . . . She swallowed hard as she reached the turning to her mother's road. Slowly, she drove in. Her heart banged. There it was. The 1960s magnolia-coloured, end terraced house she'd grown up in. She hadn't visited the house since she'd left twenty years ago. She hadn't even stepped foot in the village since she escaped its clutches. All contact with her mother had been through telephone calls and in person with her mother's biannual trips to Anna's house in Bristol.

Her mother had never argued when Anna had politely declined each of her invitations over the years. Never questioned why. She guessed Muriel knew without having to ask. Anna's strained relationship with her mum had begun the day her father had walked out on them for another woman. Anna had always considered herself a daddy's girl, so she was devastated when he left. She'd blamed everyone over the years: her mother, him, and even herself. But the full weight of her anger and bitterness had often been aimed at her mother – after all, she was the only one present and Anna believed Muriel had been the one to drive the poor man into someone else's arms in the first place.

But he'd left Anna, too. For that she'd blamed him. He'd moved to the other end of the UK – Scotland, the farthest he could get – and had broken off all contact: not a phone call, not a letter. He'd abandoned his only daughter because of something her mother had done. *That* was unforgivable.

Anna pulled the key from the ignition and, with a dragging sensation in her stomach, got out of the car.

'Bloody hell.' Anna sucked in a lungful of air. Why hadn't her mother removed the thing from the front door? It set a chill in motion, starting deep inside her belly and radiating outwards. And something else too – just outside her grasp. She imagined the attention Muriel would've got from the neighbours – she'd have revelled in that, no doubt. Approaching the front step, Anna couldn't peel her eyes away from the gruesome head pinned like a horror-film prop on the door. Her mother would've left it there so that Anna could get the full effect.

She had to admit, seeing it for herself did add the extra fright factor. If she hadn't seen it with her own eyes, she may well have dismissed Muriel's hysteria out of hand. Rather than pass the macabre doll's head, Anna retreated and made her way to the back door instead. Nothing about the house seemed to have changed – the gravel in the small square of garden to the side of the shed remained, the shed itself was clearly the original – the stained-red wood now flaky, splintered and pale from the years of battering rain and hot summers; the greenhouse, now with a few broken panes, had survived. The garden ornaments looked as though they were positioned in the exact same places as when she'd left.

Time had stood still here.

'Anna! Why are you sneaking around the back? For God's sake, child, you nearly gave me a heart attack . . . I thought someone had come for me . . .' Muriel's breaths were rapid; one bony hand was held to her chest.

'Hi, Mum. Sorry, I just couldn't—'

'No, no,' her mother interrupted. 'See what I mean, then? I'm not over-reacting, am I?'

'It appears not.' Anna approached her mother and gave her a brief hug, kissing her cheek, which was icy cold, like she was dead already. After stepping inside, she closed the back

14

door and turned to face her mother. 'So. What did the police say?'

Muriel dropped her gaze. 'I'm not bothering them with this,' she said curtly.

'But it's weird, and maybe even threatening. Why would you call me in a panic but not inform the police?' Anna could feel the annoyance flowing through her body. She'd only been in the house for thirty seconds and already she was losing her patience. She shouldn't have come back here.

'It'll be kids, won't it? Nothing better to do with their time. Nothing changes there, does it?'

'You seriously think kids hammered a head to your door? Why would they?'

'Things have moved on from the simple knocking on the door and running away game, Anna.' Her cool, blue-grey eyes penetrated Anna's, sending a shiver trickling down her spine like cold water from a shower.

'Kids or not, you have to call the police.'

'No, no.' Her mother placed a hand on Anna's arm. 'I think it's best to ignore it. They'll get bored, move on elsewhere. It's just a game to them.'

'If it's just a game, why were you so scared when you rang me?'

'A shock, that's all. When it first happened I reacted badly. I called before I had time to think about it. Silly prank, that's all.'

'But two minutes ago you said "I'm not over-reacting, am I?" And coupled with me almost giving you a heart attack and you saying "I thought someone had come for me" – I'm going out on a limb here and guessing that you're really freaked out by this and *don't* think it's just a silly game!'

'You know how it is – now you're here, I suddenly feel daft. It doesn't seem half as scary as earlier. Living alone, it does things to you, love. Makes you see things that aren't there.'

15

Anna felt even less convinced by this. 'But the head *is* there. Plain as day. You're not seeing things.'

'Yes, the doll's head is there, I know. It's more that I see meanings that aren't there – like I attach significance to something trivial, assume things, that kind of thing. Overthink everything these days. It's my age, I expect.' Muriel gave a lopsided smile, her entire face crinkling like tissue paper. Time hadn't been kind to her mother. 'Let's have a tipple. I assume you're staying the night, aren't you?'

God. No. She most certainly wasn't intending to. 'Oh, erm . . . I only asked James to have Carrie for the evening,' she lied. 'I was going to drive back home later.'

'Please stay, Anna. You haven't been back in so long and I need you now. One night won't kill you.'

It might.

Guilt surged through her. If she stayed tonight, there was a strong chance she'd be talked into staying the whole weekend – God forbid, even longer now that school had broken up for the summer holiday. James would jump at the opportunity to spend extra time with Carrie. The divorce had hit him hard, but it was the restricted time with Carrie that really hurt him. Her mother didn't have to know that, though. 'I'll call James, see what he can do. But I can't promise anything, Mum.'

Muriel's face relaxed as she took two glasses from the display cabinet and poured a large glug of sherry into each one – she knew full well she was going to get what she wanted.

She always did.

Chapter Five

2019

Lizzie

Saturday 13th July

She hadn't slept well, the night passing slowly as images of her childhood filled the hours which sleep should have. Lizzie had spent the bulk of her life trying not to remember her upbringing. Trying to bury it along with who she used to be. She wasn't that girl anymore, but she knew it was just beneath the surface, lying dormant. She'd worked hard to keep this other self hidden. And up until the opening of the letter yesterday, she'd succeeded.

'You were restless last night,' Dom said as he appeared in the bedroom doorway, his toothbrush vibrating in his mouth, white foam escaping onto his chin.

'Sorry, did I keep you awake?' Lizzie asked. He disappeared again, and she heard him spitting in the sink, then the tap running. He returned, his face now free from white paste.

'It doesn't matter. Not like I don't keep you up with my snoring is it?' He smiled and walked over to the bed. 'I guess it's payback.' He placed his hands on Lizzie's shoulders and pushed her back onto the mattress, straddling her. He lifted her top and traced his tongue along her ribcage, around the edges of her dragonfly tattoo. She wasn't in the mood, but it wasn't

Dom's fault. She gave a playful squeal and wriggled beneath his body.

Lizzie hadn't believed her luck when Dom had asked her out. Continued to disbelieve it as the years went on, but not only had he stayed with her, he'd asked her to marry him too. Despite Lizzie's insistence she didn't want children, he'd wanted to be with her. Told her he was going to spend his life with her – until they got old and died. Lifelong love, commitment, loyalty – they were alien concepts to Lizzie. The fact Dom promised all these things both thrilled and scared her. Why would he – *should* he – be any different to the others? But here they were, seventeen years later, still happy and in love.

She didn't want anything to change that. Least of all the one person who'd messed up her life over thirty years ago.

And she couldn't help but wonder how Dom would react if he found out about her past; the fact she'd kept things from him for all that time. *Marriage is based on trust; secrecy is the enemy.* She remembered those words as though he'd spoken them moments ago – they'd both repeated that mantra for the first few years, the rest of the time it was just something they'd *assumed.* Dom would feel betrayed if he knew.

'Come on, you'll be late for work.' Lizzie pushed him away.

'Okay.' A flicker of concern crossed his face. 'Anything on your mind?' Dom tucked his shirt back into his suit trousers and straightened his tie. 'Tough job coming up?'

'No. Well, actually yes.' There it was. Her get-out clause – she could say it was work-related. 'I've got to cover a story – not one I'm keen on doing if I'm honest.'

'Can't another journo do it?'

'In theory, yes. But I haven't had much on lately – being freelance you kinda have to take what you can.'

'What is it?'

'You're going to be late – I'll tell you about it tonight.'

She hated herself, lying like that. She should just tell him the

18

truth. Maybe she would later – instead of spinning him a story, she'd sit him down, open up. Finally. He would either accept that she hadn't been able to talk about it before now, or not. It'd be better to have difficult discussions now, rather than have something come out at a later date and make him even more upset with her for hiding her past.

Dom is a good man. Dom will understand.

Feeling lighter now she'd made the decision to disclose everything later, Lizzie shot up from the bed and launched herself at Dom. He let out a surge of air as she jumped at him, wrapping her legs around his middle.

'Steady on, girl. You're not as light as you used to be,' he said, staggering backwards.

'Oh, get away with you.'

She kissed him as he pulled her in even tighter, pushing himself into her. He groaned.

'Now, that would make me *really* late,' he whispered. 'Love you.'

'And I love you,' she said, lowering herself from him. 'See you tonight, babe.'

The silence in the room once Dom left crushed her. She wouldn't be working today.

Lizzie had to do something constructive; something to release the tension building in her gut. She needed to know where William Cawley was.

She had to find him, before he found her.

Chapter Six

1989

Bovey Police Station

Friday 21st July

'So, missy, your mum tells me you saw something that might help us?'

The girl stared down at her trembling hands. She didn't want to be in the dimly lit, stuffy station, she wanted to be back in her bedroom among her wall-to-wall posters of New Kids on The Block, singing along to her favourite songs on the stereo and dancing. She loved making up dance routines in her bedroom. It was what she'd wanted to do instead of going out. She should never have agreed to play that stupid game again – she should've listened to her mother.

She'd listened to her about going to the police, though. She owed it to her mum to do as she was told now. Even if it was too late. '*You have to do it for your friend,*' she'd said over and over. '*You need to do it for her.*'

'Yes . . .' Her voice shook. She turned her pale face towards her mum, who gave an encouraging smile and a nudge with her elbow. 'I saw . . .'

'Take your time,' the officer said. His wide eyes told her he didn't mean it. He was leaning forward, waiting like an impatient child who wanted their Christmas gift, and wanted it *now*. She took a deep breath and said the words in her head first; she wanted to get them right. Then she spoke out loud. 'I saw him lift her up, into the truck. And then he got in too and screeched off down the road – the one going out of Mapledon. She . . . she shouldn't have got in.' The tears strangled her voice box and the words were high-pitched. 'I don't know why she got in. I don't know why she left me.'

Chapter Seven

2019

Anna

Saturday 13th July

In keeping with the rest of the house, outside and in, Anna's old bedroom had also remained unchanged. It was as though she'd stepped into a time warp and it unnerved her – especially in the dark shadows her old Pierrot lamp cast. The ancient springs in the single mattress did little to help: digging into her hip bones if she lay on her side; displacing her spine if she lay on her back. She hadn't settled for hours. Now, as her body refused to bounce youth-like from the bed, she thought it went some way to explaining why her back was so prone to aches and pains now, as an adult. How had she ever put up with this? The floor would've given better comfort.

Not stopping to inspect any of her childhood belongings, Anna stretched – her spine giving a loud, satisfying crack – and gingerly made her way downstairs to the kitchen fridge. She needed coffee. Her stomach contracted as she sniffed the milk. She pulled the carton away from her nose with such force some of the putrid contents spilled over.

'Oh, my God!' She went quickly to the sink and turned on the tap. With her forearm pressed against her nostrils, she watched as the sour, lumpy liquid glugged down the plughole. Looking at the now empty carton she noted the use-by date was four days ago.

'Mum, your milk is off!' Anna shouted. She checked the fridge for fresh milk, but there was none. There wasn't much of anything. She slammed the fridge door. No coffee to bring her to life first thing was tantamount to hell and she'd never make it through the day. The next hour even. Especially here.

'Oh, sorry, love.' Muriel came into the kitchen, her slippers scuffing over the lino. 'Forgot to get a new carton.'

'Forgot? But it's been out of date for days – haven't you been having cereal, or drinks?'

'Oh, I just hadn't got around to getting to the shop, been using the tin of Marvel I had in the cupboard for cups of tea.'

'You've been using powdered milk instead of getting fresh? When did you last use Marvel? I didn't even know they still made it.'

'Don't be silly, dear, of course they do.'

Anna was half-tempted to check the cupboard, see if the tin was also out of date, but was afraid she'd find that it was a decade out, not just days.

'I'll take you up the shop, then.'

'Oh, you don't need me, do you? You remember where it is, surely?' Muriel slumped down onto the chair at the dining table.

'You all right, Mum? You don't look like you've slept.'

'I look like this every morning. You wouldn't know, would you?'

Anna let the comment slide; she couldn't exactly argue otherwise.

'Do you want to make me a list?' Anna offered. It occurred to her that her mum might not be taking good enough care of herself – or certainly not eating well, going by her gaunt appearance. Guilt tugged at her conscience; she'd always assumed

Muriel was okay living alone in Mapledon – she'd kept it together well after Anna's father upped and left when she was just eleven. She was fit and healthy, had good friends. But Anna now wondered if that was what she'd *wanted* to think. It was easier to believe than the alternative. Anything to avoid coming back to this village.

'Yes, that would be good, thank you.' Muriel's voice lifted; her face brightened.

'When did you go out last?' Anna frowned. Her mother's reaction to her offer to go to the shop for her seemed far too enthusiastic. The doll's head on the door was only yesterday – had other things been going on prior to that to cause her to fear leaving the house?

Muriel waved an arm dismissively. 'Oh, I can't remember – only a couple of days ago. Now, the notepad is in the top drawer of the dresser, love.' Muriel pointed towards the lounge.

'Right,' Anna said.

While in the drawer retrieving the notepad, Anna had a rummage. She wasn't sure what she was even looking for, but she had a niggling feeling. It was filled with old utility bills – thankfully none were red – and old letters. She picked up one of the yellowing envelopes. Black scrawling handwriting covered the front with little room left for the stamp. She squinted, trying to make out the postmark and date.

'Got it?' Muriel appeared in the doorway, her voice making Anna jump. She dropped the letter back in the drawer and slid it shut.

'Yep. Got a pen?' Anna straightened, hoping her mother hadn't spotted her nosing through the drawer. Going back into the kitchen she gave Muriel the pad and waited for her to write the list. Her mum's hands were shaky, the writing spiky and jagged. When she finished, Anna read it through to make sure she could decipher it.

'Here you go.' Muriel pushed a small, purple felt purse into

Anna's hand. 'The cash is in there. Should be enough. Get yourself what you need too, won't you?'

Anna squeezed the childish-looking purse. It didn't feel very full. She swallowed down another surge of guilt, avoiding direct eye contact with her mother. For years she'd stayed away from here. From her mum. She'd had her reasons, but now she questioned them.

Sitting in the car, Anna checked the purse. A single five-pound note. The list Muriel had written would cost at least twenty; maybe her mind wasn't as sharp as it once had been. She hoped it wasn't anything serious, like dementia. It's not like Anna would've noticed the early warning signs. She'd have to talk to Muriel's neighbours, see if they had any concerns.

Before setting off, Anna made a phone call.

'Hey, darling girl. Sorry not to have made it home last night. You okay at your dad's?'

'Why are you staying with Nanna? Are you coming home now?' Her voice quivered.

This, together with Carrie's avoidance of the question, made Anna's heart beat harder. James was a good dad, she had never doubted that, but she knew Carrie got anxious when there was a change in her routine. She'd got used to staying with her dad every other weekend, knew what to expect and when. Clearly, she didn't care for this current disruption.

'Nanna's not feeling too good at the moment and needs a little bit of help. I'm going to stay the weekend, but don't worry – try and enjoy the time with Daddy. What have you two got planned?'

There was a small sigh, then some rustling.

'Hi, Anna.'

James had obviously been in earshot and taken over the call.

'Is she all right? She sounds upset with me.'

'She's fine, really. You know what she's like. I've got the cinema booked for later – she'll forget about you abandoning her then.'

'Really? God, James, you know I wouldn't have asked you to have her unless it was important!'

'Yeah, sorry. I know. Anyway, what was so urgent you had to actually go to Mapledon? Didn't think anything would drag you back there.'

'I'm not sure what's going on, actually. I think Mum might be going a bit senile.'

'Oh, fantastic. Are you sure? What makes you think that?'

'A few things, but I haven't got time to talk now really. I have to go to the shop. Look, I think I'm going to be here all weekend. Are you happy to keep Carrie?'

'Of course. No problem. Stay as long as you need.'

'Thanks, James. I appreciate it. Not that I want to be here for a second longer than absolutely necessary.'

'No, I don't suppose you do.' There was a pause before he added, 'Take care there, Anna.'

Coldness spread its icy branches inside her; his words triggering old anxiety, old memories. The ones she didn't want to let in.

Keeping her gaze forward, Anna walked into Brook Cottage Store – Mapledon's only shop. Immediately, she was transported back to her childhood. How on earth had it stayed virtually the same for all these years? Anna walked past the pick-and-mix shelves – memories of filling a brown paper bag with penny sweets sweeping through her mind – and headed for the fridges. She quickly moved along the aisles, cramming stuff in her basket as she went. She didn't want to be in the shop for too long. The longer she was there, the more likely someone might recognise her; stop her and ask unwanted questions.

Anna heard more voices now, the shop suddenly filling up. She checked her phone for the time. Nine a.m. Damn, she hadn't timed her visit well – the villagers of Mapledon were beginning their day. After checking her mother's list one last time, Anna

26

popped in a jar of coffee and headed for the checkout. There were two counters with tills. That was different. Back when she was a child, there'd been just the one till and the owner of the shop, Nell Andrews, was always the one behind it. Now it seemed she'd upgraded, although it appeared only the one till was currently in use. Anna assumed Nell must've retired. That was something at least. The person serving was probably younger, new. Wouldn't know who Anna was.

There were several people ahead of her in the queue. Sweat formed on her upper lip. *Be quick, hurry up.* She tried to keep her head lowered, avoiding eye contact with anyone else. She might well know these people, but she wasn't interested in them, their lives – wasn't interested in 'catching up' with any of their news. She could hear the low murmur of conversation in front of her. Two women in the line were turned towards each other, baskets touching as they spoke. Anna could hear their supposed hushed chatter.

'Can you believe it? I never thought I'd see the day.'

'Everyone is horrified, Ali. The whole village is in shock.'

Anna turned her head, one ear towards the gossiping couple.

'Her poor mother, though. How the hell must she feel?'

Anna's heart hammered against her ribs, a sudden sensation of falling overcoming her. She popped her basket on the floor and put her hand on the bread stand to steady herself.

'Oh, I know. I really feel for them. But surely he won't come back here?'

'I don't think the villagers would allow it. And anyway, there's nothing for him here.'

'But what if we see him? Can you imagine if he were to walk into this shop now, or he moved back into that bungalow? It *has* been standing empty all these years.'

The queue surged forwards and the women stopped talking as they were served. Anna's saliva had dried, her mouth moistureless. The women could be talking about anyone. Twenty years of things Anna had no clue about had gone on in this village. The likelihood they were talking about *that* particular event was slim, she convinced herself.

Until she reached the till.

At the side of the counter was the newspaper rack. The same position it had always been. Her eyes were drawn to the headline of the *Herald Express*.

MAPLEDON MURDERER RELEASED.

The noises in the shop faded. All Anna could see was the newspaper, the bold capital letters boring into her brain.

'Everyone's up in arms about it. The whole village.' A male voice finally penetrated her thoughts.

'When?' Anna's single word was strangled with fear.

'Four days ago,' the man said, taking the items from Anna's basket and scanning them. 'No one's spotted him, yet. Mind you, I guess no one knows what he looks like now. But he wouldn't dare come back here. Mum said he'd be a fool to. She wouldn't serve him, she said.'

Anna didn't respond at first, her thoughts crashing against each other, tumbling in her head. She fumbled in her purse and paid for the shopping with her debit card. Looking properly at the man behind the counter, she realised he was Nell Andrews' son, Robert – his hair had receded, and his face was thinner than she remembered.

'Has your mum retired?' Anna asked, not because she was interested, more because she wanted to take a minute or two to recover before attempting to walk out of the shop.

'God, no. She'll be here until the end of time. I've just been covering – she's a bit under the weather at the moment. She'll be back!' The man gave a wide grin. Anna assumed he hadn't recognised her and was grateful for this good fortune – a 'wow, it's been years' conversation wasn't one she wanted now. Or ever. She thanked him and left, his words echoing in her mind: 'Four days ago. No one's spotted him yet.'

Four days ago. The same period of time her mother hadn't left the house.

The vision of Muriel's front door swam in front of her eyes.

And the doll's head hammered to it, its relevance now achingly obvious.

Chapter Eight

2019

Lizzie

All her good intentions of sitting Dom down, telling him about her past, went out of the window with one phone call. Now it would have to wait.

Lizzie shoved her hastily packed bag into the boot of her Vauxhall. She was due to upgrade her poor car, had saved for the last three years, but hadn't quite been able to part ways with her trusty old friend yet. They'd done a lot of travelling together – she knew every inch of this car, knew how to handle it. Trusted it, despite its obvious failings: the driver's side window didn't go fully up or down, had been stuck in a halfway limbo for about a year; the wheel trims had long since been ripped off, and the bumper was practically held on with luck. Dom chided her, begged her to get it seen to, but it wasn't high on her list of priorities – as far as she was concerned the faults were purely aesthetic. Knowing she was likely to change the car anyway, she'd said it was pointless spending money on it. Then she'd kept stalling on actually looking for a better one.

Some things were hard to let go of.

With an open packet of rhubarb and custard sweets on the passenger seat within easy reach, her travel mug with coffee in the cup holder and the radio on, Lizzie set off. She hoped the butterflies currently swarming her stomach would abate once she pulled onto the motorway. But then, there was a strong chance they might stay with her until this 'job' was over.

Singing along to James Blunt's 'You're Beautiful' as loudly as she could bear, Lizzie attempted to focus on the road instead of her destination – and what she'd find there. *Who* she'd find there. Within twenty minutes she'd joined the M5 motorway traffic. Now all she had to do was follow the signs to Devon.

Chapter Nine

1989

Bovey Police Station

Friday 21st July

'Now, this is important. Tell me *exactly* what you saw.'

She sat on her hands. They'd begun trembling when the policeman had first started asking questions; now, after what felt like hours, he was still asking her stuff and a funny tingling had filled her belly. Why did she need to go over this? She'd told him again and again. Maybe he didn't believe her. She'd have to say it in a stronger voice.

'The truck stopped in front of where we were walking—'

'Which was Elmore Road,' he interrupted.

'Yes, I thi— I mean, yes. It was.' She mustn't say 'think'; it seemed to make her mum and the policeman a bit jumpy. 'I held back and was going to turn around and take the cut-through to go to the park instead, but before I realised, she'd gone.'

'Gone to the truck?'

'Yes. I don't know why she did that. Why she left me.' Her eyes stung with fresh tears.

'And what did this truck *look* like?'

She was somewhat relieved at being asked this; at least it was a different question to the other ones he'd been constantly getting her to repeat.

'It was a red one,' she said with conviction. 'Dad says those types of trucks are called pickups because they have all that open space at the back to put things in.'

'And what else? Was there anything else about it you can remember?'

'Oh, yes.' She felt confident about this now. 'It had a yellow stripe all the way across the side. And as it pulled off, it turned so it almost went past me. I couldn't move. I was scared he was coming for me too.'

'But he didn't try and take you?'

'No, I don't think so. The truck slowed down, but it didn't stop. But I did see something weird.'

The policeman sat forward in his chair, his round, ruddy face lighting up. 'Yes? What was that?'

'I could see something stuck on the front, on the bit that those red noses for cars go for Comic Relief.'

'The grille,' the policeman said as he scribbled in his notebook. 'But it wasn't a red nose?'

'No. I could see a face. It was a doll's head. Just its head.'

Chapter Ten

2019

Anna

Saturday 13th July

Pulling up outside her mother's house again, Anna noted the doll's head had finally been removed – holes from the nails the only sign something had been there; the only indication she hadn't imagined it. She wished that *had* been the case. Because the alternative was far more disturbing.

Anna cautiously entered the house and rested the bag of groceries on the kitchen worktop. She didn't speak to Muriel; for the moment she was rehearsing the possible permutations of the conversation she needed to have with her mum in her head. It was a difficult subject to broach, and it required thought. The weighing up of the consequences of opening Pandora's box weren't only for her mother's benefit, she too had to be careful. Years' worth of self-preservation could easily be unravelled with a single poorly worded question.

As Anna slowly stored each item from the carrier bag into the cupboards and fridge, memories forced their way into her consciousness. She squeezed her eyes up tight, an attempt to prevent the images taking root. As she opened them again, she turned to where her mum was sitting. Muriel was staring at her.

'You heard then,' Muriel said, her eyes wide, unblinking. 'The gossips at the shop, no doubt.' There was a flatness to her tone; resignation.

At least Anna was let off the hook of being the first one to mention it, the first to dredge up the past.

'Yes. I heard. It was on the front of the paper too.' She was going to ask if that's why her mum had immediately called her, as soon as she heard the news. But she hoped, by not embellishing, that Muriel would carry on the conversation without the need for Anna to intervene with questions. Possibly the wrong questions – those that would hurt and upset, rather than those that would help tease out her fears. Although Anna wasn't sure she was the right one to be doing that, or, in fact, whether she could offer any real support at all. Because her mum's fears were more than likely the same as her own. How helpful could she be if she was scared shitless too?

'It could still be a coincidence, or kids thinking it's funny?' Muriel said.

'Yes, it could.' Anna tried to feel encouraged. 'Obviously everyone knows the tale – I expect it's been told to all the children as a warning over the years. Some teenagers are bound to have thought it was funny to pull this kind of prank. Yes, you're right. Probably harmless fun.' A false lightness attached itself to her words. It *could* be kids, it really could.

'That's what I was hoping. Of course, that isn't what I thought when I first saw it. But I talked myself down, eventually. And once you got here, I felt a bit better about it.'

'Okay then. Look, it's not ideal that he's out, but like Robert said, why would he dare come back here?'

'Nell's son Robert?'

'Yes, he was the one who served me.'

'No Nell this morning, then?'

'Ill apparently. He said she'd been feeling under the weather.'

Her mother's gaze turned to the window as she gave a *hmmm* sound.

'You think she's also worried?'

'What?' Muriel's attention snapped back to Anna. 'Oh, I don't know. I haven't seen anyone since I heard.'

'Who told you, then?'

Muriel heaved herself up from the chair and wandered into the living room.

'Mum?'

'I got a call, don't know who it was from.'

'Really? Well, when?'

'Four days ago. The day he was released supposedly.'

'Was it *him*?'

'No. No, dear, I think it was probably a journalist or some such person. Anyway, doesn't matter. It's how we deal with it, how we move on from here, knowing. Knowing that man is free. Free to do what he bloody well pleases. Can't believe they let the monster out, can you?'

'Unfortunately, life rarely means *life*, Mum. I guess he did his time.' Anna shrugged. 'It's not like they ever found a body even, is it?'

And that had always been the issue; the underlying question the family and villagers had wanted answered.

Where had he hidden her body?

Chapter Eleven

2019

Lizzie

She'd needed the satnav to reach Mapledon. It wasn't where she remembered it, but that was to be expected; she'd only been a child when she was taken from the village. It was situated south of Dartmoor – with its imposing granite rocks and sprawling moorland – and tucked away in a valley ten miles from the nearest town. What felt like hours of winding lanes, long hills and dense woodlands had passed before she'd finally come to a wider road leading to a sign stating she'd reached Mapledon.

Years of living in other parts of the country had diluted what memories of the place she'd had. Now, driving at a snail's pace through the centre of the small village, passing a spattering of old thatched-roof cottages, then a few larger, more modern houses, Lizzie's heart rate soared. So far she hadn't recognised anything. It wasn't lack of familiarity that was causing her adrenaline to shoot through her veins, though. It was the *thought* of what went on here. It was being back. If Dom had known any of her history, he'd have stopped her from leaving. But he didn't know. Her childhood secrets were hers alone. Well, almost.

There were some other people who knew.

Would they still be here, living in Mapledon?

Would *he* be here, waiting?

The reason she'd driven all this way was to find out, but now she was here the urge to turn around and leave, go back to her life in Abbingsworth, was so strong she could feel the pull. She should allow herself to be snatched from this place again – she didn't belong here.

Her foot remained on the accelerator. There was still a part of her – the part that had been in the shadow for years – which *couldn't* succumb to the pull. *That* side of her had to keep going regardless.

Thirty years. She cursed loudly. 'Fuck this place. It doesn't define me. That man does not define me.' She slammed her hands on the steering wheel, an action supporting her determination as she headed to the top of the hill. To the church. It was the first place she decided she'd go – the only landmark she could see. With luck the vicar might be there – he'd know what was going on in his parish. He'd be the best person to start with.

She could do this.

She had to close the book on William Cawley.

Chapter Twelve

1989

Brook Cottage Store, Mapledon

Thursday 20th July – the day after

Fears grow for missing child

Despite an extensive search of Mapledon and the surrounding area by police and over thirty local villagers, ten-year-old Jonie Hayes has still not been found. She has been missing for almost twenty-four hours and police say they are concerned for her safety. An appeal is due to be launched by Devon and Cornwall Police later today.

'Such terrible news. I still can't believe a little 'un could just disappear like that. Not here,' Nell said, packing the tins into Mrs Percy's shopping bag on the store counter.

'We're in shock. The whole village is.'

'Well, *almost* the whole village,' Muriel said, pushing forward in the queue to interject, her voice lowered conspiratorially.

'Are you thinking what I am? About . . . you know who?' Nell asked. A few other customers joined the women, even though they weren't in the queue themselves.

'Well, you can't help but consider it, can you? I mean, after what happened to his little girl . . .' Muriel raised one eyebrow in a high arc and stood back a little from the gathering villagers. 'I'm just saying – I mean he wasn't even out last night helping search for Jonie with all the others, was he? Wouldn't surprise me if he had something to do with it, is all.' She tilted her chin up.

'We shouldn't jump to conclusions. It's not helpful, Muriel.' A voice came from behind her, causing her to start. Muriel spun around to face Reverend Farnley.

'I'm not one to do that, Reverend.' She kept her gaze steady. 'Have *you* seen him over the last few days?'

'Muriel. Please. Gossip is a tool of the devil. Be careful, now.'

'It's not gossip if it's true, Reverend. And I didn't even mention his name, but *you* knew who we were referring to . . .' Muriel pursed her lips.

'Now I think of it, I haven't seen him, you're right,' Nell piped up in Muriel's defence, before the red-faced vicar could respond. 'Whilst it's not helpful to gossip, it would be wrong to dismiss something that might actually be key. A little girl's life is at stake, after all.'

'There's no evidence to suggest she's been *taken*, ladies, or that her life is in danger; she could merely be lost,' Reverend Farnley said. 'Anyway, I'm sure the police have a good handle on things. We should leave them to their job. But we can pray for young Jonie's safe return – put our faith in the Lord.'

Muriel turned away from the Reverend, directing the rolling of her eyes and small shake of her head to Nell and the remaining group of women. She'd been brought up to be God-fearing; however, some situations required a helping hand from those on earth. In Muriel's opinion, God could only do so much and putting all your faith in Him was a mistake. Surely, He'd want His children to sort their own mess out occasionally.

After a few polite statements the conversation turned to the Mapledon Meeting and Reverend Farnley took his leave. Muriel and Nell took turns to head the monthly get-together, the venue alternating between their houses. It normally took place on the last Thursday of each month; however, they'd brought it forward this time – both having agreed it was somewhat of an 'emergency meeting'. A small, select group of female villagers attended, usually twelve, but sometimes more if there was something pressing to discuss. Like now. Admittedly, this was one of the *most* pressing topics that had ever faced the group – although there'd been other challenging ones, Jonie Hayes' disappearance was the worst. The mothers of the group in particular were very concerned and would need support and reassurance.

'See you at seven-thirty sharp, Nell. I'll make sure I put out extra nibbles – it's going to be a busy one.'

Chapter Thirteen

2019

Anna

Saturday 13th July

'Hiding in here, worrying, isn't very productive.' Anna lowered the curtain, moving away from the lounge window to face Muriel. Since her disclosure she'd been quiet, barely speaking. Instead, she'd watched daytime TV, a blank look plastered on her face. Anna knew if she couldn't put her mother's mind at ease – if she couldn't confidently tell her that the doll's head was nothing to do with Billy Cawley – this would drag on; hang over their heads for the foreseeable future. Anna did *not* want to spend more time in Mapledon. Maybe she'd have to persuade her mum to move nearer to her and Carrie in Bristol.

'What do you propose I do? March around the village accusing the local kids of trespass, criminal damage?'

'Well, no. Although going to the police with your suspicions would be a start.'

'I told you, Anna – I'm not going to the police.' She looked past Anna, into the distance. 'That'll make matters worse.'

'For who? The kids? That's the idea, Mum. And if it isn't the kids . . .'

'It'll be him,' Muriel said.

'The police will be able to keep an eye on things. On him. He'll be on a life licence. Something like this would put him straight back to prison.'

'Or, it could stir up a hornet's nest,' Muriel said, her face stony.

That was the problem with small villages. Anna had always sensed it growing up, but now it was even more apparent. One event could cause a ripple effect – what should be contained within a family unit suddenly became the business of every person in the village. Everyone had something to say; some advice to give, solutions to problems to offer. Whether wanted or not. If word got out that Muriel thought the children of Mapledon were responsible for the macabre doll's head, then she was right – accusations would fly, uptight members of the community would be up in arms. The local council would probably seek to lay down a curfew – the teenagers would rebel. The situation would likely worsen. And then Muriel would become the sole focus of attention. But then, maybe she had already.

Why *had* she been targeted?

If it really was *him*, then this was just the start. Anna remembered that at the time every villager had been horrified at what had happened. Everyone had named Billy Cawley.

'I think I'll get some fresh air, Mum.' Anna couldn't sit inside the house waiting for the next 'gift' to be delivered to Muriel's door. It might be that others had received something similar. A walk around the village might well give her an opportunity to find out if anything else was amiss in Mapledon.

Muriel squinted at Anna. 'I – I'm not sure that's a good idea. Not on your own.'

She tried to ignore her mother's deepening frown as she bent to kiss the top of her head. 'Mum. It's daylight. I'm a grown woman – I'll be fine!'

'I didn't ask you to come here on a mission to track down the culprit, Anna. I just wanted you here to be with me.'

'I can't stay cooped up. And I'm not tracking anyone down, I'm going for a walk.'

Muriel sighed, her shoulders slumping in defeat. 'Don't be long, then.'

Taking in her mother's anxious expression, she realised Muriel's concern was not entirely for Anna. It was for herself. She didn't want to be alone in the house, just in case.

'I won't be. And I've got my mobile. Call me immediately if . . .' Anna trailed off.

'You get a full signal here?' Muriel straightened in her chair, her tone panicked.

'Well, not full, no,' Anna said. She couldn't very well lie. She'd assumed there would be areas where the signal dipped, became non-existent even. It was a small village in a valley on the outskirts of Dartmoor; it was to be expected. 'But I'll never be far away, will I? God, it'll only take fifteen minutes to walk an entire circuit of this place.'

'It took less time than that for someone to abduct Jonie Hayes,' she said bluntly.

Anna ignored the comment and left, grabbing a hoody from the hall bannister despite the warmth of the day. With the hood up, she'd maybe remain anonymous as she walked through the village. Taking a right at the end of Muriel's road, Anna headed down Fore Street. The only houses – three cottages in a row – were situated just before the road ended and joined what was the main road of Mapledon: the one that led to the church. No one was about. The cottages appeared normal as she passed. But then, had there been anything hammered to their doors, no doubt it'd been removed by now. Anna wasn't really expecting to see anything remotely strange: no doll's heads. Not really. But still, she looked. Or, maybe she was hoping to see something. She could take some comfort then; there'd be a shared fear, rather than an isolated one.

As she ambled up towards the church, passing other equally

unremarkable homes along Bridge Street, Anna found herself at the entrance to one of the cul-de-sacs that ran off it. Blackstone Close. Curiosity made her turn into it and begin walking to the end.

She stopped outside the final bungalow. The paint was peeling, the plaster crumbling. The garden was overgrown. Even in daylight there was something sinister about it. There'd been calls from angry, grieving villagers for it to be demolished afterwards. But the formidable local councillors had come up against more red tape than they could cut through. So, it had stood. Empty for thirty years. Like some strange kind of *mausoleum*.

Anna couldn't help but wonder about the man who lived there.

Would he really come back?

Was he inside it now?

Her heart jolted at the thought. She wanted to turn and walk away, but her feet remained planted. She took her hands from her hoody pockets and reached out slowly towards the wall. A voice made her snatch it away again.

'Hi, Bella. I thought you might come calling now.'

Chapter Fourteen

2019

Lizzie

Lizzie was parked just outside the church gate, eyes fixed on the entrance, her resolve wavering. There were no regular services on a Saturday – she hadn't given that a thought when she'd decided the church was the best place to start. Perhaps the vicar would still be inside, though. There might've been a wedding. Or a funeral. Doubtful, though. Surely her luck wouldn't be that great. If she didn't brave it, get out the damn car and take a look, she'd never know. But a sudden fear that her faith in the vicar was misplaced – that he'd be unable to help her at all – caused her to hesitate. It was unlikely to be the same vicar as thirty years ago, and certain events tended to cause a tight community such as Mapledon to clam up, to decide it was too hideous, too abominable to ever speak of again. A new vicar might not have any knowledge of what had happened. And Lizzie couldn't remember the name of the original one. Couldn't remember many names at all.

Just the three.

She unconsciously pulled at her hair, collecting several short, black strands in her palm whilst berating herself for not having spent some time researching before jumping in her car and setting off. That was a mistake. Local vicar aside, who would she approach to answer her questions? She brushed the hair into the footwell and sighed, the sound loud in the quiet car. Maybe the *how* was something she should've also given more thought to. Lizzie hadn't considered what effect her presence in Mapledon would have. She *could* be a "nobody" – her name was different now, after all – but that in itself wouldn't help her. She doubted Mapledon had many random visitors. A stranger in the fold would spark interest, prompt caution. A closing of the ranks.

Outsiders are not to be trusted.

They wouldn't knowingly divulge anything to an outsider. But, equally, she couldn't tell anyone who she really was, either; who she used to be. She had the sinking feeling her trip here would be a waste of time. Where was she even going to stay? She was in the middle of nowhere and it didn't seem as if Airbnb was an option. She really hadn't thought this through.

Just drive back home, back to safety. Back to Dom.

Lizzie watched as two women emerged from the church gate, one holding a pair of shears. They'd likely been tending to a grave. A pain gripped her stomach. She pushed her hands into it, clutching at the skin with her fingertips, and closed her eyes. A vision of a woman swam inside the darkness: a blurry-edged picture void of facial features. Because she couldn't remember any. Tears slipped over her cheeks and ran under her chin.

Her mother was buried in this graveyard.

Or, so she'd been told – she'd never seen for herself. A long-suppressed anger began to bubble. The details surrounding Rosie's death were vague in Lizzie's mind, what happened afterwards patchy at best. She just knew she'd experienced a lot of rage back then – an emotion she'd been unable to channel appropriately. Something she still struggled with if she ever came up against the red flags.

Maybe now was the time to change that.

Perhaps the need for change was what had drawn her back to Mapledon.

Chapter Fifteen

1989

Mapledon

Wednesday 19th July – the day of, 8.25 p.m.

In the humid summer evening, circles of lights darted over grass, whizzed over hillsides, flitted under bushes and dotted the darkening sky – like a frenzied firefly dance. But the display didn't come from a swarm of fireflies, it came from the illumination of dozens of torchlights.

'Jonie! Joniiiieee!'

Jonie's name was called again and again, each time more frantic. Desperate. One voice could be heard above others, its pitch ripping through the night, tearing through the eardrums of the volunteers, the police.

Tina Hayes' legs were weakening; her voice was not. Sheer adrenaline kept her powering forwards, her desire to find her daughter overtaking her need to slow down, rest.

'Tina?' Pat Vern ran up to her, putting a sweaty hand on her arm to stop her marching on. 'I'm not sure . . . it's a good idea . . . for you to be here.' The police officer panted, his shallow breaths diminishing his ability to form a full sentence.

'What would you have me do, Pat? Stay at home like the good little woman, waiting to see if someone else finds her?' Tina put her hands on the tops of her thighs, taking the moment to catch her breath, allowing the blood to flow through her limbs again. 'Is that what you'd do if it were Daisy?'

Pat, recovered now from the acute exertion, couldn't argue with her. He never had been able to put up a fight where Tina Hayes was concerned.

'I know. I know you think you should be doing everything to find her, and I understand, I really do. But what if she . . .' He paused. What he was thinking was: *what if you're the one to find her and she's dead?* He couldn't bear that. The last image she'd have of her only daughter would be a horrifying one – one she'd never rid herself of. But why was he thinking that at all – why *would* she be dead? This was Mapledon for Christ's sake. He'd been on the force ten years and nothing remotely bad had ever happened here, so this would end happily, he was sure.

Only he wasn't.

His gut was telling him something else – something evil – was at play. He didn't know why, but he *felt* it. He realised Tina was waiting for him to finish his sentence, impatiently stepping from one foot to the other as she stared at him, her eyes wide and red-rimmed. He pulled himself together. 'What if Jonie goes home – who's going to be there if everyone is outside searching?'

'Do you *think* she'll turn up at home, Pat, as though nothing has happened – like she'd just lost track of the time? Come on. We both know she didn't just forget the time. Her friends are all home, we've checked. So, it's not as though she'd been having too much fun or gone off with one of them somewhere and wandered too far out of Mapledon. She's not a dumb kid, Pat.'

'I know she's not dumb.' Pat dropped his gaze to his shoes. Now wasn't the time to mention what he'd heard about Jonie. 'Okay, come on. Let's press on. I don't want to waste any more time – it's going to be too dark to continue in an hour or so.'

'You might think so,' Tina said sharply, shaking her head. 'But I'll be out here looking all night if I have to. Every night. I won't stop until I find her.'

And she strode off.

Chapter Sixteen

2019

Anna

Saturday 13th July

Anna froze; the voice – soft, haunted – causing her heart to stutter.

If people had called her Bella afterwards, she'd ignored them. And, through her own choice, no one had called her that since she'd left Mapledon. She couldn't bear to hear it, didn't like to recall the memories associated with it. The last time her friend uttered it. Hearing it now transported her back to a time and place she never wanted to be reminded of.

'*Creepy Cawley, Creepy Cawley . . .*'

The hushed whisper, the goading chant, filled her skull. She shook her head, trying to shake the ghostly voice from it. But as much as she wanted to run, not look back, this was one villager she couldn't ignore. She turned around.

'Hello, Auntie Tina,' she said. 'I go by Anna these days.'

Tina's face flinched, her chin tilting up. 'Right, sure. Annabella was always a mouthful, and Anna is more grown up than Bella. Lovely that you were able to do that – grow up, I mean.' The words, edged with an iciness, made Anna shiver. She couldn't blame her for her cutting tone.

Anna opened her mouth but closed it again. For the moment, she couldn't think of a single thing Tina would want to hear. She fleetingly considered giving her a hug, but the years that had passed created a gulf between them; what had happened thirty years ago ensured the chasm was too wide to bridge with such an action. Tina was about five years younger than Muriel, but if Anna had thought the years had been unkind to her mum, they'd been downright cruel to Auntie Tina – her wrinkled skin had a grey hue to it, her dyed blonde hair was thin and patchy, making her eyes seem pale, almost albino.

Anna gazed back towards Billy Cawley's old bungalow, the memory of the game *Knock, Knock, Ginger* making her skin crawl. They'd been having innocent fun, hadn't they? Being here now, she could envisage the two of them like she was seeing the imprints of their younger selves. Ghostly figures. She'd not allowed herself to think about Jonie for a really long time before today. But she knew, despite not consciously remembering her, what had happened that sunny afternoon was part of her. Had affected her more than she'd ever cared to admit to. Now, facing Tina, everything rose to the surface. Tears slid down her face.

'Don't. Don't cry. Tears won't help anyone,' Tina said.

She'd created a shell, one that had hardened over time. They all had.

'Sorry.' Anna brushed the tears away with her fingertips. One word, weighted with guilt, years in the making. Not once had she uttered that word when it happened.

It wasn't her fault, after all.

But Tina thinks it was.

'Why are you back?'

Instinct told Anna not to mention the doll's head.

'Came to see Mum.'

'Never bothered before.'

'No, well – being the anniversary year . . .' Anna felt herself cringe; she dropped her gaze.

52

'So, you thought you'd come back to where it all began?' Tina swept an arm out in front of her, indicating the bungalow. 'Got a guilty conscience?'

And there it was. Thirty years on, the man responsible having served time in prison, and still Anna was getting the blame. Well, she wasn't that little girl anymore: the meek, mild-mannered pushover Bella. She was Anna, and she'd had to work hard to overcome her weaknesses; she'd worked hard to heal the mental scars left behind.

'No,' she said firmly, shaking her head. 'Have you?'

Chapter Seventeen

2019

Lizzie

She didn't know where to begin looking for the grave, or even if she should. Voluntarily opening old wounds probably wasn't wise. But then, coming here seeking *him* out wasn't a wise decision either. Yet, here she was. Facing her demons.

As she slowly lifted the metal latch and stepped through the wooden gate into the church grounds, Lizzie shivered. It'd only been a gentle breeze brushing against her skin – a warm one at that – but it had triggered hundreds of goose bumps to appear on her pale, freckly arms. It was like a ghost had touched her. Walking briskly to the church door, Lizzie put all thoughts of ghosts to the back of her mind. The door creaked loudly as she opened it. Inside was silent. Cool. Empty, as far as she could tell. Flowers adorned the ends of each pew and at the altar stood a huge display of white lilies, daisies and aster – all left over from a wedding, she presumed.

A stray memory came to her. She'd been inside this church before. Sunday school – she remembered being at a small table at the back, sitting with other children. She'd gone a few times, but then something had happened; there'd been a reason she stopped attending. But what was it? She filed the memory away with all the other half-formed, blurry memories of her early childhood.

There was no sign of a vicar. Lizzie ducked outside again and wandered to the far side of the graveyard; she'd work her way backwards to the entrance. It wasn't a huge area – the village had always been small. Many of the headstones were old and tilting, the writing faded. It shouldn't take too long to find Rosie's. She read the names of those she could decipher as she moved around. None of them caused a memory to stir. Until one; the name on it making Lizzie's blood chill in her veins.

Jonie Hayes.

One of the three names she did remember.

She hurried on past it, not wishing to linger. Not wanting to 'go there' yet. It was too early – she wasn't ready. *One step at a time.*

The air seemed to still as she approached the grey, granite headstone that bore her mother's name. Lizzie crouched beside her mum, eyes tightly squeezed, trying desperately to remember something. Anything about her mother. Nothing came to her. It could be because she was trying to force it – if she relaxed, didn't try so hard, something might come.

For the moment, she could only recall a snippet of one memory.

The day her mum gave her Polly.

Chapter Eighteen

1989

Mapledon

Tuesday 18th July – the day before

'Be back for lunch, Bella. And no going near Blackstone Close, you hear me?'

Her mother's shrill voice followed Bella out of the house. She called back over her shoulder, 'No, Mum. I won't!' rolling her eyes towards Jonie to prove she thought her mother's warning was something she found annoying. She didn't. She really wanted to do as her mum told her – going to Blackstone Close made her skin creep.

Of course, they *would* end up there, though. They usually did – even during term-time. Now they'd broken up from school, she knew it'd be where Jonie would want to go for the next six weeks. Jonie put up her usual convincing argument so they'd do what *she* wanted them to do. Said that it was more fun to goad Creepy Cawley than to waste the summer staying in playing stupid Barbie or watching TV. Bella had failed to impress her friend with her entertainment ideas. She'd wanted to make up some dance routines – ones like they'd been doing in PE at school. Miss Hanson had told Bella that she had "flair", whatever that meant. But she knew it was good. She didn't receive many compliments, so this was something she'd taken on board and wanted to build on during the holiday. She, Bella, was actually *good* at something.

'Come on, then. I've found a way through the back of the close, so he won't see us coming,' Jonie said, her eyes wide with excitement. Bella forced a smile. She didn't get why Jonie thought it was so thrilling to knock on someone's door and run away. It was childish. And pretty stupid. She couldn't tell Jonie that, though.

A few minutes later, they were squeezing through a small gap at the bottom of some bushes at the back of Blackstone Close. Jonie got through first and helped drag Bella through. The twigs scraped at her bare legs.

'Ouch! Mind.'

'Shh, Bella. Someone will hear us.' Jonie looked down at Bella's legs and tutted.

Bella rubbed at them. If she ripped her shorts, her mum would be mad. She hoped they wouldn't go back through the bushes when they were done.

They crouched down, across from the bungalow.

'What are we waiting for?' Bella asked, wishing she were anywhere but there.

'Well, we need to make sure he isn't watching before we go in, don't we?' Jonie shook her head. She had a way of making Bella feel stupid, shutting down anything she said immediately.

'Yes, course,' Bella said, as though she knew that.

Bella stared at Creepy Cawley's bungalow, silently praying he wasn't in. But his truck was in the driveway, so he probably was. Her stomach churned, a thousand butterflies flitting around inside it. Her legs began to cramp in their crouching position. She was too afraid to tell Jonie; she'd have to put up with the pain.

'So weird, isn't it – having all those bits of dolls everywhere?'

It *was* weird. But then, that was why he'd got the nickname Creepy Cawley. That, and the way he looked: his straggly long hair, dirty clothes, dead-looking black eyes that stared right through you. Bella shuddered.

'Yeah, why doesn't he tidy it all up?'

'Mum says it's because he's lost everything. She says he can't be bothered with himself, or the bungalow, anymore.'

'My mum said it was because he was a pee-da-something. That he lured kids there and did bad stuff to them.' Bella swallowed hard. 'Which is why we shouldn't be here, Jonie. It's dangerous.' She'd said it in no more than a whisper – not wanting to go against what Jonie wanted. But she had to say something. She didn't want to do this.

'Nah – your mum doesn't know what she's talking about. It's not *dangerous*. It's funny! Everyone does it. I heard Adam telling Nicky at school that him and John had knocked on his door dozens of times, and the worst that happened is Creepy Cawley chased them.'

'Oh.' Bella thought that *was* bad. Adam and John were quick, Bella was not – she always came last in the sprint races at school. What if he chased after them and caught them? What then?

'Right, I think it's clear. Let's go.' Jonie was up and running across to the bungalow.

Bella watched as Jonie ducked behind the dustbin just inside Creepy Cawley's driveway. She frantically waved an arm towards Bella.

If she thought this was it – the only time they'd do this – she'd feel a bit better. She'd even be okay about it if they actually knocked on someone *else's* door for a change. But Jonie had already told her they'd have to come again tomorrow, so they both had a turn at knocking on his door. It was only fair, Jonie had said.

Being Jonie's friend was hard work, Bella thought, before taking a deep breath and following – just as she always did.

Chapter Nineteen

2019

Anna

Saturday 13th July

The two of them fell into an awkward silence, both standing motionless outside Billy Cawley's run-down bungalow, neither looking the other in the eye. Anna lowered her chin, balling her hands up inside her hoody pockets. They'd all been so close, once. Muriel and Tina were best friends – they'd both been young mothers, as were their mothers before them, so they had a lot in common. That's why Anna had always called her 'Auntie' Tina. It was a thing they did back then – the mothers' good friends were always known to their kids' friends as Auntie. It was inevitable Anna and Jonie would also be best friends. Obvious to the mothers, anyway. In reality, they weren't destined to be close. They'd been too different: the balance was never right. But as their parents spent so much time together, they'd both taken it as something that just had to be.

'I haven't seen Muriel out and about in a while. She well?' Tina broke the silence first.

Anna gave a shrug. 'She's okay, I guess.' She didn't want to give anything away – not just yet. Anna needed to delve a bit more before mentioning the doll's head and Muriel's strange behaviour since. She wondered if Tina and Muriel still spoke. After Jonie went missing their relationship had faltered – so her mum had told her once after one too many sherries. Muriel had never talked about what happened, how things had been in Mapledon afterwards, and Anna had never wanted to bring it up herself, so the memories faded. The aftermath had been bad, affecting the whole community – she knew *that* – but couldn't recall any specific repercussions.

But she knew everything had changed when Jonie Hayes was taken.

'Maybe we should all get together for a coffee while you're here?' Tina said.

Anna raised her eyebrows. She hadn't been expecting that. Tina's sudden invite felt forced, like it'd been offered out of necessity. Tina wanted something, she could tell. Had *she* also been targeted with a doll's head on her door and now wanted, or needed, to talk to her old friend about it? They might not be close anymore, but maybe their shared past – the inexplicable thing that had happened – was more than enough to break down the barriers that had been built during the subsequent years.

'Yeah, sure. Pop over tomorrow morning. If you aren't going to church that is. Mum will be thrilled to see you,' Anna said, although her sentiments may well have been exaggerated. Who knew if Muriel would be thrilled? God only knew what had been going on here over the years Anna had been away.

Tina snorted. 'I don't go to church anymore, haven't done since . . .' She shook her head. 'There is no God. I'll be over at ten.' Tina gave a curt nod and walked off, back down the cul-de-sac. Anna watched her disappear around the corner before returning her attention to the bungalow. There was a reason Tina wanted to have this 'get-together' – the obvious one being Billy Cawley's release. But a prickling on the back of Anna's neck told her there was more to it than that.

60

Reassured for the moment that Billy Cawley had not returned to live in the bungalow in Blackstone Close, Anna turned her back on it and walked on. She wished she'd turned her back on it thirty years ago, too. Before the chain reaction of events following that game had become fatal. It seemed Anna's life had been filled with what ifs and if onlys.

The church came into sight almost immediately once she'd joined the main street – its limestone-rendered tower visible through the trees. She'd walk as far as the church, checking the outside of every house as she went, then return to her mum's via the road that branched off to the left, near the village hall. That way, she'd have done a circuit of Mapledon. Her hopes of finding something 'out of place' were fading, though. It might be that a more direct approach would be necessary – asking outright if anyone had experienced something out of the ordinary over the past few days. Anna thought Robert, at Brook Cottage Store, might be a good person to ask. For now, she'd continue the walk. If nothing else, it was keeping her out of her mother's hair for a bit longer.

As Anna reached the top of the village and approached the church, she spotted a woman coming out of the wooden-gated entrance. She didn't recognise her, although she didn't look much different in age to Anna. Someone she went to school with? She kept her attention on the figure for a few seconds too long, garnering a strange look in response.

'Hi,' Anna said, deciding it would make the moment less awkward now she'd been caught staring.

'All right?' The woman gave a quick, tight smile, hesitating at the church gate as though she didn't know quite what to do. Anna took her indecision and obvious discomfort as a sign of guilt. Had she stolen something from the church? Maybe she wasn't from around here at all, was some kind of chancer. Anna took a few steps towards her. The woman didn't have anything with her, not even a bag. Her T-shirt was tight-fitting – so no stolen goods could be squirrelled away beneath it. She had various tattoos on both arms, a piercing under her bottom lip. As she looked at her face, Anna noted her eyes were red as though she'd been crying, and she suddenly felt appalled at herself for jumping to conclusions. Clearly she was upset – had probably just visited a grave.

'Sorry, didn't mean to stare – just thought I recognised you,' Anna lied.

'No. I doubt that,' the woman said. She made no attempt to move past Anna. She took it as a signal to continue.

'Not many people come to Mapledon,' Anna said. 'Not if they want to leave again.' She gave a laugh, hoping this woman would take her comment as the joke she intended. Well, an almost-joke. There might well be a grain of truth in her statement.

The woman smiled – it appeared to be a genuine one. 'Yeah, I heard that about this place.' She reached a hand forwards. 'Lizzie Brenfield,' she said.

'Well, hello, Lizzie.' Anna took her hand, shaking it gently before releasing it. 'I'm Anna. I'm the one that got away.' She smiled before adding, 'Although I appear to have been dragged back.'

Lizzie cocked her head to one side. 'Well, that makes two of us.'

Chapter Twenty

2019

Lizzie

The Lord moveth in mysterious ways, Lizzie thought as she took a step back from Anna to make a quick appraisal of the situation. A moment ago she'd believed her trip here would ultimately be fruitless, but now it seemed she'd been thrown a lifeline. Whoever Anna was, whatever her reason for being here, she too appeared to have a similar feeling about Mapledon. Lizzie's journalistic mind kicked in. There could even be a story here. One that wasn't hers.

'You from here originally then, Anna?' Lizzie wondered why she hadn't offered up her surname. She'd have to work a little harder.

'Yep. For my sins.'

Lizzie arched one eyebrow. Interesting phrasing. She tried to think quickly. She didn't want to waste this opportunity to find out more about Mapledon's current goings-on, but then she also didn't want to launch into a million questions and frighten Anna off.

'Mapledon doesn't appear to be high on either of our "best places to visit in Devon list" by the sounds of things.'

'God, no!' Anna said loudly. Lizzie observed Anna's quick glance towards the church and subsequent sign of the cross, which she jabbed out over her chest.

'Don't worry,' Lizzie whispered, leaning forwards, 'I don't think He heard you.'

'You never can be too careful though, eh?'

Lizzie felt an immediate bond with Anna – as though they had something in common: a shared history. Maybe they did.

'No, you can't. Especially here in Mapledon,' Lizzie said, nudging Anna with her elbow. She meant it in jest, but her voice hadn't received that message. 'Just joking,' she added quickly.

'Actually, Lizzie, you're not far from the truth. Want to walk with me? Or do you have to be somewhere else?'

Lizzie sensed Anna wanted to be away from the church, away from the possibility of being overheard before talking more. This was good news – it meant she knew something, and more importantly, wanted to tell her about it. Perhaps her luck was about to turn.

Chapter Twenty-One

1989

Blackstone Close

Monday 17th July – 2 days before

When would the little shits let him be?

Billy Cawley saw the shadows, heard the scurrying of feet and the giggles just moments before the banging on the front door. He was tired. So bloody tired of it all. He'd lost count of how many months he'd been hounded by the kids.

Kids. Part of him wanted to let it go – they didn't know any better. But he couldn't. They *should* know better. Their parents should be teaching them better. Did they even know where their bratty children were? What they were up to? And the people of Mapledon had dared to give *him* a hard time about *his* parenting. Fucking cheek. They all needed to be taught a lesson. He'd begun chasing the kids out of the cul-de-sac – running after them, shouting like a madman. He'd almost got hold of one lad just last week, but now that he wasn't keeping himself as fit, having given up on the gym after . . . Well, after life had turned to total shit, he didn't have the stamina.

Christ – twenty-five years old and already being outrun by kids. Mind you, not only didn't he have the body or fitness of a twenty-five-year-old, he didn't have the face of one either.

That was evident when he overheard the taunts, the whispers and nicknames whenever he ventured out of his comfort zone of the bungalow – 'Old Man Cawley', 'Creepy Cawley' and the like. He had had worse nicknames though – some of the more cruel, unfounded things people said really boiled his piss. But he no longer had the motivation, the desire to look good or worry unduly about what the folk of Mapledon said about him. There was no one to impress now. Not now they'd taken everything from him.

A loud crash at the kitchen window startled him.

'Bastards!' He rushed to the door, flinging it open in time to see two boys hare down the road. He'd never catch up with them. Billy strode outside, stepping over all the crap in his garden. He kicked a doll's head hard, sending it flying through the air. It landed by his truck, then rolled awkwardly behind the back tyre. He walked around to the kitchen window, and on inspection of the ground he found a large stone. He picked it up; it was pretty weighty – he was amazed it hadn't gone right through the glass. None of the kids had done more than play Knock, Knock, Ginger before. It seemed they were getting braver.

Maybe it was time for him to do the same.

Chapter Twenty-Two

2019

Anna

Saturday 13th July

She was taking a leap of faith. Anna had no clue who Lizzie was, what she wanted – but, like her, she'd come to Mapledon for a reason. Anna wanted to ask so many questions, but also wanted to tread with caution. She needed to get Lizzie away from the church: she didn't want to be seen by any nosy villagers. Being back in this place was bad enough, being recognised even worse – but to also be caught talking to an outsider – well, that would be punishable by death. Despite knowing that to be an exaggeration, Anna did know it was the one thing the tight-knit villagers of Mapledon feared the most. Although, at this point, just because Anna didn't recognise the woman, or her name, it didn't mean she didn't have family ties here, so perhaps she was being too quick to label her as an outsider. The irony that she was acting just like a Mapledon villager herself wasn't lost.

Only one way of finding out.

'So, Lizzie – you visiting family too?' Anna turned to face Lizzie as they walked, wanting to gauge her reaction.

'Kinda, yes. No. Well, maybe . . .' Lizzie stuttered.

That solved that, then. Anna inwardly sighed. How could she proceed from there?

Anna guided Lizzie around the corner of Edgelands Lane, the small primary school coming into sight. Lizzie stopped walking, appearing to freeze to the spot.

'What's the matter?' Anna asked.

'Nothing, sorry.' She began walking again, her head bowed. 'Why did you say Mapledon had dragged you back, Anna?'

'It was only a turn of phrase, I guess. I just meant that it'd taken years to escape it – and its small-village mentality – and I never had the inclination to return once I'd left. But, with my mother still living here, well, it's like I can't quite *rid* myself of the place yet. While I still have her, I suppose it was inevitable that one day I'd need to come back here. And it seems yesterday was *that* day.'

'Is she ill, your mother?'

'I think she's showing some early signs of dementia.' Anna was surprised at herself for telling Lizzie. But then she always had found it easier to talk to someone outside of the family, someone who didn't know the people involved; couldn't judge.

'Ah. I'm sorry. It's a terrible thing watching the person you love become less like the person you've known all your life, I'm sure. Nice that you're here for her though. Are you the only child?'

'Yep. It's all on me. My mum and dad separated years ago, so Mum only has her neighbours and the other villagers to look out for her. You never really prepare yourself for a parent to deteriorate, to die – do you?' Anna gave a half-smile. Lizzie's skin had paled, and immediately Anna realised she'd put her foot in it. Shit. Lizzie had been coming out of the churchyard – what was the betting she'd been visiting the grave of one of her parents? Maybe even both. That would explain her odd 'kinda, yes, no,' response when she'd asked if she was visiting family. 'I'm sorry, Lizzie – I . . .' she faltered.

'It's fine. Really. And no, you're right, you don't prepare yourself – even in later years.' Lizzie dropped her gaze. 'But you especially don't prepare when you're just seven years old when it happens. How could a *child* ever envisage something happening to her parents?'

Oh, God. Anna flinched. 'How terrible,' she said, now wishing she hadn't begun this line of conversation. Anna had never been very good with other people's grief, and today she'd overdosed on it. As much as she wanted to move the conversation on to a brighter topic, she knew she'd opened this poor woman's wound now, so had no option but to watch the blood flow out. 'What happened?'

Anna's question was met with silence. They carried on walking, side by side – Anna led them past Major's Farm and along Langway Road, making sure to give a passing glance to each property, checking if anything unusual adorned their doors. They were almost at the turn that would take Anna back home when Lizzie finally spoke again.

'Cancer,' she said. 'My mother died of cervical cancer. She was only twenty-four.'

'I'm so sorry, Lizzie. That's shocking. It must've turned your world upside down.' Anna truly felt terrible for this woman – to have had such a young mother, then lose her. Her life must've changed dramatically afterwards. No doubt Lizzie had a long, probably painful story to tell, but Anna realised they were getting closer to Muriel's road now and she didn't really want to invite a stranger in. 'Er . . . I'm going to have to head back, actually. Mum will be anxious – I've been longer than I thought.'

''Course. Sure.' Lizzie looked around her, like she was lost. Of course. She'd dragged the poor woman quite a way from where her car was parked, through winding lanes. She was probably wondering how to get back to it.

'If you go left here it'll take you back onto the main road of Mapledon, then hook another left, back up the hill.' Anna smiled.

'Good, thanks. Oh, Anna – er . . . I have no place to stay, actually . . . so . . .'

'Oh.' Anna panicked for a moment, thinking Lizzie was angling to stay with her. Surely she wouldn't ask that of someone she'd just met? She hesitated before remembering the B&B on the edge of Mapledon. 'Have you checked out Bulleigh Barton? It's a beautiful place, rolling hillsides, quiet. I almost checked in myself rather than stay at my mother's! There's a leaflet for it in the shop window. It'll have their phone number – you'll see it when you head up the hill.'

'Great. I'd kinda left without any plan, really. And this didn't appear to be a place where I could get a cheap Airbnb deal,' Lizzie said.

'No, I guess it doesn't. There's literally just that one place within ten miles, I think. Not many visitors to Mapledon . . .'

'Not if they want to leave again, right?' Lizzie said, unsmiling. The intensity in her eyes made Anna shiver.

Chapter Twenty-Three

2019

Lizzie

So much for Anna having a 'story', Lizzie thought as she strode back to her car, her mind whirring. Visiting her mother who had dementia. Sentimental, and not exactly what Lizzie had been hoping to learn. Lizzie had failed to get Anna's surname – or her mother's name – no information regarding any recent events in this godforsaken village. She was no closer to finding out if *he* might be here. But, thanks to her new friend, she did now have a place to stay. Lizzie had finally got a mobile signal as she approached the top of the hill and booked herself into Bulleigh Barton for three nights. She reasoned that if she hadn't found what she was looking for within that time, then she never would.

A couple of people had openly stared at her as she'd stood punching the number of the B&B into her phone outside the shop. She'd been tempted to strike up a conversation but had ultimately chickened out, the thought of the questions *they'd* ask *her* putting her off. Before talking to anyone else, she required a night to prepare. She may have already said too much to Anna, who might well go straight home to her mother and repeat everything she'd said. Thinking about it, there was a strong possibility that by tomorrow the whole village would know her name. Had she been too quick to introduce herself? Giving her full name had been a mistake. Anna hadn't been that naive. But, she realised, if someone googled her, they were only likely to find articles she'd written, nothing about her past.

A journalist in Mapledon, though. How welcome would *that* be?

After sitting in her car contemplating for a good ten minutes, Lizzie reversed and instead of driving back down the main road leading out of Mapledon, she turned into the one that Anna had walked her down moments before. She pulled up outside the primary school, her heart fluttering furiously. A stream of disjointed memories had slammed into her brain from nowhere when she and Anna had walked past it. It had shocked her. So much so she'd felt debilitated; unable to move. These were things she knew she had to face if she were to have any chance of shaking off her past once and for all.

Lizzie put the car in gear and moved off again. She had an urge to see the bungalow – it couldn't be too hard to find in such a small village and she *had* recognised the school, so maybe other places would be familiar as well. A tiredness swept over her, though, so she decided it would be a task best left to tomorrow. Because if he *had* come back, then going there would be too much to handle in one day. To face him would take far more strength than she currently had. She'd rather know what she was likely to come up against, be better equipped. Her plan to get information from the villagers was the one she should follow to limit the hurt, the pain she would undoubtedly feel all over again.

As Anna had said, Bulleigh Barton was on the edge of Mapledon, barely half a mile outside, situated down a narrow lane and reached via a long driveway. As soon as Lizzie stepped out of her car she immediately felt calmer, more awake and far less anxious than she'd been in the village. It was as though the air was purer, less toxic. She was greeted warmly by the owner,

Gwen – a bubbly woman of around fifty with a soft, Irish lilt. Lizzie was offered tea and biscuits and then shown to her room, which had a luxurious double bed, a homely feel and overlooked the fields. It seemed, at least here, strangers were welcome. But maybe it was because Gwen had been an outsider herself once.

'This is perfect, thank you, Gwen,' Lizzie said, smiling.

'Let me know if there's anything I can do to make your stay better, won't you? You're my only guest at the moment.'

'Will do,' Lizzie said, her attention out the window at the cows in a neighbouring field. It was a far cry from built-up Abbingsworth. 'Oh, actually – do you have Wi-Fi here?'

For a horrible moment, as she caught the blank look on Gwen's face, she thought she was going to say no. But, with a wink, Gwen said: 'Yes – we're out in the sticks and signal isn't always grand, but we are in touch with the twenty-first century.'

Lizzie laughed. 'Great, that's good to know.'

Chapter Twenty-Four

1989

Fisher residence

Friday 14th July – 5 days before

Bella was sitting at the halfway point on the stairs, her left ear turned towards the closed sitting-room door, but annoyingly she couldn't make out what they were saying. She'd been sent to bed an hour ago, the same time as her dad had left for the pub. But the muffled voices – punctured every now and then with loud laughter – had risen through the floorboards making sleep impossible. Her mum's friends often came round for 'drinkies', as she called it, and at times the whole house was filled with women for the stupid Mapledon Meetings. But they were always on a Thursday night. Bella thought all of it was just an excuse for them to gossip and get drunk. The mornings after these get-togethers and meetings, Bella always noticed her mother wasn't herself, telling Bella she 'felt delicate' and that she couldn't cope with any of Bella's 'nonsense'. Dad would whisper 'hangover' in Bella's ear before leaving for work, or golf. She didn't know what it meant exactly, but eventually realised it just meant her mother had a headache and wasn't to be disturbed.

As her mum was drinking now, with Mrs Andrews and Auntie Tina, Bella knew tomorrow morning would be one of those times she'd have to keep her distance and let her mother be; she'd have another headache to get over. Disappointment raged through her. She'd wanted to get out of the village, maybe visit Bovey Tracey and go to some shops with her mum – have lunch in a café. Anything to take her away from the dullest place on earth. Anything to take her away from the stupid Knock, Knock games Jonie would make her play. She hated her mum sometimes.

Just as boredom was about to make her creep back to her room, Bella heard Mrs Andrews' voice more clearly. She must be right by the door. Bella ducked back a little from the open stairwell just in case she was coming out; she didn't want to be spotted and yelled at for eavesdropping.

'No one knows what he's capable of. No one *knows* him at all, not even where he came from. Just wish he wasn't *here*. I really thought he'd leave after his kid was taken.'

Bella heard murmurings, and what sounded like a disagreement, and thought she made out the words 'obviously wasn't enough', before hearing Mrs Andrews' voice clearly again.

'Anyway, I'll make sure it's on the agenda for the next meeting, even if you're not bothered, Tina. Sorry I can't stay for another—'

The lounge door swung open and Bella jumped up, moving swiftly towards her bedroom only moments before the women appeared. That'd been a close one. Bella listened as her mum and Mrs Andrews said goodbye and gave each other a kiss before the front door banged closed. The voices in the lounge became softer. Bella got back into bed. She guessed who they were talking about; he was all anyone seemed to talk about in this village. Bella wondered why he stayed too – she couldn't understand why anyone would want to be part of this place, let alone if everyone was rude and horrible to you.

What on earth had he done to make them so nasty?

Chapter Twenty-Five

2019

Anna

Sunday 14th July

At first, Anna assumed the banging on the door was Auntie Tina, but as she lifted her head from the pillow and checked the time on her mobile, she saw it was only six a.m. Who would visit at this hour on a Sunday? Then she heard quick footsteps promptly followed by a scream.

What the fuck? She launched herself from the bed, crashing against the doorframe in her rush to get out the bedroom.

'Mum, Mum! What is it?' Anna tore down the stairs, her pulse pounding in her neck almost as loud as her feet were on the treads.

Red liquid, from what appeared to be a burst plastic bag, pooled on the doormat.

'Is it real? Is it real blood, Anna?' Her mum was backing away as she repeated the words over and over.

'I – I'm not sure, Mum.' Avoiding the mess, Anna unlocked the front door, yanking it open quickly, hoping to catch the culprits red-handed. Literally. She peered out. No one was in sight, but as she drew her head back, she saw what had been hammered to the door. She didn't want to worry her mother further, but she couldn't exactly hide it either.

'What is it this time?' Muriel asked. Anna looked at her, taking in the frail woman whose shoulders were hunched in fear. This wasn't on. Someone was taking joy in terrorising a vulnerable woman and it angered her. This felt different from a kid's game. Personal.

'It's a doll's arm,' Anna said.

'This is ridiculous. Stupid kids – bags of blood shoved through the letterbox, things hammered to the door – what do they think they're *playing* at?'

'Mum, listen,' Anna said as she stepped back inside, over the red-stained mat. 'It's six in the morning – on a Sunday. How many kids do you know who'd be up this early? I don't think it's kids, I really don't.'

'So you think it's *him*?'

'I'm not saying that either. I mean, why would he? To what end? And why you? I haven't heard of anyone else receiving these doll's parts, have you?'

'No, no. But the timing . . .' Muriel carried on mumbling to herself, her thumbnail rammed in her mouth making the words indecipherable.

Yes, the timing was odd, she had to admit that; these things happening literally days after Billy Cawley's release surely couldn't be coincidental.

'Look, you go get a bucket of warm, soapy water and I'll take this outside.' Anna pointed to the doormat. 'See if I can salvage it.' Opening the door, then lifting both ends of the mat together in attempt to prevent the liquid running off the edges, Anna shuffled outside. It *was* runny, not gloopy or sticky-looking, so she was hopeful it wasn't real blood. She carefully walked with it down the side of the house to the back garden and laid it down on the lawn. Then she tilted it to let the liquid drain off. She watched as the red mess trickled into the green grass, staining it. Some had got on her hand; she wiped it in the grass too, but a pinky tinge remained. It was dye. Possibly just food colouring.

She deposited the now-empty plastic bag in the wheelie bin as she went back to the front door and pulled at the doll's arm. The nail had been driven through the upper part of the plastic arm. She had to twist it several times before it loosened. She pulled at it harder. It gave a pop as it came away and Anna stumbled backwards with the arm in her hand. The nail must've been hammered in with some force.

Anna turned the arm over in her hands, then frowned. There was something inside it, stuffed in the hollow. The opening was too small to get her fingers inside. She ran into the kitchen, almost knocking Muriel over, the water slopping out of the bucket she was carrying.

'Anna! Be careful,' she scolded, putting it down on the floor.

'Sorry,' Anna said. With the arm held on the worktop, she poked a metal skewer inside. After a few failed attempts at grabbing it, Anna finally pulled out a rolled-up piece of paper. Under her mother's watchful, and – she sensed – fearful gaze, Anna unravelled the paper, revealing bold red lettering.

SOMEONE HAS BLOOD ON THEIR HANDS

Anna and Muriel exchanged uneasy glances.

What was *that* supposed to mean?

Chapter Twenty-Six

2019

Lizzie

Lizzie hadn't attempted sleep until gone three a.m. After eating the meal provided by Gwen, she'd soaked in the beautiful claw-footed bathtub. Then, wrapped in the fluffy white bathrobe that had been hanging on the back of the door, she'd sat at the desk overlooking the garden and set about researching Mapledon and some of its residents. She'd found nothing on Anna. There was plenty of information about William Cawley, though: news articles about his conviction and the fact he'd put in a late plea bargain to the charge of the abduction and murder of Jonie Hayes, other articles about the evidence found in his truck, and the devastation felt within the 'small, tight-knit community of Mapledon'.

Lizzie struggled to read them. It was too close – too raw, even now. But she knew she had to. She'd compartmentalised all of it for years, pretending it had happened to other people – people she didn't know or care about. If she tried hard enough, she could detach herself again now, read it all as an outsider, someone with no involvement or investment.

Having had a stern word with herself, she'd continued scouring the articles for names and had noted down those that appeared most frequently: *Tina Hayes*, obviously as she was the mother of the victim; a source close to the family, *Nell Andrews*; family friend *Muriel Fisher* and local vicar, *Reverend Christopher Farnley*. She'd also been surprised to learn that a key piece of evidence was from a witness to the abduction – Jonie Hayes' ten-year-old friend, named only as '*Girl B*' for legal reasons. She hadn't remembered this. But then, she'd avoided this kind of search before, not feeling the need or desire to delve into the past.

Now, having woken with a headache and dry mouth, Lizzie reluctantly peeled herself from the comfortable double bed, stumbled to the tea tray on the unit in the corner and popped the kettle on. The names from the articles still swirled in her mind. Muriel Fisher's had come as no surprise. Hers was one Lizzie *did* remember. And once she'd seen Reverend Farnley's name, that too had sparked recall. But Nell Andrews wasn't one she remembered. The problem was that Lizzie could never be sure if any of the memories she recalled were truly *her* memories, or ones she'd taken on and remembered from what other people had told her over the years. She wondered if she'd ever really know which were hers.

Sitting cross-legged on the bed, Lizzie called Dom. He'd only sent one text yesterday to which she'd replied a brief 'all's fine', and she got the impression he was pissed off. She *had* upped and left at short notice. While he did understand her job might take her somewhere abruptly, usually she'd have at least spoken to him before leaving rather than merely leaving a brief note.

'Hey, babe – so sorry for leaving in a rush.' She got her apology in quickly, before he'd even said hello.

'Well, I was disappointed when I got home to find you gone, and without a call, or even a text . . .' His voice was distant, and it immediately set Lizzie on edge. She hated to think she'd upset him; hated the thought he was mad at her even more.

'I know, I know. I didn't have much time, sorry – once the decision was made, I didn't want to hang around—'

'Really, Lizzie? You took a few minutes at least to find the paper and write a note, but didn't have time to hit your speed dial and call me? You know there's a little button on your phone that means you can be hands free and everything, so you could have packed your bag whilst speaking to me or even called from the car.' Sarcasm dripped from his words. Lizzie had no argument, so she said nothing. The silence stretched. She heard him sigh.

'So, what was so urgent you had to rush off without so much as a by-your-leave?'

Lizzie took a moment to consider her choice of words. If she'd managed to carry out her plan to come clean about everything, Dom would now have been in possession of the facts and she wouldn't feel the need to play this down. Or lie. But she hadn't, and now – over the phone – was definitely not the right time.

'It was a breaking news story, time-sensitive, and it sounded . . .' She hesitated. 'Beefy. I wanted it, that's all, so had to rush to get here. It's near Dartmoor, in Devon—'

'Bloody hell, that's a long way away – why on earth do you want to cover a story there?'

She felt she owed him some element of truth here. She took a deep breath.

'Because once, a really long time ago . . . I lived here.' Before Dom could question her on this statement, she added, 'I can't remember any of it, I was only little and it was for a very brief time. But it intrigued me enough to make me want to come back and look into it.'

Even to her, it sounded weak. But Dom didn't press further, just asked exactly where she was. Lizzie gave him the name of the B&B and after a few minutes of general chat, she hung up.

After breakfast she was going to drive back into Mapledon and go to Brook Cottage Store to buy a few items. Stranger or not, if she wanted to make any headway, she had to speak to other villagers. She'd ask about Muriel Fisher – she might get away with saying she was a friend of the family. It was risky though, as, if she gave her name as Lizzie Brenfield – as she'd done to Anna yesterday – and they then spoke to Muriel, she would immediately say Lizzie was an imposter, a liar.

On the other hand, giving her real name would only open a big-arsed can of worms . . .

Chapter Twenty-Seven

1989

Hayes residence

Wednesday 12th July – 1 week before

Auntie Tina made the best banana cake. It was one of the high-lights of going over to Jonie's after school.

'You're lucky there's still some left – Miss Gannet Guts over there had almost half of it for breakfast!' Tina said.

Bella laughed as she shovelled the slab of cake into her mouth, causing her to cough and send crumbs flying, making them all laugh harder.

'Careful, don't choke. How would I explain that to your mum?'

Jonie gave Bella a hard slap on the back even though she wasn't coughing anymore. She moved away from her, saying she was fine. There had been no need for that. Bella thought it was just an excuse to whack her. She thought Auntie Tina noticed too, because she stopped laughing and stood in between them both, draping one arm over each of their shoulders.

'You looking forward to the school holidays?' Tina asked in a falsely bright way.

'Um, hell yeah,' Jonie said.

'Watch your language,' Tina said. But Jonie just rolled her eyes.

'I'm not that bothered, really.' Bella's words drew a shocked glance from Tina and Jonie.

'What? Are you for real?' Jonie's frown made her eyes go dark.

'I don't mind school – I like learning stuff.'

'You're such a square, Bella!'

'No she isn't, Jonie – don't say things like that.' Auntie Tina gave Bella a big smile. 'It's good to want to learn. Don't let anyone put you off, love. Knowledge is power,' she said, adding more quietly as she released her arms from them, 'and your ticket out of this place.'

Before Bella could ask what she meant, the back door opened and a man's head popped around.

'Hello, ladies. How are you all on this fine afternoon?'

The girls giggled, as did Tina. 'We're good, Pat – what brings you here?'

Bella watched as the policeman emerged from behind the door, closed it and wiped his feet on the doormat. Everyone knew Officer Vern. He 'kept an eye' on Mapledon because he had lived in the village all his life; the place was too small to have its own police station. Bella thought it must be a boring job because nothing interesting ever happened. It seemed the most he'd ever had to do was tell kids off. And if she heard her dad say: 'In my day, coppers could give you a clip around the ear and you'd behave yourself,' one more time she'd puke.

As he leant back against the kitchen sink, she noted his tummy bulged slightly over the top of his black trousers. Bella concluded he hadn't ever run after any baddies; he didn't look like he got much exercise at all. He smiled, then glanced at Auntie Tina; he hadn't answered her question, but he seemed to be waiting for something.

'Girls, why don't you both go and watch some TV, or play outside for a bit?' Tina said, her smile vanishing.

Jonie grabbed Bella's arm. 'Come on, let's go have some fun. See you later, Mum.'

Bella eyed Auntie Tina as she was being dragged out the back door. She thought she looked worried. What did the policeman want? Her tummy lurched. What if it was to do with Creepy Cawley? Had he called the police about the Knock, Knock games the kids were always playing? She'd only been to his bungalow a few times after school with Jonie, but if he'd seen them, would he have known who they were? Her mum would kill her if she found out they'd been 'terrorising' him.

Bella wished she could hear what was being said in Auntie Tina's kitchen right now . . .

Chapter Twenty-Eight

2019

Anna

Sunday 14th July

Anna wanted to go back home. She'd only agreed to stay the weekend out of a sense of duty; there'd been no plan to stay beyond Sunday. But now, with the latest development, she wondered how she could merely up and leave Muriel alone to face whatever danger was lurking. *If* it was danger that she'd be facing. Anna's optimism it was only a prank had taken a battering after the fake blood, doll's arm and the message contained within it, but there was a sliver of hope remaining.

She couldn't very well leave her mother now. What kind of daughter would that make her?

Anna called James, explaining briefly what was going on.

'Why don't you get Muriel to pack a suitcase and you bring her back to Bristol? At least then you'll be out of harm's way and after a week or so maybe it'll all have blown over. Or they'll be targeting someone else.'

'Yes, getting her away from here would be one option.' Anna chewed a fingernail while mulling it over.

'And you've called the police, I take it?'

'Not yet, no. Mum's keen not to involve them at the moment,

until we know more. She doesn't want to make the situation worse, especially if it's just kids.'

'Would kids be taking it this far, though, Anna? Look, come back here with Muriel. Carrie would enjoy spending some of the holidays with her Nanna, and you wouldn't have to feel guilty about being away from her. It makes sense.'

It did make sense. It was the niggling feeling creeping beneath her skin that prevented her from immediately packing and getting out of there with Muriel in tow. She couldn't pinpoint why, but she felt she had to stay, find out who was doing it. More importantly, she wanted to know *why*.

'I can't explain, James, but I think I have to stay for a bit longer. Put Carrie on. I'll talk to her, tell her I need to be with Nanna for longer. She'll understand.'

'She probably won't . . .' he said. Anna heard rustling as James walked around the house to give the phone to Carrie. Anna tensed. It was a conversation she knew would upset them both. She had to try and make it sound like it was an exciting opportunity for her to be with her dad. Anna would have to make it up to her.

After some coaxing, a bit of bribery and assurances that Anna loved her, Carrie finally seemed placated and Anna went back inside to her mother.

'I've spoken to James, Mum. I'm staying for a few more days.'

'Oh, that's good, love. Thank you.' Her mind was elsewhere, Anna sensed.

'I meant to say as well, Auntie Tina is popping in at ten-ish.'

'What?' Muriel shot Anna a quizzical glance. 'What do you mean, popping in? How do you know this?'

'Didn't I mention yesterday that I'd seen her?' Anna felt disingenuous, knowing full well she hadn't uttered a word about it.

'No. You most certainly did not!'

Anna was shocked at her tone. Had things really become that bad between them?

'Sorry, I bumped into her while I was walking around the village. She asked after you, and me, of course. She mentioned getting together, so I invited her for a coffee and catch-up.' Anna paused. 'I assumed it would be okay?'

Muriel chewed on her lower lip, saying nothing.

'Mum?'

Muriel shook her head and tutted. 'You should've checked with me first, Anna. I don't want to see her.'

'Why not? What on earth happened between you two?'

'It's water under the bridge, dear. It'll do no good dredging up the past.'

'We don't need to. I think she just wants to talk about now – how you are, probably what I've been doing.' Even as she was saying it, Anna got an uneasy feeling. Auntie Tina hadn't seemed as though she'd really be interested to hear about Anna's life. Yesterday, she'd come across as bitter that Anna had been the one to live at all. The visit was looking like a potential disaster. She wished she could take the invite back now.

'I doubt Tina will be wanting to talk about the future.'

'When did you last speak to her though? Maybe she's moved on.'

'She never moved on, Anna. From the day Jonie went missing, Tina changed. She's not who you knew when you were growing up. We lost our connection, really, when we lost Jonie. From that moment on I think she began to resent me, although she seemingly tried to hide it, keeping it all in for a while. But it must've deepened over the months and it came to a head a few years later. It erupted then, causing her to despise me, you – everyone who continued with their life unaltered—'

'God, *no one* was left unaltered, Mum. Surely she knows that.'

'No one suffered like Tina suffered – she made sure everyone knew *that*. Not even Mark, God rest his soul.' Muriel made a sign of the cross before carrying on. 'His grief wasn't as great, his loss not as profound. No one could understand, no one could truly know what Tina had been through, continued to go through. She looked for that girl night after night, for years. It destroyed her.' Tears shone on Muriel's dry, crinkly cheeks. 'It ripped her marriage apart, something Mark didn't recover from, and it eventually destroyed our friendship too. Even the village never felt the same again. Not *safe*. It never really recovered.'

'Did you ever tell Tina this? Like you've just told me?'

'Of course. But it didn't help. She never forgave me, you see.'

'For what?'

'For it being Jonie and not you.' Muriel looked into Anna's eyes. For a split second, all Anna saw was pain. But something else was hidden there too. Guilt? Surely the person who'd delivered the bloody message couldn't be alluding to Muriel having blood on *her* hands?

Chapter Twenty-Nine

2019

Lizzie

Brook Cottage Store looked like one of those shops that simply didn't exist in the twenty-first century. Lizzie had a sense of déjà vu when she walked through the door and a bell rang out – the gentle tinkling sound touching a memory. She closed her eyes for a moment, trying to capture it. She'd been inside the store before, she felt sure. But of course, she was bound to have been – it was the only shop in Mapledon now, so it *must've* been the only one when she lived here.

Grabbing a wire basket, Lizzie began to walk up the first aisle. As she cast her gaze about her, she wondered if she'd be stared at, or even approached by curious shoppers. But, she realised, there were currently only two other customers, and one person working the till. It was Sunday morning, so she didn't expect it was going to be teeming with villagers. Even driving up the main street she'd been surprised at how dead it was; she'd only seen one older man walking a dog.

Thinking about the likely demographic of the village, she concluded it would be the older folk up and about now, coming to the store to collect their Sunday papers – unless of course there were kids doing the paper delivery rounds. But it was the older residents she was hoping to see anyway; they'd be the ones most likely to remember what happened here, and to know about any new developments since Billy Cawley's release. Though, they'd probably be the same people who would close ranks and refuse to speak to her about any of it. Her best hope was overhearing local gossip. And she was in a prime place for that.

She thought about the guy working the till. If he worked here full-time, he'd be privy to all the chatter, all the gossip. Shop workers often were – they were the next best thing to hairdressers in that respect. Lizzie carried on browsing the products on the shelf, deciding as she went that if she didn't hear any interesting snippets of information, she'd try her luck with the till guy. She could turn on the charm when she needed to. She could get him talking. It was her job, after all.

Lizzie felt his eyes on her before she turned and saw that he was, indeed, watching her. She'd been so long browsing she'd obviously caught his attention, and now he maybe thought she was a shoplifter. She smiled and then placed another random item in the basket before ambling around the end of the next aisle. She almost said something, but one of the two other people in the shop approached the till and so she bit her tongue. She hovered within earshot.

Please, please, have a gossip.

Lizzie gave an audible sigh when the people at the till lowered their voices to such a level she couldn't make out any of their conversation. It's like they *knew* what she was there for. Frustration bubbled inside her. She'd have to think of a way in, something to pique the man's interest to enable her to ask a few questions without ringing alarm bells. She waited for the customers to leave, then slammed her basket on the counter.

'Makes such a change to have the time to peruse what your lovely shop has to offer. There aren't any shops like this one where I live now – I do miss this village,' Lizzie said. It garnered a frown from the man. She could almost see the cogs working overtime trying to place her.

'Oh? You used to live here? I don't . . .' He shook his head, giving a cautious smile.

'Years ago now, you wouldn't recognise me – I don't recognise you either.' Lizzie took a carrier and began putting the items in after he'd slowly scanned them.

'So, who do you belong to?' He said it in a light-hearted way, but Lizzie sensed the undercurrent of uneasiness. Like immediately he hadn't believed her. She had to be careful now, although at this point there was little to lose. Should she drop Anna's name, even though she didn't know her surname, or who *she* belonged to? She could play it relatively safe and mention Muriel Fisher instead. At least she had the full name and knew she'd been a villager back then. She'd checked death records and hadn't found an entry, so she assumed she was still alive. And as Anna had jokingly said yesterday, people didn't often leave Mapledon, so it was a good bet she still lived here. She couldn't remember, or didn't know, if she had siblings, though. She wondered if she could get away with saying she was a niece. Sod it, she had to try something.

'No one anymore, my own parents are gone, sadly – but I do have a cousin here. I'm making a fleeting visit before I go abroad to work.' Lizzie inwardly cringed – she didn't know where that came from, she hadn't planned to say cousin, she'd meant to just say aunt. She moved on, quickly changing it in the hope he hadn't taken it in. 'My aunt is getting on a bit now. Muriel – do you know her?'

She'd done it now. No backtracking would change it.

'Oh, of course! Everyone knows Muriel. She's a good friend of my mum's. They've been friends for donkey's years, and her daughter is roughly my age so we kinda grew up together in Mapledon.'

Lizzie smiled, but not wishing to get caught out by not knowing the daughter's name, carried on without comment. 'Yes, so anyway, being back here is a bit odd, really.' Lizzie lowered her head, watching his expression through her fringe. 'You know, the timing and all.' She hoped that would be enough to elicit a remark from him. Unfortunately, he simply said 'hmmm' and continued scanning.

She changed tack. 'I've never forgotten that poor girl. I've found myself wondering what happened to her over the years. This village holds such sad memories.' She swiped at a pretend tear.

'I know, same.' He moved his hand towards her, but withdrew it again before touching her. 'I'm sorry. It's a difficult time for so many of us. It's all people are talking to me about and to be honest, it's getting me down now. I'm hearing the same things over and over from different people. It's so draining.'

'Gosh, yes – I hadn't thought about that. It must be terrible for you, and now I'm adding to it. It's not like you can get away from it,' Lizzie said, offering a sympathetic smile. 'I assume you live in the village?'

'Yes. Still here, living with my mum. And I know, before you say it, it's such a cliché. God, it's actually sad, but I always felt I had to stay, after it all. Then, as she's aged, she's needed more help, so . . . you know.'

'That sounds perfectly reasonable – not a cliché at all,' Lizzie said, thinking the exact opposite. 'Hey – is there still a pub here?' Lizzie remembered seeing it as she'd walked up the main street yesterday.

'Yes – not that it's great, if I'm honest. Mainly old people.' He said the last bit in a whisper from behind his hand. Lizzie laughed.

'Well, do you fancy dropping the average age of its punters a bit by having a drink with me later?'

The man's eyes brightened. 'Sure, would love to. What time?'

'Say . . . eight?'

'Great. It's a hundred yards or so to the right as you go down the hill. I'll meet you outside if you like?'

That would be a good idea – she didn't want to draw unwanted attention by going in alone. 'Yes, lovely. See you later.' Lizzie took her bag from the counter. 'Sorry, I'm Lizzie, by the way.'

'I'm Robert. Rob. Bob. Bobby. Any of those.' He smiled warmly. 'Nell's son. We own this shop – in case you didn't know that already.'

Lizzie returned his smile. Nell, as in Nell Andrews. Perfect.

Chapter Thirty

1989

Blackstone Close

Saturday 8th July – 11 days before

Billy lifted his head from the arm of the sofa, immediately regretting doing so: it felt heavy, clogged, painful. His tongue was dry too, sticking to the roof of his mouth – he had to free it with his forefinger, causing him to gag; it made a strange suction sound as it released. He rested his head back gently while dropping his arm and feeling around, exploring the floor beside the sofa with his fingertips until he located the can. He took a swig from the remaining content – the warm lager tasted foul, but he continued to gulp it down anyway – anything to relieve the dehydration.

A sinking feeling surged through his gut. The can was his last. How would he get through another night of loneliness, of guilt and regrets, if he didn't have alcohol? He'd need to replenish his stock, but couldn't face going to Brook Cottage Store to buy it. Couldn't face the judgement, the accusations. And he dare not drive outside of Mapledon to acquire some – if he got stopped, he knew his blood alcohol level would put him over the limit. Though incarceration might actually be better than how he was living right now, he would never turn this around if he were in prison.

He snorted. If he was being honest, and taking a good, hard look at himself, then he would never turn it around by diving into the bottle every time he hit a stumbling block either. He needed to pull himself together, get back to work. The problem with working for himself was having no one else to answer to and having a plethora of excuses for why he couldn't find any carpentry jobs. The people of Mapledon wouldn't employ him. He had to go further afield – and in his current state of mind it was too much effort. Much easier to lie about all day and wallow in self-pity.

God, he missed her.

He'd let her down so badly.

His forced solitude was suffocating him. If only people could give him a chance, instead of believing all the terrible stories flying around. If only he had company. Being by himself all the time wasn't good for him. Never had been. He needed, *craved* someone to understand him. To be beside him and love him. To trust him.

But, did he deserve any of that after messing up so badly?

Chapter Thirty-One

2019

Anna

Sunday 14th July

Anna paced the lounge from the doorway to the window and back, the edge of one thumbnail jammed between her teeth, chewing on it vigorously as she waited for Auntie Tina to walk down the path.

'For goodness' sake, love, you're making *me* nervous,' Muriel said. 'Stand still. Or better yet, sit.'

'I can't. Not now you've told me I've done the wrong thing inviting her here. If she hates me for merely living, then why does she want to come for coffee? Is she going to lace it with arsenic?'

'And I thought I was the one who blew things out of proportion,' Muriel muttered, giving Anna a knowing look. Anna smiled weakly. Did her mum know that's what she often said about her – what she told other people – that her mother was inclined to dramatise?

The doorbell startled her, in turn making Muriel jump.

Anna shot a wide-eyed glance towards her mum and headed to the door.

'Morning, Auntie Tina,' Anna said.

'You going to keep me on the doorstep?'

Anna stood back quickly. She hadn't realised she'd frozen. 'Sorry, yes – come in.'

Even though the morning was warm, Anna felt a chill as Tina brushed past her and walked into the lounge. She took a slow breath in, closed the door, then headed into the lion's den.

'Haven't seen you out and about for a while, Muriel,' Tina said, as soon as she sat at the dining table.

'The way it goes sometimes.' Muriel gave a shrug.

Anna faffed about with the coffee and mugs, trying to busy herself until the awkward first comments were done with.

'Surprised me, that's all – I assumed you'd be the first to be gossiping at the shop, not avoiding everyone.'

'I'm not avoiding anyone. I've been a bit under the weather, that's all.' Muriel's tone was defensive.

'Ah. Yes. I noted Nell was "under the weather" too,' Tina said, repeating Muriel's words while making air quotes with her fingers. 'Must be catching.'

Anna wasn't sure of the relevance of Tina's observation, but something was passing between the two of them that Anna wasn't privy to.

'Here we go,' Anna said as she placed a mug in front of Tina. 'Biscuits?'

'No, thanks. I might choke.'

Anna bit her lip. She may not know exactly what had gone down, what had caused this frostiness, this animosity, but she was close to telling them both to grow the fuck up.

'Why are you here, Tina?' Finally, her mother had voiced the question burning in Anna's throat.

'Obvious, isn't it?'

'I do remember the anniversary. I do every year.'

'This one is particularly significant though, wouldn't you agree?'

'Because of him?'

Tina sipped her coffee, then banged the mug down. 'He's out. He's free. He's back.'

A shiver travelled the length of Anna's spine and the way Muriel's face had lost all its colour indicated she'd had a similar reaction.

'What makes you think he's back?'

'No need to be coy, Muriel. I *know* you've had one too.'

So, Tina *had* received a similar macabre message hammered to her door. Were they the only ones?

Anna stared at Muriel, watching as she struggled to look Tina in the eye.

'Yes, Auntie Tina. She had one. Two now, in fact.'

Tina's mouth gaped. 'When?'

Muriel lifted her head. 'First one was Friday. Second was this morning. You?'

'Just the one. Friday. But I imagine there'll be more to come.'

'I think you might be jumping to conclusions, Auntie Tina. Mum thinks it's probably teenagers with nothing better to do. I mean, why would Billy be doing this? It doesn't make sense – surely he'll just land himself back in prison.' Anna joined them at the table, her questioning gaze darting from her mother to Auntie Tina.

'After all that time locked up, perhaps he can't handle being out – back in the real world. He might *want* to be put back inside,' Tina said. 'Or . . .' Auntie Tina ran her fingers through her thinning hair. 'His desire for revenge outweighs the risks.'

'Revenge? For what? He's the one who committed murder!' Anna shouted. 'And it's deplorable that he never disclosed where he hid poor—' Anna stopped, aware her angry outburst might not be appropriate for the mother of the victim to hear.

'Oh, Bella. Your naivety is less endearing now you're an adult.'

'I told you, it's Anna now.' The huffy tone made her sound childish, which angered her even more than Tina's snide comment. She'd not been that innocent. And besides, she'd only been ten years' old when all of this happened – how was she supposed to remember everything, understand all the details and subtleties surrounding the events?

'Sorry, *Anna*. All I'm saying is Billy Cawley felt wronged by the people in Mapledon. For numerous reasons.'

Anna was going to ask what the specific reasons were, but got the feeling she might not be told the truth. Or even whether she really wanted to know.

Chapter Thirty-Two

2019

Lizzie

Lizzie had arrived at the pub ten minutes early. She was now sitting waiting on the wooden bench at the bus stop opposite the building, trying to appear inconspicuous. She'd left the car near the church again and walked, thinking she'd draw less attention to herself – but now, as she felt eyes on her, Lizzie wondered if that plan had failed.

Two men in their late fifties, she approximated, were sitting at a table in the small, gravelled area beside the entrance of The Plough. They were nursing pints, and each had a cigarette between their fingers – plumes of smoke curling above their heads. Their eyes turned towards her several times as they spoke, their deep voices drifting across the road, but Lizzie couldn't make out what they were talking about or if their topic of conversation was 'the stranger on the bench'.

As she considered getting up, crossing over, and entering the pub just to stop the curious glances, she caught sight of Robert. He was exiting the side alley to the right of the pub, one that also ran alongside Brook Cottage Store. It was good she'd been able to identify another villager who'd previously just been a name in an article – finding out he was the son of 'family friend' Nell Andrews had been very helpful prior to this meeting. She stood, and began walking to meet him, relieved she'd no longer be alone.

'Hi, Rob,' she said, deciding in that moment he was more of a Rob than a Bob, or a Bobby. He was dressed casually – jeans and a short-sleeved shirt. His hair was slick with gel, which only served to accentuate his receding hairline, but he was attractive in a boy-next-door kind of way.

'Wasn't sure you'd show,' he said in return.

Lizzie raised her eyebrows, questionably – uncertain what he meant.

Rob smiled. 'I thought you might have been joking there in the shop, asking to meet at the pub.'

'Oh. I wouldn't have asked if I hadn't meant it. Why would you think that?'

'Sometimes people say things they don't really mean,' he said, shrugging.

'Oh, dear. That sounds as though you have prior experience.'

'Well, yes – it's been known. But it's been more usual for me to ask someone out, not the other way around. I think some just said yes to get out of the awkward situation and then left me hanging. Although, it's not like there are many ladies in Mapledon who are eligible *and* in the right age bracket. The pickings are very slim in the first place . . .'

'I see. So, that makes me feel *real* special.'

'Oh, my God. I didn't mean that to sound . . . you don't live here – I don't mean you,' he said, flustered.

Lizzie gave him a gentle knock in the shoulder with her fist to indicate she was teasing him. But then had a surge of panic. She was acting as though she was keen on him, *wanted* to be special. Christ, she was only meant to be charming him in order to get information, not coming across as wanting more than just a drink. She'd have to rein it in. Maybe mention her husband, quickly, before she led this poor guy on. He seemed nice enough; she didn't want to be *that* disingenuous.

'Anyway, you caught me on a good day. I was feeling generous, so turned up,' she said.

'Oh great. First round's on you, then.' He grinned, then swung the door open, standing back to allow Lizzie to walk in first. She ducked under his arm and entered what she could only describe as a dingy dive. The place probably looked the same now as it had thirty years ago. And, after a quick glance around the small bar area, she reckoned the few punters were likely the same ones who drank there thirty years ago too. Now, as it'd been then, it was the only watering hole for about ten miles. For a second, she wondered if any of these people were Billy Cawley, but then dismissed the idea – if he was back, she couldn't imagine the locals would allow him to drink in their pub.

'All right, Dave,' Rob said as he approached the bar. 'Pint of Hunters Premium, please, mate. And . . .' He held his hand, palm up towards Lizzie. 'What about you?'

'Oh, erm . . . gin and slimline tonic, please.' Lizzie smiled at Dave, who didn't return the gesture. She already felt uncomfortable being there. 'I'll just go and sit down, then.' She walked to the table farthest from the bar and the other drinkers – which, she realised, wasn't far enough. She could hear them talking and caught 'bloody outsider', and 'no doubt after a story' and sank a little lower in the chair. She knew it would be this way, but that didn't make it any less awkward. Lizzie got the impression she wasn't going to be winning friends anytime soon. In a moment of madness, she almost shouted, 'Don't you know who I am?' She was damned sure they'd be all interested if they realised. Interested, or angry. Probably neither was an outcome she really wished for. Best to bite her tongue and take the hostility on the chin.

'There you go, Lizzie. I got him to jazz it up a bit.' He smiled, indicating the glass. Lizzie gave him a frown in return. Rob, obviously realising she didn't have a clue what he was referring to, added: 'Ice and a slice? *Plus* a straw. As jazzed up as it gets here,' as way of explanation.

'Oh, I was rather expecting an umbrella.'

'Really? I can—'

'I was joking, Rob.'

'Oh. Sorry. City humour . . . guess I'm not used to it.'

Lizzie shook her head mockingly. They sipped at their drinks for a while without speaking. Her mind was working overtime to formulate the questions she wanted to ask him in a non-threatening way. She needed to frame them so Rob thought she were merely curious to find out what had happened in her absence, rather than grilling him as though it were the sole purpose for meeting him. A blush travelled up her neck. For the first time ever, she felt ashamed for using someone in this way.

'If you don't mind me asking, how come you're spending what precious little time you have before you jet off abroad here with me, when you came to spend it with Muriel and Bella?' Rob asked, breaking the silence.

Lizzie hesitated. Bella must be Muriel's daughter – she'd told Rob she was there to see her cousin before she mentioned her 'Auntie' Muriel and, as he knew them, he'd put two and two together. That was helpful.

'Well, I've got tomorrow still. Maybe even the Tuesday; it all depends.'

'Oh? On what?' His smile reached his grey-green eyes and they twinkled, even in the dull room. She averted her gaze, realising she was making the whole situation more complicated. He was openly flirting with her and she was allowing it. Worse, encouraging it. *God, if Dom could see this.*

'Depends how desperate I am to escape from Mapledon.'

'Right.' For a moment he looked hurt, like he'd taken her statement as a personal insult, but then his face relaxed again, and he leant across the table, his upper body close to hers. 'I get that,' he said in a hushed voice. He turned his head to look around him before carrying on in his whispered tone. 'You were lucky to escape the first time, really. In fact, I'm surprised you considered visiting again, however fleeting. Just in case.'

Lizzie's blood ran cold. 'You're not the first person to say something like that.' She pulled back from him slightly. It wasn't a normal thing for people to say, and yet both people she'd met had given the same creepy warning. Or what felt like a warning. She couldn't dismiss the possibility of it being a thinly veiled threat. *Stay too long and you'll never leave,* or maybe *dig deep enough and you'll unearth secrets that could get you killed.* She was over-exaggerating now, her mind galloping. She should get a grip. They'd only been joking. Hadn't they? Whatever the reason for Anna's and Rob's flippant comments, Lizzie was feeling more anxious with each 'joke'.

She wondered who'd be next to suggest she leave Mapledon while she still could.

Chapter Thirty-Three

1989

Mapledon Church

Sunday 2nd July – 17 days before

'Reverend, I need to speak with you. In private.'

'Right now, Muriel?' Reverend Farnley's brow furrowed as he laid the book he'd been reading to the children on his lap. The group of three girls and two boys stared up from their sitting position on the rug in the corner, quietly waiting for the story to resume. 'I'm in the middle of telling the story of Noah.'

'Sorry, but I don't think this should wait,' Muriel said, her eyes travelling to the floor where Eliza Cawley was sitting, her body turned away from the rest of the group, then back to Reverend Farnley.

'Oh, well, then. Give me a second and I'll see you in the vestry.' He stood, then beckoned to Wendy, one of the other Sunday school helpers, to come and take over from him. He strode to the vestry.

'What is the matter, Muriel?'

'Well, as you are . . . *aware* . . .' Muriel gave him a knowing look '. . . something isn't quite right with little Eliza Cawley. I need to ask for your guidance. *His* guidance, Reverend Farnley.'

'I see. What is it that has concerned you now?'

'It's the very sensitive matter we touched upon before. It's not something that can be ignored any longer.'

'Go on, Muriel. I will need the full facts, though.' He raised his eyebrows.

'She's a strange child—'

'There are no strange children, Muriel. Only troubled ones.'

Muriel shook her head impatiently. 'Yes, well, troubled then. In any case, I've been keeping an eye on her behaviour: the way she doesn't, or can't, interact with the other children her age, the things she says, the things she plays with – and giving me the most concern, the *way* she plays with things – is not normal.'

'Have you spoken with Eliza since our last discussion?'

'You mean, have I asked direct questions about her home life?'

'I mean, have you asked her anything at all about this?'

'I have, yes.'

Reverend Farnley shuffled his feet; his face became solemn. 'And?'

'I think there *is* abuse, Reverend,' she whispered.

Reverend Farnley took a step back, his face blanching. 'Right, I see. That accusation cannot be made lightly, Muriel, and not without evidence. I thought we'd spoken of this.'

'I think there is evidence. I just need your help to ensure she's safe.'

'I'm not sure I follow.'

'Everyone knows Billy Cawley isn't going to win a father-of-the-year award, and no child has ever been allowed to go and play after school with Eliza. He keeps her to himself – I'm surprised he allows her to come to Sunday school, but then I think that was due to your encouragement, was it not?'

'Yes, I did work rather hard to get her included,' he said, running his fingers along the edge of his smooth chin.

'There are bruises on that girl—'

'All children of her age get bruises from playing, Muriel. That in itself doesn't mean anything.'

'It does when the bruises are on her wrists, as though she's been restrained.'

'I'm worried we're jumping to conclusions here.'

'I asked her earlier about why she pulls the heads and limbs off her dolls. And do you know what she said?'

'Go on.'

'She said it makes her feel better if the dolls suffer too. She doesn't feel as alone. How terrible is that?'

'I agree that is very troubling. We should keep a closer eye on her.'

'No. We should do more than that. We need to make sure he can't hurt her.'

'How?'

'We've already got it planned and I've been able to put some things into action . . . but I'm going to need your help for the next bit, Reverend.'

'I'm not sure it's a good idea for me to get involved in this, Muriel.'

'Oh, I think it is, Reverend.'

Muriel stared at his face – at the worry etched in his features.

'Sit down, Reverend. We need to discuss this now.'

Chapter Thirty-Four

2019

Anna

Sunday 14th July

The three women sat around the dining table, now on their second cups of coffee.

'What are we going to do about it?' Tina asked.

'We have no proof it's him. Not at the moment. We need to catch him in the act, maybe?' Anna said.

'Don't you think that might be too risky?' Muriel's attention seemed to be lost in her mug of coffee.

'Mum – I know you want this to just blow over, but if Auntie Tina is right, Billy Cawley is out for revenge. I don't think he'll stop at a few bloody doll's parts. That's just the beginning. He'll be working up to something. We have to inform the police. At worst, we're right – but then they'll put him right back inside.'

'And if we're wrong?'

'Then we can try and find the little shits who've been doing it.'

'If we're wrong, Anna, he'll be angry with us that we've implicated him, and that could actually make him do something against us.'

'Do you still hold the monthly Mapledon Meetings?' Anna asked.

A strange look passed between Muriel and Tina. 'They were . . . well, *disbanded*, so to speak.'

'Maybe now is the time to reassemble the group. It affects everyone, doesn't it? Everyone should come together for this.'

'I'm not sure,' Tina said, lowering her gaze. 'It'll feel like a manhunt all over again.'

'How do you feel about the man who murdered your daughter being free, Tina? Free to terrorise this community again.'

Tina snapped her head up, her glowering stare fixing on Anna.

'That's unfair. You weren't aware of everything that went on – you were too young. Then, when you were old enough to understand, you buggered off, never came back. Well, until two days ago. Don't start flinging your weight about now. It's nothing to do with you.'

'It is when he's threatening my mother!'

'You don't know enough to say how we should handle it now, though. It was *my* daughter. *My* hell. *I* should be the one to say how we deal with him.'

'Well, you let me know what you two come up with then, yeah? And I'll just sit back and watch you make another huge mistake.' Anna slumped against the back of the chair, folding her arms tightly across her chest. 'I wonder who'll suffer the consequences of your poor decisions *this* time?'

Chapter Thirty-Five

2019

Lizzie

They'd been in the dimly lit pub for an hour and Lizzie didn't feel as though she'd made any progress. Apart from finding out another name – Bella – she'd come no closer to getting to the heart of the matter: Billy Cawley. Surely, she'd done enough chit-chat and groundwork now to gain Rob's trust and be more direct without setting off alarm bells. She had to go for it.

'Auntie Muriel is worried about Billy Cawley, I think. I mean, she hasn't said it in so many words, but she seems distracted, anxious.' Lizzie thought it was a general enough response that not just Muriel, but other villagers from that time might feel. It would hopefully ring true.

'Yes, I think you're right. I haven't seen her for a few days, which is unlike Muriel. I'm not being funny, but well . . . she is a bit of a busybody usually. No offence.'

Lizzie laughed. 'None taken. I am quite sure it runs in the genes.' Her faced burned. She was beginning to feel guilty about her lies.

'And it's their age, I reckon. It's like they've less to think about so they have to create a bit of drama to keep their minds active. Running the shop is what's keeping my mother going.'

'But she's not been working?'

'Nope. And, coincidentally, she's felt under the weather since Friday. I get the vibe from her that she's scared to leave the house. Which is really unlike her as she'd usually delight at being at the heart of this kind of village gossip. It only comes along once in a blue moon.'

'In thirty years,' Lizzie said, absently.

'Exactly. And both times it's been related to the same man.'

'Do you remember anything from back then, from when Jonie went missing?'

'Not a whole lot, no. I was still at primary school, my last year I believe. I only really remember the stupid game we all played back then – Knock, Knock, Ginger – and the fact we targeted Billy Cawley's bungalow a lot more than any other house. It was because it was the biggest thrill, of course: he was the strangest, most scary adult we knew. It's weird, looking back, because we all thought he was so old. Old Man Cawley, the village weirdo. God, he must've only been in his late twenties. How mad is that?'

'Twenty-five, actually.'

'Shit, is that all? Why do I have the image of some ancient old man then?'

'Our recall will do that. We were kids. Don't you remember also thinking your teachers were at death's door? And that your parents were old fogies?'

Rob laughed. 'Yes, that's true. I still see some of the teachers who were at our school, and they don't seem any different!'

Rob was talking as though Lizzie had been at the school at the same time, experiencing the same things. She hoped he didn't ask her any specific questions because she recalled very little of her school years. She was younger than Rob, though, so he wouldn't remember her from his class at least. But there had been fewer than a hundred pupils in the entire school, so there was a possibility he'd realise her name didn't match any from that time.

What will happen when he realises I'm not exactly who I say I am?

She drove the thought from her mind. 'Remind me again, how *did* they figure out it was him? How did they catch him?'

'Ah, well – a lot of it was circumstantial evidence to begin with. Timing of when Jonie went missing, what he had been like in the run-up to her disappearance—'

'What he'd been *like*? How do you mean?'

'His behaviour, you know. He'd never been what you could call stable, but when they took his daughter, well—' Rob shook his head '—he kind of flipped out, mentally. People reckoned he was trying to replace her. That's why he took Jonie.'

'Which people reckoned that?'

'At the time, like a few weeks before Jonie was taken – and as I said, I was young and can't say for sure what I remember is correct – the mums were all freaking out about Billy's daughter, saying he was hurting her and that she was acting very bizarrely, and something needed doing. They talked about abuse. Of course, at my age I hadn't realised quite what they meant, but later, I came to understand. Everyone believed he'd sexually abused his own daughter. Makes me shudder.'

Lizzie looked down, focusing on her drink while she let his comment sink in. 'And they took her away from him. So, as revenge, or as a replacement, he took one of *their* daughters. A daughter of one of the villagers who'd been instrumental in taking his away?'

Rob shrugged. 'It's a theory. He never did tell anyone his motives. Never told anyone where he dumped little Jonie's body.'

'That's because he said he was innocent, didn't he?'

'To begin with he denied everything, yeah. Then his lawyer must've told him to plead guilty in return for a reduced sentence, rather than whole life. He wasn't innocent, Lizzie. Couldn't have been. No smoke without fire, as they say.'

She paused. 'Depends who started the fire.'

Chapter Thirty-Six

1989

Blackstone Close

Friday 30th June – 19 days before

'Eliza, come on in. Now!' He barked his order, his voice hoarse from the remnants of the flu, and the chest infection he'd had on top of that. His forty-a-day smoking habit hadn't gone any way to help matters either.

The girl, sitting in the dirt of the front yard among her dolls, had heard her father's demand, but she'd caught sight of a movement at the end of the cul-de-sac, which had taken her attention. She pulled the head off the doll she'd been holding and placed it carefully down beside the arms. The legs could wait. She stood up and slowly walked towards the driveway entrance, her hands hanging loosely by her sides. She hoped it was a cat. She liked playing with live things.

'Here, pussy, pussy,' the girl called – her lisp making it sound as though she were saying 'puthy'. Laughter erupted from the darkness of the bushes to her right. She stood still, putting her hands on her hips. She was disappointed it wasn't a cat, but it might be someone she could play with.

'Hello? Who is that? Can you come and play?' she called. She knew she'd be in trouble though – her dad had just called her in for tea. She shouldn't invite anyone in; he wouldn't like it. She was never allowed anyone to come to play. It was unfair.

There was more laughter before she heard voices whispering: 'Eliithaaa, Eee-liii-thaaa!' She huffed and turned her back. They didn't want to play, they just wanted to be mean. She might only be eight years old, but she knew when people were making fun of her.

'Never mind,' she called out. 'I'm going in now.'

As she turned and began walking to the door, something hard smacked into her back. She screamed out in pain. Her back was stinging. She wanted to cry, but instead turned to face her attacker and shouted. 'You shouldn't hurt people. Not if you don't want to be hurt back.'

Eliza heard the squeals as they disappeared into the distance. She swiped at the tears rolling down her face and kicked the stone they'd thrown at her. Why did they have to be mean to her? What had she ever done? Her dad was right: she didn't have any friends.

She didn't have anyone but him. It was him and Eliza against the world.

Chapter Thirty-Seven

2019

Anna

Monday 15th July

Anna's third night in her childhood bed had been no better than the first. Her back was aching even more, and she felt as though she'd aged twenty years overnight. Sitting on the edge of the bed, she cupped her chin in her hands. She wasn't ready to face the day yet. Or her mother. She'd only managed a few fitful hours of sleep in between dark dreams – disembodied heads floating helplessly, dolls' mouths twisted and screaming, women wailing. Her mother in the middle of it all, calm and strong. Is that how she wished her mother was now? The calm, strong one? When she'd been a child, and when all of the stuff with Jonie was happening, as far as she remembered it *was* Muriel who held it all together. Muriel who'd guided Anna through the horrors. Muriel had been strong. Strong-minded, strong-willed – so much so, even Anna's father hadn't been able to live up to the impossible standard she'd set.

Years after her parents' separation, Muriel had still stuck with the story that Eric had been traumatised and unable to come to terms with his little girl being so close to being the one taken and the after-effects had caused a rift in their marriage. She'd simply told Anna that her father had sought comfort in the arms of another, without much further explanation. Anna didn't entirely believe that, though. She could understand the strain of it all – of course she could – but to leave his family, travel to the other end of the United Kingdom to live? It didn't ring true. The explanation he was going to Scotland because that's where his new partner and her family were from seemed a stretch. Anna later decided her father had wanted to get as far away from Muriel as was humanly possible and that's why he chose Scotland. That made more sense.

But Anna had never forgiven him for leaving her like that. Just when she'd needed her daddy the most, he'd abandoned her. What was it with the menfolk of Mapledon? Were they all useless at being fathers, husbands? Jonie's dad hadn't played a huge role in her life if Auntie Tina was to be believed, and Billy Cawley's daughter was so damaged and neglected that social services removed her from his care.

Now Anna came to think of it, there did seem a disproportionate number of single women in the village from her mother's age group. Perhaps it was all linked to Jonie Hayes' death – all the families struggled in the aftermath of her abduction and the parents' relationships crumbled when she was never found. There had to be something in it – a huge shared traumatic event had to have a lasting impact. Anna rubbed her hands over her face. How tragic it had been. And now, with a surge of anxiety, Anna wondered if, somehow, it hadn't quite finished.

More trauma was to come.

With a reluctance that dragged her down so much it made her feel heavier, Anna forced herself off the bed. A hot shower might ease her muscles. And give her thinking time. Her thought processes were always sharper while she was in the shower. With luck, her brain would come up trumps and provide her with a plan, a way forward. Because if she were to stay in Mapledon any longer, it wouldn't only be her physical health that would suffer. She needed to either work out who was playing the new, macabre version of Knock, Knock, Ginger – and why – in the hopes of bringing it to an end, or, she would have to do what James had suggested. Take Muriel to Bristol to stay with her and Carrie for a while.

The latter option motivated her enough to get in the shower and make a start on her day.

'Anything happen in this place during the week?' Anna asked after she'd knocked back her first coffee of the morning.

'The village hall tea and cake morning is at ten-thirty today and that's about your lot until Thursday. Then the church wardens hold their coffee morning at the old Red Cross hut.'

'I'm surprised that place hasn't been converted into a house yet.'

'I think some have tried, Anna, but not much gets past the local councillors. Unless, of course, the idea came from one of them in the first place.'

'God. Nothing changes. Let me guess, the new councillors are the offspring of the ones who were throwing their weight about when I was growing up?'

Muriel gave a loud sigh. 'You don't hold this place in high regard, do you?'

'Well? Are they?'

Muriel muttered something before answering, 'Yes. Most of them are.'

'Proof is in the pudding, eh, Mum?'

'*The proof of the pudding is in the eating*, actually,' Muriel corrected, with a shake of her head. 'Anyway, what are your plans for today?' she said as a way of changing the subject.

'I guess I'm off to the village hall for tea and cake,' she said, smiling. 'And you're coming with me. Get ready, then.'

'Oh . . . er . . . Anna. I'm not really feeling up to—'

'It wasn't a request. You have to get out of this house. We need to find out what the word is in Mapledon about bloody Billy Cawley and I can't do it alone. You're the one people know in this village. You're the one people talk to and confide in. If anyone can find out what's going on, it's you.'

'Well, thank you for the glowing appraisal; however, things have changed. It's not how you remember it, Anna. I'm not the person you remember, either.' A sadness swept across Muriel's face.

The statement unnerved Anna. She'd tended to assume everything in the village had remained how it was at the time she'd left. That her mother was the same as the day she left her behind. But her visit had shed an uncertain light on Muriel's health and well-being, and now Anna wondered what other differences there were – ones she hadn't had the opportunity to find out about yet. The fact her mother and Auntie Tina were no longer best friends was shocking enough, but what if the other villagers had turned against Muriel too? Anna had to prepare for the possibility.

Anna brushed away Muriel's words with a hand. 'Nonsense. Right, shall we walk? It seems a shame to waste this lovely sunshine, and as you've been cooped up here for days, I think you could do with a hefty exposure of vitamin D.' Anna rose from the sofa and smiled encouragingly at her mum. Muriel didn't look at all convinced. 'Mum?'

'I'm scared, Anna.' Muriel wrung her hands together. 'What if we see him?'

Anna took a moment to consider it. 'Then we'll know better what we're dealing with.'

Muriel visibly inhaled and then stood. 'As long as you're by my side, I guess he can't do anything.'

'Mum, he could be wheelchair-bound for all we know. You could be worrying over nothing – we have no idea what effect all those years in prison may have had on him or his health.'

'Yes, maybe you're right – it must've taken its toll on him. I have to face this fear head on, not hide away from it.'

'Exactly. It's not like you to shy away from anything. You always fought for what you believed in; you were always strong. No reason why you shouldn't be that person now.'

Muriel put her arm around Anna. 'Thank you, my darling girl. I know I didn't often tell you, but you were everything to me. You still are. I may not have made the right choices, or good decisions, as you were growing up. But what I did, I did because I loved you and wanted to protect you. You know that, don't you?'

'Of course, Mum. Of course.' Anna ignored the niggling sensation creeping up the back of her neck, and with her mum in tow, left the house to walk to the village hall.

Chapter Thirty-Eight

2019

Lizzie

Lizzie woke up early, the sun streaming through the gap in the curtains the likely cause. She got up, filled the basin in the bathroom, and swilled cold water over her face. An attempt to wash the guilt away: she'd gone too far yesterday. She smacked the palms of her hands against the white china of the sink. 'Stupid, dumb-ass move that was, Lizzie!' she told her reflection.

It could've been worse.

That was the phrase she'd repeated to herself since she'd left Rob outside his house. It was a kiss, nothing more. It wasn't a snog. It wasn't sex. But her conscience knew. It was physical contact and it was not with her husband. Therefore, it was wrong. She couldn't even blame alcohol. She'd stuck to just the one G&T, drinking Diet Coke after that. She'd overstepped the line, even if it had only been meant as a 'thank you' kiss. That type of kiss would usually be a peck delivered to the cheek, not a lingering one smack-bang on the lips. She'd broken the trust. *Marriage is based on trust; secrecy is the enemy,* she heard Dom's voice saying.

And having committed this act of betrayal, what exactly had she gained?

It was only a kiss.

But she doubted Dom would see it that way. Did Rob?

She was playing with fire and wasn't even sure to what end. Rob had opened up a little about what he thought Billy Cawley had done and why, but an internet search would've told her that. She *had* found out about the Monday tea and cake morning – but she knew that piece of information was probably in the shop window. Spending an entire evening in the pub with a man she'd met once was not really required to gain it. Also, because of her lie about being Muriel's niece, she wasn't sure rocking up to the village hall for cake would be the brightest of moves. Having said that, maybe Rob wouldn't have time to mention to customers that he'd met Muriel's niece, and as he wouldn't be at the village hall, she might be able to go and mingle and not be called out.

Given she had very little else to go on, Lizzie made the decision to sort herself out and drive to the hall. She never could say no to cake.

The village hall was opposite the church and there was a small car park off it. Lizzie sat in the car for a while, watching as a few old people slowly, painfully, entered the building. She was going to stick out like a sore thumb. Even more than at the pub last night. She hoped she didn't spot anyone who'd been in the bar. What if they'd seen her kiss Rob? She pulled her fingers through her hair. 'Don't think about it,' she said out loud. After giving herself a quick glance in the visor mirror, Lizzie jumped out of the car before she could change her mind.

There were half a dozen or so rectangular tables dotted around the hall with sturdy metal chairs covered in orange-coloured cushioned fabric arranged at them. A hatch linked the main room and the kitchen where a few ladies were arranging plates of buns, muffins and slices of cake. The laminated sign informed Lizzie each item was two pounds, a cup of tea or coffee one. Juice with a biscuit was twenty pence. Lizzie looked around briefly; there were no children there, but presumably some were expected.

'Hello. Can I help?' a woman, rounded like a barrel, asked her curtly.

'Oh, hi. Yes, I'd like a coffee please,' Lizzie said, then when the woman's stare didn't waver, made a big deal of perusing the cakes on offer, adding: 'And that yummy-looking lemon drizzle cake. Did you make that? It looks delicious.' Lizzie smiled as widely as she could manage.

'Erm . . . yes, actually, I did. Thank you.' The barrel woman blushed. Lizzie had pushed her off-track. Amazing how a well-placed compliment could massage someone's ego enough to force them to be nice. Lizzie could tell the woman was itching to ask who the hell she was, though. But she'd make her wait. She needed to suss out who people were first, make sure she didn't drop Muriel's name before she even knew what she looked like, or if she was there in the hall.

'Thank you so much. I'll enjoy this, I feel sure. I might be up for a second slice in a moment.' Lizzie grinned again before paying and finding a seat. She chose the table on the far side so she would have time to see people walking in and make a quick appraisal. She also needed time to perfect her 'pitch'.

As she took a bite of the cake, which was every bit as good as it looked, Lizzie's heart leapt. She sat forward, cake crumbs falling into her lap. She couldn't believe it – Anna, the woman she'd met the other day had just walked into the hall. She was with a delicate-looking older woman – the elderly mother she'd spoken of? Lizzie's arm was raised before she'd consciously decided to do it, and she waved Anna over.

'Hi, Anna. Thanks so much for your B&B recommendation – it's fantastic,' Lizzie said enthusiastically. 'This must be your mum . . .' She trailed off, in the hope Anna would introduce them.

But instead, she simply said, 'Yes, it is.' Then politely added,

'I'm so glad you found the accommodation to your satisfaction.' The whole episode seemed fake and falsely bright, which in turn caused a bead of sweat to run down Lizzie's spine. Had Anna found out who she was? The real reason she was in Mapledon? She certainly seemed standoffish now, compared to their first meeting.

'Would you sit with me? I feel like Billy-no-mates here.' Lizzie smarted, immediately regretting her turn of phrase. Bloody hell – how stupid. She rushed into further conversation, hoping to brush over her faux pas. 'The cakes are amazing – I miss this kind of thing. No one has these types of coffee mornings in Abbingsworth.'

'No?' Anna was distracted, her gaze bobbing around the room rather than focusing on Lizzie. Lizzie directed her next comment at Anna's mother, whose attention had also been elsewhere since they'd approached the table. 'Do you bake . . . Mrs . . . er . . .'

The woman faced her; their eyes locked. They seemed to penetrate Lizzie's, looking deep within her. Lizzie gave an involuntary shudder, a strange sensation sweeping through her.

'It's Mrs Fisher,' Anna's mother said. Her voice was weak, a whisper of air. She didn't take her eyes from Lizzie's. Anna seemed not to notice. 'Don't you remember me?'

The question threw Lizzie completely. She sat back, shock preventing any words from forming. How, after thirty years, had there been any recognition?

'Mum, are you going to sit down? Mum?' Anna pulled a chair around and tried to get her mother to sit down. 'Hello? Earth to mother!' Anna's voice became irritated. She looked across the table at Lizzie and leant in closer. 'See what I mean?' she said quietly, shaking her head. Lizzie felt her whole body relax. Mrs Fisher probably didn't remember her at all, which was why she'd asked Lizzie if she remembered her. It wasn't because she'd recognised Lizzie from when she was a child.

124

'Oh, I'm so sorry,' she whispered back. 'Yes, you did say you were worried about her . . . er . . . health, didn't you?'

'I am here, you know, no need to talk over me.' Mrs Fisher pushed the chair back in under the table. 'I am not losing my marbles. I just don't want to sit here, thank you.'

'Oh, okay, Mum. No problem, we'll grab a different table.' She guided Mrs Fisher away from Lizzie, mouthing an apology over her shoulder. Lizzie found herself glad they'd gone. *Mrs Fisher*. Muriel Fisher, the name Lizzie had given as her auntie. Which made Anna her daughter.

But Rob had told her that Muriel's daughter was called Bella.

The memory of their first meeting at the church gate shot into her mind, the words Anna said when she introduced herself: *'I'm Anna. I'm the one that got away.'*

Bloody hell. Anna *was* Bella. So, Lizzie wasn't the only one hiding her real identity. There was definitely more to Anna's story than she'd first thought.

Chapter Thirty-Nine

1989

Blackstone Close

Tuesday 27th June – 22 days before

'Why aren't you at school today, Eliza?' Muriel asked. She'd stopped by Billy Cawley's driveway, to the side of his red truck, not daring to step inside the boundary – she didn't want him to see her if she could get away with it. Not before she'd been able to talk with his little girl, anyway. It was a risky move; even being there was. But she was willing to take the chance on this occasion. *Someone* had to. There were too many warning signals to ignore. It was wrong to stand by, do nothing. Her conscience couldn't take it, and she felt sure the others would agree. She hadn't told them she was going to approach Eliza – she didn't need their permission.

Muriel didn't need their *permission* to keep the children of Mapledon safe. But she might need their help.

Eliza turned her face towards Muriel. Her breath caught. There was a distinct yellowing mark on Eliza's temple. A fading bruise. It confirmed Muriel's suspicion.

'Are you poorly?' Muriel tried again. She crouched down and smiled. Eliza knew Muriel from Sunday school, she wasn't a stranger – so hopefully she could coax her to talk.

'You don't look poorly.'

'Daddy said I'm sick,' Eliza said.

'Did he? Oh, well, if Daddy thinks you should stay off school, then I guess he must be right.'

Eliza gave a half-smile and continued to pull her doll apart.

'Don't you like that dolly, Eliza?'

Eliza looked up, a puzzled expression on her dirty face. 'Of course I like her. She's just like me.' She held the dismembered torso of the plastic doll up for Muriel to see.

'Oh. I'm not sure I understand. Why is she like you, Eliza?'

Muriel thought she saw the flutter of the curtain in the front room of the bungalow, and her heart gave a jolt. If Billy had seen or heard her, she'd best be quick and get out of there. It wasn't like she could say she happened to be passing, not when his bungalow was the last in the cul-de-sac – she had no reason to be there.

'Because she hurts too,' Eliza said simply as she let the body drop. Then, Eliza looked back down to the ground and picked up the head. Muriel watched in stunned silence as Eliza shoved a broken arm inside the head's cavity, her lips stretched into a huge smile as she did it. Something about the scene was so bizarre, so disturbing, that Muriel wanted to run away from it. This child was damaged.

And there was only one explanation as far as Muriel was concerned.

She wasn't sure she wanted to speak to Eliza anymore. Maybe she'd got what she came for. As Muriel straightened and prepared to walk away, Eliza stood up. Her dress was filthy with dried mud from the ground. But a splash of red stopped Muriel in her tracks.

'Oh, sweetie – are you bleeding?'

Eliza looked down at the red stain on her dress and smiled. 'Oh, no. That's not my blood.'

Muriel's mouth opened and closed, no words escaping it.

'What the hell are you doing?' a voice bellowed, loud and angry.

Muriel gave an involuntary shriek – it'd taken her totally by surprise. She'd been too preoccupied to notice Billy coming outside.

'Sorry,' she rasped. 'I was only asking Eliza—'

'I suggest you bugger off! Nosy cow.' He spat at the ground in front of Muriel before sweeping one hand around Eliza's middle and lifting her up. With her squashed under his arm like a rugby ball, he strode back inside his house, her cries of 'No, Daddy, no!' fading as he went.

Muriel's legs shook. Hot tears tracked down her face. For a moment she stood, frozen to the spot, her brain refusing to send the correct signals to her limbs.

Billy Cawley was every bit the monster they'd believed him to be.

She had a lot to tell them at the Mapledon Meeting on Thursday. If she could hold off for two days.

Chapter Forty

2019

Anna

Monday 15th July

After the awkward moment between her mother and Lizzie, Anna hoped there'd be no further episodes with anyone else at the coffee and cake morning.

'You feeling okay, Mum?' Anna didn't know if it was being out of the house, or being at the hall itself, but her mother appeared very stressed and, right now, almost vacant – staring off into space as though she'd forgotten where she was.

'What? Yes. Fine.' Muriel's attention finally turned to Anna. She gave a tight smile. 'Trying to put things together in my head, that's all.'

'Maybe we should see what friends of yours are here.' Anna searched the room for Nell, or someone she recognised. 'It would be good for you to catch up and we could do a bit of gentle nudging, see if they've been getting any unwanted attention too.'

'Nell's not here,' Muriel stated, without looking up.

'Well, I'm sure there *are* people here you could chat with. Look, it's filling up.' By which Anna meant there were now more than ten people. She had another sinking feeling. Mapledon really was a dying village by the look of it – she'd yet to see anyone other than Rob, Nell's son, and Lizzie, who were under the age of fifty. And even fifty seemed the lower end of the scale – most of the people in the hall were approaching their birthday card from the Queen.

Muriel mumbled something that Anna didn't catch. She was beginning to think this outing was just another waste of time – her mother didn't seem keen to mingle, and Anna didn't recognise anyone, nor did she feel confident enough to strike up a random conversation with someone.

'I'm going to get us a cup of tea, Mum. You want cake too?'

'Yes, go on then. May as well now you've dragged me here.'

On the way to the hatch, Anna weaved deliberately slowly in between the tables, hoping to pick up something interesting in the conversations. She heard everything from, 'I'm not able to get in and out of the bath anymore,' to 'The cramp is terrible in the night; I have to stand on a cold floor to ease it.' But no mention of doll's heads or Billy Cawley. Why weren't people talking about it? They seemed to be openly discussing him at the shop on Saturday morning. Surely, he hadn't already been forgotten a mere two days later.

'Haven't seen you for some years, Bella,' the woman behind the hatch said, her large chins wobbling as she spoke. 'I wasn't sure it was you at first, but I put two and two together when I realised you were with Muriel.'

'You have one up on me, then – I'm afraid I can't place you.' She was going to have to get used to people here calling her Bella. Even though she'd encouraged the use of Anna before she left, they'd known her as Bella for far longer here.

'Angie. I'm a friend of Tina's.'

'Oh, yes. You do seem familiar now. I don't remember you being Tina's friend though.' Anna's recollection of Angela Moore was that Tina hated her. She wondered how, or why, they'd become friends. Unless Angie was telling her own version of the truth, of course.

'Friendships often grow from tragedy,' Angie said. 'And even adults have some growing up to do sometimes.'

Anna badly wanted to contradict Angie's statement – she hadn't experienced a great deal of tragedy, but the one she had, had *lost* her a friend, not gained her one. She did, however, agree on her latter point. Instead of debating it, though, she thought she should take this opportunity to mention recent events.

'Yes, you're right, Angie. And this village had the worst kind of tragedy. I'm glad you and Tina were able to forge a friendship from it. I'm sure she must be especially grateful for it at the moment, what with *him* being let out of prison last week.'

'Oh, gosh, it's terrible news, isn't it?' Angie leant towards Anna conspiratorially. 'I don't like to speak out of turn,' she said in a hushed tone, 'and I swore I wouldn't say anything here today – I don't think it's something the villagers want to talk about – but I've got a very bad feeling about it.'

'About Billy?'

'Yes. I mean, he still has his place in Mapledon. I think he'll come back.'

'I wondered that too,' Anna said, matching Angie's quiet voice. 'But I'd have thought he wouldn't be allowed within a certain distance of his victim's family, wouldn't you?'

'Probably not, but do you think a murderer who's been inside for thirty years will do exactly what he's supposed to?'

Which was just what had been bothering Anna. Billy might have to attend meetings with his probation officer and comply with certain conditions – but she assumed he wasn't tagged, so in between those meeting times he could go where he pleased as long as he wasn't caught.

'But you haven't seen him, or heard that anyone else has?'

'No, not yet. But I'm keeping my ear to the ground,' Angie said, whilst tapping her forefinger on the side of her nose. For a split second, Anna found it comical and had to suppress a laugh, though deep down none of it was in the least bit funny.

'Do you remember that game us kids used to play?'

'Oh, goodness, yes. Knock, Knock, Ginger – you little horrors plagued the life out of Billy back then.'

'I remember. As I'm sure he does.'

'He actually called the police on numerous occasions. Pat Vern used to round the kids up and give them a stern telling-off, all the good it did. My, my, Bella. If it hadn't been for you two playing that stupid game, maybe—'

Angie stopped speaking, her face turning pink. She didn't need to finish her sentence. Anna knew the ending. And Anna knew Angie wasn't alone in her thinking.

'Well, hindsight is a wonderful thing, Angie. As well you know.'

Anna hadn't meant anything by her comment – she just thought she'd add it for impact. But the look of guilt on Angie's face told its own story. The villagers of Mapledon all had their part to play in Jonie Hayes' death.

'Right, well, must get on. Did you want a cup of tea?'

'Two please, and two chocolate muffins.'

As Anna placed the cups and plates on the table in front of Muriel, Lizzie caught her attention from the next table.

'Here you go, Mum.'

'You were a long time chatting to Angie. Anything interesting?'

'Not really. Didn't know she was mates with Auntie Tina, though.'

'Ah, yes. Strange if you ask me. Would never have put those two down as friends, not in a lifetime.'

'I thought it odd too. But she said their friendship had "grown out of tragedy".' Anna mimicked Angie's voice.

'Hmm. Or the need to stick together.'

'What do you mean?'

'Nothing, ignore me. Bitter old woman. Sour grapes. All that stuff,' Muriel said with a wave of her hand.

'Sorry to go off again, Mum, but I want to have a quick word with Lizzie.'

'Yes, you do that.' Muriel raised one eyebrow. 'But take what she says with a pinch of salt. She lies.'

Anna's stomach dropped. What a strange thing for her mother to say. Was it part of the suspected dementia – coming out with odd things out of context? She needed to look into it, and make a doctor's appointment soon. 'Will do,' she said as she turned and took a seat back at Lizzie's table.

'Hi, again. Sorry about Mum acting a bit . . . odd.' Anna gave what she hoped was an apologetic expression.

'No worries. But I really think your mother believes she recognises me, Anna.'

'She might well do. It's not as if Mapledon is a big village – and back then everyone lived in each other's pockets. She probably remembers you even though you only lived here briefly.'

'You don't, though, do you?'

'No. But trust me, there's a lot I don't remember from my childhood. We don't tend to, though, do we? I mean, as adults, there's not a lot of recall from before the age of ten or so. Personally, I struggle to even remember much about my teen years.'

'Oh, yes, I agree. But there's something . . . more . . .' Lizzie fiddled with her mug. 'It's the *way* that Muriel looked at me.'

'Mum, Mum, come here a sec,' Anna called.

'Oh, no, seriously, don't bother her now. We can talk another time.' Lizzie's voice sounded panicky.

Muriel rose from her chair and, cup of tea in hand, wandered across to them.

'Mum. You remember Lizzie, don't you?'

Muriel nodded very slowly, almost comically.

'From when she lived in the village?' Anna coaxed.

'Yes. From when she lived here. With her dad.'

'Look, really – I'm sure I look like many other people. I wasn't here long. I don't think you really can – it's probably someone else you remember.'

'No, no. I would recognise those eyes anywhere. And the fact you've chosen now to come back makes me think I'm right. I know who you are.'

In the pause that followed it was as though the whole world had silenced itself – its breath held.

'You're Billy Cawley's daughter, Eliza. And it's obviously you who's been terrorising me.'

Chapter Forty-One

2019

Lizzie

Muriel had now let the cat well and truly out of the bag. It would be a matter of minutes, hours if she were lucky, before the entire village knew her true identity. She wondered how long it would take them to run her out of the place. Not long if Muriel had anything to do with it, she guessed. The dark look, the penetrating stare she was currently being treated to, was one that hurt – even though she'd predicted what would occur when people found out she was Billy's daughter.

She wasn't the person who'd done wrong. She hadn't taken and murdered young Jonie Hayes. In fact, if anyone was to blame, it was Muriel. And she was itching to tell her as much.

Lizzie turned away from Muriel's death stare and looked at Anna. Her face wore a shocked mask.

'Anna, I'm sorry. I should've told you when we spoke, but, well . . . it's not the easiest confession to make. Under the circumstances. And I think you understand really, because I got the distinct impression you weren't honest with me, either.'

Anna stuttered. Then, failing to utter a sentence, sat back heavily on the chair.

'I'm just a little . . . dumbfounded? That might be the word,' Anna said, finally.

'I'm sure you aren't going to be the only one,' Lizzie sighed.

'What are you doing here?' Muriel said. She'd also seated herself back at Lizzie's table. 'Is it revenge you want?'

'God, Muriel. Revenge for what? My dad—' She lowered her voice, sitting further forward, closer to Anna and Muriel. 'My dad deserved what he got. The reason I didn't want to disclose who I was, was because I assumed, and probably rightly, that the people of Mapledon would want some form of retribution themselves, and if faced with the daughter of child killer William Cawley, I might be the one they focused that revenge on. *I'm* certainly not after any form of payback here. Not from the innocent villagers, anyway.'

'What do you mean, innocent villagers? Do you think there are guilty ones, and you just want *them* to pay?' Muriel said, her voice rising in pitch. A woman on the next table gave them a curious glance.

'Please, listen. Stop all this revenge talk,' Lizzie whispered. She shifted in her seat again. 'The only reason I'm here is to find out if my father came back. And to face *him*. My being here has nothing to do with any of the others.'

Muriel looked unconvinced. 'So, you think he'd come back here, to Mapledon? Why?'

'He still owns the bungalow. Where else has he got?'

'But I've just had this conversation,' Anna said. 'He couldn't come back here even if he wanted to. There will be restrictions in place – boundaries and whatnot. His victim's family still lives in Mapledon. He wouldn't be allowed within a certain distance. His solicitor will probably sell his bungalow. Haven't you been contacted?'

'Yes, I had a letter. But I didn't read it all,' Lizzie admitted.

'Maybe you should, then. You'd be able to find out where he is through the solicitor, too. He might be at the other end of the country and we're all worrying for nothing.'

'Fair point. But I have this gut feeling – I can't explain it. I

136

was drawn here, like I knew deep down he was here, waiting for me.'

'Did you never visit him in prison?'

'God, no! He wrote some letters that were passed on to me through the solicitor, but I haven't set eyes on him since I was taken away from him.' Lizzie shot Muriel a sideways glance. She had her head down, looking at her hands in her lap.

'Social services took you into their care?' Anna said, her face softening. It was the pity look Lizzie always managed to elicit when talking about her removal into care.

'Yep. Accusations of neglect made them decide he wasn't a fit parent.' Lizzie didn't go into more detail, certainly didn't want to repeat what Rob had said about sexual abuse. That was something she suspected had evolved from village gossip, and despite the mention of it as she was growing up, she'd pushed it to the back of her mind.

'What about your mother?'

'Dead, as you know.'

'Oh, yes. Sorry. Do you . . . well, remember much about it, like how he . . .' Anna stumbled over her words.

Lizzie cut in, helping her out. 'Do I remember how he treated me, you mean?' No one ever really knew how to talk to her once they found out the reason behind the authority's decision and she didn't like talking about it because it might mean she had to face up to the possibility he really *had* abused her. 'No. I barely remember a thing from that time. Snippets of broken memories, that's all. I suppose I remember the *feeling* I had, though. It lasted for many years. Like a heaviness, as though there were something sitting inside my stomach. And I sensed a darkness: I could almost reach out and touch it, it was so tangible. And something else . . .'

'What else?' Anna asked.

'A missing link, or something that was present but which didn't fit. I've never been able to distinguish which. I know it's

137

important, but don't know how, or why.' Lizzie looked up into Muriel's eyes, then back to Anna. She caught the confusion in her expression. Or maybe it was discomfort. Perhaps they both thought her unhinged. 'It's very hard to put into words. I suppose what I'm saying is, *I'm* the one who has to put it all together. I know it. Like an incomplete jigsaw, I have to find the missing pieces and make it whole. And once I do, I can move on. And every fibre in my being tells me it's here,' Lizzie said, flinging both arms wide as she cast her gaze around her before allowing it to settle back on Anna. 'Here in Mapledon is where it began, and where it must end.' Even to herself, she sounded like a crazed fortune-teller.

Chapter Forty-Two

1989

Mapledon Churchyard

Sunday 25th June – 24 days before

Billy knelt beside the mound of earth. It was still raised, hadn't had time to sink; to settle like the other grave plots. He hadn't had time to settle either. It was hard raising a child alone. Hard to be the dad he knew Eliza needed, the dad Rosie would've wanted him to be.

'There's too much to think about, Rosie. And I miss you so, so much.' Tears choked him. He regularly visited Rosie's grave in the dead of night – usually between midnight and two in the morning. It was the best time: quiet, calm. Deserted by all bar the dead – and he wasn't afraid of them. No one bothered him there. He'd left Eliza tucked up in bed; he always made sure she was asleep before he locked her in.

Billy let out a wail, swiping at the head of the roses he'd placed there a few days ago. He was too young for this to be his life – for it to be over before it had properly begun. He was pissed off that he'd been dealt these shitty cards. Eliza had been an accident – a moment of uncontrollable lust between two teenagers. Then, later, he'd done what he thought was right – married Rosie. From that moment on he'd had to work like a dog to get the money to support them all. He'd been lucky, if he could call it that, that his father had died not long after they'd got hitched at Gretna Green. The money he'd left Billy in his will was substantial. He could've started his own business with that money, but instead he bought the bungalow in Mapledon and settled for getting the odd carpentry job here and there.

Biggest mistake of his life. He'd never had the chance to attain any of his goals, never had the opportunity to *be* someone. Apart from the 'Village Weirdo'. He'd managed that all right. He let his head loll back, his gaze travelling over the glittering night sky, wondering if Rosie were one of the brightest stars. Then the stars seemed to fade, and blackness replaced them. He felt the weight of the dark pressing against his skin, then lowering further and entering him. As it often did.

'Eliza is all I've got, Rosie,' he said, placing both hands on the ground that was mere feet above his dead wife. 'But she's not all I *need*. I have needs too – who sees to those now you're gone, eh?' He'd tried to suppress his desires, drank them into oblivion – but he couldn't simply put them aside. They kept resurfacing whether he wanted them to or not. He required an outlet, a way of expressing his thoughts, feelings of hurt, anger, frustration and sexual desire.

He realised now he was never going to have that in this village.

Mapledon was not only small in area, it was small-minded too. And they'd made their minds up about Billy Cawley. He wouldn't change them now. But he had no means of leaving. He *could* sell the bungalow – but he'd also be getting rid of the memories, of what lay beneath. He wasn't ready to do that. There had to be another way.

'I need help, Rosie. Help for me *and* help for Eliza. She's not right. And the more I do for her, the worse she seems to get. I've tried to be everything to her, told her she only needs me, not the vile kids in this place. I'm striving to make her stronger, you know? She has to be hardened in order to survive. The other kids are mean to her, but she doesn't see it; she's too *innocent*. She tries to be friends with them. I keep telling her she's different to them; they'll never accept her. She doesn't help herself, what with the way she destroys those dolls. It's unnerving. I caught her doing really . . . really, *odd* things to Polly, the doll you gave her – the only one she hasn't de-limbed. She looked so guilty when she saw me watching her. And then today she seemed distant. I think it's to do with those God Freaks.'

Billy involuntarily looked over his shoulder towards the church. '*They* are putting stuff into her head!' he spat. He turned back to Rosie, lowering his voice. 'When she came back from Sunday school earlier, she wouldn't even look at me. Didn't speak a word or come near me for hours. Just sat in the garden, pulling her dolls to bits. Then, when she did finally come in, I tried to put her in her nightie for bedtime and she smacked my hand away, like she was telling me off. She said, "It's wrong to touch, Daddy." And she told me to leave her room. She's never done that before. They are saying things to her, I know it.' Billy pushed himself up from his kneeling position.

'I need to keep her away from them, Rosie. This village and its people are poison.'

Chapter Forty-Three

2019

Anna

Monday 15th July

They'd left the village hall not long after the revelation that Lizzie was Eliza, the daughter of murderer Billy Cawley. Lizzie offered them a lift home, which Anna accepted. She felt zapped of energy and didn't relish the thought of the walk back anyway. The shock hadn't abated; Anna still felt numbed by it. She wasn't sure why, because none of what had happened had been Lizzie's fault. She'd only been eight. Why would, or should, Anna feel so taken aback?

She couldn't even remember much about Eliza Cawley: what she looked like, or what she did – but she did recall the rumours for some reason. Or maybe she'd grown up hearing about the day social services had taken her from the bungalow. Her only memories of Eliza were related to her and Jonie *talking* about Eliza – about what she used to do to her dolls and seeing the bits strewn haphazardly in the yard of the bungalow after the girl had gone. And what with a major piece of evidence having come from Anna herself about seeing Jonie getting into the truck with one of Eliza's doll's heads on it, she supposed that was the sum of what she knew.

Thinking about it now, Anna wondered if it were that piece

of evidence Billy Cawley had focused on all these years. Obsessed about, maybe. If Anna hadn't informed the police she'd seen him, had watched as Jonie climbed in beside him in the cab, maybe the jury wouldn't have convicted him. Was that why her mother's house was being targeted now? Because it was Anna's childhood home?

The police still had the necklace they'd found in Billy's bungalow, though, she reminded herself. Jonie's. Auntie Tina had identified it. So even without Anna's witness statement, they likely would've found him guilty. Wouldn't they?

If it were hers and Tina's statements that ultimately led the jury to believe he was guilty, maybe that was why they were the ones who'd received the dolls's heads on their front doors. Was Muriel right to suspect Lizzie? But surely now her father had been released there was no need to seek any kind of vengeance. Years had gone by, why would Lizzie want to do something like that *now*?

Unless she was doing it *for* Billy. He had restrictions; his daughter did not. She could be doing it for him, for his revenge.

'You're quiet, Anna,' Lizzie said.

'Mind is elsewhere, sorry.' Anna kept her gaze to her left, out the passenger window. Her mum's road was approaching. She opened her mouth to direct Lizzie, but stopped short. Lizzie had already taken the right turning and was driving up the road. Next left was Muriel's. Lizzie indicated and turned in, coming to a stop right outside Muriel's house. Anna swivelled a bit in her seat so she could face Lizzie.

'Thank you for the lift back,' she said, her eyes locked on to Lizzie's.

'It's fine. Thank you for not making a big deal about who I am.' She smiled, but seemed guarded. 'Maybe we could chat later? I could come and get you.' She leant into the passenger footwell and retrieved her phone from her bag. 'What's your number so I can let you know when I'm on my way?'

Anna's instincts were telling her to say no. Not to get involved.

'Sure,' she found herself saying before rattling off her mobile number. Lizzie immediately rang it.

'Great. And now you have mine,' Lizzie said, smiling.

It seemed she never could learn – ignoring her gut instincts had done her no favours in the past, yet here she was again, leaping in blindly, going against her body's self-preservation impulse.

'I don't think so,' Muriel piped up from the back seat.

Anna got out of the car and opened her mother's car door. 'Mum. It's fine, come on, let's go inside.' She spoke in her firm, don't-mess-with-me-voice in the hope Muriel would get the message and leave it. 'Nothing will happen while I've gone.'

'How can you be so sure?'

'Let's go in and get a cuppa, shall we?'

'We've just had one!'

Anna screwed her eyes up and took a slow, deep breath. Why was she suddenly being so awkward?

'Actually, why don't you take your mum in, make sure she's all right and come back to Bulleigh Barton with me now? We could have lunch in the garden. Save you coming out again later?' Lizzie suggested. Maybe she, too, was becoming impatient with Muriel's behaviour.

'If you can wait here for five, I'll come back and let you know.' Anna ducked her head back inside the car and gave Muriel's arm a gentle tug. She finally, but slowly, climbed out of the back seat.

'What has got *into* you, Mum?' Anna hissed as she opened the front door and did a quick check of the floor to make sure there'd been no other deliveries.

'I don't trust *her*.' Muriel jabbed a finger towards the waiting car.

'I know.' Anna ushered Muriel further inside. 'Look, you might be right not to trust her. She just drove straight to your

144

door without asking for directions. I mean, I know Mapledon is pretty small, and she *did* walk this way with me on Saturday, but we were still a few roads away. How did she know exactly where you lived?'

'Because she's been here before,' Muriel said, her eyes fixed on a point beyond Anna.

'Exactly. So maybe she *is* the one hammering dolls' heads to doors. When she was a child, she was always tearing those dolls to bits. It makes sense it's her doing it now.'

'And you want to go and have lunch with her?'

'I thought it would be a good opportunity to dig a bit deeper.'

'I don't really like the idea of being left here alone, Anna.'

'Pop next door and have a catch-up with Sandie. It would be a perfect opportunity to ask her if she's had anything strange happen, seen anything or anyone unusual. And anyway, if we're right, nothing will happen while I'm with Lizzie, will it?'

'Fine. Be careful, though, Anna,' Muriel said, her eyebrows raised. 'Sometimes when you go digging you unearth things you're not looking for.'

Chapter Forty-Four

2019

Lizzie

The short drive to Bulleigh Barton passed in relative silence, Lizzie struggling to gauge how Anna was taking the news of her being Billy's daughter, Eliza Cawley. She'd spent a lifetime pretending she was someone else – who would want to be the daughter of a child killer? Why couldn't her dad have been like the other kids' dads? Someone who blended in, rather than sticking out like a sore thumb. But no. He'd lost his way in life; lost his ability to work. Had turned instead to some dark side that Lizzie couldn't, and didn't want to understand. How do supposedly normal people carry out such hideous crimes? How do they hide their real selves from everyone else? But then, she had kept a part of *herself* hidden for most of her life. Maybe that's just what her dad had done too.

She couldn't remember living with him, either before her mother had died or afterwards. Her brain had done a good job blocking the unwanted childhood memories. Which is why she needed help now to unblock them. To finally move forwards, she had to cleanse herself. She had to exorcise William Cawley once and for all. She'd got Rob onside, although he might well back off once he found out she'd lied, and she had Anna. Together they might be able to piece the jigsaw together.

'Well, hello. I see you've brought a guest,' Gwen said as they walked into the house, her Irish accent washing over Lizzie like warm water. There was something soothing about her voice. Kind, honest. 'Did you two want some lunch in the sunshine? I could set you up on the picnic table beside the pool if you like?'

'Thanks, Gwen, that'd be perfect. I'll pay for the extra lunch, of course.'

'Ooh, no, not at all. It's my pleasure. What can I get you – I have baguettes with various fillings, or salads, some sandwiches perhaps?'

'A ham baguette with some salad would be lovely, thank you,' Lizzie said.

'The same, thank you. No onion though.'

Gwen gave a nod. 'I'll pop it out the back in ten minutes or so,' she said, before disappearing into the kitchen. Lizzie led Anna to the back of the house, out through the patio doors and onto the decking area.

'It really is a beautiful B&B, Anna. Thanks for the heads-up.'

'That's okay. It's not like there was much of a choice though, eh? It is lovely, though, and Gwen seems to be a fab host.'

'Don't you know her?'

'No. This place had different owners when I left Mapledon. It belonged to the Timothy family then. Their son went to my . . . *our* . . . primary school. He was a bit, well, strange.'

'Even more so than me? I find that hard to believe. By all accounts my head spun and I threw up green vomit and everything.'

Anna laughed, which acted as an ice-breaker. Even though Lizzie had felt a connection to Anna when they'd met at the church gate, since her 'unmasking' today, Anna had been very off with her. Understandably.

'Do you remember anyone from Mapledon school?' Anna asked as she sat down at the wooden picnic table. Lizzie swung her legs over the opposite bench, so they were facing each other.

'It's difficult to explain. I don't think I remember *people* per se; I feel certain connections instead – I thought I felt that when we first met, for example. It's like, I know I knew them, but can't locate any specific memories concerning them. I didn't recognise any of the houses as I drove up the main street on my first day here, but when we were walking and I saw the primary school, a jolt, like an electric shock almost, hit me. I knew the place. But I wouldn't be able to tell you anything about what it looks like inside, or even give you names of other kids or teachers.'

'I suppose when I left I was eighteen, so my childhood memories had been talked about, reinforced by sharing them with other village kids, my mum, and to a lesser extent my dad. Because you left at eight, didn't even get to go to comprehensive school with the village kids, too many other significant memories must have come after and replaced them – or overlaid them. Perhaps the more you talk to people in Mapledon, the more things you might recall.'

'I guess that was my hope. That and to find out more about *him*. There's unfinished business for me, as you can imagine. It's like there's a thousand-piece puzzle that needs to be put together to answer the questions I didn't even realise I wanted answered until I read the release letter.'

Gwen stepped out from the patio doors with a tray and headed to where Lizzie and Anna were sitting.

'Here we go, ladies.' She put the plates in front of them and placed a basket of condiments in the centre of the wooden table. 'What would you like to drink?'

After they'd told Gwen what they wanted and she'd disappeared back inside, Anna spoke.

148

'I don't think the villagers will make that easy, Lizzie. I have a feeling you'll get so far, but be unable to complete that puzzle without the bits they've been hiding for thirty years. And I doubt if some of them even remember what, or where, those missing pieces are.'

Chapter Forty-Five

1989

Fisher residence

Saturday 24th June – 25 days before

'Are you off out again, Bella? You're never in lately. What about your spelling homework? The test is on Monday. Have you finished learning your words?'

'I already know them, they're easy ones. I can spell them backwards.'

'You don't get marks for that I'm afraid, my little one,' Eric called from his armchair in the lounge.

'Oh, you're funny, Dad,' Bella said in the stroppy teenage voice she'd adopted despite being only ten. 'Test me later, I'll prove it.'

'I'm going out in a bit, and you'll be tucked up asleep by the time I get back. But tomorrow you can prove to me how clever you are.'

'After Sunday school then – it's a deal,' Bella shouted. Moments later the front door slammed.

'Oh, so I'm going to be left alone then! I do enjoy my weekends.' Muriel's brow creased and she put both her hands on her hips. 'I'll take myself off to Tina's then. It would be nice to have *some* company.'

'Don't sound so hard done by, love.'

'I'm fine. I'm sure we can come up with an enlightening topic – maybe what can be done with the abandoned barn on the edge of the play park. Some of the kids have broken the door and are using it as some kind of den; it's not safe. I don't think it should wait until the next Mapledon Meeting, so I'll discuss with Tina how we should approach the councillors. They really need to do something about it right now.'

'You're acting like you're the bleedin' high priestess of a witches' coven, you are, Muriel!'

'Are you jealous, dear – would you like to be the high priest? It can be arranged,' Muriel said with a tight smile. 'But I'd still be the one to make decisions, so don't let's get ahead of ourselves.'

Eric shook his head, tutting. 'I'm just saying, you don't have to be the one to make *every* decision, that's all.'

'I'm not, Eric. And I'm sorry, but you don't have the first clue what we even discuss at the meetings, and well, that's the way us ladies want to keep it. You men have the pub, your golf, your *gambling*,' Muriel said, shooting him a knowing look. 'Don't think you've got that past me, dear.'

Eric shuffled in his chair, his eyes now averted from Muriel's. 'Nothing bloody gets past you,' he mumbled.

'Language, Eric,' she scolded. 'Leave us to our business and I'll leave you to yours. And don't worry, we would trust you and the other men to help us if it were required.'

'Oh, well, don't do us any favours. We might not want to help just when it suits you.'

'I'm sure you would do what needed to be done for the good of the community, wouldn't you?'

'Yeah, yeah. We always do, don't we? You might think you run the village, Muriel – you and your cronies – but it's us men that you all count on. Couldn't do without us, could you?'

Muriel kissed the top of Eric's head.

'No, love. I couldn't,' she said.

'Oh, meant to say – a letter came for you. Was official-looking. I put it on the sideboard.'

Muriel went to the dining room and looked at the white envelope propped up against the silver bowl. She took it and, without opening it, slid it into the bottom drawer between her cardboard box of birthday cards and her address book. She'd deal with it later, when Eric had gone to the pub.

'Anything important?' Eric called from the lounge.

'No.' She swallowed hard. 'Just some information I requested a while ago. Ironically something related to our Mapledon Meeting agenda.'

Eric stood as Muriel walked back into the room, and strode forwards, taking both her hands in his. 'I know I joke about the meetings, about the women only getting together for wine and gossip, but I am aware that's not all you do. I know you do a lot for this village and it's a better place for it. I can always rest assured you ladies are keeping things running smoothly, making sure the village kids have a good, safe place to grow up in. Making sure our Bella is safe and secure. I'm only teasing you, you know that, don't you?'

'Yes, love. Of course. And, let's face it, getting intoxicated and gossiping without an agenda is something we leave to our men,' she said, smiling.

'Touché.' He kissed her. 'And on that note, I'm off to the pub.'

Chapter Forty-Six

2019

Anna

Monday 15th July

So far, Anna had kept her conversation to topics Lizzie seemed happy to talk about – she hadn't asked many questions. From what she'd spoken of, Lizzie appeared to be in Mapledon purely to see if her dad had returned, and to find out what happened thirty years ago. Much the same reasons Anna had stayed beyond the weekend. But Anna only had Lizzie's word she hadn't been in contact with Billy since she'd been taken into care. Only her explanation for why she'd turned up in the village asking questions.

Anna couldn't extinguish the feeling of unease she'd had when Lizzie had driven her and her mum straight to their front door that morning. And until she had evidence to the contrary, she wouldn't rule out the possibility Lizzie was involved in the macabre mutation of the Knock, Knock 'game' that had begun on Friday. Lizzie *and* her dad could be doing it.

'When did you first arrive in Mapledon again?' Anna asked, then took a bite of her baguette.

'Saturday. I hadn't opened the solicitor's letter for a few days, then I ummed and ahhed about coming. But then I got a call that made my mind up for me.'

'Oh? How come?'

'It was someone saying they knew his plans.'

Anna's heart dropped. 'Who?'

'They didn't say. It was a woman's voice, and it came to the landline, not my mobile.'

'Did they say how they knew?' Anna's throat tightened. She put her baguette down, unable to take another mouthful just yet.

'Nope. But they knew I was a journo because they said I'd be interested in the story.'

'You're a journalist? You didn't mention that.' Anna's discomfort about being continually on the back foot wasn't doing her stress levels any good.

'Freelance, yes. But I'm not here after some sensationalist story, Anna. I'm just here for the truth.'

'The truth? I don't understand.'

'I'm not sure what exactly went down the day Jonie Hayes went missing, Anna. But I *am* sure there was more to it than you or I know.'

'I don't think there was. The evidence pointed to your dad, and I am sorry for that – it can't be easy for you knowing what he did – but there was no other explanation for what happened.'

'Because the police, and the people of Mapledon, stopped looking, Anna. They assumed they had their guy, and as you say the evidence pointed to it being him, so they wrapped it up, no further questions asked.' Lizzie looked Anna straight in the eye. 'I'm here to start looking again.'

'But why now? Why not before, when he was in prison?'

'Because I was one of those people who'd spent all those years believing he'd done it. Assuming he'd taken Jonie and then murdered her, dumping her body. Because that's the story I'd been fed.'

'And now you don't? Just like that? What changed your

mind?' Anna's questions tumbled over themselves, her mind racing.

'During my childhood, moving from one foster home to another, I was told various things about why I'd been removed from my father's care. Initially, it was the straightforward "after your mum died, he was unable to cope and he neglected you" line I was given. As I got older, though, that story developed; things were added on. I was told other, less straightforward things – stuff I don't want to get into right now. So, over the years I built a picture of what my time with Billy must've been like, what kind of person he was . . . and what a monster he must be to have killed a child. When I was driving here all I could think about was how I was going to "put William Cawley to rest".' Lizzie made air quotes with her fingers. 'And up until today, that remained my plan. But I felt something . . . odd . . . today. I'd say it was a memory, but it wasn't tangible – it was a *feeling*, something deep down, buried, rather than an actual memory. A sense, a knowing, that all was not as it seemed. Whatever happened here, we don't know the full story.' Lizzie bit into her lunch. It appeared she'd said all she was going to say for the moment. It was as if she'd delivered her speech and now wanted Anna to chew it over.

They both continued eating in silence, Anna's brain working overtime. Lizzie could well be right – they didn't know all that went on back then. But she still believed that Billy Cawley was responsible for abducting Jonie Hayes. After all, *she'd* witnessed it – the police had taken her statement and that had been a key piece of evidence. Perhaps Lizzie didn't know that. After swallowing the last piece of baguette and washing it down with the rest of the tea, Anna leant forwards on the table, resting her chest on her folded arms.

'You do know I saw it, don't you?' she ventured.

'Saw what, exactly?'

'Jonie Hayes getting into Billy's truck. Him driving out of the village.'

155

Lizzie's eyes squinted. 'So, *you* were the one.' Lizzie shifted, moving her body back, away from Anna.

Anna frowned. 'The one?'

'You were child B. The major witness. The *only* witness,' Lizzie said, her voice cold, monotone. A shiver ran the length of Anna's spine, despite the summer sun beating down on her.

'Well, yes. I assumed you knew.'

'No. You weren't identified; how would I know?' Lizzie's words sounded sharp, snappy.

The whole tone, the atmosphere of their lunch, had altered, and Anna now felt even more uncomfortable. She wanted to get the attention off herself.

'I suppose you wouldn't. Although you *are* a journalist, and you do seem to have found out where my mother lived easily enough, so no doubt your contacts could've found out that information?'

Lizzie's frown grew deeper, but her eye contact didn't waver. 'Fair play.'

She didn't expand. With an attempt to hold Lizzie's intensity of eye contact, Anna asked the burning question.

'So, who told you the address?'

'No one,' Lizzie said without hesitation.

Anna's pulse picked up. 'Then how . . .'

'I've been there before.'

'You said you didn't remember anything about Mapledon, only the school when you saw it. Why on earth would you have remembered where my house was? I was never friends with you.' Maybe Muriel was right then. It had been Lizzie who'd hammered the doll's head to the door.

'No. That's right. I didn't. But seeing your mother sparked something and I just knew where to go.'

'Do you remember when and why you went to my house?'

'Your mum, and someone else I think, took me there. But no, I don't remember exactly when. I certainly don't know why.'

'Who was the other person?'

'Look, Anna. I don't really remember. I think the best person to ask is Muriel, don't you?'

Yes. And she was going to ask more besides. What had her mother been up to? And why hadn't she ever told Anna about Lizzie being at their house?

Chapter Forty-Seven

2019

Lizzie

Two missed calls showed on Lizzie's mobile. Both had been while she'd been lunching with Anna Fisher – whose surname she'd found out was now Denver. One was from Dom, the other, Rob. Both had left voicemails. She plugged her mobile in to charge; she'd listen to them later. For now, she wanted to go online and do some more background reading of the Cawley case. The more she spoke to Mapledon's inhabitants, the more she became aware there were secrets to uncover here. And she wanted to be the one to do it. Lizzie opened her laptop, and with the view of the fields calming her, began to compile some new files, labelling them:

MURIEL FISHER
ANNABELLA FISHER – 'Child B' – aka ANNA DENVER
NELL ANDREWS
ROBERT ANDREWS
REVEREND FARNLEY
TINA HAYES
JONIE HAYES
WILLIAM CAWLEY

She inputted all she knew so far about each person.

Anna was an interesting one. Lizzie got the distinct impression

Anna didn't trust her, and currently that feeling was mutual. She'd looked surprised when Lizzie had mentioned she'd been at Muriel's house before – it appeared genuine. But she'd observed Anna's change in demeanour: suddenly tense, immediately on the defence. Protecting her mother? Or herself? Lizzie had been equally shocked to learn that Anna was Child B. That's the piece of information she would concentrate on for now. Lizzie needed to draw out more about what Anna remembered of that day. Then she would try and elicit information from Rob, and move on to the others. Cross-reference it all. She'd also need to find out who the other key people were and find out about spouses and any other children they had, too, of course. This was going to be a huge task, but one Lizzie felt would be worth it in the end.

If she got the answers she was looking for.

But what if she was wrong? If she did all this digging around and only reached the same conclusion the police, and the villagers of Mapledon, had back then? She'd not only have wasted hours of her life on that man – again – she'd also be left with no doubt she shared the genes of a child killer. But then, she'd come here assuming that was the case, anyway. So, would it damage her further if that were right? If she didn't look into it, and left now, she'd be forever wondering. And that was the opposite outcome to the one she'd come here for. No. One way or another, she was leaving Mapledon with the truth.

Lizzie left her room and rang the bell at reception. A few moments later Gwen appeared from the side door, which Lizzie assumed led to her private side of the B&B.

'Gwen, hi.'

'Hello, my lovely, is all okay?'

'Yes, thank you. In fact, I'd like to extend my stay, please. If possible.'

Gwen popped behind the desk and opened a ledger. 'How long for?'

'I'm not sure, exactly. I don't suppose we could do it as an indefinite stay . . .?

'Oh, erm . . . It is going to get a bit busier come beginning of August – tends to be my busiest time. But looking here, your room isn't booked again until the end of July. After that there will be another room available if you're happy to move?'

'Lovely, thank you.' Lizzie had yet to see any other guests and wondered why July was quiet. Especially given the weather. It was *very* rural, though, not to everyone's cup of tea. How did Gwen make the place pay? Maybe she had another income.

'Grand. I'll pop it all on the computer and we'll do it per week, then. It'll be cheaper for you to book per week than per night,' she said, smiling.

'That's very kind of you,' Lizzie said, then added, 'Oh, and Gwen?'

'Yes, Lizzie.'

'I wondered if I might . . . pick your brains, as it were, later?' Her smile wavered and she looked unsure.

'I'm keen to find out what I can about the history of Mapledon while I'm here.'

'Oh, I'm not really sure I'll be of much use there, lovely. I've only been here six years.'

'You must know more than me,' Lizzie said. She made sure she gave her biggest smile. 'And you could definitely enlighten me on the villagers who live in Mapledon now, I'm sure.'

Chapter Forty-Eight

1989

Mapledon Park

Wednesday 21st June – 4 weeks before

Beams of sun broke through the tall, leafy trees, like shards of glass. Tina watched as the shimmering lights cast patterns on her dress. She'd been sitting beneath the large oak, its gnarly roots digging uncomfortably into her bottom, for twenty minutes now, waiting patiently for Pat. She knew he'd turn up, even if it was past the agreed time. He must've just got caught up on some police business. She'd often wondered why he'd hung around the Mapledon area. He'd had a promising career in front of him. He'd been keen and ambitious at one time and had been earmarked for the accelerated promotion scheme, but then, nothing. He just stayed local. He'd never talked about why. Although Tina had her suspicions.

Hearing heavy footsteps, Tina jumped up and brushed her dress down with both hands before straightening.

'Morning, Tina. Looking lovely and summery.' His smile brought one to Tina's lips too. He wasn't what she'd consider good-looking, but his smile always radiated warmth and it was contagious. And the fact he always complimented her made her feel good. Mark rarely told her she looked lovely, or even just nice. It gave her a boost when Pat looked at her the way he did. She'd always known he liked her, even back when they'd been teenagers it'd been obvious. But she'd been into the bad boys then, the thrill and excitement they could offer. Pat was . . . comfy. He was quiet and kind. And he'd ended up with the equally quiet and kind Zoe.

It was only now that it was dawning on Tina that she'd made an error in judgement by choosing Mark. She wouldn't do anything to jeopardise Pat and Zoe's marriage now, of course, but she *could* use his feelings for her to gain some information – and it was what the others were also counting on. Although he was very much by the book, if Tina asked him to look into something – someone – for her, she felt certain he would. *For the good of Mapledon.*

'Thanks, Pat – you're too kind,' she said, looking down at herself, then back at him. She returned the broad smile.

'We having a picnic?' he asked, casting his eyes around the empty area of the park Tina had asked him to meet at.

'Ah, I should've brought you something. A doughnut at least. Sorry.'

'Watching my waistline anyway,' he said, both hands jiggling his belly. He had put a bit of weight on, Tina noted. But she refrained from saying.

'Look good to me, Pat,' she said, instead.

'Okay, so you have me to yourself in an almost-abandoned park. If we aren't having a picnic and we're not engaging in an affair—' he winked at her '—then what have you asked me here for?'

Tina sighed. 'I'm worried, actually, Pat. About a certain person in Mapledon.'

'Oh, let me stop you there, Tina.' He put his palms up. 'I'm not going fishing around making trouble for someone who should just be left alone to get on with his life.' He turned and began walking away from her.

Damn. Tina hadn't expected him to already know who she was referring to, much less walk away without even listening to her.

'Wait, Pat. Please wait!' She ran after him, grabbing his arm. 'It's not some whim, nor is it a witch-hunt – I know what the village men call us behind our backs, you know. It's for the safety of our kids. For Jonie, her friends. Your Daisy. Don't you want them to be safe in their own village – the one we grew up in happily with not a care in the world? That's all I want for them, too.'

Pat blew out a long breath. 'He's just lost his wife, Tina. Yes, he's a little . . . odd. But it's not his fault the kids are drawn to him and play those god-awful Knock, Knock games on *his* property. It's not like he's the one seeking out trouble, is it? He's in his *own* bungalow minding his *own* business. I think it's the parents of those unruly kids who should be teaching their offspring some manners and respect. Don't you?' Pat's face was beetroot red.

Of course, he did have a fair point. But kids would be kids. They didn't see the harm, couldn't foresee any danger in what they were doing. Hadn't they played those games too when they were growing up?

'Come on, Pat. We're not so old as to not remember the shit we got up to. What they do is pretty harmless—'

'It's trespass, actually, Tina.'

'Okay, I understand where you're coming from. And I will make sure I disseminate that at the Mapledon Meeting next week, even though I don't want to go – they are getting *so* tedious. But, in the meantime, please could you just run a quick search, see if anything comes up. He hasn't lived here long enough for us to know him, and the fact he was an outsider is making everyone uncomfortable when it comes to letting our kids roam freely. Especially given the way his daughter is. Something isn't quite . . . well, *right*. You understand their . . . *my* concern, don't you?'

'I do, of course I do.' His voice softened. Tina knew she had him now.

'You're a good man, Pat. I'm glad we have you. I'm really grateful for anything you can manage – I know it's not something you feel comfortable doing, but if you have suspicions, you do need to act on them. How bad would you feel if something happened to one of our own?'

Tina felt a twinge of guilt. She'd laid it on a bit thick. But it worked. Pat moved closer to her, giving her a kiss on the cheek. 'I'll do some preliminary searches. And if you can bring me actual evidence of your suspicions about his little girl being . . . harmed, or abused, then obviously I'll report it immediately and do things through the *correct* channels.' He turned again to walk away, then added: 'But when I say if you can bring me evidence, I don't mean you lot should play bloody detective and go seeking it out. I mean if you *come across* it, if Eliza tells the school something, stuff like that. Tell me that. Don't you dare go snooping and putting me in an awkward position. Promise?'

Tina caught the concerned tone in Pat's voice. He knew he'd said the wrong thing about taking evidence to him. He seemed scared, probably quite rightly, that the women of Mapledon might take it as a green light to do some of their own digging.

Chapter Forty-Nine

2019

Anna

Monday 15th July – evening

The revelations, tense conversations and sense of unease had all taken their toll on Anna and now, slumped on her mother's ageing, saggy sofa, she felt utterly drained. Numb. And yet, her mind wouldn't settle, wouldn't quieten. Loud, annoying thoughts and questions swamped her tired brain. She wouldn't sleep if she didn't at least attempt to get rid of a few of them. Get some of her queries out, maybe even get some answers.

Strangely, her mother hadn't quizzed her when she'd returned from lunch with Lizzie. She'd fully expected to be given the third degree, but instead she'd been met with indifference; Muriel didn't even ask what Anna'd assumed to be the burning question: was it Lizzie who'd left the doll's head and arm? Anna hadn't said much either – if her mother wanted to know, she'd ask. Perhaps it'd been too much for her, too. A day filled with unexpected twists. She was probably too tired to care.

Anna had taken the opportunity to call Carrie. She'd been excited to share what she'd been up to – James had taken her to the cinema, as promised, and then for fish and chips, which they'd eaten on the seafront, guarding them with their lives while seagulls swooped. It was lovely to hear her upbeat chatter, but it also created a deep ache in Anna's stomach. She should be the one spending time with her daughter, enjoying the school holidays. She shouldn't be running about the countryside on some wild goose chase with Muriel and the daughter of a child murderer – her childhood friend's killer. It didn't seem right, somehow. But Carrie reassured her they would still have plenty of time – five more blissful weeks without school. Anna repeated 'plenty of time'. Would they still have lots of time to spend together? She supposed it'd only been four days so far – but there didn't seem to be an end in sight yet. It could easily be another four days. More, even, before Anna felt it was safe to leave Mapledon. Leave Muriel to her own devices. Or, take her home to Bristol – temporarily at least. She was beginning to realise this might be the only course of action. Unless she could get Muriel talking. Dig under the surface, find out the real story behind Billy Cawley and his abduction of Jonie Hayes.

'Fancy a Horlicks, Mum?' Anna said, pushing herself into a better position on the sofa. Muriel's eyes appeared glazed, as though she'd been asleep with them open.

'Sorry, what?' She blinked several times and turned to Anna.

'Had you zoned out?' Anna gave a nervous laugh. The vacant look had unnerved her a bit.

'Yes. Yes, I was deep in thought then. Sorry. Now, what did you say, love?' Her voice now light and cheery.

'I was going to make Horlicks, do you want one?'

'Ooh, have I got any? I don't think—'

'I picked some up when I went to the shop on Saturday. Remembered it was your favourite.'

'Lovely. Yes. And then maybe we can have a heart-to-heart?'

Anna's pulse quickened. Muriel suggesting a heart-to-heart? What was coming?

They both sipped tentatively from their mugs, facing each other at the dining-room table, Anna sitting in what used to be her dad's chair. It'd been a long while since he'd vacated it, but it was still his. Funny how some things just *were*; the passage of time didn't alter everything – despite the fact he'd been gone for longer than he'd been present, certain things stuck. It was almost as if he'd died, rather than left of his own accord.

'How is Carrie? I haven't seen her for such a long time. I miss her.'

'She's good, thanks. You should come visit during these holidays. Perhaps when *this* is sorted?'

'I'd love to. I could come back with you tomorrow, and stay for a few weeks.' Muriel spoke so quickly and enthusiastically, Anna thought she was having a funny turn.

Anna nodded her head, slowly. 'That would be nice. But I don't think there's a big rush. Don't you want to know who's doing this to you, Mum? Make sure it stops?'

'Don't you want to make sure I'm safe? You were the one concerned that these awful . . . these . . . abominations, were threats. And now you're acting as though it's nothing to worry about again. How come you've changed your tune?'

'I know. I realise I've been swinging from one thing to the other. If I'm totally honest I don't understand any of it. Speaking with Lizzie today, it's just confused me further.'

'What claptrap has she been spewing?'

'Mum! Why do you dislike Lizzie? She was only eight when all this happened with her father. Hardly her fault, is it?'

'No. And I don't dislike the girl. I merely mistrust her. She was so damaged, Anna. You won't remember much, aside from the dismembered dolls that is. It was the way she looked, the way she acted. He'd damaged her. It wasn't enough to lose her

167

mother to cancer, more hurt and pain came her way via him. And it had a terrible consequence. Well, more than one . . .'

'Oh? What do you mean?'

'Nothing. Like I said, she was harmed. To such a degree I think it affected her. Made her moody, nasty and unpredictable.'

'Didn't she have help from professional psychiatrists or anything? Poor girl.'

'I was trying to help her. I did what I could.' Muriel's attention had drifted again, she seemed lost to another place, her eyes wide, unblinking. Anna's mind went back to Lizzie's earlier comment about having been taken inside Muriel's house before she was removed from her dad's care.

'What did you do, Mum?'

Muriel didn't answer.

'Mum?' Anna got up and gave her a gentle shake. 'Anna to Muriel,' she said.

'Enough for tonight, Anna,' Muriel said, finally. She rose from her chair, placed her empty mug in the sink, filled it with water, then walked past Anna and headed to the stairs.

'I'll lock up, then.' Anna called after her.

What a strange exchange. Anna got up and locked and bolted the back, then front doors. Her mum had been the one to suggest a heart-to-heart, but had shut down almost immediately. As Anna turned out the downstairs lights and was about to climb the stairs, a thought occurred to her.

The letters in the drawer. She'd clean forgotten about them. They might not be important at all, just letters from a friend maybe. But the thought they might be from her father, Eric, intrigued her. Muriel never spoke of him, and Anna hadn't tried to contact him herself. But if there were letters, she'd perhaps learn more about what went on at the time of Jonie's disappearance.

Retreating, Anna switched the hallway light back on and walked into the lounge and across to the dresser. She slid the top drawer open. The letters weren't there. She rifled deeper, then tried the other drawers. Not a single one.

Muriel had moved them. She must've seen Anna holding the one she'd found on Saturday morning. They were letters she clearly didn't want Anna to read.

Chapter Fifty

2019

Lizzie

Tuesday 16th July – 1.15 a.m.

It was gone midnight when Lizzie finished speaking to Gwen and she immediately went to her room and opened her laptop, clicking on the files icon. At 1.15 a.m. Lizzie pulled on a jumper, grabbed her phone, then tucked her room key in her jeans pocket. She left through the main door of Bulleigh Barton B&B, reversed her car out of its space in the courtyard and took the winding lane towards Mapledon. She was wired, her mind too busy for sleep. Gwen had been more helpful than she realised, and Lizzie had been able to add to her notes; the further information she'd gleaned changed some things.

Lizzie parked directly outside the church gate. No one would need access at this time of night. She got out of the car, and quickly checking her mobile for the time – 1.24 a.m. – switched its torch app on. Her heart rate had doubled, or that's how it felt, crashing against her ribs like waves against rocks. She had a feeling – a premonition, almost – that this was where she had to be. With her mother, Rosie. Even with the torch app, the graveyard was eerily dark. If she was one to believe in ghosts, she'd be turning back about now and heading for the safety of the car. But the only ghosts she believed in were those in her head – her memory, or her imagination. She tripped on uneven ground but managed to right herself. She took it more slowly. At least she knew where to find Rosie's grave; that made the walk across the ground slightly easier.

Something smashed against her shin.

'Ow!' She stooped to rub the painful lump that had already risen. She'd walked into a small gravestone – she didn't stop to read the inscription. It was probably that of a child. As she cast her phone around where she was standing, the beam picked up movement.

'Hello?' Her voice wavered. She hadn't even meant to call out.

There was a rustling noise, then she heard breathing.

She froze. *Shit. Why the hell did you come here alone?*

She forced herself to breathe more slowly. A panic attack would not be helpful in this situation. The sounds of movement had stopped. She could no longer hear breathing. Had she heard her own panicked breaths? Lizzie moved cautiously forwards, her eyes keeping focus on the area ahead of her. She risked hitting another headstone, but she didn't want to take her attention away from where she thought she'd seen something. Or someone. If it turned out to be the church cat, she'd feel so stupid.

There it was again. The movement was slower this time, as though they were trying to avoid detection.

'I can see you. I know you're there. No point trying to hide,' Lizzie said, her voice sounding braver now: confident and strong.

What first appeared to be a dark blob of a shadow, lengthened and spread – became solid. Lizzie's mouth dried, her pulse pounding in her ears, drowning out any other sounds.

'I think we're here for the same reason,' she said, making her way more quickly to the figure now. Lizzie's hand trembled, the light from her phone wavering wildly, but she kept her arm outstretched.

'What makes you say that?' A deep voice broke the silence, tore through the darkness. Lizzie suppressed a yelp of surprise, forcing her other hand across her mouth to prevent its escape.

'Billy?' she whispered.

The man turned sharply and shot off, away from Lizzie, away from Rosie's grave.

'Don't run, please. I want to speak to you.'

The adrenaline coursed through her veins, and she was saying the wrong things. Frightening him away. But maybe that was a good thing. Was she really ready, or able, to face the man who'd ruined her life and those of so many other people?

Calm the fuck down, Lizzie.

She squeezed her eyes tight and took some steadying breaths. He'd disappeared, but without thinking, she shouted after him.

'Dad! It's Eliza. Your Eliza. I just want to see you.'

The silence was fragmented by the odd chirp of crickets, but nothing else. He must have left via another gate. Her shoulders slumped. She was unsure as to why, but she felt disappointed. She'd missed her opportunity to confront him. But she'd been right – he *had* come back to Mapledon. Even if only in the dead of night to visit her mother's grave. Maybe he'd come back again tomorrow night. But now he'd been rumbled, he might not risk coming back at all.

Lizzie crouched in front of Rosie's headstone, one hand on the cold granite.

'I wish I could remember you, Mum,' she whispered.

Lizzie felt the weight of a hand on her shoulder and she fell sideways, her legs scrambling to get purchase on the earthy ground.

'Shitting hell!' she shouted.

'Sorry, sorry. I didn't mean to frighten you,' the man said, his hands up in front of him, fingers splayed indicating he came in peace.

'Well, you did. I thought you'd gone.'

'I had, but I heard what you said, and it forced me to come back.' He kept a comfortable distance between them, and Lizzie felt herself relax a little.

'I had a feeling you'd be here.'

'So, you're Eliza, are you?'

Lizzie caught his faint smile in the illumination of her phone light.

'Yes. It's been a long time, Dad.'

Tears shone in his eyes and Lizzie was lost for a moment, she didn't know what to say, how to be. She'd been told a great deal of second-hand information about a man she'd no memory of: the man now standing in front of her. Awful things, disturbing things. She felt unsure, wary. But she didn't feel how she imagined she should – no fear, no disgust. This moment wasn't as she'd expected. *He* wasn't as she expected. It was dark, she knew, but he appeared younger than she'd imagined. He was grey, with a growth of stubble that suggested he hadn't shaved in a few days, probably since his release – but he wasn't old when she considered he'd been in prison for thirty years. For all the things she'd wanted to say, had rehearsed so many times in her mind – now faced with William Cawley, she was lost for words.

'I know you'll remember the bad things. I suspect you hate me, or at least have grown up with hatred in your heart. But you're here for a reason. What made you come looking for me after all this time?'

'I guess I want the truth. Straight from the horse's mouth.'

'You could have got that if you'd visited me in prison. You could've known the truth years ago.'

'Yes, but I didn't know then. I thought I knew the truth already, which meant there was no point seeing you. I didn't want to put myself through it. Yes, I hated you. You ruined my life. You took away my childhood. Why would I even consider visiting a child murderer?'

Billy frowned and made a deep, grunting sound, like a hurt

animal. Lizzie noted his fists were balled, by his sides. She may have misjudged this situation. Put herself in the direct line of fire.

'What's changed?'

'I came here. And since I stepped foot in this village, I've seen things differently.'

He nodded, a smile playing on his lips.

Was she being naive?

'If it's the truth you want, it'll take some time. It's not a short story. I suggest we do this in the daytime, somewhere neutral. I can't be seen here.'

'Okay. Let's agree to meet later this afternoon. Where are you living?'

'I've got a caravan. It's on a farmer's land on the outskirts of Bovey Tracey. Close enough to secretly visit Rosie's grave, but far enough to keep within my restrictions.'

Lizzie didn't like the sound of it. Too remote to be on her own with Billy Cawley. Whilst she had the overwhelming feeling there was more to what had happened than had ever been told, she also believed there was no smoke without fire. He might not be responsible for the murder of Jonie Hayes, but he might still be responsible for the abuse she'd been told she'd suffered as a child. She couldn't put too much trust in him.

'I'm staying at Bulleigh Barton B&B. It's a little way—'

'Yes, I know of it.' He took a moment to mull it over, then agreed to meet the following day after he'd reported in with his probation officer. Lizzie watched as he left, then took the opposite path and quickly got in her car and drove off.

She'd met her father. After thirty years. For the moment, Lizzie didn't quite know how to feel about it. And a nagging feeling tugging on her insides told her she might have made a huge mistake letting him into her life again.

Chapter Fifty-One

1989

Brook Cottage Store

Tuesday 20th June – 29 days before

'Can I go and play with Eliza?'

'Robert Andrews, what have I told you about coming into the shop when Mummy's working?'

'Dad's not home yet,' he said, as though that should answer the question.

'Hang on there a second, please. Wait until I've finished serving Mrs Fisher.'

Robert did as he was asked, stepping away from the counter. He pressed his back against the newspaper stand so he was out of the way and he stood still, straining to hear what Mrs Fisher was whispering to his mum. He heard 'not a good idea', but that was all. Grown-ups were weird. He eyed the shelf of penny sweets opposite, and decided while he waited he'd get a selection for him and Eliza to share. He picked out some sherbet flying saucers, dropping them into the white paper bag. Then added some fizzy cola bottles, his absolute fave, and some fried eggs. He was about to pop in a candy lipstick for Eliza when his mother shouted for him. He quickly shoved them in, hid the bag behind his back, and went back to the counter.

'I'm sorry, love,' his mother said looking at him, her head to one side. Robert knew it was going to be a 'no'.

'Why not?' His voice came out like a girly whine. He looked down at the floor.

'It's just not a good idea at the moment. You know she lost her mummy not very long ago . . .'

'I know. We had an assembly about it.' Robert looked up to Nell, his expression thoughtful. 'Which is why it *is* a good idea, Mum. It can be "a very lonely time" – it's important she has friends to help her.' Robert watched his mother's face intently. Tears shone brightly in her eyes, but they didn't fall out.

'Robert, you are such a kind little boy. I'm so proud of you. But for now, I would like it if you'd wait a while. Until things settle a little for Eliza and her dad. I think they need time to heal. Do you understand?'

'Not really. And it's sad because she doesn't have any friends. If you died, I'd want someone to be kind to me.'

Mrs Fisher, who'd been standing there the whole time, suddenly butted in.

'Robert, you need to listen to the adults. We know more than you do.'

Robert curled his lip – he hadn't meant to, it just happened. He doubted they *did* know more. Why did grown-ups think they knew it all? He'd lost this battle though, that was obvious.

'Fine,' he said, sulkily. 'I'll go back into the house then.' Tucking the hand holding the bag of sweets into his trouser pocket, he retreated. Sometimes he was allowed to take some things from the shop, like last week when his mum told him to take two Pot Noodles for himself and Nick for an after-school snack. But he had to have permission. He couldn't ask for it now – she'd see right through him and know he was taking sweets for Eliza. Robert had already made his mind up he was going anyway. His mum would be in the shop working for another two hours at least, and his dad wasn't due home from work at the local brewery until seven. There was plenty of time to sneak out, see Eliza, and get back before anyone knew he'd been gone.

His heart beat so hard as he crept out the back door. He was careful not to be seen by any adults, particularly those heading towards the shop – he didn't want them to dob him in. He'd made sure he'd given enough time for Mrs Fisher to have walked down the road – she was so nosy and annoying – she'd *definitely* rat on him if she saw him leaving.

Eliza's house wasn't far from the shop; it wouldn't take him long to reach it. He'd only ever been there with some of the older kids when they'd knocked on Creepy Cawley's door and run away. Robert felt scared now as the bungalow came into sight at the end of the cul-de-sac. He knew the things people said about Eliza's dad, but he wasn't sure they were true. Even so, his tummy twisted and bubbled as he approached. Creepy Cawley's red truck was in the gravelled driveway. He really hoped Eliza was outside playing. That way he wouldn't have to knock on the door and ask for her.

Robert hesitated by the front wall; his hands were hot in his pockets, the paper bag of sweets felt warm and squidgy. Eliza wasn't in the garden. He stood, unable to go forwards yet unable to walk away either. He'd come this far; he had to be brave enough to knock. He wished he knew which window Eliza's bedroom was. He'd just knock on that and she'd probably come outside.

He heard the word, *chicken*, repeated in his head.

Come on. Do it.

His hand was raised, inches from the door before he realised he'd even walked up the path. He had a moment of sheer panic as his knuckles rapped on the glass. What was he doing here, really? He'd never even spoken to Eliza before – most of the kids at school picked on her, said she was weird like her dad, and 'one sandwich short of a picnic'. And even Robert agreed she was. Eliza was bound to tell him to go away now, and if she didn't, her father surely would. He was so stupid. His mum and Mrs Fisher were right. It wasn't a good idea to be here.

There was no answer anyway, so Robert turned his back, his legs ready to make a run for it. But what if Creepy Cawley thought he was playing Knock, Knock, Ginger? He'd chase him down the street. Robert dithered on the step, not sure what to do.

Stay. Grow up. You're almost ten years old, not a baby.

He knocked again, then shut his eyes tight. His heart was going to leap out from his chest any minute. A breeze swept across his face at the same time he heard a whooshing noise. The front door had been opened so quickly he'd felt the movement of air. He held his breath, for good measure, and waited for the shouting to begin.

'Open your eyes, boy!' A booming voice came from in front of him. Robert's eyes sprung open. A pain in his groin gripped him and he held onto himself in the hope he wasn't about to pee his pants.

'What do you want?' Creepy Cawley's frown seemed to take up his entire face – creases upon creases, making him look like a scary old man. No wonder all the kids were afraid of him. Up close he was even worse than how Robert had imagined him. An ogre, even. Robert opened his mouth, but only a squeak came from it.

'I – er . . . I—'

'Spit it out, boy! If you're meant to be playing that stupid game, I'm afraid you've not grasped the point. You're meant to knock, then run away?' He raised both eyebrows, displaying wide, dark eyes.

'I'm not . . . I wasn't playing it.'

'So? Again, what do you want? I haven't got all day.'

'I wanted to see Eliza,' Robert managed to say through his tightening throat.

178

'What for?'

Robert put his hand in his pocket and took the crumpled bag out, holding it up towards Creepy Cawley. 'I brought her some sweets.' His voice sounded weak. Scared. He coughed and took a deep breath before speaking again. 'My teacher said it's nice to do things for other people when they're sad.' He dared to look into the man's eyes and give a small smile.

'Right. I see.' Creepy Cawley nodded, slowly, and Robert thought he saw the hint of a smile on the man's thin lips. 'You'd better come in, then.' And he swung the door open wider to let Robert walk inside.

Robert swallowed his fear and took a step into the hallway. He couldn't hear Eliza's voice. He really hoped she was home.

The door slammed loudly behind him.

Chapter Fifty-Two

2019

Anna

Tuesday 16th July

The fact her mother was hiding the letters from her made Anna wonder what else she was keeping secret. What could possibly be in them? Not that Anna should be privy to her mother's private mail, of course. And maybe that's all it was – the desire for privacy. It's not like she'd want Muriel reading any letters of hers either. It didn't necessarily mean they contained anything untoward just because she'd moved them.

But it did *feel* like that was precisely why her mother had taken them from the drawer. Because she didn't want Anna finding something out that she shouldn't. Or something Muriel didn't want her to know, at least. Curiosity, however, would ensure Anna carried on searching for them. She assumed Muriel had hidden them away in her bedroom now. One of the places Anna wouldn't go sneaking around in. Or couldn't, as her mother would know, being that she didn't leave the house without Anna. So, there'd be little chance for Anna to go rummaging around in her bedroom. Plus, it would be wrong to abuse her mother's trust in her.

She wished *she* trusted Muriel.

Too many niggles underpinned their mother–daughter relationship as far as Anna was concerned. Too many incidences that couldn't be swept under the carpet – irregularities that couldn't be explained. Having met Lizzie, and heard what she had to say, Anna's niggles had only increased. With Lizzie saying her memories of her childhood in Mapledon were sparse, and the only thing clear in her head was that she'd been brought into this house by Muriel and someone else when she was a child, Anna felt she might be the only one who could now piece the jigsaw together.

But she could only do that if Muriel were to be compliant – if she openly shared the facts surrounding Jonie Hayes' abduction and subsequent murder with her. And maybe with Lizzie. The three of them *could* deduce who was hanging doll parts on Muriel's door if they worked together. And if it did, in fact, turn out to be Billy Cawley, his own daughter might be the one to stop him. Allow Muriel to live in peace. Allow Anna to go back home, alone, back to Carrie and the life she'd created away from Mapledon – the village of the damned. Anna laughed out loud at this description. But it was an uneasy laugh. Behind the jokey nickname she couldn't help thinking it was the perfect phrase.

Anna swung her legs out of bed, did her usual stretches to realign her spine and then headed for the shower. She could hear movements from Muriel's room as she walked along the landing – drawers being opened and closed – she was obviously choosing clothes and getting dressed. Or, maybe she was moving the stash of letters again. She'd need to get her mother out of the house in order to have a good look. It was about time she popped next door for a coffee, Anna thought. She'd try and convince her to do that after breakfast.

Having let the hot water pound her body, Anna felt refreshed and less achy. With a towel wrapped around her, she headed back to her bedroom. She met Muriel coming the other way. She was still in her nightie.

'Not getting dressed today, Mum?' she said, lightly.

'Oh, I might shortly. Just feel like a lounge day today. Didn't really sleep well.'

Muriel's eyes – dull, with dark circles beneath them – backed this up.

'Oh. I guess that's to be expected given the circumstances.' Anna put a hand on Muriel's shoulder and gave it a squeeze. What had she been doing in her bedroom all the time Anna had been in the shower if she hadn't been getting dressed? 'But maybe if you grab a shower and get dressed, you'll feel better. You always used to tell me that, remember?'

Muriel looked blankly at her. 'Oh, did I?' She frowned. 'I used to say such stupid things. Would've told you anything if it meant you got ready for school on time.' She gave a weak laugh.

'Oh, I see – it's all coming out now, isn't it?' Anna shot Muriel an over-enthusiastic smile before adding: 'What other lies did you tell me, eh?' She said it in a joking way, although obviously meant it. Taking in the look on Muriel's face, Anna could tell she'd also taken her comment seriously.

'What's that supposed to mean?' Muriel's eyes, which a moment ago were dull, were suddenly wide, her pupils dilated.

'It was a joke.'

Muriel pushed past and went down the stairs, leaving Anna standing on the landing with a knot in her stomach. It was clear her mother really had lied to her; it was the only explanation for her reaction. She hurriedly dried and dressed and headed downstairs too. She wanted to speak more with Muriel – tease out some of the things that were bothering her.

Anna's eyes were drawn to the mat by the front door. It was clear. No blood bags or the like. But was anything on the exterior of the front door? Her hand hovered over the lock, but she withdrew it. Finding something now would detract from the conversation she needed to have with Muriel. If there was

182

something hammered to the door, it would still be there after breakfast – she'd deal with it then.

Her mum was sitting in her armchair in the lounge, eyes fixed to the TV screen.

'Haven't you got a drink yet?' Anna asked.

'Thought I'd watch the news first.'

'I'll make it then. What do you want for breakfast?'

'Toast will do,' Muriel said impatiently, her attention not wavering from the TV.

'What's happening in the world, then?' Anna wondered what was so captivating it prevented Muriel from looking away.

'A girl's body has been found on the moors,' she said bluntly.

'What? Really? How terrible. Near here?'

'Yes. *Shush*, love. I'm trying to hear.' Muriel scowled, turning the volume up to thirty-six.

Anna mumbled an apology and walked into the centre of the room so she could see the screen properly. The report was from Spitchwick, an area about five miles from Mapledon and part of the Dartmoor National Park. It had always been a popular place for families to picnic and swim: a large, grassy bank ran alongside a bend in the River Dart. Teenagers also flocked to the area in summer, the cliffs further up the river drawing them like a magnet – they dived from them into the water like lemmings. Had that been what had happened now? A girl had been killed diving into the water? The report was almost over. She'd missed the key points.

Before Anna could ask any questions, Muriel jabbed the off button on the remote and stood up. 'Right, are we eating then?'

'Oh, you're done are you?' Anna let the sarcasm ooze.

'It was a new body,' she said, before slipping past Anna into the kitchen.

'Right, and so . . . that means?'

'It's not Jonie.'

183

The penny dropped. Her mother had been so engrossed in the report because the headline had merely stated: *Body of girl found on Dartmoor*. Muriel had thought it could be Jonie Hayes' body, finally found after thirty years. Anna felt a dragging feeling in her gut. Sadness? A hope that her childhood friend could be put to rest – her family, the villagers of Mapledon, finally relieved of their burden?

Or, was the dragging sensation fear?

Anna closed her eyes for a moment, a dizziness washing over her. Why should she be fearful of Jonie's body being found? Surely it could only be a good thing.

Unless deep down she knew there was a reason to be afraid.

'Were you expecting it to be her?' Anna asked as she flicked the kettle on.

'Not really. But the mention of a girl's body and being found close to here – there had to be a chance, didn't there?'

'Do you think Auntie Tina saw the news and would've thought the same as you?'

'If she saw it, yes – she would've. She's been preparing for news like that since Jonie went.'

'Did she ever believe Jonie was still alive?'

'I can't remember now. I suppose at the beginning she must've.' Muriel's eyes clouded. 'We all did,' she added quickly. 'But with the evidence piling up . . . the hope was replaced by the knowledge she was gone for good.'

'Tina must despise Billy Cawley. Not only for taking Jonie away, but also never revealing where her body was. It's so cruel.'

'She did become bitter, as you know. Not sure about how she felt towards Billy though. By that point we weren't as close, so she didn't confide her feelings to me anymore.'

'Very sad. What do you remember about the time Jonie went missing? Because I must admit, my memory of it all is really hazy.'

'I don't want to drag it all up again, Anna. I'm so tired.'

Excuses. Anna realised Muriel always made an excuse for why she didn't want to speak about that time.

'It bothers me, though. Like, I have this niggling feeling – almost an ache – that I've forgotten something important. I think you could help me get rid of it, Mum.'

'I doubt I'd be much use.'

'I think you would be. You could tell me about Lizzie – *Eliza* – for starters.'

'No, love. I'm afraid I can't do that. Now, are you getting that toast for me or not? I'm hungry.'

Chapter Fifty-Three

2019

Lizzie

She didn't think it was the best idea inviting Billy to the B&B, but it was the safest. For her, anyway. Gwen wouldn't know what he looked like, so Lizzie had dropped into conversation at breakfast that her uncle would be visiting later. Yes, it was a lie, and she didn't like to deceive Gwen, but for the moment it was the only option. Soon enough everyone, including Gwen, would know she was the daughter of a murderer, and at that point Lizzie felt sure her welcome here would be revoked, so adding to that one white lie wouldn't make a whole lot of difference to the inevitability of the outcome. To be fair, she might not be giving Gwen enough credit – she might actually be fine with Billy Cawley being at her B&B – it wasn't as if he were staying in a room there.

Lizzie's fingers trembled as she dialled Dom's number. Anticipation of the meeting with her dad, coupled with the fact she'd not been honest with her husband, had caused anxiety and guilt to combine; it was a heady mix.

'Hey, babe. How's it going back home?' she asked, keeping her voice light and breezy.

'Missing you. Work's shit. I'm bored. You?' he rattled off.

Despite his abrupt opening line, Lizzie smiled, her heart lifting

186

at hearing Dom's deep, smooth voice. 'Ah, you know. Busy, but missing home,' she said. Then added quickly, 'Missing you, of course.'

'Thanks for remembering me right at the end there.' He laughed. But Lizzie thought it sounded hollow. He really was upset with her.

'I love you, stupid. Obviously, I'm missing you – it goes without saying.'

Her statement was met with silence.

'Is everything okay, Dom?' Her heart fluttered nervously, an uneasy feeling creeping through her.

She heard a long sigh.

Shit, what's wrong? What's happened?

'Dom?'

'It's nothing, don't worry about it.'

Lizzie let out her breath, but her concern didn't dissipate. Something in Dom's voice told her she *should* worry. She wrestled with the idea of pressing him, versus letting it go for now. If there was something bothering him, it would be better to speak about it face-to-face, not now, while they were a hundred miles apart. And not just prior to the visit from her father. Another pang of guilt hit her. She really should tell Dom about Billy.

'Are you sure? We can chat if you need to.' Lizzie swallowed the lump that had formed in her throat.

'Really? I'm not sure you can talk to me, can you?'

That was it. Whatever was on his mind was to do with Lizzie, to do with the things she'd been hiding from him. He knew something. But what?

The solicitor's letter.

Where the fuck had she put it? She'd been in shock when she'd opened it, had only partially read it. She felt sure she'd torn it up and thrown it in the bin. But maybe she hadn't. Or, he'd somehow retrieved it, read it. In which case, he already knew she'd lied to him – had been lying during all their time together. She had to try and salvage this.

'I'm not sure what's up, Dom, but of course I can talk to you. Although, maybe now isn't the best time. I think we need to talk in person—'

'Come home, Lizzie. Now. Leave Mapledon and drive home. We can talk tonight.'

Lizzie hesitated. As much as she was desperate to talk to Dom and limit the damage, she had to see this thing through now. Had to meet Billy, find out what he had to say. Then continue to put together the shattered pieces of her childhood. Get to the bottom of whatever happened here thirty years ago.

'I can't travel back today, Dom. I really want to speak with you properly – I've got some things I have to tell you. But I need to finish up here first. It's an "I've started so I'll finish" kind of thing I'm afraid. I'm making headway on the story. I just need a bit more time.'

'Fine. Take all the time you need. I guess I'll be here when you decide to come home. When you decide you want to confide in your bloody husband.'

The line went dead.

Lizzie felt weak. Drained. The last thing she wanted was to mess up her marriage. She was being irresponsible. She owed her life to Dom; she shouldn't be shutting him out. She certainly shouldn't be prioritising her murdering father over him. What was it she'd told herself before coming to Mapledon? She wasn't going to let the man who'd ruined her life thirty years ago do it again.

Yet here she was, allowing him just that opportunity.

Chapter Fifty-Four

1989

Mapledon Primary School

Monday 19th June – 1 month before

'I'm going to play elastics with Amber – we need a third person, so you have to come and play,' Jonie said as she dragged Bella by her upper arm into the playground. Bella spluttered a few words in dispute – she was about to go into the hall for lunch – but quickly realised she was wasting her breath. If Jonie had decided she was playing, she was. Food would have to wait.

'I snapped mine. Do you have yours?' Amber asked Jonie when they reached the area to the side of the field. They always played elastics there so the boys who were playing football on the grass could see them. That was Jonie's idea too; Bella wasn't in the slightest bit interested in the grubby, disgusting boys at their school.

'Yeah,' Jonie said, pulling the white length of elastic from her school bag. 'I pinched it from my mother's sewing basket last night. I think it's long enough.'

The girls stretched it out, then knotted the ends together.

'Perfect,' Amber said. 'Right, I'll start; you two stand at each end.'

'Get over!' Jonie shouted. 'It's my elastic. I'll say who goes first.' She scowled at Amber. Bella lowered her head, not wishing to make eye contact with Amber, to see her embarrassment. Jonie was such a cow sometimes. Always having to be boss. But at least she wasn't shouting demands at Bella. Yet.

'Go on then,' Amber said, stepping into the elastic and placing it around her ankles. Bella did the same.

'Hope you're ready to be beaten. You know I can get to necksies, don't you?' Jonie sounded so assured, it annoyed Bella. She found herself wishing, *praying*, for her to trip. Fail for once. But as they chanted: 'England, Ireland, Scotland, Wales, inside, outside, inside, on!' at ankles, then kneesies, thighsies, waisties, then armpits . . . each stage getting more boring than the next for Bella and Amber, they realised Jonie wouldn't fail. Of course she'd reach, and complete, necksies.

Jonie had her back to Bella as she began the song, her jumps high, her legs clearing the elastic – but as she was about to straddle the elastic, on the word *outside* – Bella sneakily pushed the elastic further out. Jonie's right leg missed, her foot landing heavily on the inside of the elastic. She pivoted quickly, her angry stare fixing on Bella's face.

'What did you do that for, you bitch?' Jonie's face was a deep red.

Bella's mouth dropped open. Jonie had never sworn like that before, and especially not at Bella.

'Well? You that pathetic you have to *cheat*?' Jonie stormed towards Bella, her pinched features almost touching Bella's face, her finger jabbing into Bella's chest.

'It was an accident,' Bella lied. 'Sorry. Go again if you want.'

'I will! And I'm facing you this time. You can't be trusted.'

'It's only a game, Jonie,' Amber interjected, trying to defuse the situation.

'Only losers say that,' Jonie retorted. And then, her eyes trained on Bella's said: 'And only losers cheat.'

'I didn't even want to play. I just wanted my lunch.' Bella

could hear the tears in her voice, and knew Jonie would also pick up on the fact she was about to cry.

'You're so boring, Bella.' Then she laughed. 'Boring Bella, Boring Bella,' she sang. 'Maybe we should make those the new words, instead of England, Ireland.' Her wide grin was filled with a viciousness that made her face ugly. Bella felt her own face grow hot. Inside her head she was screaming: '*You're ugly, Jonie. Jumped-up Jonie, Jumped-up Jonie.*' She really thought she was something special and could get away with treating people badly. But, Jonie was probably right – she *was* boring. And she was weak. She'd never stand up to Jonie Hayes. Which made Bella hate herself almost as much as she hated Jonie.

Chapter Fifty-Five

2019

Anna

Tuesday 16th July

'Why don't you go next door, have a morning coffee with Sandie, Mum? It would do you good.'

'I'm not feeling very sociable.'

'Which is why it's a good idea. Force yourself, otherwise you're going to end up a recluse.' She silently added: *like Billy Cawley was*. Muriel shook her head.

'Seriously, please. You're really worrying me now.'

'I'm fine. Just because I don't want to go around to my neighbour's does not mean I'm becoming a recluse, Anna.'

'Sorry, I'm only trying to help. This house feels like it's suffocating us both, that's all.'

'Well, *you* go next door then,' she said.

Anna was as good as smashing her head against the wall. 'Maybe I will,' she replied, her voice shrill. She was taken back to her teenage, childish outbursts when she and Muriel would do battle on a regular basis, particularly when Anna was attempting to go outside of Mapledon on nights out. It had been tedious as a teenager to grow up in a tiny Dartmoor village, miles from any excitement. Of course, they'd all wanted – been *desperate* – to escape and flock to the brighter lights of the nearest town. Although, in reality, they weren't that bright. There were more pubs in Bovey Tracey, but that was about it. The closest club was twenty miles away and until they were a bit older – able to successfully get in with fake ID – there was no point in arranging transport to get there; it was too much hassle just to be turned away and made to feel stupid. Anyway, anything had been better than The Plough in Mapledon, the pub where all their parents frequently drank, so at least Bovey had given them something.

Muriel shot Anna a disgusted look.

'What?' Anna shouted, rolling her eyes at her mother.

'You're beginning to irritate me.'

Anna bit her lip, suppressing the urge to fire back 'not as much as you're irritating me', but knew it would get her nowhere. She got up and walked away without saying anything further. She would go into Sandie's – it might actually give her a good opportunity to find out what Muriel's behaviour had been like over the past weeks and months. She'd quiz her about whether she'd seen anything strange in the neighbourhood too.

Anna unlocked the front door. Stepping outside she glanced back, her heart sinking as she noticed what was pinned to it. Another limb.

'Jesus Christ!' she said, reaching forwards and ripping it away from the wood. The single nail came away, the plastic leg attached. Anna walked to the top of the path, eyes searching up and down the road. Of course, no one was there. Must've been left in the early hours of the morning; they hadn't even heard it. Anna pulled the nail out and examined the leg. Inside the hollow, the same as before, was a piece of paper. She couldn't reach it with her finger, so she used the nail to hook it out. For the moment, she pocketed the leg and paper, not wishing to read its contents outside, and then carried on up the path. She'd check it after she'd spoken with Sandie.

Sandie's house was slightly smaller than Muriel's as it was mid-terraced. The neighbour to her other side was an elderly man who'd moved into the property after Anna had left Mapledon. Sandie, however, had been Muriel's neighbour since she moved in with Eric just after they'd married. Anna remembered Sandie well – she'd always been popping in and out while Anna had lived there – coming in for a cup of tea and a chat with Muriel, leaving several hours later with her mug still in her hand. Nobody knocked on doors back then, they merely called 'cooee' as they let themselves straight in. Anna almost did the same now as she stepped up to Sandie's front door. She gave a small laugh. Funny the things you remembered, and strange how years later old habits were still strong. Anna rang the bell, and as she waited, studied the door for nail holes. It was intact. Clearly, Sandie hadn't been the recipient of any doll parts.

'Yes?' Sandie's face, small and heart-shaped, peeked around the door.

'Hi, Sandie. It's Anna, it's been a while.' Anna smiled but realised there was no recognition in the woman's eyes. 'Muriel's daughter,' she added.

'Oh, my goodness. Little Bella!' Sandie opened the door fully and burst from behind it, her arms open wide. She grasped Anna in a tight hug, then, still holding on to her, extended her arms again. Sandie looked her up and down, appraising her. 'I'd seen you coming and going the last few days – I did wonder who you were. I was moments from nipping in to have a nose.' She gave a wink. 'Gosh, I can't believe it's you. How long has it been?'

'Oh, well – a fair few years,' Anna said. 'Twenty or so?'

'You'll come in for a coffee, yes?' Sandie's gaze searched the path and then she turned her head towards Muriel's house. 'No mum?'

'Er . . . no. She's in a bit of a funny mood. One of the reasons I'd rather speak to you alone, actually.'

194

'Ah. I see.' Sandie nodded in a way that conveyed an understanding.

Unlike Muriel's house, which internally had largely remained the same as when it was newly built in the Sixties, Sandie's had been transformed since the last time Anna had stepped inside. The lounge and dining room were now integrated, and it ran seamlessly into the L-shaped kitchen – modern decoration and updated kitchen units made the house feel totally different.

'Wow, Sandie – it looks really great in here.'

'Well, I have Ian. He does so much DIY still – he loves tinkering about in the house. Although I don't let him have a say in the colour scheme; he's completely uncoordinated when it comes to matching colours.' She gave a laugh, and went to the kettle, grabbing two china mugs from the cupboard above. 'Tea or coffee, love?'

'Coffee, please. Although I consume too much caffeine really. I should cut down.'

'Shouldn't we all?' Sandie smiled and dropped a heaped teaspoon of coffee into the mug. 'Muriel tells me you're teaching still. How is that going?'

'Yeah, good thanks. It has its challenges, but it suits me and means I get the school holidays to spend with Carrie. Well, I usually do, anyway.'

'Isn't she with you?'

'No. It was an . . . *unexpected* visit, let's say. And I didn't want Carrie being dragged into Mum's drama.' Anna felt her cheeks flush, guilt at bad-mouthing her mother surfacing.

'Ah.' Sandie pursed her lips as she handed a mug to Anna. 'Where do you want to sit? Comfortable sofa or dining area?'

'I'm easy,' Anna said.

'I have the feeling this conversation may require a comfy sofa.' She smiled again, placing a hand on Anna's shoulder as she moved back into the lounge. Although Anna hadn't intended to dive right in and talk about her mother behind her back, the warm reception from Sandie – coupled with a familiar, friendly face – triggered an outpouring. After what seemed to be an hour of monologue from Anna, Sandie finally sighed and began her appraisal of the situation Anna had detailed.

'Firstly,' Sandie said, 'I don't think you need worry about dementia, or Alzheimer's. Apart from some odd lapses of memory, I think Muriel is fine – or fine for our age, should I say.' She smiled warmly. 'Secondly, no – neither I, nor anyone else I've heard about, have received any such macabre items hammered to our doors. Tina hadn't mentioned she'd had this happen to her when I saw her last. I can't say I've seen anyone hanging about either. Which is odd, as I do like to know what's going on in the street and often sit in the chair by the front window to watch the world go by. My guess is they have been performing this "game" for want of a better word, very late, or in the early hours when no one is about. The streetlights going off at one in the morning doesn't help. Whoever is doing it, kids or adults, will be able to keep in the shadows and go virtually undetected. Now, as for your third point about contacting the police due to your suspicion it's Billy Cawley, I'd advise caution there, love. You remember what this village is like, don't you?'

'The villagers all huddle together and act as one when there's a problem.'

'Quite. Sometimes I feel it's a little like a vigilante group. If they get wind you think Billy's back . . . well, they'll form a lynch mob or something. You need to be sure it's him.'

And Anna wasn't. As much as everything *pointed* to it being him, she couldn't rule Lizzie out. Before she could say anything more, Sandie echoed her thoughts.

'It may seem obvious to you that it must be Billy, given the timing, but you can't be sure it really isn't teenagers. It's not the same world now – teenagers play far more risky games than the ones the kids played back in your day. Simple *Knock, Knock,*

Ginger wouldn't cut it nowadays. They're all so obsessed with the internet and games and the like – kids now would need to up the stakes. All they'd have to do was search the internet and find out all about Billy Cawley and what happened in Mapledon, and together with what their parents would've told them as they grew up – that would be enough.'

'You could be right,' Anna conceded. 'I need something more. Actual evidence.'

'Yes, I think that would be a better idea. Stay up, put up a camera, anything. But make sure you have something solid, then take it to the police.'

After some further, more light-hearted, conversation, Anna finished her coffee and got up.

'I'd best be getting back to Mum.'

'Of course, love. Well, it was really great to catch up at last. Don't be a stranger, eh?'

Anna smiled, but in truth, she was aiming to be just that. As she was leaving, she remembered Pat.

'Does Pat Vern still live locally?'

Sandie frowned. 'Yeees, although as you know, he's been retired for some time now. Why?'

Anna hadn't known that, but continued. 'Well, he was an officer at the time and would remember a lot from then. Plus, he may be able to offer some advice about the situation. He'd be worth chatting to, unofficially. Is he still in the cottage on the edge of the village?'

'Didn't your mum tell you?'

'Tell me what?'

'He's with Tina, love. Has been living with her for over ten years.'

Anna narrowed her eyes, deep in thought. Why hadn't her mum, or Tina, mentioned that? Seemed a strange omission. She was surprised; she would never have put Pat with Tina. She recalled he'd been to Tina's house a few times while she'd been over playing with Jonie. Had something been going on, even back then? Behind Mark's back? An affair?

'No, she didn't say a thing.'

'Don't suppose she thought to mention it; it's old news now. It was no surprise, really, after Mark. To have lost her daughter to murder, then her husband to suicide . . .' Sandie let out a long breath. 'Pat was a godsend, a huge support. Everyone knew how he felt of course; it was no secret that he'd always carried a torch for Tina. When this all happened, he kind of slipped in, moving into Mark's shoes so to speak.'

'I don't suppose anyone could begrudge her some light after all the dark.'

'No, love. Just a shame for Zoe and Daisy. Another broken family in Mapledon.'

Anna nodded in agreement – the memory of Eric leaving her and Muriel flitting through her mind. 'Okay, well, thanks so much, Sandie. You've been really helpful. And if you could keep an eye on Mum when I've gone, that would be great – put my mind at ease a bit about her living alone. James had suggested I take her home to Bristol with me, but I can't quite see it working particularly well.'

'Goodness, no. Neither can I. And to be honest, I don't think you'd ever get her to leave Mapledon anyway – no matter what was going on or how frightened she might be. This place is in her blood.'

Chapter Fifty-Six

2019

Lizzie

Nerves had prevented Lizzie from eating breakfast, and now, as the time rolled on towards lunch, her stomach growled. She'd been sitting in her car for the past half an hour, waiting, watching the driveway, her fingers drumming on the wheel. She assumed Billy must have transport – how else would he have been visiting Mapledon from his caravan in the farmer's field? He'd said he had to be outside a ten-mile radius to keep to his conditions, so walking would surely be out of the question. She checked the time on her mobile for the twentieth time.

Had he changed his mind? Decided it wasn't worth the risk?

Lizzie glanced back towards the B&B and noticed a shadowy figure lurking behind a curtain in one of the upstairs rooms. It must be Gwen. She mentioned she'd be getting more rooms ready for guests. She was probably wondering why Lizzie was sitting in her car. She was drawing attention to herself, so if Billy did turn up, Gwen was bound to be even more curious about him. She needed to be more nonchalant. Hoping Gwen was still watching, she got out of the car, her attention on her mobile phone. She held it up, casting it around as if to find a signal. Maybe Gwen would think she'd been trying to make a call all that time.

Lizzie stood by the front door, eyes still searching the driveway. It was the only way into the B&B. Perhaps she'd go for a walk – at least she'd be out of sight and could catch Billy before he came up the drive. They could walk and talk; they didn't need to sit in full view of Gwen. Their conversation would be more private. But what if he came another way – through the trees, across a field or something? She'd miss him if she wasn't right here. Her stomach was one big knot. The ringing of her mobile jolted her out of her thoughts. No caller ID. She accepted the call.

'Hello?'

'Hi, Lizzie, it's Anna. We need to talk.' The intensity of her voice set Lizzie's pulse racing.

'Um . . . okay. Now? On the phone?'

'No. In person. I need to show you something. Can you come here?'

'Not right now, I've got . . . er . . . something on.' She found herself stammering, afraid Anna would sense from her tone that she was about to meet Billy Cawley. Stupid, she knew – how could anyone know but her? And especially not merely from her voice. Her face reddened at the thought of her idiocy. Just knowing she was meeting with a convicted child killer, who happened to be her father, the one who reportedly abused and abandoned her as a child, was enough to bring to the surface a whole range of emotions. Dread. Insecurity. Anger. All of which made her feel her world was spinning, rotating in the wrong direction at high speed. Made her feel as though she and her thoughts were transparent.

'Later this afternoon then? It's important.'

'Sure. I'll ring when I'm on my way.'

The call ended. Lizzie's blood fizzed as Anna's words rang in her ears: 'I need to show you something. It's important.'

What now?

Anna's attention was drawn to a sound. A crunching – tyres over gravel. But not a car.

200

Billy Cawley's hunched figure came into view, his legs slowly pumping as he cycled up the drive. Lizzie lurched forwards, and on shaky legs ran to him, hoping no one had seen his approach.

'Stop there. We'll walk back the way you came,' Lizzie said. Her voice was more solid than she felt. 'Leave the bike behind one of the trees.'

Billy silently obeyed her order. He turned back to face her. In the bright, midday sunshine, he looked very different from last night. Light caught the white-grey streaks of his hair, making it shimmer. It was cut short at the sides, the top slightly longer and swept back with gel, or oil, revealing a receding hairline. He'd worn it longer when she was little, and it had been blond and straggly, more unkempt. Not that she remembered him – it was his photos from the newspapers she was recalling now. He was heavier set, not scrawny as he'd been then. He had that typical 'hard man' quality, she thought. He reminded her of Ray Winstone, the actor who always seemed to play gangster-type roles. Maybe Billy had always had that air about him, or maybe he'd gained it from years of incarceration.

She drew in a deep breath to control her rising anxiety. She could be making a huge mistake being here with him. Alone. No one knowing. She regretted not confiding in Anna on the phone just now. She needn't have said *who* she was with, just that she had a meeting with someone, and it might turn nasty, and if she didn't call Anna back by three, to alert the police or something. Lizzie put her hand in her jeans pocket, touching her mobile phone. It didn't offer a hundred per cent reassurance, though – the area wasn't great for signal, and the further into the lanes she went, the likelihood of being able to make any calls, even to 999, was slim to non-existent. It wasn't just *her* network that was dodgy; she'd been told no network was reliable in some areas of Mapledon.

Lizzie walked to the side of Billy, their backs to the sun, her head down, looking at the driveway, which had now gone from gravel to a dusty, muddy track. She felt trickles of sweat running down her back. Lizzie sensed Billy was watching her as they walked. He hadn't spoken a word yet – not even hello. One of them had to break the silence soon; it was uncomfortable. Why had he come if he wasn't going to speak?

Impatience – her downfall – took over. 'So, do you have anything to say? Anything you want to get off your chest?'

'Like?' he asked, simply.

Lizzie bristled. Was he really going to make this as hard as possible? Make her drag every last word from him? 'Like, why did you do it?' She turned to look at him directly now, wanting to see his reaction.

'Do what, exactly?' A frown wrinkled his forehead.

A loud huff left Lizzie's mouth.

'I'm not trying to be awkward, Eliza. But you need to be more specific.'

Hearing herself being called Eliza caused a strange sensation to wash over her. It didn't sound right. Didn't sound familiar at all, although she guessed she must've been referred to as Eliza at some point when she was little. For as long as she could remember, she'd told everyone to call her Lizzie before officially changing her name by deed poll at sixteen. She'd taken on the surname of the last people to have fostered her: the Brenfields. She'd liked their name more than she'd liked them, but they'd been decent enough.

'Fine. Is this specific enough?' she said before launching into one question, then another, and another, all of them suddenly spilling out of her like an erupting volcano. 'Did you kill my mum? Did you abuse me as a child? Did you abandon me? Why did social services take me away? Did you kill Jonie Hayes? Where is her body? Why didn't you let her poor parents know where their dead daughter was? How could you do this to me? How could you murder a child?'

Breathless, she stopped and rested against a tree, tears falling down her cheeks. Sobs filled the quiet countryside lane. Billy laid a hand on her shoulder.

'Shhh, shhh. It's okay. I get it, there's a lot of questions you want answered. I understand you've had years and years of hearing all the horrible things I was meant to have done, years of building up enough hatred for me to last a lifetime.'

His voice was smooth, comforting almost. But Lizzie knew she mustn't let him manipulate her. She had to stay strong, dig deep to find out the truth. 'So? Go. Answer away,' she said, her voice monotone and cold.

Billy gave a short, sharp laugh. Lizzie's blood chilled. What the hell was funny?

'I might have forgotten the running order now.' He smiled as he backed up, creating some distance between them. 'You may have to prompt me, but I'll give it a go.'

'It's not amusing, Billy.'

'No.' He dropped his head. 'Sorry, I know. I'm just nervous, that's all. It's been a very long time since I had a real conversation. It's been too long since I saw my little girl.'

'Save the pity-talk – I'm not the one who's likely to give you any sympathy.'

'Right. Sure,' he said, his eyes darkening. 'Okay, then. In answer to your first question, I loved Rosie with all my being. But we did marry very young. Of course, that's not to say I wouldn't have married her even if she hadn't been pregnant with you, but I'm sure we would've waited until we had more money. But we managed. We had help to get the bungalow in the form of an inheritance from my father, and we thought it was perfect. However, right from the start we didn't fit in. We were never "one of them". They were a funny bunch, the villagers of Mapledon, and despite trying so hard to be liked, we were never accepted. And before long, Rosie fell ill. At first, we thought it was exhaustion – looking after a young child, sleepless nights and all. But as time went on, she developed other symptoms and she was finally diagnosed as having cervical cancer. It was too late by then. No treatment would've worked: it would've prolonged her life, but she was terminal, so she declined the treatment. I didn't kill your mother, Eliza. Cancer did.' He swiped a tear from his cheek. Lizzie averted her eyes. She didn't want to see his emotions. She didn't handle her own well; she wanted no responsibility for his.

'Then you were left with me,' Lizzie said.

'Yes, and that's when I lost all control.'

'So, you gave up on me? Neglected, and even *hurt* me?' Hot anger flared.

'No, Eliza. I never hurt you, not on purpose. You hurt me, though. You used to lash out – punch, kick and bite me. You wanted to punish me, I think. You didn't understand why your mum had left you, and I was swamped with grief, unable to understand enough myself. Unable to take proper, good care of you. I lost all interest in work – it'd been difficult enough to find decent carpentry jobs around the village to keep the money flowing, even before Rosie got bad, but then I stayed home to be with her. After she died . . . well . . . I guess I gave up even looking. I'm surprised you weren't taken from me sooner really, and at one low point, I actually thought perhaps it was for the best – you'd seemed so troubled and I didn't know how to handle that, maybe better people would. But if someone had given me a chance, supported me, *helped*, then things might have been different. If I knew then what I do now . . . But no.'

His tone became harsher, his voice louder. 'Everyone was too keen to point the finger, blame me for anything and everything that went wrong in the village. They were always baying for my blood, Eliza. They did everything to drive me out. I didn't fit, nor did you. Two weirdos in their perfect Stepford wives bloody village.' Spit flew in thin strands from Billy's mouth. Rage bursting from him like flames. 'I didn't take Jonie Hayes. I didn't kill her. So how could I ever confess to where her body was?'

'But you pleaded *guilty*!'

'Yes, because there was little choice and that's what I was advised to do. But I didn't do it, so I couldn't tell the police where Jonie was. I didn't know then and I still don't. But I have had a very long time to think about it all. And now I've got some debts to repay.'

'What do you mean, debts to repay?'

'I owe a few people.' His smile was menacing, unnatural. 'Not money. No. I owe them justice.'

Lizzie sucked in a breath. That didn't sound like a debt that could easily be paid back. It sounded like Billy wanted to dish out his own kind of justice. Maybe revenge.

'Like what, and how?'

'Sorry, Eliza. You've asked enough questions for today. And there are some answers you really don't want to hear, trust me.'

Chapter Fifty-Seven

1989

Mapledon

Saturday 17th June – 32 days before

'Come on, come on! Enough of that, kids.' Officer Pat Vern walked purposefully towards the group of boys hanging around the entrance to Blackstone Close.

'What you talking about, mister? We done nothing wrong,' one of the boys on the bike shouted across to him. 'We're riding our bikes. That illegal now, is it?' He was a confident, bolshie lad. As Pat got closer, he recognised him as Adam Furlong. Pat guessed his confidence came from the knowledge his dad was local councillor, Eddie – an equally bolshie adult who believed he ran the village. Pat's lip curled involuntarily. Nothing he loathed more than self-appointed, pompous know-it-alls who were, essentially, just bullies with a wish to control others.

'Nope, but trespassing is. And it's Officer Vern to you!' Pat was standing on the pavement adjacent to the group now. There were only eight of them, mostly on bikes, but he noted two bikes were lying on their sides, abandoned. He walked further into the cul-de-sac until he could see the last bungalow in the row – Billy Cawley's – and then he caught sight of the missing riders. They appeared to have just exited Billy's driveway. They were awkwardly running towards the rest of the group, bent over, laughing. 'And what've you two been up to?'

'Nothing, Officer Vern,' they sang, before doubling over with laughter again.

'Come on, we're going,' Adam shouted to them, shooting Pat a smug look. They mounted their bikes, smirking the whole time, and started to pedal.

'If I catch any of you on private property, harassing Mr Cawley, there'll be trouble, you hear?'

The bikes whizzed past Pat, the riders cackling like a bunch of witches. Pat watched them disappear up the road, waiting until he could no longer hear their voices. Then he walked back in the direction of Billy's bungalow, just to check no damage had been done. As he approached the walled garden, he heard other voices, hushed, urgent. They weren't coming from Billy's; they seemed to be from the direction of the thicket of bushes at the end of the cul-de-sac. He crossed over, and edged towards the sounds, hoping he'd not been seen. Had the lads cycled around to avoid his detection – come to finish their stupid game? They must've pedalled damned quick.

He crept up beside the hedges, ears sharpened, focusing on the voices. Girls, not boys. He relaxed, straightening. He was about to walk away, but then he caught what they were saying.

'Don't believe what Jonie tells you. Really, she's a nasty bully and will say anything to get what she wants,' one girl said.

Then a different voice: 'I heard what she did to Eliza. Do you think she really did that?'

Pat stiffened. He didn't want to listen to any more. It was just kids' talk. Gossip. He didn't want to hear bad things about Tina's girl – that would be awkward. But the other girl started talking again, and he couldn't walk away. He carried on listening.

'She was inside. Actually *inside* the bungalow. I mean, she might be a bully, but she's a brave one. I wouldn't go inside, would you?'

'No way! But why did she go in?'

'Apparently, it was a dare. Robert told me. She told him he was next, that he had to go inside, otherwise she'd tell.'

'Tell what?'

'That's the point, no one knows.'

'Wow. We're not going to do that dare, are we?'

Pat heard the quiver in the girl's voice.

'Don't be daft, no way – I just told you I'd never go in there. My mum said he's nasty and hurts people; that's why Eliza is so weird. He hits her and locks her in a cupboard. Mum said if he got someone inside the bungalow, they'd probably never come out again.'

'But Jonie did. If what you say is true.'

'Yeah, but only because she let him do stuff to her.'

Pat couldn't bear to listen to any more. These kids were about ten, eleven at most and shouldn't be talking like that. He shuddered. Where was the naivety, the innocence? What was the world coming to? But, more worryingly, what was Jonie playing at? The almost-harmless Knock, Knock game seemed to have progressed to a more dangerous one, one he really didn't like the sound of at all.

Chapter Fifty-Eight

2019

Anna

Tuesday 16th July

When Anna left Sandie's house, her mind had been filled with questions about Tina and Pat. She'd walked back down her mother's path, but instead of going in the front door, she'd slipped down the side and into the garden shed, her fingers curled tightly around the doll's leg. She hadn't wanted to show Muriel. And she'd wanted to be alone when she uncovered the words on the paper. The arm and note from the other day were also safely stowed away in the old wooden storage unit at the back of the shed – her dad's – the one where he used to keep all the odd bits of junk: spare plugs, nails, plant stakes, garden scissors and small tools and God knew what else. Most of it still remained in the drawers, which hadn't surprised her given the rest of the house, but the cupboard part had enough space to fit the additional items.

But what had her mother done with the doll's head? Anna had forgotten to check last Saturday when she'd come back from the shop as she'd been too relieved to find it gone from the front door. But now, given the latest parts, she wanted them together in a safe place while she figured out what to do next. Whether to inform the police or, at the very least, Pat. Although now he might not be of any real assistance. He was with Tina; he was too close. He was involved, and therefore not objective – but still, he could have a better memory of the events of July 1989 from an official perspective. Anna had called Lizzie, partly in desperation – because she felt she wanted someone to show, someone her age and who might be able to help her put the pieces together – and partly to watch her reaction. See if there was a glimmer of guilt – a sign that would give her away as the culprit. The Knock, Knock game that had been relentlessly played on her father now being played out by his daughter – there was a certain irony to that. Anna had assumed the game was being played on Muriel, but in fact it might be aimed at Anna herself. She'd been one of the key players of that game back then – her mother didn't have anything to do with *that*.

Maybe this was Lizzie's way of getting Anna here, back in Mapledon, to exact revenge against her. Muriel could merely be the conduit; the target was really her. She'd have to be careful around Lizzie. Trust was a luxury she couldn't afford. But first, she needed the head. Which meant asking her mother where she'd put it. Anna hadn't looked inside the head's hollow, and to her knowledge neither had Muriel – there was probably a note stuffed inside that too, which they'd missed. It could hold vital information.

'Mum, when you took the head off the door, where did you put it?' Anna asked as soon as she walked into the kitchen.

'Oh. Where've you been? You were gone ages; I was worried.'

'Next door, having coffee with Sandie, like you told me to do. No need to have been worried.'

'Well. You two certainly seemed to have a lot to talk about then!' She seemed put out. Jealous even.

'It's been twenty years, Mum. We had a lot to catch up on.

And you never told me Pat was with Tina now,' Anna said, suddenly side-tracked.

'Didn't think of it. Not particularly relevant is it?'

'I guess not. But would've been nice to know. Strange though, isn't it? How long after Mark's passing did that happen?'

Muriel's gaze faltered. She slipped away, her mind elsewhere. Irritation growing, Anna went back to her original question. 'Didn't you put the doll's head in the shed?'

'No. I threw it right in the bin. Disturbing-looking thing, didn't want to *keep* it!'

'Shit. We haven't had bin day since, have we?' Anna felt the panic rising in her voice.

'No, not until tomorrow.'

Anna rushed out of the door, ran to the black wheelie bin and flung the lid open. It banged against the side. Relief flooded her. Underneath a bin-liner and some wax cartons, she spotted dirty-blonde hair. Reaching in, she grabbed a handful and dragged the head out. She hoped if there *was* a note, it was still tucked inside. She didn't relish the thought of having to empty the entire contents of the bin to find a scrap of paper. She tried to angle the head so the light was right and she could see inside. Yes, there was something in there. Another white piece of paper, just like those found within the limbs. Anna pushed two fingers inside and was able to grasp hold of it and withdraw it.

She quickly returned to the shed and deposited the head inside the cupboard. The pieces of paper were lined up on the top, in order of receipt, weighted down with jam jars that now held screws and nails. Three notes. Three threats, if you wanted to take it that way. Which Anna did now, as she read them in order:

SOMEONE KNOWS THE TRUTH

SOMEONE HAS BLOOD ON THEIR HANDS

SOMEONE HAS TO PAY

She wondered what Lizzie would make of them when she got here. She still hadn't called to say she was on her way. Had she chickened out? Perhaps she'd realised Anna was on to her.

No matter. At least she had evidence. It was about time to pay Pat a visit. She'd give Lizzie another hour to turn up, then go across to Tina's.

Chapter Fifty-Nine

2019

Lizzie

As soon as Lizzie had parked up next to Muriel's house, Anna appeared in the doorway.

'I didn't think you were coming,' she said, her voice lowered so Lizzie could barely hear her. 'You said you'd call when you were on your way.' Anna closed the front door cautiously and stepped outside.

'Sorry, I was distracted, didn't realise the time,' Lizzie said. Which was true. Her walk with Billy had taken longer than she'd anticipated. 'What's so important?' she asked. Lizzie felt a pang of unease as she looked at Anna's pale face – worry had etched its lines across her forehead.

'Follow me,' she instructed as she marched down the side of the house. Lizzie gave a furtive glance around, then followed. She wondered where Muriel was. It seemed Anna didn't want her involved. This sneaking around, trying to catch her before Muriel saw her set alarm bells ringing.

When Lizzie caught up, Anna was disappearing into a garden shed. She assumed Anna wanted her to go inside. Something caused her to hold back, the uneasy feeling she'd had a moment ago doubling in intensity. But, bearing in mind she'd just spent two hours with a convicted murderer, she weighed up the risk

213

this petite, boring teacher-type woman posed and decided she'd be safe. For now, at least.

It took Lizzie a few moments for her eyes to adjust to the sudden darkness. There was a dim light inside the shed, emanating from a single electric pendant light hanging from the ceiling, but it took a while for it to be bright enough to make out her surroundings.

'These are what's been hammered to Mum's front door,' she declared, pointing to the items laid out.

Lizzie's gaze followed, and for a split second she thought she was imagining it – seeing what wasn't really there. But then her body reacted: her palms becoming hot, her armpits clammy. Tears sprang to her eyes, tears she tried but failed to swallow down, the lump in her throat preventing it.

She stared at the doll's head, unable to tear her eyes from it.

Her breath stuttered and caught in her lungs, trapped. Her trachea tightened. She was going to choke.

It looked just like Polly.

The last doll her mum had given her. *Could* it be her? She thought she'd taken the doll with her when she'd been taken into care. But now, staring down at it, she felt sure it was Polly. Not just the head, but the leg and arm also resembled her beloved doll. The only doll she'd never ripped apart. But now, it appeared someone else had.

She was aware of sounds – slowed-down speech, like a record playing at the wrong speed, coming from her right. An arm on hers: the touch light, unreal. It was as though she were experiencing an out-of-body episode. There she was, hovering above herself and Anna, each of them looking down at the surface of the wooden cupboard – at the head, arm and leg lying harmlessly, still. Inanimate. No need to be afraid, she told herself.

Only there *was* a reason to be afraid.

Someone was messing with her, playing around with her

emotions, tossing her life into turmoil. Why was someone hammering parts of Polly to Muriel's door?

Lizzie had the sensation she was moving. Air swept around her body, her face. Anna was talking. She could hear more clearly now – not in slow motion, not as though she had cotton wool in her ears.

'Lizzie! God, are you okay? I think you fainted.'

Lizzie gasped air, trying to force as much of it in and out of her lungs as she could manage without hyperventilating. She was reassured when her breathing became easier, less painful, steady. She wasn't going to die.

'It . . . it was a panic . . . attack,' she managed to say.

'Shit, it was scary. I'm so sorry, I shouldn't have taken you in there. I didn't think it would have that effect.'

'No. It's fine.' Lizzie sank fully to the ground, sitting cross-legged, her hands on the grass. 'It was claustrophobic in there, and so hot – just got to me. It was so sudden I didn't have time to get out.'

'I'm glad you're okay now. I'll get you a drink,' Anna said, and disappeared into the kitchen.

Recovered now, Lizzie stood and, checking all was clear, went back inside the shed. She grabbed the head. Polly's eyes stared at her accusingly. Poking her fingers inside, Lizzie retrieved what she'd seen tucked within it. Obviously Anna had missed it, taken out the paper and thought that was it. But lining the head was a small piece of material. Lizzie quickly shoved it into the top of her jeans and returned to the garden.

Not only was someone messing with her, they were also leaving clues only Lizzie could know about. And the only conclusion she could reach was that her own flesh and blood, Billy Cawley, was behind it all. Who else would know about Polly, let alone keep her for all these years? And Lizzie had allowed him to talk to her, had given him a chance to explain, clear his name.

Lying. Fucking. Bastard.

He must be laughing hard right now, thinking he'd won her over. Believing she believed him. What a gullible fool she was.

Again.

He wouldn't get away with it this time.

She had a friend now.

Chapter Sixty

1989

The Plough, Mapledon

Friday 16th June – 33 days before

Reverend Christopher Farnley was sitting at the bar nursing a warm pint of bitter while listening to the group of men discussing everything from their wives and children to work and golf . . . and Billy Cawley. It seemed everyone always got back to the topic of Billy, however the conversation initially started. He sighed as he took a sip of the insipid liquid, wishing he'd asked for a whisky instead. If he could bear sitting there listening further, he might ask for that next.

Chris tended to keep himself to himself outside of church. There were few men he wished to converse with; not many of them had anything interesting to talk about in his opinion. He missed the city life: the diversity and stimulating discussions, although it'd been over ten years now since he'd moved back to Mapledon to head the church. He sometimes also craved the anonymity a large town had offered him. His father had been instrumental in the posting – having lived in Mapledon and serving as the local vicar for most of his adult life. Now Chris was literally walking in his footsteps after years of trying to escape them to walk in a different direction. His path, it

217

appeared, was preordained. He'd probably die here too, as his father had.

He made the best of it – his life in Mapledon hadn't been a bad one. Boring, but not unbearable – he'd become accustomed to the small-mindedness, the power-hungry, the gossipmongers, the top dogs, the underdogs. And Billy Cawley was most certainly the latter. He'd never really stood a chance. The only reason Chris had been accepted was because he'd lived there once, his roots firmly established – he came from a long line of Farnleys, so was classed as an insider despite his time away from the village.

Chris had tried to intervene by speaking about inclusion and community spirit in his sermons – impressing on his congregation the importance of being kind and supportive, of being non-judgemental like the Lord Jesus – but nothing changed. He'd then gone for the more direct route, visiting Billy at his home and trying to make him and his family feel welcomed. But his attempts had been met with a disapproving grunt and the door slammed in his face. And that had been before Billy's wife, Rosie, had passed – before Billy became a drunk and virtual recluse.

Rosie had been to church, though, on numerous occasions following her diagnosis. Not at services – she would sneak in when the congregation had dispersed, crouching down behind a pew, making herself as small as possible. For peace, and an element of comfort he presumed; she never spoke with him about her illness, about her worries. She seemed a closed book. She had, however, asked Chris not to mention to anyone that she'd been visiting the church – especially Billy. How he was meant to ever mention it when Billy refused to speak with him anyway, he didn't know, but he'd assured her he wouldn't tell him or anyone else. He'd often wondered why Rosie appeared afraid of Billy, and against his wishes, he'd found himself questioning the things people said about him. Were they true?

But God didn't judge, and nor should he, he kept reminding himself.

Everyone had a cross to bear. Some had several.

'What do you think, Rev?' The voice jumped into his thoughts, and Chris turned sharply. Eric was standing beside him, eyebrows raised, appearing to be waiting for a response.

'Oh, sorry, Eric. Miles away. Say again?' He picked his pint up and took another sip.

'We were just discussing what to do with Billy. What do you reckon?'

Chris felt his insides contract. Getting dragged into such talk would not be a good idea. He allowed the silence to stretch, pretending he was considering the question. He made a mental note to avoid The Plough in future – he'd be better off buying alcohol from the shop and drinking alone in the comfort of the rectory. He had a sudden feeling of affinity with Billy Cawley.

'I'm not sure what you mean, *do* with him?' Although Chris could make an educated guess. Eric was a meddler, the same as his wife, Muriel – he hadn't reached her level as yet, but together with the other husbands, the group of men were always keen to make their mark. Ensure their presence was felt and to drive home the fact their wives might well hold the Mapledon Meetings, but it was they who were really in charge. Some of them were also on the local board of councillors, which only added to their self-inflated sense of power. As much as Chris would like to assert his own authority as a man of the cloth, he also did not wish to get on the wrong side of the Mapledon Mafia. That was a place of nightmares, and he couldn't afford to be in that particular position.

'We—' Eric swung his arm around the bar, indicating the other men sitting around the largest table '—don't really want him here, in Mapledon. We think it's time he moved on.'

'Well, I'm afraid it's not as simple as asking someone to "move on", Eric. He owns property, his daughter goes to school here.

It would be a huge upheaval for them, particularly so soon after Rosie's passing.' Chris pushed his lips into an unsteady smile. Then, as Eric hadn't responded, added: 'Maybe we should think about offering support, or practical help—'

'Are you joking?' Several raised voices erupted from the table of men. Chris's shoulders fell, his eyes closing as he awaited the onslaught. 'The man is a straight-up freak,' Eric continued. 'If he's not abusing that girl, I'll eat my hat. You can't say there's nothing wrong there, Reverend, can you? I mean, you only have to look at her, see what shit – pardon my French – she does to them dolls of hers to know something ain't right. And then he has our kids hanging around him all the time. That's not normal.' Eric shook his head.

Another man, Mark – Tina Hayes' husband – stood up, shouting across the room. His words left Chris in no doubt where this could go if it were to get out of hand.

'If that paedo does so much as lay one finger on any of our kids . . .' And he drew his forefinger across his throat to indicate Billy Cawley's fate.

Chapter Sixty-One

2019

Anna

Tuesday 16th July

It had felt like an age before Anna managed to help Lizzie out of the shed and she'd recovered from her panic attack. Had she known Lizzie was claustrophobic she wouldn't have taken her into the humid, dark shed. That, together with the doll's parts, must've tipped her over the edge.

Anna pressed a glass of cold water into Lizzie's hand. 'Drink this,' she told her.

Lizzie gulped it down.

'Thanks,' she said, wiping her mouth with the back of her hand. She came across as a vulnerable girl, sitting cross-legged, pale and shaky on the grass. Anna saw her mum at the kitchen window; she hadn't been able to prevent her from knowing Lizzie was there once she'd rushed into the kitchen for water. It was inevitable she'd ask questions now and Anna would have to disclose the latest find and tell her she'd found a note in the doll's head.

'You feeling better?'

'Much.' Lizzie pushed herself into a standing position. 'Maybe we could go inside? Have a chat?'

Anna nodded, and they headed in through the back door, Muriel's puzzled gaze following them.

'What's going on?' she said. She was standing with her arms crossed firmly, her features carved into an accusatory glower.

'There's been another one, Mum.' Anna told her as they all positioned themselves at the dining room table.

Muriel sighed. 'Right. Well, I'll make us a cuppa then, shall I?'

She didn't wait for a response, sliding back off her chair and walking to the kitchen area. Anna noted that she avoided looking at Lizzie.

'I have a bad feeling we're going to receive the entire doll piece by piece,' Anna said. 'What do you think will happen once the doll is complete?'

'I don't know. But only three more parts to go? Then we'll see, I guess.'

'Should I involve the police?' Anna whispered, hoping Muriel wouldn't hear her above the noise of the boiling kettle. 'Mum really doesn't think it's necessary, but the more this goes on, the less inclined I am to go along with that.'

'I honestly don't know, Anna. I'm not sure the police can really help—'

'Of *course* she doesn't want you to involve the police, Anna. Because she is probably the one behind it all,' Muriel said, her mouth contracted into a tight pout as she plonked two mugs in front of Anna and Lizzie.

'Mum!' Anna tutted. Her mother could be so rude; too direct, sometimes.

'What? You weren't thinking the same thing?'

'Look, can I just remind you that you didn't want to involve the police either, so does that mean *you* have something to hide too?'

It was meant as a way of closing her mother down, giving Lizzie a chance, but her reaction and Lizzie's caused Anna to sit

222

back. She saw a look pass between Muriel and Lizzie – each was drawing a battle line; each knew something about the other and was deciding whether they should be the one to throw the first punch.

Anna, it appeared, had been left very much in the dark about something.

'Are either of you going to tell me what the hell is going on, please? What is it you know that I don't?'

'Nothing,' Muriel stated defensively. 'There's nothing to tell.'

'Bollocks.'

'Anna! Refrain from using that language in my house.'

'Then refrain from lying to me. I'm not having it.'

Lizzie placed her hands on the table, hard. 'Right. It's about time we all took some responsibility for this . . . this . . . *predicament* – for want of a better word – that we find ourselves in. We're *all* involved, whether we like it or not. Let's get real, and maybe we can figure out who's doing this, and why, and put a bloody stop to it before someone gets hurt. So, Muriel – over to you. You can start, don't you think?'

Anna's hands felt tingly, her fingers numb. She wasn't sure she was ready to hear this. She placed both her elbows on the table and cupped her chin in her hands. To steady herself. To prepare for whatever was about to be said.

'I'm all ears.'

Chapter Sixty-Two

2019

Lizzie

All Lizzie could do was watch and wait to see how the situation unfolded. She didn't really have much idea what Muriel might or might not know – but Anna seemed confident her mother knew something and, given one of Lizzie's only childhood memories related to being brought to Muriel and Anna's house, she was sure Anna was right. Lizzie only had one thing on Muriel – and that had come from her dad earlier on. It was ammunition, if required, but she couldn't be certain it was true. The lines between truth and lies appeared to be blurred beyond recognition where Mapledon and its inhabitants were concerned. The toxicity of the place was beginning to take over, sinking into her like poison from a snake bite – she wondered how long it would be before it took a firm hold and dragged her down, away from her life, away from Dom.

Lizzie almost felt sorry for the old woman sitting in front of her, her eyes weak and watery, filled with uncertainty and maybe a glimmer of fear. Muriel Fisher had aged in a matter of minutes. What could be so bad to have caused such a reaction? Lizzie sat back in her chair, ready now to find out. Hoping she wasn't about to be told yet more lies.

'Go on, Mum,' Anna said. Lizzie thought Anna's eyes looked

dark, lifeless. Not like they'd appeared the first day she'd met her at the church gate. She, too, should get out while she could.

'It's been thirty years,' Muriel said shakily before pausing. Lizzie suppressed a laugh. She'd immediately remembered a similar line spoken by the old woman in the film *Titanic*, and half expected to see Muriel's appearance change from the one in front of her to the thirty-eight-year-old Muriel from 1989, when all this started. Lizzie coughed, putting her hand to her mouth to disguise the smile. None of this was remotely funny; she recognised her reaction as one she used to employ when she was a child – a defence mechanism, she'd later realised.

Muriel's attention was on her hands, her fingers turning the gold band of her wedding ring round and round. For a moment Lizzie was mesmerised, then she remembered the point of this chat.

'Are you okay, Muriel?' she asked.

'Yes, yes. Just thinking.' Finally, she looked up, making eye contact with Lizzie. Her heartbeat jolted as Muriel's gaze, her non-blinking eyes, penetrated hers. 'I thought I was saving you. Saving Eliza.'

'So, it was you who got social services involved?'

'Yes, I suppose I was the one who got the ball rolling. I didn't act alone. I wouldn't have interfered had it not been for the others agreeing.'

'I see. But why did you bring me here?' Lizzie said, scrunching her face up.

'We needed to get you away from *him*. You were never allowed to speak with anyone when he was around. That's why Reverend Farnley convinced him to enrol you in the Sunday school too, to distance you – get you alone. But that wasn't enough. They wanted evidence.'

'Who, social services?'

'Yes. It wasn't enough for us to be suspicious, for us to think he was neglecting you, abusing you, even. Mad, really. What *would* it have taken? For him to murder you?' Muriel looked away. 'I mean, they only had to look at you, see what you were doing with your toys to see you were disturbed.'

Lizzie flinched. 'Taking dolls apart doesn't necessarily equate to abuse though, surely?'

'No, but together with the other things, we felt it did.'

'And by "we" you mean the other villagers?' Lizzie asked.

'No, not all of them,' Anna said. She'd been silent up till then. 'You mean the women who were part of the Mapledon Meetings, don't you.' It wasn't a question, it was a statement – bordering on an accusation, given the tone of Anna's voice.

Muriel shifted in her seat. 'Yes. The topic of Billy Cawley had been one discussed at pretty much every meeting since he moved into that bungalow.'

'You didn't like him, right from the start, did you? Didn't want to even try,' Anna said.

'It wasn't like that. Not really. I agree, he didn't fit in – he didn't try to. So inevitably that got some people's backs up. It's a tight-knit village. We all pull together, all get involved for the good of the community. Billy Cawley wasn't interested in all that; he didn't care. He was often rude, abrupt, and he kept Rosie and Eliza on a tight leash, which in our minds rang alarm bells. Once Rosie died, he seemed even more determined to keep you to himself.' Muriel looked to Lizzie and sighed, as though remembering that time.

'I didn't have any friends, did I?' Lizzie stated.

'No, love. Although some kids did try. Young Robert for instance.'

Lizzie sat up straighter. 'Rob? As in Nell Andrews' son from Brook Cottage Store?'

'Yes. There was one time in particular, I remember. Nell had finished work late one afternoon, and found that Robert had left the house, even after being told not to. Transpired he'd been *inside* the bungalow; Billy had actually let him in. Rumours flew around afterwards because Robert seemed scared, distant when he'd returned home. Refused to ever speak about that afternoon. Something had spooked him. Or someone.'

Lizzie thought about her evening with Rob. He'd been adamant he didn't remember anything specific about Jonie, and hadn't mentioned this incident with Billy or Eliza. What was he hiding? Or, perhaps it wasn't that he was *hiding* something; it could be he'd buried a terrible memory. Had her dad done something to him too?

'Anyway, carry on, Mum,' Anna coaxed.

'There isn't much more to say. Suffice to say Billy was angry when Eliza was taken away from him—'

'Hang on,' Lizzie said. 'You're jumping ahead. You mentioned social services wanted evidence. What convinced them they should take me into care in the end, then?'

Muriel sighed. 'We videoed you,' she said, quietly.

'*Videoed* me? Doing what?' Lizzie felt her voice rise. She didn't like where this was going.

'Me and Nell set up the camera and brought you here. We'd done it several times in the hopes of getting you to admit what your father was doing to you.'

'*Get me to admit?* Christ, that sounds more like coercion! Or did you go a few steps further and waterboard me to force me to say what you wanted?' Lizzie's face blazed. She'd been a child, and these women had manipulated her. She shot Anna a look of disgust. Did she *know* what her mother had done?

'No, not coerced,' Muriel said. 'We were gentle – tried to get you to open up to us by being supportive and encouraging, that's all.'

'Two grown women took me, and I'm guessing without my father's permission, and kept me in their house to drag some kind of sick confession from me?' The anger was building, Lizzie's heart pounding. 'Is that not abduction? Maybe it was *you* who took Jonie Hayes!'

The words hung between them – Anna and Muriel's expressions stunned at her accusation.

'Lizzie, please calm down,' Anna said as she rose from her chair and put her arm around Lizzie's shoulders. She shrugged her off.

'I *am* calm. For a woman who's just found out that not only had her own father let her down, she'd also been manipulated by other adults as a child.'

'But you did tell us, eventually.' Muriel's voice was confident now, as if the end had justified the means. 'Poor little Eliza, it broke my heart.'

'What broke your heart?' Lizzie's eyes immediately stung with tears. It'd been building to this.

'You had a doll, Polly you called her . . .' Muriel paused, looking up to Lizzie.

Here we go. 'Yes, I remember her.'

'It was the only doll you seemed to love; the only one intact.' Muriel took a deep breath. 'And you showed us, using the doll. You showed us what he'd done to you.'

Chapter Sixty-Three

1989

Hayes residence

Monday 12th June – 37 days before

Mark grabbed Tina around the waist, grasped both her hands and then pulled her in to him. He twirled her around the kitchen, dancing to Jason Donovan's 'Sealed With A Kiss'. Jonie jumped out of their way, eyes rolling. 'Yuk,' she said, her nose wrinkled.

'What do you mean, yuk? We're just dancing.'

'It's gross.'

'Oh, really!' Mark said, coming to a stop in front of his daughter. 'You won't think so one day – you'll be dying for a boy to sweep you off your feet and dance with you.'

'Boys are stupid. And I can dance on my own, or with Bella. I don't need a *boy*.'

Mark laughed, sharing a knowing look with Tina. He'd remind Jonie of that when she was a teenager and crying over some boy. He ruffled Jonie's hair before turning his attention back to Tina. Her indigo-coloured shirt made her cool, blue eyes pop; their intensity seemed to penetrate his very soul. He wished he could see contentment – happiness – behind those eyes. He longed for the love he had for her to be reflected in them. They didn't argue, or not often, but he'd felt a distance between them over the past year. Maybe he was neglecting her, spending too much time at the pub with the fellas. He should make more of an effort, he thought.

'Fancy a barbecue at the weekend?' he asked, brightly. 'We could invite everyone, make the most of the good weather.'

'Sure.' Tina shrugged, turning to Jonie. 'That sounds like fun, doesn't it?'

'If you say so.' Jonie's response appeared indifferent.

'What's wrong with you lately?' Mark cut in. 'You're only ten and already acting like your mother does when it's her time of the month.'

'Mark!' Tina jabbed a finger into his ribs.

'Well, it's true. You're young and pretty, Jonie – not like your mother – why so miserable?' He winked at Tina.

'Dad. It's boring in this village. There's literally nothing to do. I'm not miserable, I'm fed up.'

'So, a barbie will give you something to do, then, won't it; something to look forward to. You can be in charge of the music, get a playlist together, and let the King of the Barbies do his magic.'

Jonie smiled.

'Oh, my goodness, be careful, honey,' Mark said, rushing over to her, placing his hands either side of her face and squeezing. 'You almost cracked it then.'

'Ha. Ha. Very funny.' Jonie pulled away from him. 'And King of the Barbie *dolls* is more you, Dad.' She poked out her tongue and skipped out of the back door.

'Where are you going now?' Tina shouted after her.

'Dunno. Out to see who's around.'

Tina looked at the wall clock, then sighed, looking to Mark for his input.

'It's only five o'clock, not too late?' he said, as a question, putting the onus of the decision back onto Tina.

'I suppose it's fine for her to go out and play for a couple of hours, although it *is* a school night.' Her face showed concern. She ran to the back door. 'Be back at seven, on the dot, please!' Tina shouted in the direction of Jonie's disappearing form as she ran out of view behind the wall. 'Do you think she's okay, Mark?' Her brow was creased as she walked back in and leant against the worktop.

'A bit moody, but otherwise just our sweet, charming daughter.' He laughed.

'Seriously, though, I'm worried. She's so snappy, irritable. You joked about it being the time of the month, but maybe you're right – she's becoming hormonal.'

'Bit early, isn't it?'

'Not necessarily. I got my first period when I was at primary school.'

'Maybe time for a mother–daughter chat, then.'

'Yeah, if I can pin her down. She makes any excuse to be out of the house, and when she's here, she shuts herself away, playing music as loud as she can get away with. I wonder if she's fallen out with Bella, or another friend.'

'At her age, it's bound to happen. Kids fall in and out of friendships daily, don't they? Especially girls.'

'Sexist pig,' Tina said, shaking her head in mock exasperation.

'True though, babe. Just sayin'. Us males don't appear to have that problem.'

'I beg to differ.'

'Oh, well, there are always exceptions. That freak, Billy Cawley, for one. He's mega weird now; he *must've* been like it as a kid.'

'Don't be so mean. If he had a difficult time when he was growing up, it would explain why he's not interested in bonding with you lot now, as an adult. I mean, it is slim pickings in this village – perhaps he just dislikes you all. Being a loner doesn't make you weird, Mark.'

'Oh, right. And that's what you ladies have been chatting

about at the Mapledon Meetings, is it? How he's not weird at all, just misunderstood, or some such twaddle.'

'Actually, I'm a little fed up with everyone's attitudes towards Billy, and I don't join in with the discussions about him. In fact, after the last meeting, I might not bother even going again.'

'Really? That bad. The witches out for him, are they?'

'You can joke, but it does feel a bit like that if I'm honest. The guy's never actually done anything wrong, has he?'

'He's not been *caught* doing anything wrong, no. But where there's smoke there's fire, love. And he stinks of smoke.'

'Well, I for one think maybe he should be cut some slack. If everyone wound their necks in, let him get on with his life, the village kids would give him a break too. They only play those Knock, Knock games on him because they've heard what their parents say about him. It's the adults at fault. We should be leading by example, not teaching our kids to bully other people.'

'It's not bullying, for Christ's sake!'

'What would you call it, then?'

'Keeping our village safe. That's what I'd call it. You'd think the same way if anything ever happened to any of the kids.'

'But it hasn't!'

'No. *Because* we're keeping a close eye.'

Tina raised her hands in defeat. 'Whatever. But you know, this kind of behaviour might well push him into doing something he wouldn't have if everyone had just left him alone.'

Chapter Sixty-Four

2019

Anna

Tuesday 16th July

After her mother's revelation about videoing Eliza and informing social services about the alleged abuse, they'd all sat in silence around the table. As a teacher, Anna had undertaken child safeguarding training to gain awareness of the signs of child abuse and neglect, how to detect them, and what steps they should take if they suspected one of the kids in the school was a victim. Thankfully Anna hadn't needed to put those steps into action thus far in her career. Her mum had probably done what she thought was the best thing at the time, despite it seeming rash and inappropriate now – it wasn't as though *she'd* had any training relating to spotting the signs and the best way to handle suspected abuse.

Now, having decided that it was time for Muriel to see the notes they'd already received, Anna retrieved them from the shed and spread the pieces of paper out on the dining table, flattening each with her palms. The three of them stared downwards, taking them in. Having listened to what her mother had told them, it now seemed obvious to Anna that the notes were aimed at Muriel. She'd been the one instrumental in getting Billy Cawley's daughter put into care. As much as it was a terrible thought, what Muriel had done could have been the catalyst for what Billy did next: abducting and killing Jonie Hayes. It certainly explained why parts of a doll were now being hammered to her front door. It was some kind of message, a sign that Billy blamed her.

The trouble was, did he now want revenge for it? For taking away the only thing he'd had left in the world?

She wondered how his conviction for Jonie's murder fitted in with this, though. Was Billy just beginning? He could be working his way through the people he felt had wronged him. In which case, Anna imagined there was a long way to go yet. Next he'd probably want revenge on who he saw as responsible for getting him sent to prison.

Unless, of course, he was killing two birds with one stone on that front. Muriel and Anna in one hit. She didn't really understand why he'd be concerned with Anna, though. She'd merely told the police what she'd seen. *He* was responsible for his actions, not her. An entire jury had decided his guilt. Not one young girl. Why should she suffer?

Muriel, she could understand.

The villagers had suggested, even speculated in the press, that Billy took Jonie as direct retaliation for Eliza being taken from him. So why did he take Jonie, and not Anna? Had she been lucky? Is that why Auntie Tina was so bitter? That would make sense. Tina suffered terribly from something Muriel had done. And Muriel's daughter had escaped.

She'd be pissed too.

'There's more to come, then,' Lizzie said, her fingertips pushing the bits of paper around the table.

'I'd guess so. As I said earlier, I think we're going to get the entire doll. Perhaps the idea is for us to put it back together again. Rebuild it.'

'The reverse of what I used to do to them.' Lizzie gave a sharp laugh.

Anna nodded. She'd almost written Lizzie off as the culprit, but now wondered if it was some kind of symbolism. Lizzie had been abused, felt as though she'd been taken apart, now she wanted to rebuild herself. And maybe to do that, and gain closure, she had to face her past, her abusive father, and put Polly back together. She may have been the only doll to have survived when Lizzie was in Mapledon, but what about when she'd been taken into care? Her life then must've been filled with upset and turmoil, with no understanding of what had happened to her or why. Maybe Polly, who'd once been her beloved doll – a final, parting present from her dying mother – had come to represent everything bad that had happened to her. All the evil.

It was a theory. Probably far out; too outlandish. And it was one that Anna was unable to share at this point in time. But she probably shouldn't rule Lizzie out just yet.

There were a couple of people Anna would love to talk to about it all. She'd already decided to visit Pat Vern later. Now she added Robert and Nell Andrews to her list.

Chapter Sixty-Five

2019

Lizzie

Lizzie hadn't asked for further details; she didn't want to hear any more. The images conjured up by Muriel describing how her eight-year-old self used Polly to depict what Billy had done to her were enough. A sick ache crushed her insides. She was glad she couldn't remember it. Any of it. The strange thing was that, during her time in care, she'd been told much of what had happened and knew she'd been taken from her father because he wasn't looking after her properly, but mostly it had been focused on what her father had supposedly done to Jonie Hayes, not to her, his own daughter.

And what she *had* heard she'd firmly placed in a compartment at the back of her mind, never to revisit. Part of her hadn't believed the tales. They'd come from people who couldn't have really known – it was all speculation, gossip. They couldn't be trusted to tell her the truth, or give an accurate account – too much had been written in the tabloids and people believed what they wanted, added more shocking and 'interesting' details to those known. Did Muriel have any reason for lying to her now? Lizzie couldn't see what an old woman would gain from it, especially as it made her look bad too. Why would she put herself in the firing line? No, Lizzie had the distinct feeling Muriel was scared. Afraid her past actions were coming back to haunt her now.

But, there could be the possibility she was remembering it wrongly. Or that she'd misinterpreted eight-year-old Eliza's actions in the first place.

That's what her dad had told her, just that morning. '*Muriel Fisher was a meddler,*' he'd spat. '*Instead of messing around in our lives, she should've been looking more closely at her own.*' His words came back to Lizzie now. As did his seething accusation.

'Are you all right, Lizzie?' Anna's concerned voice broke into her thoughts.

'Yeah. I'm okay. It all had to come to light one day, eh?' She managed a tight smile.

'Billy's release has brought a lot with it – unearthed all that pain and harm he caused. We're all going to suffer again. He shouldn't have been let out,' Muriel said, sharply.

'But he has. And now we have to deal with it, and everything that comes with it. Including *this*.' Lizzie flung an arm out, motioning to the pieces of paper on the table. 'Clearly whoever is leaving these doesn't feel the truth is out there. As far as I can make out, they must believe someone *else* is to blame for Jonie's disappearance. Not my father.'

'Do you believe he was responsible, Lizzie?' Anna asked. Her eyes searched Lizzie's.

'Honestly? I don't know. I grew up believing he was guilty, obviously. And I came to Mapledon thinking that too. But then . . . I, well, now I'm not quite as sure as I was.' If she confessed to Muriel and Anna that Billy Cawley was back, and that she'd seen him, there'd be no doubt left in their minds that he was the one hammering dolls' bits to the door. And given she was convinced it was her doll, Polly, being used for this bizarre game, together with the notes, it was hard not to conclude it was Billy.

But there was a *little* doubt. Something niggled at her like an itch she couldn't reach to scratch.

It was too obvious.

But then, didn't they say the simplest explanation was usually the correct one?

Maybe she was looking for a different answer because she was grasping at the chance to get to know her father again after all these years, and hoping against hope he wasn't the guilty man everyone assumed he was.

Not guilty for all of it, anyway.

Chapter Sixty-Six

1989

Fisher residence

Sunday 11th June – 38 days before

Bella was sitting on the middle stair, elbows digging into her thighs, chin cupped in her hands. She hadn't heard her mum and dad arguing before, not that she could recall anyway. They thought she was out, having got back from Sunday school and stripped out of her Sunday best, quickly pulling on her jeans and T-shirt and diving back out the door to go to the park. But she'd forgotten her purse that had her pound coin in for some pop and sweets and so had slipped back in, clearly unnoticed by her parents.

'You tell me off for interfering, then do that? What were you thinking? You're going to ruin it, undo my hard work!' Her mother's anger burst through her words. Bella could almost see her dad cowering.

'Well, make your bloody mind up: you either want my help or you don't. Stop picking and choosing what works for you, Muriel. I'm doing my best to support you here.'

'Maybe you shouldn't bother. We were doing all right without you going to his place.'

'Yeah, I can see that. Clearly you've done a stellar job.'

Bella was confused. Her dad's tone was sharp. Did he mean her mum *had* done a good job? Or was he being nasty? She had a sick feeling in her tummy; she shouldn't be eavesdropping. She started to creep back down the stairs; she'd leave again – they were shouting so loudly they wouldn't hear her.

The final step let out a loud creak as her weight shifted from it. She froze.

The lounge door swung open.

'I thought you were out.' Her mum's face was red and blotchy, as though she'd been crying.

'I forgot my purse,' Bella said. She turned to leave.

'No. Hang on. Come back in.'

Bella's shoulders slumped. Now she was going to get yelled at for listening. As she followed her mum into the lounge, her dad pushed his way past and left, slamming the front door behind him.

'I'm guessing you heard all that?'

Bella screwed her eyes up. She wondered if she could say no and get away with it. But before she answered her mother continued.

'It was only a bit of a disagreement, nothing to worry about. But, Bella?' Her mother took her by the arms and lowered her face to hers. 'You can't repeat anything you heard, okay? It's between us. If someone found out, it would just cause problems. You don't want your dad getting into trouble, do you? You know how much he loves you – he'd do anything for you. He'd be so upset if you told anyone. And so would I.'

Bella frowned. She hadn't even heard very much. What was her mother talking about – why would her dad get into trouble? She shrugged.

'I mean it, Bella. This is serious; we can't have people thinking your dad was with Billy.' Her eyes were wide. '*Creepy Cawley,*' she added, as if Bella wouldn't know who she meant.

'Why was he with *him*?' Bella couldn't stop the question from escaping.

'He wasn't. Not really. Look, enough now. Your dad wasn't there, remember?'

Bella felt so confused she just wanted her mother to stop speaking. She shook her head. 'Fine. Dad wasn't there.'

Her mother released her grip from Bella's upper arms and Bella took a step back. Muriel stood up straight, her face relaxing. Bella, relieved at obviously having said the right thing, took the opportunity to bolt out the door. She ran most of the way to the park, eager to put as much distance between herself and her mother as possible.

What was going on?

Whatever it was, she'd do as she was told and not utter a word about it again. The last thing she wanted was to get her dad into any kind of trouble.

Chapter Sixty-Seven

2019

Anna

Tuesday 16th July

Anna gazed silently at Tina's house; the last time she'd set foot inside was with Jonie, thirty years ago. She pushed her shoulders back and opened the rickety wooden gate leading to the front door. The house was one of three in the small terraced area just off the main road, each having joint access to the back gardens, the paths running the full length of the row. It'd been one of the fun aspects of going to Jonie's – they often played hide-and-seek in the neighbour's gardens without their knowledge, or permission.

Anna paused at the door, hand poised to knock. The likelihood of Pat Vern being there on his own was slim, and she wasn't keen to face Tina again. Particularly as she wanted to grill Pat about Jonie's disappearance. It would be less awkward if she approached Pat on more common ground, like at The Plough, if he still drank there. It would be easy to find out. She backed away, but as she reached the gate she heard the door being opened.

'Can I help?' a gravelly voice asked. At least Pat had answered and not Tina. Anna smiled as she turned to face him.

'Hi, Mr Vern.'

He stood still, a puzzled look momentarily covering his face. Then his frown transformed into realisation, and he inhaled deeply. 'Bella? Is that you?'

'Guilty as charged,' Anna said, her attempt at humour falling flat.

'Now what do you want? Haven't you upset Tina enough?'

'I didn't realise I had upset her.' Anna flushed, knowing full well she had. 'I'm sorry. Look, I was only dropping by to speak with you, but if I'm going to cause grief, I'll leave. As I was about to anyway.' She walked through the gate and turned to close it.

Anna saw Pat look back over his shoulder into the darkness of the hall, then he stepped outside, pulling the door to. 'Well, she *is* upset, whether that's what you intended or not. But if you want to talk, it's best we meet elsewhere. I'll be at the pub in twenty.' And before Anna could speak again, he'd turned and disappeared inside.

Anna gave a wry shake of her head as she seated herself near the door inside The Plough. All these years later and it was still very much the man's domain if the current punters were anything to go by. Her presence there had already garnered some curious glances.

Mapledon – the village that time forgot.

Thank God she'd escaped. She couldn't begin to imagine what living here was like – it set the women's movement back fifty years. She hadn't seen many younger people, she noted. Had her age group all taken the opportunity to leave the second they were able to? The population did seem to be mainly above the age of fifty.

With her back to the wall, Anna sipped her Pinot Grigio, the fruity flavour hitting her taste buds. It felt like weeks since she'd had a nice wine. Her mother's 'drinks cabinet' – the ancient one she'd had since the Seventies, which still housed the plastic Babycham Deer bar sign – contained only sherry, and a single bottle of wine that had clearly been opened years ago and was now cloudy and smelt of vinegar.

Her mother hadn't been enamoured with Anna's decision to go out – leaving her, if only for a few hours, was risky as far as she was concerned. Anna could understand her fear, but didn't offer to take her along, not even letting on that it was Pat she'd arranged to meet. She felt she'd be too much of a hindrance to get to the truth. Anna knew she'd be better off without Muriel playing sidekick – Pat would be more willing to talk freely. Or that was the hope. Anna had made sure Sandie was aware Muriel was alone; her kind neighbour would keep an ear out and her mother had been somewhat reassured by that.

Anna was halfway through her glass of wine, and almost ready to knock the rest of it back in one, give up and go home, when Pat finally put in an appearance. In the dull light of the pub, he appeared dishevelled, tired. It seemed Billy Cawley's release had taken its toll on many of them.

'Hey, Pat. Thanks for coming, what can I get you?' Anna stood up, ready to go to the bar.

'Nothing. We can't talk here, come on.' And he was out the door again as quickly as he'd entered. Anna reached for her glass and gulped down her remaining wine – no point wasting good alcohol.

The air outside had cooled, but Anna didn't need the cotton jacket she'd brought on her mother's insistence 'just in case' – it was still a bearable level for a summer's evening. She slung it over her arm and hurried to catch up with Pat, who was marching on up the hill towards the church.

'Slow down,' she said, her breath coming quickly. 'What's the rush?'

'Don't want anyone tittle-tattling, that's all. Tina's got enough on her plate.'

'Where are we going?' Anna said as they took a left. Her heart missed a beat. Was he taking her to Blackstone Close?

'Somewhere we won't get bothered.'

Shit, he *was* taking her there. A nervous flutter filled her stomach. He seemed angry. Was it wise to follow him? She fumbled in her handbag as she walked, closing her fingers around her mobile phone. Regardless of the uneasy feeling she had, she continued to follow him along the street, taking the turning into the cul-de-sac leading to Billy Cawley's bungalow.

'I don't think we need to go there, though,' Anna said.

It was pointless putting up an argument now; they were directly outside the bungalow. It was even more eerie in the dark, the only illumination coming from the streetlight halfway down the road and the weak lighting shining from the windows of the bungalow next door to it.

'You were very keen on spending your time here as a kid.'

'Kids haven't learned to be afraid,' she said simply.

'Really? I heard enough squealing and saw enough kids running away that said different.'

'It's not the same kind of fear, though, is it? Not the kind that comes from experience, from learning the hard way that people can be vicious and cruel. Evil.'

'Kids can be all of those things too, though, remember.'

'Oh, I didn't say they couldn't be, just that as kids the fears aren't entrenched, and kids don't think about the consequences; they don't weigh up all the possible outcomes of an action like adults do. Or most adults, anyway.'

'Sounds like you're speaking from experience now.' He tilted his chin, then looked her straight in the eye. 'What do you remember about that day, Bella?' he asked softly.

'It's Anna,' she said wearily. 'The day she was taken you mean? Not an awful lot, weirdly. You'd think it'd be engraved in my mind, wouldn't you? The thing is, I'm not sure I can separate what I *actually* remember from then, with what I remember

245

after the fact, or years later. Snippets of other people's memories, of newspaper articles, news stories – they're all jumbled up in my head. Whose memory is whose?'

'That's what I thought.'

Anna narrowed her eyes. 'Meaning?'

'Meaning I don't think you can accurately remember something that happened when you were ten – however traumatic that event was. And in fact, I'd go as far as to hypothesise that it was *because* it was traumatic that you can't remember it well.'

'Okay, so I don't recall the events very well now, but at the time – when I was ten and my friend was taken – I would've been able to tell you exactly what happened. Accurately. It's only now, years later, that things have become jumbled.'

'Maybe.' Pat shrugged. 'Maybe not. Anyway, what did you want to ask me?'

Anna pushed down her rising sense of annoyance. Who was he to say what she could remember or not and why? Now wasn't the time to get into a debate about memory, though.

'I wanted your version of what happened the day Jonie went missing.'

'I was at Bovey station dealing with a teenage tearaway who'd taken his dad's car for a joyride when I got the call.' Pat sighed, staring off into the distance. 'Tina was concerned that Jonie was late back home. I told her not to worry – she wouldn't be far away. Jesus. I can hear myself saying those words. Anyway, I left the station and drove back to Mapledon, assuming by the time I reached Tina's Jonie would already be home, and Mark would've chastised her for her lateness. But obviously that wasn't the case. It was about eight o'clock when the search party began looking for her. Tina had said she'd called all of the parents of Jonie's friends and none had seen her. Apart from you. But Muriel had told Tina you'd got home at six. So that left a two-hour gap to account for.'

246

'But I told you about her getting into Billy's truck, you knew that. The police knew that.'

'That wasn't the day she went missing, Bel— sorry, Anna. You and Muriel didn't come into the station until the Friday, about thirty-six hours after she was reported missing.'

'That can't be right, surely? It must've been the same day, or maybe the day after if it was late . . .' Anna placed her fingers on her temples, trying to remember.

'No. It's right. It was the reason I felt so anxious. And angry, if I'm honest. Had we had the information straight away . . .' Pat tailed off, his eyes sliding away from Anna's.

'Shit. If I'd given the information right away, you'd probably have caught him before he killed her.' A huge lump lodged in Anna's throat; tears stung her eyes.

'You were just a kid – you probably didn't realise the gravity of the situation. You said yourself a minute ago, kids don't really think of the consequences. You wouldn't have necessarily thought about the danger Jonie was in.'

It hit Anna then. She *would've* known. She must've. It was Billy Cawley – she'd been scared of him, frightened that he'd somehow get them back for the Knock, Knock pranks. If she'd seen Jonie getting into his truck, why hadn't she said something immediately?

'I think I would've known the danger, Pat. Every kid was scared of Billy – God, even some parents – I must've just been terrified – in shock or something, surely?'

Pat looked thoughtful for a moment, then gave a nod. 'Yes, actually, I do remember that's what your mother said at the station: that you'd been in shock and hadn't spoken a word. She said she'd had to coax it out of you slowly, and once you'd told her, she'd immediately taken you to the station.'

That made more sense to Anna. She'd been a timid thing, no doubt she'd have been traumatised by what she'd witnessed. But, nonetheless, a sense of unease rocked her, sending a tingling cold sensation, like icicles, cascading down her spine.

Had she *wanted* Jonie to be in trouble with Billy? Could that also be a reason why she'd stayed silent until almost two days later? To punish her?

Chapter Sixty-Eight

2019

Lizzie

Tiredness came in waves over her. It'd been a long, stressful and emotionally charged day. All she wanted was to eat, shower and sink into her large, soft bed. But Gwen's opening statement as she entered the reception brought those wishes crashing down.

'You've got a visitor,' she said with an exaggerated wink.

'Really? Are you sure it's for me?' Lizzie's voice sounded as exasperated as she felt.

'Oh, yes. He definitely belongs to you,' she said brightly. 'I showed him into the lounge. I'll bring you some tea.' She disappeared, leaving Lizzie to plaster a smile on her face before entering the door leading to the lounge.

'Dom!'

Dom grinned as he bounded up to her, looking like an excited puppy who'd not seen his master for a week. 'Hey, beautiful. God, I've missed you,' he said, squeezing the life from her and kissing her hard. She was part annoyed he'd turned up unannounced and part relieved he seemed to be okay with her – their last conversation hadn't been good and had ended abruptly, negatively.

'I've missed you, too. You didn't mention you were travelling down, though.'

'I thought I'd surprise you.' His smile faltered.

He'd certainly managed that. And although Lizzie was really pleased to see him, the timing wasn't the best, and she was afraid of the real reason behind his shock visit. It wasn't like him to turn up whilst she was on a job; this must be because of what he'd said. Because of what he'd found out. Lizzie was too tired for this kind of confrontation.

'Congratulations.' She forced a smile. 'You've definitely succeeded!'

'Yeah, well, try not to look too ecstatic.'

Thankfully, Gwen chose this time to bring in a tray of tea. 'Here you go, my lovelies. Now, I assume you'll both be wanting some supper?'

Lizzie hesitated a moment too long. Dom jumped in, thanking Gwen and accepting the offer of food.

'That's grand. I'll come back shortly with the options.'

There was an uneasy silence once Gwen had left the room. Lizzie had to break it, before it broke her.

'So, what did you want to talk to me about?' Lizzie sat down in the wing-backed armchair, purposely avoiding the sofa.

'You said you wanted to talk to me. That you had things to tell me but wanted to do it face-to-face, so here I am.' He cautiously moved towards Lizzie, and knelt down in front of her, taking her hands in his.

Lizzie's muscles tensed; her hands felt clammy in his cool ones. 'It could've waited until my return.'

'But I didn't know when that would be. And to be honest, I *didn't* think it could wait.' His face took on a worried look. 'Not after I found this.' He pulled one hand away, reaching it into his pocket.

Lizzie knew what he'd have in his hand without needing to look. Her pulse skipped. She was going to have to have this conversation now whether it was good timing or not.

'I'm sorry, Dom. Please forgive me?' Tears welled, her lower lip trembling.

'I just need to know what's going on, Lizzie. You're my wife – we shouldn't have secrets.' Now removing his other hand, he brushed away the tears on her cheeks with his fingertips.

'It's a long story, Dom. And I'm so tired.'

'There's no rush.' He stood up and, taking her hand, pulled her across to the sofa. 'But at least make a start now.' His eyes – kind, trusting – focused on hers.

Where should she begin?

'I haven't told you everything,' she said. 'Because I didn't want to ever speak about him – if I didn't talk about any of it, it wasn't real. It didn't happen. It was the only way I could cope, the only way I could move forwards, get any semblance of a life after a dreadful childhood. I'm sorry I didn't confide in you, I really am.'

'I understand, I do. Really.' Dom gave her a reassuring smile. 'So, who is this William Cawley? Why did this letter set you off?' He held out the crumpled paper.

'He's my father. Birth father.'

'Okay.' Dom nodded gently. 'I didn't realise you even knew who your father was.'

'Oh, I knew, unfortunately.'

'What had he been in prison for?'

The question Lizzie had dreaded.

'When I was eight, I was taken into care. And not long after, he abducted a young girl and killed her.'

Saying the words out loud made her feel sick to her stomach. Seeing Dom's shocked reaction brought bile into her mouth.

'See why I didn't want to acknowledge his existence?'

'God, Lizzie. That's some heavy shit.'

'Quite.' Lizzie attempted a weak smile. 'And now he's out, he's free, and I needed to come here to see if he'd returned. I wondered if he'd come back for me.'

'And?' Dom looked worried. Lizzie didn't want to alarm him, but now she'd been honest, a weight had been lifted and she felt the need to share the rest.

251

'He's here. Nearby. I met him yesterday.'

'Jesus, love. Was that a good idea? I mean, you don't know him, don't know what years' worth of prison would've done to him.'

'I know. I was aware it was risky.'

'Why? Why put yourself through this?'

'Closure? Some kind of explanation. The truth. All of that, really.'

'The truth? About what?'

'About my alleged abuse – the reason I was taken away from him, about Jonie Hayes' abduction and murder. And to ask him where he disposed of her body.'

'Oh, my God. And what makes you think he'd tell you these things? Or what he says will be fact? He's had years to concoct whatever narrative fitted – his version may not be the truth, Lizzie.'

'I know that. I guess I thought I'd know the truth if he told it to me – that I'd see it in his eyes. Ridiculous, I know,' she said, shaking her head.

'So, you've spoken to him now. What conclusion have you come to?'

'He says he didn't take Jonie, and he didn't kill her. As far as he's concerned it's all lies and he was framed.'

Dom huffed. 'Standard,' he said, raising his eyebrows.

'Yes. But a huge part of me believed him. And having spent some time in Mapledon, I have to admit, there are secrets here. Secrets that the villagers are hiding.'

Lizzie suddenly felt awake, invigorated by the discussion. As she was speaking, the strength of her feelings intensified. Maybe she *did* believe her father was innocent. And that would change everything.

Chapter Sixty-Nine

1989

Brook Cottage Store

Thursday 8th June – 41 days before

'How're you getting on with the action points from last week's meeting?' Nell asked as she picked up the items and punched the price into the till, her long, red nails tapping annoyingly at the keys.

Muriel turned her back fully, to shield herself from the man in the queue behind her, before she spoke.

'I've had some success, yes.' Muriel smiled. Then added quietly: 'But we need a chat, in private.'

'Let me just serve Malcolm,' she whispered, 'then we can nip into the storeroom.'

Muriel took her shopping bag and hovered near the door to the storeroom at the rear of the shop. A few moments later, Nell rushed towards her.

'Come on in,' Nell said, ushering Muriel through. 'What's up? Is it what I think?'

'Possibly,' Muriel said, her eyebrows raised. 'Tina?'

'Yes! My goodness, has she had some kind of personality transplant? She's acting so strangely. What is *up* with her?'

'She seems so distant, doesn't she? She appears to have lost interest in the meetings – she doesn't offer any suggestions anymore, barely says a word. It's making me nervous.'

'Should we cut her out? Even Mark doesn't seem to be able to talk sense into her. I think she may have lost her way.'

'I think we should perhaps give her another chance? Maybe see what she's like at the next meeting at the end of the month. It would be awkward for me to cut her out altogether, Nell. We've been friends for so long, and Bella plays with Jonie all the time.'

'But, Muriel, if she's not committed to the cause she shouldn't be privy to the discussions. She should be replaced by someone who is.'

'I know. I'm wondering if there's something wrong between her and Mark. I'll try and have a heart-to-heart; it might not be anything to do with our action points. She's always been supportive of our community work in the past. I can't see why she'd change her mind now.'

'Unless she has a vested interest . . .' Nell lowered her head, raising her eyes over the top of her glasses to shoot Muriel a knowing look.

'You can't seriously still be suggesting that, Nell, surely? I'd *know*.'

'Would you? As you said yourself, she's been distant lately, and now suddenly disinterested in what we're trying to achieve. I'm adding two and two here, that's all. You must've heard the rumours.'

'Of course. But there's no way. I mean, *why*?'

'There's nowt so queer as folk, as my dear grandmother would say.'

Muriel nodded. 'Fine. I'll pay her a visit soon, pretend it's something to do with the next meeting. See if I can get her chatting. We need to know what she's playing at.'

Chapter Seventy

2019

Anna

Wednesday 17th July

Anna was greeted with a worried look from her mum as soon as she got to the foot of the stairs.

'I was going to say, "good morning", but from your expression I'm guessing it's not so good?'

'You were right,' Muriel said. 'There's been another.' She took Anna's arm and half-dragged her towards the kitchen. There, sitting ominously on the dining table, was a doll's leg. Polly's leg, Anna assumed.

'Have you taken the note out?'

'No. I was leaving that for you.'

'Well, cheers,' Anna mumbled as she sat down, squinting at the leg. 'Can I at least get a coffee first; my eyes aren't even in focus yet.'

Muriel hurried to the kettle, shook it to check the water level, then switched it on. She tapped her fingers on the worktop.

'A watched pot never boils, Mum.'

'Are you going to recite back to me every saying I've ever uttered?' Her voice was strained, the stress seeping from her.

'No. Sorry. Look, I'm going to show this all to Pat later.'

'What? Why?'

'Because he knows the history. Because he's an ex-cop. Because he could be of assistance. Lots of reasons, Mum.'

'But we agreed no police involvement. It'll aggravate the situation.'

'But we don't know where this is all leading, do we? What if there's a *pièce de résistance*?' Anna stopped herself from finishing her thought. She didn't want to put any more worry on to her mother. But it was a real concern – if Billy Cawley truly wanted revenge, who knew where this would end? Getting police involved might be the only thing that would prevent a tragedy. Another one. Anna shuddered. 'Anyway, he's only going to offer his opinion and Tina's probably told him all about it anyway. He didn't seem surprised when I mentioned it last night.'

'You spoke to him about it last night? Is that where you went – to meet Pat?'

'Yes. I want to get to the bottom of this, find the truth; and I thought he would be a good source of information.'

'Please, Anna. I've told you – there's no point digging up the past.'

'I disagree. So would Lizzie.'

'Well, she didn't seem happy about what she's found out so far. What makes you think getting *your* hands dirty in the depths of history will do you any good either?'

'Doesn't the truth matter to you? What about finding out what really happened to Jonie Hayes? What about finding her body? Doesn't that matter?'

'After all this time? Maybe not.'

'How can you say that?' Anna's eyes widened in shock at her mother's attitude. 'You amaze me sometimes. Auntie Tina could finally rest, for one. The dark cloud that's hovered over Mapledon for thirty years could be lifted. It would be awful for Tina to go to her grave never knowing where her daughter was. How would you feel if that were you?'

'Yes, I know. Right, here's your coffee,' Muriel said.

The fact her mother wasn't keen to dig up the past was disconcerting. It couldn't just be that she was concerned about some video she and Nell had made of Eliza to prove Billy was abusing her; that she was partly responsible for Eliza being taken into care. There was something else, there had to be. Another reason she didn't want this to all blow up, for the police to get involved. Maybe in digging further, Anna would find something far worse.

Was she prepared for that?

Anna sipped the coffee and placed it on the coaster. She ran her fingers through her hair, then got up. 'Right, come on then, let's see what we've been left.' She got a skewer from the drawer and stuck it inside the cavity of the plastic leg, hooking the paper out. She took a deep steadying breath, then unfolded it.

SOMEONE KNOWS WHERE SHE IS.

'Well, that's obvious,' Anna said, her shoulders slumping. She was disappointed; she'd hoped for something a little more solid. A clue that might actually point them in the right direction.

'This is stupid. Whoever is doing this knows absolutely nothing. This proves it. It's someone who thinks they're being clever, but they have zero proof of anything and they're just fishing. Of *course* someone knows where she is. That evil good-for-nothing Billy Cawley does, and that's the end of it,' Muriel said, shaking her head while pacing the kitchen.

'Calm down, Mum. Come and have a seat.'

'I can't. I'm too on edge. And annoyed.'

'I feel at a loss as to what to do now. Are we going to wait, sit it out? If there's an end point to this game, I'm not sure we should be sitting ducks, awaiting whatever comes next. This is one game of Knock, Knock I'd rather not play.'

'You didn't like playing any of them,' Muriel said flippantly.

'No? I can't really remember.'

'You hated that Jonie made you play. *I* remember.' Muriel looked off into the distance. 'You used to prefer playing on your own – making dance routines up in your bedroom.' Muriel gave a short laugh. 'The ceiling would shake with all your jumping around. You drove your dad nuts.'

'Is that why he left?' Anna snapped.

'Don't be stupid, of course not.'

'Why did he, then?' Now the opportunity to talk about her dad had arisen, she wanted to take full advantage – see if Muriel stuck to her usual lines.

Muriel sighed, and Anna saw tears gather along her lower lids. 'You know why. Because he wanted to be with the other woman.'

'Who was she? You never told me anything.'

'No one you knew. There was nothing to tell. We had our problems and he didn't love me; it was that simple. He loved you, though.'

'Well, that doesn't make any sense now, does it? If he loved me, he would've stayed in contact – visited me, or at the very least called. He never even sent me birthday cards. That's love, is it?'

'You wouldn't understand.'

'No, you're right. I can't see how he would leave me, and you can sit here and still say that he loved me. That's nonsensical.'

'When Jonie was taken, it changed him. He couldn't accept how close you'd come to being taken away from him. He was destroyed by the very thought. He'd never been emotionally strong – he depended on me for that. I was the strong one.'

Anna so badly wanted to make a comment about that statement, but instead said, 'If that was the case, why didn't he stay with you?'

'Our marriage became very strained, very quickly, and after I found out what he'd been up to, we both thought it best if he left straight away. With her.'

'I still don't see why your marriage being strained and Dad being overly upset about what happened meant he had to go to the other end of the UK, Mum. And never have contact with me? Or you? That's weird.'

'I can't speak for your father, Anna,' she said abruptly. 'He had his reasons.'

'So, you basically treated him as if he were dead, not speaking of him, not telling me anything. That was the best thing for me, was it?' Anna's voice broke; she felt the old anger resurfacing.

'It was easier for us all.'

'It was easier for *you*, you mean.' Resentment spilled from her. 'My God, you're a piece of work.' Anna got up and strode into the lounge. She couldn't look at Muriel right now. Was this one of the patches of dirt her mother didn't want her digging in?

She wondered what else lay beneath the surface, waiting to be unearthed.

What other truths had been buried in Mapledon all these years?

Chapter Seventy-One

2019

Lizzie

Wednesday 17th July – evening

Dom had been extremely understanding, albeit hurt that she'd felt unable to tell him about her father before. Lizzie had poured it all out in a matter of an hour – every sordid detail she could remember about her childhood, all the things she'd come to believe because of what others told her. How she'd been classed as 'disturbed' by her caregivers for most of her young life. It was only later that teachers, doctors, specialists had taken the time to have her assessed professionally and she'd begun to receive the help and support she so badly needed.

It was only when she'd met Dom that she truly began to look after herself, consider herself worthy of love. Even then, she'd struggled to believe she wouldn't be abandoned, cast aside for something, or someone, better. She still struggled. She hadn't wanted to purposely build a wall around herself, but she'd considered the barrier to be a requirement – a back-up, just in case.

Lizzie perched on the edge of the bed watching Dom as he slept. The journey down, the emotionally draining evening, and maybe the relief from his point of view that her sudden departure hadn't been anything to do with him, had all taken its effect. It never took much for him to crash. And tonight, Lizzie was glad he had. It would make it easier for her to sneak out. After the revelations at Anna's house, hearing Muriel's confession and also her belief something had happened to Rob Andrews when he'd visited her as a child, she had to go and find out more. Delve into *his* memories. He might be like her, and not remember anything, but she had to try. Together, they might be able to slot in some pieces of the puzzle.

Rob had responded to her text almost immediately. He'd jumped at the chance to meet her. Lizzie had suggested they meet at the churchyard, but Rob asked her to go to his. After a fleeting moment of uncertainty, she agreed, telling him she'd be there in ten minutes.

During the brief car ride, Lizzie went over what she wanted to say and the questions she wanted answered. At this point, she wasn't sure if he'd found out she was Eliza Cawley – and if he knew, what sort of response she could expect upon her arrival. If he didn't already know, then he was about to get a shock.

Rob opened the door before she'd rung the bell. His face was solemn, fixed into a grim-looking expression.

'Hi,' Lizzie said, tentatively. He didn't respond, just stood in front of her, staring. 'Is it all right to come in?'

'Sorry,' he said, standing aside. 'Yes, come on in.'

Lizzie stepped over the threshold and found herself in a small square hall, stairs on the left, and two doors going off to the right. Both were closed. They stood silently, awkwardly, in the hallway.

'I'm sorry,' Lizzie said. A glimmer of emotion flashed in his eyes. Lizzie was unable to identify whether it was hurt, anger, fear or sadness. But in that moment, it was clear he knew. Knew she'd kept her identity from him. Lied to his face. She wondered how she could repair the damage, then remembered her lines – the ones she'd been rehearsing on her way there. 'I didn't tell you who I was because I was scared, Rob. I was afraid of everyone's reactions if they were to realise whose daughter I was. I didn't like misleading you.' She drew her lips into a smile, waiting for him to respond.

'I get it. I don't like that you did it, but I understand. Doesn't stop me feeling as though you've conned me, or tried to trap me, though. Mum said you're a journalist. Were you after some scoop, or something?'

'No, Rob. I was after closure. I'm still looking for that. Searching for the truth.'

'I'm not sure you're going to find that here.'

'Oh, I am determined I will.'

'At what cost?'

'What do you mean?'

'There's always a cost, Lizzie. Someone will suffer – truth or lies – things can still hurt.'

'What is it that you know, Rob?'

He lowered his head. Then turned and walked to the first door, opening it and going through. Lizzie assumed he wanted her to follow.

'Sit down. Wine? Or lager?' he asked.

'If it's cold, I'll take a lager, please.' The heat in her throat needed cooling.

He disappeared and Lizzie took the opportunity to look around the room. It was like a drawing room, rather than a lounge – a large dark-wood desk stood in the far corner, bookshelves packed haphazardly with paperbacks lined two walls. Picture frames hung on the other two in diamond formations. Lizzie studied them. She continued even when Rob re-entered the room. He silently waited for her to finish.

'It's weird, seeing these,' she said, finally. Rob passed her a bottle of lager and she took a large gulp, the liquid coating her throat.

'It's like a time capsule,' he said. 'I rarely come in here – it creeps me out.'

Lizzie laughed, but didn't say anything. He was right.

Somehow it did feel creepy in this room. Like it held secrets. All those faces trapped in time, lining the walls. Snippets of history. Of Mapledon's past; its residents.

'You're in one of them, did you see?' Rob said, approaching the first wall.

'No, where?'

He pointed to one that depicted what looked to be a village fete. 'This was May Day. I was about nine or ten I think, and I'd been counting my lucky stars I'd got out of dancing like a prat around that bloody maypole.' He laughed. 'Some of my mates hadn't been that fortunate – there's Adam, and Nicky.' He laughed again, pressing a fingertip against the glass, indicating the boys. 'And there's you, sitting in the middle. The younger kids always sat around the pole while the older ones danced, weaving the ribbons into patterns. Do you remember?'

She had a vague memory of coloured ribbons flying around. 'I think so. I don't remember ever dancing, though.'

'You wouldn't. You'd gone before you were the age to dance.'

'Wow, that sounds unfair, doesn't it?' She forced a smile. 'Who are the people around the edge, watching?'

'Um . . . gosh, not sure, almost all the villagers came out in force on May Day. Let's see . . .' Rob moved closer to the photo and began rattling off names. 'There's my mum and Muriel – obviously, there was never any show without Punch – Eric, Mark, Reverend Farnley, Tina, Billy and Pat.'

'Wait, Billy? Really?' Lizzie pushed her head next to Rob's. 'I didn't think he ever went out. By all accounts he was never made to feel welcome. And most people's memories point to him not being bothered in the slightest with village events.'

'Well, the camera never lies. And he is there, standing right next to Tina.'

Lizzie noted the straggly hair, the hunched shoulders, recognising her father from the many pictures she'd seen in the media. 'He was keeping an eye on me.'

'Or just going to see you take part in the May Day celebrations?' Rob offered.

'No. You can see from his posture, his gaze – look.' Lizzie pointed. 'It's like he's afraid I'm going to come to harm or something. I'd heard that he'd become overprotective of me after Mum died. This must've been near then.'

'Didn't your mum die at the end of May, though? This would've been before that, being a May Day thing. I could ask Mum.'

'No need.' It didn't really matter about the timing. What was interesting was how closely her father was standing to Tina. Jonie's mum. Was Jonie one of the girls dancing? Looking more closely, Lizzie wondered if it was Jonie her father had such a close eye on. Not her. A shiver shot through her. No. She was reading too much into it. Hadn't she decided that she was more inclined to believe Billy was innocent of the crime? She had to make her mind up, come down on one side of the fence or the other.

'I was talking to Muriel today,' Lizzie said, changing the subject. 'She mentioned you had tried to be friends with me. Is that true?'

Rob backed away from the wall and sat down on a large, flat stool. It resembled a big mushroom. When he looked back up to Lizzie, she saw his face was red.

'I told you the other night, I don't really remember much.'

'Bollocks.' Lizzie heard herself saying it before she could control her mouth. Rob looked away sharply. 'Look, I know I lied about who I was,' Lizzie said, 'we've covered that. But there's no need to lie now. Is there?'

'It's awkward, Lizzie. I mean, like . . . uncomfortably so. I've never spoken about it and if I'm honest, I don't want to start now. Nothing good will come of it. Just more hurt and pain.'

'For me, or you?'

'You, mainly.'

'Well, can you let me be the judge of that?'

264

'Okay, and me, then. If you don't believe me, then—' He held his head in his hands, his eyes masked. 'You'll think I'm some weirdo.'

'Oh, come on. *I'm* the weirdo – you can't take that crown off me.' Lizzie attempted a laugh, but it sounded hollow.

'I wanted to help, somehow. We'd been told in a school assembly to be kind to others. And I knew you got a rough ride from everyone. Just about every kid teased you – their parents stopped them from playing with you. You were certainly never invited over to someone's house for tea, and despite some horrible kids trying to befriend you just so they could get a look inside Creepy Cawley's house, no one had stepped foot inside or been allowed to even play in your garden with you. I felt sorry for you.'

'So, you snuck out, away from the shop, and came to the bungalow to call for me?'

'Yep. God, I actually remember it clearly. I had a bag of sweets to share with you. They were stuffed in my pocket, getting gooey in the heat. I was scared stiff when I knocked on the door. Even more scared when your dad answered it. But he let me in.' Rob's eyes narrowed, his face crumpling.

'Did he hurt you, Rob?' Lizzie asked softly. Her heart banged hard against her ribs as she awaited the awful answer.

'No. He didn't touch me.'

'Oh. Okay, then. Why has it been such a big deal to you all these years then? Why the silence?'

'This is so . . . so hard, Lizzie.'

'You've come this far, go on – get it off your chest.'

'It was you. *You* who touched *me*. And you made me touch you.' Tears tracked down his face.

Lizzie's jaw slackened. 'What the hell, Rob?'

Chapter Seventy-Two

1989

Mapledon Church

Sunday 4th June – 45 days before

Muriel hurried through the church gate, patting her dress down, then dragging her fingers through her hair to neaten it. She swiped the back of her hand across her forehead, clearing the dampness from her skin. Rushing up the road in the heat hadn't been a good idea, but she was late. She'd never been late for Sunday school. Reverend Farnley would be wondering what had held her up. The truth of the matter was that she'd been too preoccupied with the minutes from Thursday's Mapledon Meeting, keen to get the action points written down. Keen to make progress with at least one of them. The main one.

She opened the heavy church door as quietly as she could, so as not to disturb any reading the vicar might be in the middle of, but she was lucky – he was nowhere to be seen as she entered. It was uncharacteristically quiet. Muriel looked around for the other wardens, but they weren't there. Had Sunday school been cancelled without her knowledge?

'Hello,' she called out, tentatively.

Nothing.

Where were the kids?

An outing. Muriel tutted. She'd forgotten all about the walk. Reverend Farnley had said last week they'd be taking the children around Mapledon to talk about its history. Odd that she hadn't encountered them on her way up through the village though.

A noise from the vestry caught her attention. Muriel strained her ears, moving closer to the room. There were voices coming from inside. She lifted her hand to knock on the door, but froze. The deep voice, muffled by the heavy wooden door, seemed urgent. It was Reverend Farnley, Muriel felt sure. Why hadn't he gone along with the others? Rather than knock, she pressed her ear to the door instead. She didn't know why she felt compelled to listen, why she hadn't just let her presence be known – it was a feeling, an inkling something wasn't right. His voice lowered to the point she couldn't make out any words. She stepped away from the door, deciding to wait in the main church for the others to return. Maybe he was making an important call. She shouldn't disturb him.

Muriel busied herself with tidying the kids' corner, straightening the kneeling pads in the pews and neatening the pile of hymnbooks. After ten minutes or so, she heard the vestry door opening. Finally, Reverend Farnley was coming out. Muriel walked towards him, but the look of dismay on his face made her stop short.

'Whatever's the matter, Reverend?' Muriel shot him a worried look. 'Are you unwell?'

'Muriel. I . . . you . . .' he stammered, then took a big breath, composing himself. 'You weren't here when the others left. I assumed you weren't coming today.' He kept turning his head to look behind him as he spoke.

'I'm sorry I was running so late; I had some urgent business to attend to.'

Farnley raised an eyebrow, but didn't comment. He seemed to be hesitating, undecided whether he was going to walk back into the vestry or come out into the church.

'Right,' he said. 'Yes, I had rather the same predicament.' He smiled – but it was an awkward one.

'Oh? Is everything all right?'

He turned his head again, back towards the vestry. 'It's Eliza,' he said quietly. 'She's been sick, and I was trying to get hold of Billy to come and get her.'

Muriel craned her neck around the Reverend to see inside the vestry. But the door was pulled to.

'Well, we shouldn't leave her in there on her own,' Muriel said, moving towards the door. Reverend Farnley caught hold of her arm. 'She's fine now, Muriel. No need to fuss.' Something in his voice caused her to pause.

'I can drop her home, Reverend. It's no problem.'

'Give her a moment.'

'Why?' Muriel couldn't keep the bewilderment from her tone.

Reverend Farnley's face flushed. Muriel, her patience wearing thin, walked forwards and pushed the vestry door open. Little Eliza was sitting on the floor – on cushions taken from the wooden bench – clutching her doll, crying.

'Oh, poor Eliza. Are you feeling poorly, love?' Muriel crouched down beside her. Eliza nodded without looking up. 'Come on, sweetie.' Muriel held out her hand. 'Let's get you home. Maybe you need to go to bed and rest.'

As Muriel straightened, Eliza's hand now in hers, she felt Reverend Farnley right behind her. She turned, banging into him.

'Sorry,' she said, backing up and moving around him to reach the door.

'Muriel, wait a moment. I need a word with you.' Reverend Farnley's face was set in a solemn expression. 'Alone. Eliza can wait for a bit longer.'

It hit Muriel then.

'Has she told you something?' A flash of hope that Eliza might have divulged what her father had been doing to her bolstered her. Muriel would finally have a way of getting rid of Billy Cawley from her village.

'Not really, no. But I think it's best if you don't mention it to anyone.'

'Mention what? That she's sick?'

Reverend Farnley gave a deep sigh. 'No, Muriel. That there is . . . well . . . *suspicion*, let's say, that Billy is in some way . . . er . . . *neglecting* her.'

'So, she *did* say something.' Muriel pursed her lips, her face becoming stony. 'Look, I'm sorry, Reverend, but you can't keep that sort of thing to yourself. It's important—'

'It's important we don't rock the boat unnecessarily, Muriel. It wouldn't look good that I was trying to coax her to tell me something now, would it? What if she goes back home and tells her father that I'd been asking questions?'

'What if he really hurts her and you knew about him all along but had done nothing? How would it look if the person she confided in, who happened to be a *vicar* no less, stood aside and allowed such a thing to happen?'

'Well, I'm asking you not to say anything *for now*, Muriel. There is no solid proof and the poor man has already had a rough ride since moving into Mapledon,' Reverend Farnley said in a calm but firm tone, giving Muriel a look that left no room for interpretation; he might as well have said 'because of you, Muriel'. 'I don't want to be the one to instigate a persecution, do you understand?'

Muriel nodded, thinking that from where she was standing, the Reverend seemed as afraid of Billy Cawley as the village kids were. She opened her mouth to say as much, but Reverend Farnley put his hand up to silence her.

'You know how people talk, Muriel. You of all people know. As I say, I would rather Billy wasn't put under scrutiny merely as a result of one conversation with a child – one who is clearly vulnerable. It could produce all kinds of problems. I shouldn't have tried talking to her without a professional – a social worker, or at the very least a teacher. It was foolish of me and Lord knows I should've known better . . .'

'Are you telling me to *ignore* my suspicions, Reverend? *Allow* her to be abused by her own father?'

'No, Muriel, of course not.' He sounded exasperated. 'We're both after the same outcome here, I think?' He raised both eyebrows, his deep honey-brown eyes boring into Muriel's. 'If you help me out here, I can help you out with your "mission"?'

Muriel raised her eyebrows to match the Reverend's expression. What exactly was he saying? She questioned if he really *knew* about her mission, because his current suggestion led her to believe he couldn't. He seemed too keen to *protect* Billy rather than rid the village of him, which was her aim.

Unless he knew something she didn't. He was privy to things she wasn't, being a servant of God. And lots of villagers entrusted him with their personal business. Maybe he had information she could use. 'I do have something I'm working on, actually,' Muriel said, finally. 'I'm sure at some point down the line you'd be useful.'

He smiled, baring his large, square teeth. 'That's good. God moves in mysterious ways, Muriel. He will ensure the safety of the flock.'

Muriel wasn't so sure about that. She couldn't place so much faith in the Lord, only in herself.

Chapter Seventy-Three

2019

Anna

Thursday 18th July

Anna held her mobile up higher, trying to get a full signal before calling Carrie. She'd walked to the end of her mother's road, not just because of the signal, but also because she wanted to be out of earshot. After she chatted with Carrie, she wanted to tell James what she'd found out about her dad. She needed someone who knew her, someone who knew her history, to talk it through with.

Finally gaining four bars, Anna dialled. Carrie picked up on the first ring.

'Mum! Where have you been? Why haven't you called me?'

Anna's heart plummeted. Her poor daughter was suffering from her absence.

'I'm so sorry, love. I don't think I'll be much longer.' Anna winced; she shouldn't make false promises. 'If it looks like it'll take more time, I'll bring Nanna home with me.'

'Why can't I come there with you?'

'You'd be so bored here, Carrie. There's literally nothing to do. Don't you remember me telling you how tedious it was for me growing up here? Trust me, nothing has changed.'

'But I'd be with you. I miiiiisssss you,' she wailed.

'I miss you too, honey. I have a feeling things might sort themselves out in the next few days.' And she did have that feeling – she wasn't lying about that. In her gut, Anna knew it was coming to a head – some grand finale was due. Given that the thirty-year anniversary of Jonie's actual disappearance was tomorrow – Friday 19th July – it seemed the most likely day that this, whatever 'this' was, would end. How it would end was the worrying, unknown factor.

After giving Carrie further assurances she'd see her soon, she was happy to pass the phone to James.

'So, things not going to plan, then?'

'Not really. On the plus side, I no longer think Mum has dementia.'

'Oh? Then why was she acting so strangely?'

Anna gave him a brief run-down of what had been happening, hearing a sharp intake of breath every now and then. She finished her monologue with the part where her dad had supposedly abandoned her due to Muriel's behaviour. The reason for never contacting Anna seemed to be because it was easier for her *mother*. He'd apparently loved Anna. Even vocalising it to James made her shake her head in disbelief.

'What does that even mean?' he asked.

'Precisely! If he loved me, he wouldn't have given up so readily. It doesn't add up, does it? Why make my mother's life easier, not mine?'

'I suppose we don't know how Jonie's abduction and the subsequent assumption that she'd been murdered affected him and your mum's relationship. Or you for that matter. Thankfully it's not something we've ever had experience of. We can't *know* the reasons your dad chose to leave for another woman and shack up with her in another country; we've only one side of the story.' There was a pause before James spoke again. 'Is it wise, dragging this up now? I mean, you've had years to question this . . .'

'Don't you start,' Anna huffed. 'Everyone seems to have an aversion to digging things up!'

'Sorry, but why now?'

'Because of the situation,' Anna said, her tone shrill. She took a deep breath. 'This is why I don't visit Mapledon, James. This is why I rarely see my mother. Because now I *have* spent lots of time in her company, I can't help but question everything. It's easier to let sleeping dogs lie when there's distance.'

'Hmm,' he said. 'Maybe that was your dad's view too.' His voice was almost a whisper as though afraid of Anna's reaction.

Anna wanted to be angry with him, shooting a sarcastic comment back, but it was as if all her energy left her. 'Whatever.'

'Have you got contact details for him—'

'God, no, James. I'm not speaking to him, or seeing him. I don't care what his reasons were. As far as I'm concerned, they weren't good enough to leave a ten-year-old daughter. Would you leave Carrie?'

'Well, no. Of course not.'

'Exactly. Nothing could cause you to abandon her. My dad was selfish and weak, end of. And my mother let him walk and is now trying to somehow justify his actions by saying he'd left because of her, not me. You know, because he still loved *me*. Well, that's bollocks.'

'I agree, it's weak. But maybe he deserves to put his side forward, rather than having Muriel speak for him?'

Anna closed her eyes, her mind conjuring her dad's sandy-brown hair flopping over his high forehead. His cool-blue eyes. She could hear his calming voice, feel his warm hugs.

'One day, maybe. For now though, I need to see this through here.' She brought the conversation back to the present; she'd deal with her past another time.

'Do you think you're in danger? Or that Muriel is?' James's voice was edged with concern.

'I change my mind about that almost hourly, James. I've

spoken to an ex-copper about it, but still haven't gone to the police officially.'

'I think you should. Couldn't they place a patrol car outside the house? At least you'd feel safer.'

'Possibly.' Anna became lost in her thoughts. It was the obvious solution – get the police involved. The doll parts, together with the notes, were surely evidence enough someone meant them harm? The police would do *something*. 'Mum still seems keen to avoid police involvement.'

'Why?' James's voice was incredulous.

'She believes it would aggravate the situation, make it worse. Maybe she feels he'll up his game, or just find another way of getting to her. I don't know. But there is the possibility she's still not telling me everything. She's holding back key information, I feel sure. And that's why she doesn't want to call the police – because it'll bring up the past she's been trying so hard to keep buried.'

'Then I think it's about time she came clean, at least to you. For your sake, Anna. For Carrie's. Currently her behaviour is putting you at risk. Does she really want that?'

James's words rang inside her head as she walked back to the house. The front door was bare. No new body part had been hammered to it overnight. Anna wondered when it would come. When Pat had come over the previous evening and Anna had shown him the doll's parts and the notes, he'd offered to sit outside in his car and watch the house. Muriel had declined, of course.

But it'd made Anna think that maybe *she* should stay up – keep a vigil – see who was leaving them. She should've set up a camera as soon as the second item had been left, to catch them in the act herself, as Sandie had suggested. But she supposed whoever it was would be clever – they would've factored in something like that, and they'd be disguised. Still, having any kind of visual evidence would be helpful to them – at least it might be possible to tell if it were a man or woman. Being able to eliminate Lizzie as the suspect would allow Anna to fully confide in her. Realistically, she was the only one Anna could work with to get to the bottom of what happened to Jonie Hayes.

Anna felt buoyed at the thought of doing something more constructive. She hadn't even ventured out of Mapledon since getting there – a trip into Bovey, the closest town, to buy a security camera would be a relief. Allow her some release from the village, which in some ways was beginning to feel like a prison.

Anna had enjoyed the few hours away from Mapledon – and her mother. It was as though a stormy cloud had been lifted the second she left. Anna remembered that feeling – it was the same she'd experienced twenty years ago. But Anna's light mood darkened the moment she pulled her car into her mother's road. Even from a distance she could tell there was something on the door. If only they could've waited until she'd set the camera up. It's as if they knew what she was planning.

She slowly got out of the car, trying to delay the inevitable. There it was: the next body part – an arm. Anna stood still in front of it, the bag carrying the camera in her hand. Damn it. Only one more part to go. Or that was the general consensus anyway. The torso would be the final piece, and Anna guessed it would be tomorrow's offering. There was one last chance to get the perpetrator on camera.

'Mum!' Anna called out as she walked through the door. 'Mum?'

Anna pushed through the lounge door, but there was no sign of Muriel. Popping the bag on the dining room table, Anna walked out into the back garden, calling as she went. A door banged.

'Here!' Muriel shouted, and Anna watched as she emerged

275

from Sandie's back door. Finally, she'd ventured in to see her neighbour, and typically that had been when the arm had been attached to the door. 'You took your time,' she said, her words cutting.

'Sorry, it wasn't easy to find a shop in Bovey that sold the type of camera I wanted. It had to be one with night vision.'

'You managed to get one, though?' Muriel closed the gate that separated hers and Sandie's houses and ambled to the back door. She was more hunched than she'd appeared before: her shoulders rounded, her spine curved. She looked so much older than sixty-five – Anna had seen sprightlier ninety-year-olds. It was like she was shrinking, disappearing further inside herself with each new day.

'Yes. And we got another doll part, too.'

Muriel's face blanched. 'I thought we'd got away with it today.'

'Yes, me too. Didn't you hear anything?'

'No.' Muriel shook her head, sighing. 'Nothing. Sandie and I were in the kitchen. If we'd been in the lounge I might've. Right, so what's this one got to say?'

'Let's look, shall we?'

They both sat at the table, Anna with the skewer poised ready.

'Go on, then,' Muriel said. Anna dug out the piece of paper: SOMEONE HAS TO CONFESS. NOW! YOUR TIME IS RUNNING OUT.

Muriel muttered something under her breath and rose from her chair. Without looking at Anna she walked into the lounge. Anna sat for a while, thinking.

Someone has to confess. Now. Your time is running out. What was going to happen when the undisclosed time ran out? That was the question. If the person didn't confess, what were they going to do about it? There couldn't be enough evidence of wrongdoing or surely they'd be taking it to the police, not terrorising her mother. They had to be bluffing, or they were about to take matters into their own hands and dish out what they believed to be justice. If this person was so convinced Billy Cawley was wrongly convicted, how far were they willing to go to clear his name? If it was Billy himself behind it – Anna would bet he'd go quite far.

But maybe that wasn't the intention.

As she'd already thought, there couldn't be enough evidence for the police, so this must be a way of getting back at someone purely for their own satisfaction. Rightly or wrongly they'd decided Billy was innocent and someone else guilty. Lifting the blame and pushing it onto someone else was maybe a way of ridding themselves of the guilt. Or sharing it.

The only thing Anna knew was that her mother had been instrumental in Eliza's removal from Billy's care. But what if it hadn't ended there?

Chapter Seventy-Four

2019

Lizzie

Dom had been snoring gently when she'd returned to the room the previous night. Lizzie had watched him, silent tears tracking down her face. She was still reeling from Rob's recollection of what had happened in her bedroom when she was eight years old, his words echoing in her mind:

'*It was you. You who touched me. And made me touch you.*'

She'd never felt so horrified.

Her own reaction had been quick, drenched in disbelief:

'*I was eight years old, Rob – why are you saying this? Why would you lie about something like this?*'

But, as he'd crumpled into the chair, his head buried in his hands, she'd known. He wasn't lying. After he'd composed himself, he'd told Lizzie everything he remembered from that afternoon. How he'd freaked out. How he'd thought Billy was going to kill him if he'd seen, or if Eliza told him. Who'd believe an older boy over an eight-year-old girl? Certainly not the girl's father. She would be seen as the victim, not him. Rob said he'd run out of the bungalow and legged it back to the safety of the shop and been afraid for weeks afterwards that Billy Cawley would come for him.

He'd never spoken to anyone about what happened. After

years of ignoring it, it'd been put to the back of his mind – other problems had replaced the incident: Eliza had been taken away, Jonie had been abducted and killed. He'd told Lizzie how, at first, he believed he would somehow get the blame for Jonie. Like someone would find out about Eliza and him and add two and two together and come up with ten. Assume he was a delinquent, someone who touched up girls – and people would think he'd harmed Jonie too.

Lizzie's heart had ached for him. His childhood had been upturned, ruined. Innocence lost.

The same as Lizzie.

Only *she'd* caused Rob's distress.

'I'm so sorry,' she'd said.

'You can't blame yourself. You were a child, for God's sake, and kids experiment. It's just what you did was more, well . . . adult than most. Blame *him* – the abuse he inflicted on you.'

Lizzie had turned from her sleeping husband and slowly slid open the bottom drawer of the dresser, retrieving the piece of cloth – the one she'd found in the doll's head. She'd sat silently, turning the bloodstained strip of material over in her hands. She'd studied it. The material was from her dress – she recognised the now-faded yellow flowers from a photograph of Eliza wearing it. One of the few photos she'd seen of herself from childhood. Instinct had told her to take it when she'd been inside Anna's shed.

It must've been her father who'd placed a strip of her clothing inside the doll's head. But why? Lizzie had been working on the understanding that Billy was trying to show he was innocent of Jonie Hayes' abduction and murder. And maybe show who *he* thought was really responsible. But Lizzie couldn't understand what relevance bloodstained clothing of *hers* had to any of it.

For a split second, a horrifying thought had crossed her mind. Had she *been* there? Had she been present when Jonie Hayes had been killed?

She'd shaken her head, taken deep breaths. No, of course she hadn't. She'd already been taken into care by that time. The red stain could be her own blood, or dye. Nothing to do with Jonie. Hearing Rob's story and holding the piece of her clothing had unsettled her and her mind was jumping. She had to keep emotion out of it, think logically.

Now, in the cold light of day, having only had small snatches of sleep, Lizzie opened her laptop. Dom had woken early and had showered and gone for a walk around the gardens of the B&B to 'take in the country air'. She'd avoided getting into a conversation with him. Her mind was too full – she needed peace to get her head together. Lizzie started reading through the notes in the files she'd made on each person of interest. Somewhere in there could be a link to the missing piece of the puzzle. The photographs on the wall in Rob's house were also on her mind. May Day. Tina Hayes watching as Jonie danced around the maypole. Billy Cawley standing beside her, shoulder-to-shoulder.

If she could bear to see Rob again, it would be good to take a closer look at the photos, and to ask Nell if she had any more from that time. By searching the old photos she might gain the truth, find out what the villagers of Mapledon were hiding. Lizzie picked up her mobile to compose a text to Rob. A stream of pings sounded. She frowned. That was an awful lot of notifications since last checking it. The signal came and went, though, so it was likely a load of messages had suddenly filtered through all together. She scrolled through them to see if there was anything pressing to deal with. All seemed non-urgent – one from the editor who'd commissioned the Billy Cawley piece needed answering, but the others could wait.

Then one caught her attention. Anna had texted her Wednesday afternoon. There really was a delay in getting the notifications if it had taken that long to come through.

Hi Lizzie,
Just to keep you updated – we got the leg as expected. Note inside: SOMEONE KNOWS WHERE SHE IS. Have spoken to Pat Vern about it, but Mother still adamant we shouldn't bother the police. I want to go and see Nell and Rob – thought it would make sense if we went together. Could you make tomorrow afternoon?
Anna.

Lizzie was surprisingly nonplussed about the leg and note – as Anna said in the text, it was expected. But she *was* disconcerted about her suggestion they go to see Nell and Rob together. After last night's revelation, Lizzie would rather go back alone. She didn't relish the thought of it all coming up in front of Anna. She took a few moments to consider it before texting back.

Sorry, just received your text this morning. I can come over after 2pm if that's OK?

She'd have to put what had happened to the back of her mind – she was good at doing that. She'd had a lifetime's practice, after all.

Chapter Seventy-Five

1989

Inside Billy's truck

Friday 2nd June – 47 days before

He'd tried for the longest time, he really had. And still all he'd gained was grief, not acceptance. That bitch of a woman, Muriel Fisher, her husband – all the husbands in fact – horrible people the lot of them. What were they so afraid of? Just because his wife had died, it didn't mean he was after theirs. God, who'd be interested in those fake women anyway?

Billy's eyes were staring forwards. He watched her intently from the safety of his truck, the engine idling. She was prettier than the others. Not just physically – she was prettier on the inside too. Or she was when she wasn't with *them*. If he could get her on her own, be alone with her for a while, he might be able to release some of the pent-up anger. If the pressure was released from inside him, from inside his head, he'd be better able to cope with Rosie's death – with the knowledge he now had to bring Eliza up all on his own.

'Can we go to the shop and buy sweets, Daddy?' Eliza asked. She brought his thoughts back to the here and now. She'd been sitting quietly beside him while his attention was elsewhere.

'Not from there, no. We'll drive into town.' He shifted the truck into gear and sped off. Away from her. He'd have to watch her more, find out her routine. Figure out a good time to approach her.

'Ohh, but it's so far,' Eliza complained, slapping her hands hard onto her lap.

'But there are better sweets in town. You need to be patient, Eliza. Good things come to those who wait.'

Chapter Seventy-Six

2019

Anna

Thursday 18th July

Anna rushed to the front door, calling to Muriel over her shoulder as soon as she spotted Lizzie's car turn into the road.

'Won't be long, Mum. Ring if you need me.'

She didn't wait for a response. Muriel had appeared slightly more reassured once Sandie's husband had set the video security camera up on the wall to the left of the front door – inside the alcove so it wasn't easily visible – its lens trained on the door. Anna had tested it prior to Lizzie's arrival – walking towards the house several times and reaching up to the point the doll's parts had been left. She then made sure it had recorded, checking the quality of the captured images. Though Anna felt happy with her purchase, she was annoyed with herself for having waited this long to do it.

'You ready for this?' Anna asked, as she got in the car and pulled the seatbelt over her chest.

'As I'll ever be,' Lizzie said, her voice monotone. Then she added, 'I'm keen to get some answers, to find out who the "someone" is who knows where she is.'

'Oh, there's been another since that one,' Anna said. 'It was the other arm. The note read, "Someone has to confess. Now! Your time is running out." One more to go?'

'Christ. Well, I hope that is the case. As much as I enjoy unearthing my stories, I must admit, this has been too close to home. I'd quite like it to be over now.'

'Oh, me too. I'm done with Mapledon.'

Lizzie gave Anna a weak smile. 'Thank you,' she said.

'What for?'

'Believing it's not me attaching Polly's limbs to your door.' Lizzie's eyes glistened. But she blinked rapidly and reversed the car sharply, driving back out of Muriel's road without saying more. Anna didn't respond. She couldn't very well tell her that she still had doubts. She also refrained from mentioning the new camera. Trust had to be earned, and she wasn't sure Lizzie had reached that level yet. One more day, or night, and she would be sure.

Lizzie parked in front of Brook Cottage Store and Anna got out. Lizzie didn't move.

'You coming in?' Anna asked, ducking down to look at her.

Lizzie blew air from her puffed-up cheeks. 'Yep. I guess so.'

'What's the matter? It's like you don't want to do this. If you want me to go—'

'No, no. I do. I'm just working myself up to it.'

Anna frowned as Lizzie finally exited the car.

'It's difficult, Anna – revisiting demons I'd suppressed so much that I don't have a memory of them anymore. It's like opening an old, deep cut.'

'Yes, you're right. That's exactly what we're doing.'

The two women made their way around the side of the shop, to the accommodation behind, and rang the bell. Nothing.

'Could they both be working in the shop?' Lizzie asked.

They went back around the front, Anna walking into the shop first, Lizzie hanging back reluctantly.

'Afternoon, Nell,' Anna said. Nell Andrews was standing at the end of the nearest aisle, pulling items forward to the front of the shelf.

'Hello, Bella. I'd heard you were back.' Nell turned to face her. 'Oops, sorry. Robert did tell me that you prefer *Anna* now. How's everything, love? Mum okay?' she said brightly.

'Yes, she's doing all right, thanks. Are you feeling better?'

Nell gave her a quizzical glance before answering, 'Oh, er . . . yes. Thank you.'

'That's good. Is Rob about?'

'In the storeroom. What do you want him for?' Her tone changed immediately.

Anna was taken aback by her abruptness. 'Oh, just a quick catch-up. But hoping he can help with something too, before I head back home.'

Nell's brow creased. 'Well, I guess I could spare him. But I can't sort the delivery on my own, and that's due any minute, so . . .'

'I won't keep him, Nell.' Anna forced a smile.

Nell disappeared into the storeroom, leaving Anna standing alone in the aisle. She'd been gone a few minutes and there was still no sign of Rob. Anna crept towards the closed door, straining to hear voices. It sounded as though Nell was having a go at Rob, her voice harsh, demanding. She couldn't hear what she was saying, though. Footsteps came closer; Anna scuttled back from the door.

'Hey, Anna,' Rob said as he burst through the door, his face blotchy-red.

'Rob, hi. Can I tear you away from your work for a bit?'

He looked furtively around at Nell, who was directly behind him. 'Er . . . yeah, I can spare a few minutes.'

Anna knew she wanted him for longer than that, but went along with it. 'Good. Lizzie's here too,' she said, motioning outside.

'Oh.' His face fell. Anna wondered what had gone on between the two of them, remembering Lizzie's reluctance to leave the car.

'Can we go inside? Into your house?'

'Sure.' He shrugged. He walked out the shop door, greeting Lizzie without making eye contact, and strode around the side of the shop. Anna and Lizzie followed.

The musty smell assaulted her nostrils as Rob showed them into the first room on the right as they walked in. Anna couldn't remember having been inside when she was younger – she and Rob hadn't been particularly friendly; they hadn't hung around with the same crowd. She was immediately drawn to the framed photographs covering two of the walls, going up close to study them. Lizzie came up behind her.

'What do you notice in this one?' she asked, pointing to one depicting Mapledon's May Day celebrations. Anna let her eyes travel over the picture. Her heart gave a jolt.

'Billy Cawley is there, watching the girls dancing.'

'Yes, but look who he's with.'

'That's Auntie Tina,' she said, straightening, unable to keep the surprise from her voice. 'But that doesn't really mean anything – most of the village, if not all of it, would've been there.'

'But that close? They're touching, see? They don't need to be. There's plenty of room around them – it's not like they're being squashed together in a crowd.' Lizzie sounded excited now, like she'd been drinking energy drinks and they were just beginning to kick in.

But she was right – Tina and Billy looked very comfortable standing shoulder-to-shoulder. Anna searched the image for Mark, but couldn't see him – only her mum and dad, Reverend Farnley and Nell.

'But to be honest, Lizzie, the fact he's with Tina Hayes only points to a connection between your dad and Jonie. If, as I assume you're suggesting, he and Tina were close – having an affair even – all that proves is he had access to Jonie. It *increases* the likelihood your dad abducted her, as far as I can tell.'

'No. You're missing the point, Anna.'

Anna gave an exasperated sigh. 'What point are you trying to make, then?'

'My dad being in any kind of relationship with Tina doesn't automatically mean he would abduct her daughter! That thinking is ludicrous. What *I* think it proves is that my dad wasn't the man everyone made him out to be. And Tina saw that. She saw something good in him where no one else could – or would – even attempt to. He was hounded the entire time he lived in this village, and *she* might've been the only person he had on his side. I bet that didn't go down well with the women at the bloody Mapledon Meeting.' Lizzie jabbed a finger at the photograph further along the wall. 'They're the ones who are key, I think,' Lizzie said. 'The ones who know.'

Anna moved along the wall, her focus following Lizzie's finger.

'What makes you think that?' Rob had finally found his voice, having been silent since he'd shown them in. 'They're just photos. The village isn't big; you're bound to see the same faces cropping up again and again. It doesn't mean anything. And neither does that one.' He nodded his head towards the photo Lizzie and Anna were now standing in front of.

'That's the women from the Mapledon Meeting.' The voice, loud and sudden, made Anna start. She turned as Nell entered the room.

'Yes, so I see,' Anna managed.

'Why are you so interested in these?' Nell closed the door behind her.

'I love looking at old photographs – they can tell you so much,' Anna said.

Nell pursed her lips. 'They do say a picture can tell a thousand words, but I'm not sure I agree. You can't tell everything, can you? People hide themselves, even if in plain sight. I mean, you can't see the evil lurking in *him*, for example, can you? Not from this photo.' Nell pointed to the May Day one they'd been looking at before she came in.

'Maybe because there's no evil to see.' Lizzie spoke so quietly her voice was barely audible.

Nell huffed. 'You would say that.'

Anna felt the atmosphere shift and butted in quickly before things could get heated. She was interested in the women in the photo and wanted to find out more.

'This photo,' she said. 'It's dated Thursday, 1st June 1989. You must've had a million meetings; why was this one taken?' Anna noted that the women standing at the forefront of the picture – Tina, Muriel, Nell – seemed to be 'in charge'. It was as though they were the most important.

Nell shrugged. 'No idea. Probably one of the few meetings everyone was present at or something, or maybe it was an anniversary – however many years since we first began them. I can't remember.' Nell stepped back. 'Anyway, I need Rob back in the shop. I've left it unattended.'

'Maybe Rob can go back in and you stay here for a bit?' Lizzie asked suddenly.

Nell bristled. 'I haven't got time for this nonsense.'

'There's something in Tina's expression that's unsettling, don't you think?' Lizzie said, ignoring Nell's comment. 'What did you discuss at these meetings, Nell?'

'Mrs Andrews to you,' she snapped.

Anna hadn't seen Nell for many years prior to this visit; maybe she'd always been sharp, snappy. But she didn't think so. Lizzie had hit a nerve.

'Sorry. What went on at the meeting, *Mrs Andrews*?'

Nell puffed out her chest. 'All sorts,' she said. 'How am I meant to remember now? We covered a lot of topics: how to raise money for new playground equipment, how to make the roads safer for the children, that sort of thing.'

'And how to make the children safer in general?' Lizzie asked.

'What do you mean?'

'Well, none of the villagers made a secret of the fact they mistrusted my dad, did they? He wasn't liked. So, did you discuss *that* at your meetings? Did you talk about what to do about *him*?' Lizzie's voice rose as she spoke, her face turning a deep shade of pink.

'It's so long ago, no point digging up the past,' Nell said.

Anna's blood chilled in her veins. 'Funny,' she said. 'That's word-for-word what my mother said.'

Nell bowed her head.

Anna wondered now, more than ever, just what had gone on at those meetings. Why were her mother and Nell so cagey about them? It was almost as though it were some kind of secret society. As if Lizzie had read Anna's mind, she walked up to Nell and said: 'Mapledon has a whole Stepford wives vibe about it, doesn't it? I don't know how you bear it – it's suffocating. You're trapped, aren't you. I think the truth would set you free, Nell. Sorry – *Mrs Andrews*.'

'I don't know what you're talking about.' Nell backed away from Lizzie. 'You come here, pretending to be someone you're not, raking up the past for your own benefit. You're disgusting. Just like your *father*.' Nell's face scrunched up into an unattractive ball of wrinkles, spittle forming at the corners of her mouth.

'Mum!' Rob said, a hand raised towards his mother. 'Enough.'

'Well!' Nell shook herself, as if to rid her body of something clinging to it. 'If it wasn't for the pair of them, this village would've carried on as normal. And poor Jonie Hayes would be here now. When you went, you weren't meant to *come back*,' Nell said, her words almost hissing like a snake.

Anna, Lizzie and Rob remained silent as Nell stormed out of

290

the room, each seeming to be as shocked as the other by the outburst.

Anna turned to Lizzie. 'I think we've found out enough for now. Let's go, shall we?'

If Anna was certain of one thing, it was that those women had done something more than just get Eliza Cawley taken away from her father.

Chapter Seventy-Seven

2019

Lizzie

Lizzie drove in stunned silence back to Anna's house. Whilst she'd been glad the topic of Rob's childhood visit to their bungalow hadn't come up again, she hadn't expected the turn of events that had unfolded. She was so pleased Anna had been present. She was another witness to Nell's outburst.

'I think you should be here tomorrow,' Anna said when Lizzie pulled up outside her house. Her body was turned towards Lizzie, her eyes staring, intense.

'Because it's the anniversary?'

'Yes. After that *bizarre* display, I think we should face whatever is coming together.'

'Okay. But we won't know *when*.'

'You could stay here for the night, just in case?'

Lizzie wrinkled her nose. 'I'm not sure. My husband turned up last night and he's staying at the B&B too now.'

'Oh? How come?'

'Long story. But basically, he didn't know.' Lizzie slumped. 'As in, he didn't know who I was. Who my father is. His release has had such a huge impact. Greater than I imagined it would, actually.'

'I'm sorry. Everything you went through, and now you're reliving it – like watching the DVD but with bonus material.'

Lizzie laughed.

'Oh, well I'm glad you can still laugh,' Anna said. 'That's something.'

'What's the saying? If I don't laugh, I'll cry?'

'Yup!' Anna turned away and opened the car door. Before closing it, she lowered her head back inside. 'Whatever happens, Lizzie, whatever truth we find – if we do get to the truth – I hope you can finally move on. Enjoy your life as you should.'

Lizzie swallowed the painful lump in her throat. 'Thank you. I really hope the same for you, too. Let's pray the truth isn't as painful as the lies have been.'

Anna nodded and slammed the door. Lizzie watched her walk down the path and in through the front door. She drove to the end of the road and stopped to make a call while she had a few bars of signal. The phone still went straight to voicemail.

'Hey, Dom. Sorry, but I'm not coming back to the B&B just yet. I have to make a trip into town to interview someone of interest. I'll give you another call when I can – signal is iffy, so don't worry if you don't hear from me. I'll be back by dark.'

She hung up, then clicked on Google Maps, searching for farms situated around ten miles from Mapledon. She hoped there weren't too many places with caravans in the vicinity. Two farms showed up: Blasedale and Haytor Vale. Lizzie decided Blasedale fitted the description her dad had given. Anticipation growing in her stomach, she set off.

The steering was heavy; she needed to really pull at the wheel to manoeuvre the car up the dirt track approaching Blasedale Farm. She abandoned it at the side of a barn, and continued on foot towards the gate, which looked to lead to the back, and, with luck, the caravans. She wondered how many were on the land, and how easy it would be to locate Billy's. It would be preferable to find him without having to ask anyone – she wasn't sure what details he would've given and didn't want to say the wrong thing. Lizzie lifted the wooden gate, walking through and closing it behind her. No one was in sight; she couldn't even hear any noises she'd associate with a working farm. Maybe it *wasn't* a working farm anymore.

Lizzie felt her muscles relax as she rounded the corner and saw just two caravans in a field not far from the farmhouse.

Please let this be the right place.

She trudged into the field and approached the first caravan, tiptoeing to peer inside the window. It looked empty. If the other one was, she'd have to drive to the next farm. What if Billy had lied about where he was? The thought crushed her. There would be no other way of finding him. She'd have to wait for him to come to her. She almost laughed at the irony.

She held her breath as she looked through the only clean spot on the dirty window of the second caravan. Then released it in a rush of air. Billy was inside. She took a few moments to compose herself, then knocked on the door. Her knuckles made a hollow sound on the plastic.

'Well, well. This is a surprise,' Billy said as he opened it. 'I didn't think I'd see you anytime soon.'

'Me neither, if I'm honest,' she said.

'Come in, if you like?'

Lizzie stepped up inside the caravan, a faint smell of gone-off food wafting towards her. She cast her eyes around the small space.

'It's not much. But it's better than a prison cell.' He smiled as he quickly cast his eyes around the caravan's interior. 'Sit down. What is it that you want?'

Lizzie cautiously moved to the end of the caravan and sat, her back rigid. 'I want to know the full story. The *real* one. No lies, no bullshit. Straight-up what happened to me, why I was taken, why the Mapledon villagers wanted you gone so badly. All of it. I need to know what they did and whether you're here to take revenge.' Lizzie took a breath.

'Hmmm . . .' Billy said, perching on the edge of the square-looking sofa that ran along one side of the caravan. 'You didn't seem like you were ready, or even willing, to hear about it when I saw you the other day.'

'No. I wasn't ready then. But I am now.'

'Fine, I'll tell you what you want to know. But you have to believe what I say. Not all of it will make sense to you. Most of it won't *sound* believable. One part specifically. But I promise you now, what comes out of my mouth will be the truth. I'm not going to lie to you. You need to be certain you want to know. You need to be sure you can handle the fallout. Because all I want is a quiet life now, and somehow I get the feeling after this conversation, shit will hit the fan, so to speak. As seems to be the popular saying in Mapledon – if you don't want to get your hands dirty, don't go digging in the dirt. And you, my girl, are digging deep.'

'I'm aware of that. But it's time, Dad. Time for the truth. Even if that means more pain.'

Billy nodded and slipped down so that he was sitting on the sofa cushion beside her.

Lizzie caught the scent of Old Spice. She angled her body so she was fully facing him. He was clean-shaven today, and wore a plain black T-shirt, untucked from his dark blue denim jeans. He'd tidied himself up since she'd first met him. She almost smiled – for some reason his neatened appearance – the fact he was making an effort and taking pride in himself – made her feel a warmth towards him. He seemed calm and in control when he spoke again; he started slowly, his voice low and measured. 'The lies began early on. The ones circulating the village about me abusing you being some of the first. But the biggest lie of all came two days after Jonie Hayes went missing. And that's when I knew.'

'Knew what?' Lizzie shifted awkwardly on the firm-cushioned sofa, creating a little more distance between her and Billy.

'Knew that whatever I said was a waste of time. No one was going to believe weirdo Creepy Cawley, were they? Who'd believe a loner and a child molester?'

'But you hadn't been convicted, no charges came about for abusing me, did they?'

'Because I was innocent!' he shouted suddenly, running his fingers through his grey hair. 'But it didn't matter by then. Shit sticks, Eliza. No smoke without fire, as they say. And they *knew* that. That's how come it worked.'

'How come what worked?'

'Their plan. They knew I'd struggle to get out of the mess they'd created for me. The stage was set, and I was the number one suspect. The only suspect in their minds. The only one they ever wanted.'

Chapter Seventy-Eight

1989

Fisher residence

Wednesday 19th July – the day of, 6.15 p.m.

Bella couldn't catch her breath. She'd run home all the way, not stopping once. She couldn't; she was too afraid. Too afraid to look back. Now, safely behind her front door, she collapsed in a heap, gasping for air.

'Whatever's the matter, Bella?' Her mother appeared from the lounge doorway and then rushed towards her, bending down in front of her.

Bella couldn't speak.

'Slow it down, take deep breaths,' she coaxed, taking Bella's hands in hers and waiting for her to calm. 'You're shaking,' she said, her brow creasing with concern.

Bella heard a sob. It had come from her – from deep inside, bubbling up and erupting noisily. Tears stung her eyes.

She shouldn't have run. But what other choice had there been?

The shaking got worse, her teeth chattering together violently. Muriel pulled Bella in close to her, wrapping her arms tightly around her trembling body. She brushed Bella's golden hair down with her hand, whispering comforting 'shushings' into her ear.

They rocked together on the floor, saying nothing.

'I'm home!' Eric called as he opened the back door. He turned to bang his boots against the back step to dislodge mud.

'You're late,' Muriel said.

'What's going on here?' he asked, ignoring her statement as he entered the lounge, his eyes squinting at Muriel and Bella huddled together on the sofa.

Muriel glanced up at him, shaking her head gently. 'I don't know, Eric. But it must be bad – she hasn't spoken a word yet. She's been in this state since she ran in an hour ago.'

'Come on, love,' Eric said, crouching down in front of them. 'Tell Daddy what's happened. Have you fallen out with Jonie again?'

Bella's sobs started up again.

'What's she done this time?' Eric bellowed. 'Tell me, and I'll go over there right now and sort it out.'

'Eric! That's not helpful,' Muriel said, glowering at him. She turned her attention back to Bella. 'Dad's worried. I'm worried. You need to tell us what's happened, darling.'

Bella pushed herself away from her mum and, with tears cascading down her still-red cheeks, took some deep breaths. She stared into her father's eyes, searching them. Eric looked away.

Bella's stomach hurt. Her limbs still burned from the running. She wanted to go to her room, dive under her duvet and never come out. But she knew she couldn't. She had to say something.

'He – he . . . chased . . . us,' she stuttered. 'Billy.' A sob racked her body. 'It's . . . Jonie . . . I left her. It's . . . my fault.'

Chapter Seventy-Nine

2019

Anna

Friday 19th July

A nervous, tight ball sat heavily in the pit of her stomach.

Today was the day. Exactly thirty years ago, Jonie Hayes went missing. Thirty years ago, to the day, Anna's life changed. She stopped being Bella. She stopped being a child. Her memories of that Wednesday afternoon were still vague, the timeline hazy. The other night Pat Vern had told her she and Muriel hadn't reported Jonie's abduction to the police until the Friday, which she still found hard to comprehend. She would obviously have been suffering from shock, but since she realised there'd been a time lapse, Anna had wondered whether she'd deliberately held off telling anyone because she'd secretly wanted Jonie to get into trouble. Wanted her to suffer.

But those reasons seemed too incomprehensible to be true; the fact she was even considering it horrified her – ten-year-old Bella wouldn't have been capable of that thinking. She'd been too young, too innocent. She'd seen her friend being taken by Creepy Cawley. That would've frightened her and the fact she'd done nothing for almost forty-eight hours must've been due to feeling numb with shock. It was the only feasible explanation. She just wished she could recall exactly what had happened to put her mind at rest.

Anna stared at her mother as she picked at a piece of cold toast. Muriel had always sliced toast into four, neat triangles. Anna remembered how her mother would pop the triangles into a shiny, silver toast rack, place a pot of butter and one of jam onto a plate and present it to Eric on the dining room table. That had been her father's breakfast every day for the years he'd spent at home. For the ten years of Anna's life he'd been around.

'Have you checked the front door?' Muriel asked.

'No. I was gearing up for it. I didn't sleep much, kept jolting awake at every small sound. I didn't hear any loud banging or anything, though. Maybe there's nothing. Yet.'

'I glanced at the doormat first thing but was waiting for you to check the door. Not sure my poor heart can take any more, if I'm honest.'

'Ditto,' Anna said. 'And if there's going to be a "big one", it'll be today. I feel it.'

'Should we check the security camera first?'

'Yes, good idea. We'll be prepared then.'

Muriel and Anna both made their way upstairs to the spare room – the box-room at the front of the house where the recorder and monitor were set up. Anna peered out through the curtains. No one was about.

'Do you know how to work it, Anna?' Muriel took her glasses off her head, perching them on the end of her nose, and stared over them at the blank monitor screen. Anna smiled. Why put glasses on and then look over the top of them? She didn't bother to voice the question.

'I had a practice; it's very straightforward,' Anna said.

'Well, it is for you youngsters, not so much for me.'

'Don't worry. Let's hope you don't need to become an expert . . .'

Anna pushed a few buttons and the image of the front door popped up on the screen.

'Damn.'

'It's the body,' Muriel said, her tone defeated. 'I didn't hear it. Must be going deaf as well as daft.'

One of her mother's favourite sayings.

'Okay, well we can at least go back through the recording. Maybe we'll catch them in the act and be able to identify the fuc—'

Muriel shot Anna a hard stare.

'Sorry. I stopped myself, didn't I?' Anna protested, feeling like a child again.

'I'm scared to see,' Muriel said quietly.

'Don't watch then. I'll find the right bit, see if there's anything helpful. You can make your mind up if you want to know afterwards.'

For a moment Muriel looked confused, but then she straightened and agreed it would be better if Anna checked first. She backed out of the room.

Anna went to the beginning of the recorded footage. She watched minute after minute of the infrared grey-white, non-moving image of the front door. Then, with the time showing at 2.13 a.m., Anna noticed a shift in brightness. A torchlight on the door? She sat forwards, her heart racing at the thought she was about to see someone. The person who'd been leaving the doll's parts, leaving the notes. She held her breath as a dark figure approached the door.

A gloved hand reached up, steadying what must be the doll's body, as the other hand pushed something against it. They didn't appear to have a hammer; it must just be a pin. But Anna's attention had left the gloved hands. It was focused on the hooded figure. She'd known she wouldn't be able to tell the identity of the Knock, Knock player – they would've been prepared and covered themselves as much as possible. But

Anna *could* distinguish their build, as she'd hoped would be the case.

And Anna was certain she was not watching Billy Cawley at her door.

She rewound the footage and watched again, and again.

It was a woman, she was sure.

Had Muriel been right all along? Was it Eliza Cawley – Lizzie?

The woman had reached up quite high to pin the body to the door. Maybe that would indicate how tall she was.

Anna rushed down the stairs and flung the door open, revealing the torso. Polly's torso. It had only been attached with a large pin, no nail this time. To ensure she and Muriel *couldn't* hear her this time? Had the unidentified woman seen, or known, about the camera too?

'I've checked the camera footage, Mum.' Anna walked into the lounge, the torso in her hand.

'And?' Muriel turned and her face fell as she noticed what Anna was holding. 'Oh.'

'It's a woman. It's not Billy doing this to you.'

Muriel seemed to shrink a little. Relief relaxed her face. 'That's something. But why? Why is a woman doing this? Unless I was right, that Lizzie can't be trusted, that it's *her* and she's the one who wanted revenge for her dad.'

'It's a possibility. We have to work on the assumption it is her for now, I think. She did seem particularly upset at finding out how you and Nell had recorded her confession. And she was very keen on pushing the attention onto Tina.'

'Tina? How come? You never told me that.'

'Only just happened, I haven't had a chance to discuss it with you. Lizzie thinks there's some kind of Stepford wives thing going on in Mapledon – that the monthly meetings the women had were in some way the key to the bad goings-on in the village. Key to getting her father put into prison.'

'That's absurd,' Muriel said. 'The more you say, the more I'm certain it's her. She's a very damaged young woman, Anna. You need to be careful there.'

'I will. Anyway, let's see what this torso has for us.' Anna pushed two fingers inside the hollow – through the hole where a leg should go – and pulled out a piece of folded paper. She was about to put the body on the table, when something else caught her eye. 'There's something else in this one.'

'Oh, now what?' Muriel sounded deflated.

Anna *had* expected something in addition to the doll's body, something significant being that it was the anniversary, but still she felt a surge of panic. Her fingers shook as she grasped the small, round item and pulled it clear. She stared at the cloth-covered ball sitting in the palm of her hand.

'Open it,' Muriel said. Her voice had lost all power. She was scared. Which scared Anna.

She carefully unravelled the small parcel. Anna sucked in her breath as she realised what she was holding.

'Shit!' Anna breathed. Muriel didn't chastise her language use. Anna sensed she was thinking the same. 'How? Why?' Anna couldn't order her thoughts.

In her hand lay a small, silver, heart locket on a dainty chain. And they both knew whose it was.

Neither of them looked at the other.

'The note might explain,' Anna whispered.

'No! Don't read it!' Muriel lurched forwards, grappling to take the paper from the table. Anna was quicker.

'God, Mum! Why? We may as well – and actually we *need* to. We have to know who had this and why? Not to mention, *how*?'

Muriel's face contorted. Tears escaped her screwed-up eyes. Anna's chest tightened. What the hell was this reaction?

'Don't, Anna. It'll be lies, rubbish. Just like everything else. No good can come—'

'Of digging up the past. Yeah, I know. You and Nell have been very keen on telling me that. You are both hiding something

– don't think I don't know. Now, come on. It's time for the truth to surface.'

Muriel shook her head, tears still spilling down her face.

Was Anna about to find out what Muriel had done? *She* obviously thought it was all about to come out. That's why she didn't want Anna to read the note.

With her eyes watching her mother carefully, Anna unfolded the paper.

SOMEONE HAS TO CONFESS, NOW!

Anna was about to shout, to say how this was a repeat of the note found in the leg. But the words continued.

Anna's legs weakened. Her arm felt heavy – she dropped her hand to her side, the note falling from it. Muriel slowly bent down to retrieve it. She read it, then reached a hand out to Anna.

'Darling, I'm sorry.'

Anna stared, open-mouthed. It didn't make sense. The words were wrong. She must've misread them. She snatched the paper from her mother's hand and looked again.

No. She hadn't been mistaken. She read the words aloud this time.

'AND THAT SOMEONE IS YOU, BELLA.'

Chapter Eighty

2019

Lizzie

'I think you need to go back a few steps. Tell me from the beginning.'

'You got all night?' Billy smiled, weakly.

'I've got however long it takes,' Lizzie said. She took her mobile phone and tapped out a text to Dom. There was no service, as expected, but he'd hopefully get it before he had time to really worry about her. Then she set her phone to record, placing it on the small, square, melamine table in front of them.

Billy closed his eyes, sighing deeply. 'It's odd. I've kept this inside for thirty years. Almost as long as *I* was inside. It feels wrong, almost, to speak of it again now. Maybe I should let sleeping dogs lie.'

'But what good will that do? If you're innocent, like you say, then someone else is guilty. Why should they get away with it?'

'I don't expect you to understand, Eliza.'

'Can you call me Lizzie, please?'

'Sure. Seems no one wants to be themselves anymore. Maybe I should change my name too.'

'I think you should, actually. Anyway, enough stalling. I want to hear your side. I need to know. I realise it must be difficult for you to talk about it all these years later, but it's important to me to know the truth. Don't you think I deserve it? And Tina Hayes? That poor woman has been suffering terribly, wondering where her girl is.'

At the mention of Tina, Lizzie noticed Billy's face lose its colour. She'd been right. When she'd seen how close they were standing in the photo, she'd known there was more to them than anyone else knew. It was her name that now seemed to be the magic word to get Billy Cawley to begin his story.

'Right. Okay. So, Muriel Fisher started it. The whole campaign to drive me from the village came from her. She was the force behind it all. At first, I thought her heart was in the right place. You were a strange child.' Billy looked into her eyes, putting his head to one side. 'Sorry, but it's true. Not that it was your fault . . .'

'It's fine. I get it. Go on,' Lizzie said.

'I think she saw the damage inside you before I really understood it. But instead of looking for the real reason, she assumed I was . . . abusing you . . .' He struggled to say the words. 'Once she'd got that notion in her head, there was no stopping her. She looked for evidence of it, but when she didn't find any, she decided to make it up instead. I'd already given her the ideal background – you know the kids of the village had decided I was a weirdo and hounded me?'

'Yes. I don't have any memory of it, but I heard all about the Knock, Knock, Ginger games and how you were always the main target.'

'Yes, and after a while – bearing in mind I was grieving and a mess – I gave in to it and played along.'

'What do you mean?'

'It got so tiring, the constant banging on my door, the stones thrown at the windows. The copper wasn't going to do anything – the kids outran that fat bugger every time.'

'Pat Vern? He's with Tina Hayes now,' Lizzie said.

'Yeah, I know.' Billy shrugged. 'Anyway, I thought if I couldn't beat the little shits, I may as well have some fun with them. So, I began chasing them myself. Ran after them down the cul-de-sac screaming blue murder, threatening to give them a hiding they'd never forget. Hearing them scream like babies gave me an element of satisfaction. Sometimes I'd have a giggle when I got back home, puffed out and red-faced. Those ended up being the only times I ever laughed!'

'But it added to your scary persona. Reinforced everyone's belief you were a weirdo and the kids should be afraid of you. All it did was make you more of a target because you became a challenge. If a kid could get close to the bungalow – or even inside – it gave them greater kudos with their mates.'

'Exactly. Which all came back to bite me on the arse when Jonie Hayes went missing.' Billy leant forwards, resting his clasped hands on his thighs. 'She'd been one of the kids who'd regularly played Knock, Knock. Her and the *liar*.'

'The liar?'

'Yeah. The one who told the police what she saw that day.'

'Bella Fisher.'

'Yep – the bitch's daughter.'

'She gave the description of your truck, which was easily recognisable to everyone around here, and told the police she'd seen Jonie get into it and you drive away. Out of the village.'

'That's what she said, yes. But the girl lied, Lizzie. She had to have done.'

'But they found DNA evidence in your truck?'

'Oh, you mean the *planted* evidence? Yes, well. What they found was a piece of clothing, a dress, with blood on it. They may as well have set the dogs on me there and then. No one in the village even waited to find out whose it was. And it just so happened that it was Eliza's—*your* dress. It was *my* blood. But instead of them thinking "Oh, we were wrong", that piece of so-called evidence seemed to be the final nail in the coffin. If I could hurt you, I could hurt Jonie Hayes. They thought I'd taken her to replace my daughter. To replace you. To do to her what they always thought I did to you. But I never touched you. As I say, the blood was mine. You hit out at me several times. You acted so oddly, you actually scared me. I put it down to the shock of losing your mother. It was more than that, but I didn't have the chance to find out. Because that fucking bitch manipulated you into telling social that I did stuff to you. Hideous stuff. Unthinkable. It destroyed me.'

'Yes, I know about that now. Muriel confessed.'

'It wasn't me though. I wasn't the one abusing you.'

Lizzie frowned. 'Meaning what? You think I *was* abused?'

'Oh, yes. I know it.'

'Who? Who did it? Do you know?'

'I have my suspicion – I'll get to that later. But, like everything else in that fucked-up place, the villagers hid it. They looked after their own. *I* was the obvious culprit. They didn't bother looking elsewhere. I was set up for that, then they pinned Jonie on me, too. On the outsider who had nothing left to lose.'

'How, though? I get you'd built a bit of a reputation, which was then reinforced with me being taken away, but to be charged with abduction and *murder*? I don't understand how anyone could've achieved it.'

'A lot was circumstantial. Even the dress – which they later found out was yours – and the blood, which was mine, wouldn't have held up in court. But a little girl's witness statement to the police, one detailing my vehicle and saying how I'd chased her and her friend Jonie, how I'd then grabbed Jonie and bundled her into the truck – well, they listened to that, and they believed it. Because I didn't have an alibi – or rather no one would admit to seeing me anywhere else at that specific time – this was deemed the key evidence. And when the police searched the bungalow . . . that's when they found it.'

'What?'

'Her necklace. They said I must've taken it as a trophy.'

Chapter Eighty-One

1989

Fisher residence

Wednesday 19th July – the day of, 7 p.m.

'Is Bella home with you?'

'Yes, Tina. She's been home for a while,' Muriel said. Would Tina note the shake in her voice over the phone?

'And Jonie isn't with her? *Was* she with her? Can you ask her?'

'Calm down, love,' Muriel said lightly. 'Yes, she was with her earlier – they were playing that *stupid* game over at Blackstone again. But Bella said she got fed up and convinced Jonie to go into the village park instead.'

'So, she left Jonie at the park? Is that the last place she saw her?'

'I'm not sure, Tina. I'm sorry. She was upset when she got back – I think Jonie went off on her own. Bella hasn't said much since.'

'For God's sake. Where the hell *is* she?'

'Maybe she went to another friend's house – have you tried everyone?'

'Not yet. I rang you first because I assumed she'd be with Bella.'

Muriel could hear the tears thickening Tina's voice. Her heart stuttered; her mind went blank. She couldn't think of the right thing to say.

'I'm going to ring off now then,' Tina said. 'Try others. Can you speak to Bella again please? She might have forgotten something. Maybe Jonie told her where she was going.'

'Will do. Keep me posted.' Muriel hung up and turned to Bella. 'It's okay,' she said. Bella's red-rimmed eyes were stark against her milky-white face. Muriel put her arms around her. 'Don't worry. It'll be all right.'

Bella's sobs were muffled in Muriel's shirt. Muriel squeezed her eyes tight, willing her own tears not to come. She had to be strong.

Everyone would need her to be strong.

After a few minutes, Bella pulled away from Muriel's chest. 'Where's Dad?'

'He went to look for Jonie.'

'Oh.' Bella looked thoughtful. 'Did he go to where I said?'

'Yes, love. He left as soon as you told us where you'd last been.'

'When will he be back?'

'I don't know, Bella. I expect he'll call on the others to help too. He'll be as long as he needs to be.'

'Until he gets Jonie back? I want her to come home now, Mum.'

Muriel looked down at Bella, cupping her face in her hands. She couldn't head off her own tears any longer.

'Whatever it takes, my darling girl.'

Chapter Eighty-Two

2019

Anna

Friday 19th July

'Confess to what? What the hell did *I* do?' Anna slumped into the chair. 'Mum? Why did you say you were sorry? Because I'm getting the bloody blame for something *you* did?'

'I'm sorry,' she said again. Muriel had her head bowed.

'Why can't you even look at me? What did you do, Mum?'

'I did what I felt I had to do.' Muriel's voice was void of emotion. Dead. Anna could feel her anger rising and tightening in her chest – sticking there like a hot lava ball. It was typical that Anna would now have to suffer for her mother's high-drama antics from thirty years ago.

'What have you dragged me into here? For Christ's sake, Mother – I've got Carrie to think of. Being here all week away from my daughter has been bad enough. But now I find you've been keeping things from me, and probably knew the whole time what this fucking Knock, Knock game was all about – and don't you dare chastise me for swearing, I have every right – but somehow it's *me* who needs to confess? *Me* who this person wants to seek some kind of revenge on? How is that fair?' Anna ran out of breath.

Her head was swimming with false knowledge, with disjointed memories – with an anger she realised now had been germinating for a long time. Whatever had happened in Mapledon all those years ago, whatever lies had been told, whatever truths buried – Anna knew her mother was behind them all. And now Anna was going to pay the price. This woman who'd been leaving the doll's parts, the notes, clearly believed it to be Anna who needed punishing.

What was next?

'Dad,' Anna said. A sudden, clear memory shot into her brain. 'He was late home the day Jonie went missing. I remember you asking him why he was late. But then he left again. I was upset at the time, didn't think about it. Where had he been and where did he go?'

'I don't remember.'

'Yes. You do.' Anna stood up, walked into the lounge and began pacing. 'The necklace.' Anna frowned, then went to the dining table to retrieve the small cloth ball that had been stuffed in the doll's torso. She walked back in, coming to a stop in front of Muriel. 'It was found in Billy Cawley's bungalow. It was one of the key pieces of evidence, apart from my witness statement.'

Muriel stared unresponsively at Anna.

'I had an identical necklace. I remember Jonie's dad giving them to us at a barbecue that summer. He said he'd got the same ones for the "terrible twins". But I don't remember anyone ever mentioning that when the necklace was found in Billy Cawley's place.' Anna took the silver necklace from the cloth, shoving it in Muriel's face.

'It wasn't your necklace they found,' Muriel said, taking a step back. 'So, there was no need to mention it.'

'How do you know that, though?'

'Because you had yours, obviously.'

'But I didn't.' Anna shook her head. 'I can't remember ever seeing it again after Jonie went missing.'

'Well, your memory of that time has always been hazy – you said it yourself. You just can't *remember* having it. But you did.'

'No . . .' Anna said, her mind now in overdrive. 'You took mine, didn't you?' A sudden and shocking realisation hit her. A dizzy sensation swept over her. 'Did you make Dad put it inside Billy's bungalow so the police would suspect Billy of taking Jonie?' The accusation sounded incredulous, even though she was the one saying the words. She prayed she was wrong.

'But Billy *did* take her, Anna. You saw him with your own eyes.' There was a pleading in her mother's voice. Anna's skin turned to gooseflesh, her mind awash with snippets of conversation, a collage of images – none of which made sense in this moment.

And her mother had not denied her accusation.

Chapter Eighty-Three

2019

Lizzie

Armed at last with what she truly believed was the correct story, Lizzie reversed her car back out of the farm and sped through the lanes towards Mapledon. It was late, the night closing in quickly around her now the sun had set. She'd listened intently for hours to what Billy Cawley – her father – had to say. She felt as though she were on fire – all her synapses firing at once, her adrenaline crashing through her veins at breakneck speed. All her focus was on one thing: finally airing the dirty secrets Mapledon had been hiding for thirty years; hanging the villagers involved in the cover-up out to dry. She'd felt the darkness the moment she'd driven into Mapledon six days ago. Then she'd questioned accounts, delved into the background of the story, as well as the inhabitants of the Stepford wives' community – and now she had answers.

But she couldn't carry this off alone; she needed help. Someone to be a witness.

As soon as she got to the outskirts of the village, she stopped to make a call while she still had signal. The recipient didn't seem surprised to hear from her, even giving her some further important information. Nothing else could shock her now. They'd agreed to meet Lizzie at the suggested location. Her phone pinged with notifications. Dom had tried calling and had texted her seven times. Lizzie quickly hammered out a reply, a brief explanation. Then she started the car again and turned in to Mapledon.

Chapter Eighty-Four

1989

The Mapledon Meeting

Thursday 20th July – the day after

'Thank you for coming. I know the timing seems . . . difficult. But actually it couldn't be better. We can do something to help. Something positive,' Muriel said.

'Like what, though, Muriel? Jonie's missing, the police haven't found any trace of her. We were out last night combing the village, the moorland on the outskirts – and nothing. What more can we do?' Allison, Councillor Furlong's wife, said.

'We can make sure whoever did this doesn't get away with it! Come on – we all know who's responsible, let's not make any bones about it. Billy Cawley took her and whatever he's planning to do with her, we can assume it's not good. We know what he did to his own daughter . . .'

The women, all fifteen of them, began mumbling between themselves. Muriel and Nell exchanged glances.

'Ladies, ladies, quieten down a moment. This is important. Muriel has brought this meeting forward for good reason,' Nell said.

'Thank you, Nell.' Muriel stood up in front of the women. 'We need to come up with a plan.'

'To do what?'

Muriel sighed, rolling her eyes dramatically. 'To make sure the police get him, obviously.'

'How? We don't have any evidence he took her, Muriel.' Wendy, one of the members who was usually very compliant, shook her head and the noise started up again, a loud buzz of conversation filling the lounge.

'Well, that's where you're wrong!' Muriel raised her voice.

The women all stopped their chatter and stared at Muriel.

'If you have evidence, why haven't you told the police already?' Allison asked.

'Tomorrow. I'm taking her tomorrow.'

Nell stood up and went to the lounge door.

'What's going on? Taking who?' another woman piped up.

'Come in, sweetie, it's okay.' Nell grabbed Bella's hand and pulled her inside the room and positioned her next to Muriel.

'As you are aware, my daughter is best friends with Jonie. And she was with her.' Muriel smiled at Bella, stretching her arm out to embrace her. 'Good girl, it's going to be fine. Don't worry,' Muriel whispered in her ear before turning to address the women. 'She was in shock. She wasn't able to tell me until just before you arrived. Bella, darling. Just tell them what you told me.'

Bella began to cry, and Muriel squeezed her shoulder tighter. 'It's fine. Go on,' she said more firmly.

'I – me and Jonie . . .' Her bottom lip trembled. 'We were playing all afternoon . . .' She snivelled and wiped the back of her hand across her nose. 'Knock, Knock Ginger. As usual. He chased us.' Her voice rose. 'We got away, but Jonie thought it was funny and wanted to do it again.' Bella paused, her eyes looking to Muriel.

'Go on, tell them what happened next.'

'I— ca . . . can't,' Bella sobbed and broke away from Muriel's grip, running out of the room. Her footsteps crashed loudly as

317

she bolted up the stairs. Her bedroom door slammed shut moments later.

'She's distraught, poor thing. It's taken ages for her to open up – she's barely uttered a word until now; my darling Bella was traumatised and in deep shock,' Muriel said, accentuating the word 'deep'. 'I can't get her to speak to the police just yet – she'll freak out. And she was witness to it, so her statement will be important; she has to get it right first time.'

'What did she see, Muriel?'

A hushed silence fell on the room.

Muriel allowed the pause to stretch before answering. 'Bella saw Jonie getting into Billy's truck.'

'Christ! Is she sure?' Wendy said.

'Of *course* she's sure. That truck's not exactly common, is it? She knows what she saw.'

'Then you have to let the police know *now*, Muriel. You can't waste time with this. He might be doing awful things to poor little Jonie as we speak and there's already been too much time wasted.' The women all muttered their agreement with Allison's statement.

'I know, I know. But I have to protect my daughter too, don't you see? This could ruin the rest of her life. She feels so guilty that she left her best friend when she needed her most, running away in fright and not telling anyone what she saw. I can't allow her to come to harm because she was in shock and afraid. I won't have people saying it's her fault. I won't let that happen, do you hear me? And anyway, *we* are the adults. *We* will take care of this. The village will pull together as it always does. And it'll get through this.'

'If it's not a good outcome, Muriel, then I don't think it'll be so easy for Tina Hayes to get through it.'

'I get your point, Wendy,' Muriel sighed loudly. 'I'll talk to Pat Vern after the meeting, give him a heads-up so he can start looking at the right person. But, Wendy?'

'What?'

'Remember you're a member of the Mapledon community, and you're part of these meetings. You know we work for the good of the whole village. Don't forget that.'

'I suggest we keep a few of the more productive – and *faithful* – members here after the others have gone, Muriel?' Nell whispered when the others were all talking among themselves.

'You're right. We'll make a proper plan then.' Muriel spoke quickly before moving on to the next item on the agenda, and the room once again became quiet.

'How did the meeting go? Did you come to an agreed plan of action?' Eric asked as they climbed into bed.

'Yes. We've agreed. I'll take Bella into the station tomorrow,' Muriel said. She kept her eyes averted, not able to look at her husband.

'Mark's destroyed. Tina is going mad with worry. I'm not sure I can handle it.'

'You have to, Eric. What's done is done. You should've thought of the consequences before, shouldn't you?'

'Likewise, Muriel. Likewise.'

Chapter Eighty-Five

2019

Anna

Friday 19th July

'I'll make us a Horlicks,' Muriel said, her voice bright and breezy as though they hadn't been sitting in complete silence, neither making eye contact, for the last few hours. Muriel had said nothing following Anna's accusation. Having thought about it, Anna now felt sure her dad would never have agreed to plant fake evidence to ensure blame was placed on an innocent man. Her mother wasn't *that* persuasive; he would've stood up to her. Wouldn't he?

'What time is it?' Anna asked.

'It must be late.' Muriel walked into the kitchen. 'Nine-twenty,' she called.

Anna was exhausted. Mentally and physically. If she could go to bed now, she would. But she knew she wouldn't sleep. And the uneasy feeling the day wasn't over – that there was still far more to come – hung around her, loitering like a malevolent force waiting for the right moment to release its devastation.

'Okay. Sure,' she said.

Muriel came back into the lounge ten minutes later with a drink in each hand and set them down on the coffee table.

'Can you grab another coaster, Anna? They're on the dresser.'

Anna reached across and took one of the old coasters – they'd bought them on a family daytrip to Looe, in Cornwall, a lifetime ago – and as she did, she remembered the letters that had been in the top drawer. She hadn't had the opportunity to search her mother's room, and with everything else going on, she'd almost forgotten about them. But now, concerned her dad might've been involved in getting Billy sent to prison, the content of those letters was even more significant. If they *were* from Eric, of course. Even if they weren't, there was a reason Muriel was keeping them, and the fact she'd hidden them from Anna was a firm indication they were linked to what was going on now. To what went on back then.

'Here you go,' Anna said, placing the mat down and popping the mug onto it. 'Mum?' She waited for her mother's attention. 'When I arrived last Saturday, you asked me to get a notepad from the top drawer.' Anna pointed to the dresser. 'I saw a bundle of old letters in there.' She watched for Muriel's reaction.

'Yes, don't know why I keep such things. Terrible hoarder,' she said, shrugging.

'Who were they from?'

'You always were a nosy one,' Muriel said, taking a sip from her drink.

'No. I really wasn't, Mum.' Anna knew her mother was stalling. Not wanting to divulge the author of the letters. 'They're from my dad, aren't they?'

'No, no. Just a pen friend. Goodness, your father would never put pen to paper.'

'I don't believe you.' Anna could no longer bother with the nicey-nicey, drawn-out approach she'd been taking with her mother. 'Show me.'

'I – I shredded them. They were taking up too much space . . .'

'When did you do that?'

321

'Oh, I don't remember. The other day, when you were next door with Sandie I think.'

'Really?' Anna got back up from the sofa and bent down in front of Muriel. 'Look at me, Mum.'

'What? What now, Anna?'

'You're lying to me. Shit. You've lied to me all my life, haven't you?'

'Of course not,' Muriel said. But there wasn't an ounce of conviction in her tone.

Anna's jaw muscles clenched; her teeth jammed together painfully. She had to keep her temper – losing it now wouldn't get her anywhere.

'I realise you've told some untruths,' Anna said, knowing she was putting it very mildly. 'And I know you're probably worried about what I'll think of you. How I'll react. But, Mum – I need to know now.' Anna took Muriel's hands in hers. 'This is getting out of hand and I'm afraid people will come to harm because of what you did, or what Dad did. Or what the villagers of Mapledon did. I realise what's done is done – we can't alter the past, but we can ensure no one else gets hurt *now*. All I want is for you to confide in me, to tell me the truth. It has to come out eventually. Whatever you did – I'll forgive you.' Anna attempted a warm, encouraging smile. She wasn't sure she *would* be able to forgive her, but she felt it's what she had to say to get Muriel to talk.

'Oh, Anna. It's all such a mess. None of us had any idea it would come to this, I promise you.' Muriel put her head in her hands.

The knot in Anna's stomach intensified. *None of us?*

'It's okay, Mum. Did your attempts to get Billy to leave Mapledon snowball? Did you *use* Jonie's disappearance to ensure you got what you wanted?' A cold sensation crept over her skin.

'It wasn't just that,' Muriel said. As she looked up, Anna saw the tears slide down her face, their path meandering through the deep wrinkles. Christ. Had her mother *caused* Jonie's disappearance?

'What else?' she asked. Her voice shook with apprehension, fearing the answer.

Muriel began shaking her head, the movements getting more and more violent.

'Mum! Stop that, you'll give yourself a headache.' Anna placed her hands either side of her mother's head to stop her.

'I'm sorry, Anna,' she said.

'What for? *Tell* me.'

Anna's phone pinged, the sharp tone making them both jump. She sighed. Couldn't be worse timing; talk about being saved by the bell. Muriel looked relieved when Anna straightened and retrieved her mobile from the arm of the sofa.

'Christ,' she breathed. She looked up at Muriel. 'Well, I get the feeling whatever you're holding back might be about to come out in the wash,' Anna said.

'Why? Who is it?' Panic spread on Muriel's face.

'It's a text from Lizzie. She says it's urgent. She wants to meet us.'

'Not now, surely? It's gone ten o'clock.'

'The text was sent an hour ago by the look of it,' Anna muttered. The damn signal in Mapledon was driving her mad. 'But yes. We have to leave now. And, Mum . . .' Anna looked directly into Muriel's watery, pale blue eyes.

'What, Anna? For goodness' sake, don't draw this out so dramatically!'

'She wants us to go to Blackstone Close. To Billy Cawley's bungalow.'

Chapter Eighty-Six

2019

Lizzie

Lizzie parked on the drive at Blackstone Close. It felt odd – particularly as the place didn't bring back many memories. She'd clearly done a very good job compartmentalising them, burying them deep inside a part of her brain where they were irretrievable. She climbed out of the car, fetching the backpack from the rear seat. Gravel crunched underfoot as she approached the front door. Billy had given her his key. He'd also given her strict instructions.

Nerves clutched at her insides as she slid the key into the lock and pushed the door. It resisted; she had to give it several hard shoves before it opened. Piles of unopened post lay wedged behind it; it was no wonder she'd struggled. She kicked most of it out of the way and took a tentative step inside – muggy air, a damp smell and dust quickly clogged her nostrils. She sneezed three times, then covered her nose with her sleeve. She flicked the nearest light switch knowing full well it wouldn't work as the electric had been switched off long ago, then continued on through the hallway. Using her spare hand to direct her mobile phone light, Lizzie headed towards the front room – the one overlooking the garden. She wanted to see the people arriving.

Lizzie hoped what she was about to do would work. Hoped Billy Cawley would finally get what he deserved.

Atonement.

Car headlamps flooded the end of the cul-de-sac, the beams of light hitting the ten-foot hedges, momentarily blinding Lizzie. The car came to a stop just outside the bungalow, across the driveway – blocking Lizzie's own car in. She guessed they'd be leaving before her, though. Then Lizzie spotted two figures walking slowly along the pavement. Cautious in their movements. Following closely behind, a further two people.

At least they had come. Lizzie was surprised – she assumed they'd be reluctant, that she'd have to work harder to get them to agree to meet her at Billy Cawley's. It seemed everyone was curious enough to want to find out what Lizzie had called them together for. She wondered how long that would that last.

How long before their curiosity gave way to anger, fear and self-preservation.

Not everyone was going to make it, Lizzie knew that. Some of the people involved with the lies, the cover-up – they would not be present: Mark Hayes was dead – Lizzie's research had revealed it to be suicide; Reverend Farnley was in a residential care home – unable to string a sentence together according to her father's ex-cell mate who'd made 'some enquiries'; Eric Fisher – he'd been AWOL since Billy Cawley's incarceration, and some villagers who'd had a part to play and had continued to allow the secrets to remain buried – they were more minor players and Lizzie hadn't bothered with them. Lizzie, and Billy himself, weren't interested in those smaller fish. Just the big players – the ones who'd lied and manipulated for their own ends.

Lizzie lit the two oil lamps she'd brought with her, then walked purposefully to the front door; she wanted to appear calm, confident and in control, however much she felt the opposite. She stood aside to let them in. Muriel and Anna. Tina Hayes and Pat Vern. Nell and Rob Andrews.

They were the chosen ones. They were the ones who'd perpetuated the lies, covered the truth and were happy to let those really responsible slip away and remain hidden. Remain guiltless in the eyes of the law.

They'd been the ones who'd been portrayed as the innocent, damaged-by-a-tragedy members of the village of Mapledon. Although there *were* some people present who were more innocent than others, each had to be present for the full story to emerge. Lizzie wanted them *all* to know.

'What's going on, Lizzie?' Rob was the first to question her, the first to even utter a word. The others were solemn, pale and twitchy. Lizzie experienced a strange buzz of satisfaction. But then, she had always troubled these people. They'd always thought Eliza Cawley strange, damaged goods. A child who repulsed them. She guessed they still felt that way, even though she didn't rip the limbs off dolls anymore.

Unless some of them believed she did, of course – and that she was the one hammering dolls to doors.

How short-sighted they'd been.

'You're all here for one reason,' Lizzie said as she ushered them into the lounge. The thick dust, the dark shadows, the smell of rot – all added to the atmosphere, made them cower just a little bit more.

'Which is?' Anna asked.

Lizzie stared at her for a moment before answering, taking in her slumped shoulders, her pinched expression. Something had altered – there was a coldness in her eyes that hadn't been there before. Hopelessness? When Lizzie had first met her, she'd felt a connection – had immediately related to her. She hadn't come across as someone with dark secrets.

'You'll see,' Lizzie said.

'This is preposterous! What is your problem, young lady?' Nell demanded. 'Stop playing games. We've better things to do with our time.' She turned and fumbled her way to the lounge door.

'I wouldn't,' Pat Vern said.

Nell turned back sharply. 'I *wouldn't*?' she repeated. 'That sounds like a threat to me, Pat?'

'No, Nell. Of course it's not.' He sounded exasperated already. 'But you need to stay. Eliza has things she wants clearing up. She deserves to hear from you, too.'

'Hear what? Look, Pat, I appreciate this must be a difficult time for Tina and you,' Nell said, pointing a finger at the silent Tina. 'But dragging up what happened to poor Jonie, without being able to bring any kind of closure, is mean. It's selfish. And Eliza – *Lizzie* – is only here to witness more distress, and to try and vindicate her abusive, murdering *bastard* of a father!'

Lizzie heard a gasp from Muriel's direction. That woman was something else. How could Muriel be so offended by a bit of bad language after what she'd done?

'Who said I couldn't offer any closure to Tina?' Lizzie said.

Shocked faces all turned to look at her.

'As I said,' Lizzie continued. 'You're here for a reason. That reason is to uncover the truth. Although I'm aware some of you *know* aspects of the truth, others only know very little of it.'

'Go on, Lizzie,' Tina said. Her voice was a small sound from the corner of the room. Lizzie nodded to her.

'Okay.' Lizzie gave a feeble smile. An attempt to soften what was to come. Some of the later revelations would hit Tina hard. She looked to Pat, who tilted his chin in acknowledgement before wrapping an arm around Tina.

'You lied, Anna,' Lizzie said as she turned, directing her mobile phone light onto Anna. Lizzie watched as Anna's face seemed to lose its shape – the muscles slackening. She wasn't enjoying seeing Anna's discomfort, but it was a necessary part of the reveal. Lizzie allowed the words to hang for a few beats, then added: 'Little Bella Fisher didn't tell the whole truth, and nothing but the truth. Did she?'

Chapter Eighty-Seven

1989

En route to Bovey Police Station

Friday 21st July – 36 hours after Jonie Hayes' disappearance

Muriel took the narrow roads slowly to avoid the Dartmoor ponies and to allow her time to pull in for any cars coming from the opposite direction. And to give her time to go over the script with Bella. She had to get it right.

'Again,' she said. 'You need to sound more confident.'

'I'm tired, I can't.'

They passed Haytor, the car juddering over a cattle grid. Bella's head banged rhythmically against the passenger window, but her blank stare never wavered.

'You must, Bella. Now, from the beginning: where were you when you first saw Billy's truck?'

She sighed. '*Fine.* Jonie and me were heading to the park, so we walked along Elmore Road, and that's when I saw Billy Cawley's truck.'

'Okay. Right, well don't *say* it's Billy's truck to begin with. *Describe* it,' Muriel coaxed.

'Red truck, yellow stripe, doll's head. Yes, mother, I've got it.'

'Don't snap at me, Bella.'

'Well, I don't want to *do it*, Mum.' Fresh tears glistened on her cheeks.

'I know, darling. But we need to. You understand, don't you?'

Bella turned her head, her eyes finding Muriel's and locking with them. 'Yes. I understand. I just wish we could go back to before. I wish we'd never started playing that stupid game. I wish I . . .'

'Enough, Bella. No point going over the *what-ifs* and the *I wishes*; there's nothing we can do to change what's happened. We can only try and fix it as best we can.'

'There's no fixing it, though, is there? Jonie's gone.' Her gaze left Muriel's and returned to the sweeping countryside, her face expressionless.

'But we can make it easier for Auntie Tina.'

Bella huffed. 'You mean easier for you and Dad.'

Muriel drove on in silence, hoping and praying her ten-year-old daughter would come good once she was in the police station.

Their future depended on it.

Chapter Eighty-Eight

2019

Anna

Friday 19th July

The realisation hit Anna full force.

She hadn't seen Jonie Hayes being taken by Billy Cawley.

Her younger self – little Bella Fisher – hadn't even seen the truck where she said she had.

Everything she'd told the police had been a lie. A story her mother had tutored her to get right. A fleeting memory of rehearsing the story before going to the police station flashed through her mind.

That must have been why there'd been a delay in informing the police; why she hadn't told them what she'd seen immediately.

Because it hadn't happened.

And her mother had come up with a story that made Billy Cawley look guilty to get rid of him from the village. A story that would see her mother's agenda come to fruition.

Anna wanted to vomit.

All eyes in the room were on her, waiting for an explanation she couldn't – didn't want to – give them. Her memories were still so jumbled, she didn't trust herself to speak. Didn't believe she would be able to give any kind of accurate account after all these years.

'My memory . . . it's . . . well, it's hazy . . .' she stuttered.

'Yes, I'm sure it is. You were a kid, I get that,' Lizzie said softly. 'I'm the same. But there *are* things you do know, Anna. Things you remember; but maybe you've put those memories aside because they're not ones you care to recall. They don't fit the stories you've been told all your life. The people of Mapledon haven't done us any favours, Anna. Both of us have suffered at their hands one way or another. We were *both* manipulated. You can see that now, can't you?'

Anna's breath was coming in ragged bursts. The room was closing in; the lies smothering her. Lizzie was right, there were things she remembered, and those memories were hers, not ones she'd formed over the years due to her mother retelling the story she'd wanted Anna to take as truth.

'I can. Yes,' she said.

'Anna, stop,' Muriel cut in. She turned sharply to Lizzie. '*You* are the liar.'

'Hear, hear,' Nell piped up. 'The only reason you came here was to stir everything up for your own gain. You're a journalist – you'd try and dig up anything and manipulate it to make a good story. You're just here for the money.'

'No, you're so far from the truth it's scary.' Lizzie laughed – it sounded hollow in the sparse, dusty room.

'Really? Then why do we have evidence of you hammering your doll's limbs to my door?' Muriel stormed forwards, her finger jabbing Lizzie's chest. 'You and that evil man are playing games with us. Everyone knows you're both wrong in the head and want to make others suffer just because both of you did!'

Anna felt something give; some part of her mind gave up. Her mother was still pushing her agenda all these years later, despite the evidence now stacking up against her. Anna wanted to stop her mother from speaking, but she didn't have the energy. Let her dig herself into a bigger hole – Anna was almost past caring.

'I'm not sure what evidence you think you have – but it's not me doing it,' Lizzie said. 'Did you fabricate that evidence too, Muriel?'

'You're talking nonsense. And I have *real* proof – I caught you on the security camera Anna set up to watch the front door,' she said, her voice filled with smugness.

'Ah. I see,' Lizzie said.

Anna felt her body slacken. Her mother was running with it, but she was wrong. She'd realised Lizzie was too tall after standing on the doorstep and re-enacting the woman's stretch to pin the doll's torso to the door – it couldn't have been Lizzie caught on the camera – it was someone shorter.

'I'm glad you have that footage, Muriel,' Lizzie said. 'As it will prove my innocence – just as I'm here now to prove my father's. The woman who's been playing her version of Knock, Knock, Ginger isn't me. It's her.' Lizzie raised her hand, pointing her finger. Anna followed it, her gaze landing on Tina Hayes.

Chapter Eighty-Nine

2019

Lizzie

'Go on, Tina. Now's your chance to explain,' Lizzie said.

Pat Vern released his arm from around Tina's shoulders as she moved forwards. He'd told Lizzie he suspected it was Tina who was playing the macabre game. When he'd talked to Lizzie on the phone earlier, he'd confided how he'd been noticing changes in Tina over the past few years. How he'd watched as she had become more and more angry, yet subdued at the same time – not going out as much, becoming more introspective and withdrawing from friends and social gatherings. She'd stopped going to church a long time ago, but she'd still been involved in many village events – yet the last ten months in particular had seen her drop out of everything. Instead, she'd become obsessed with Jonie's case again. Returning to all the old clippings she'd kept from the time of her disappearance and from Billy Cawley's trial. Pat said she was convinced everyone had got it all wrong.

That Billy Cawley was innocent after all.

'It was all so obvious I can't believe it took me all those years to *see* it; to piece it all together,' Tina said. Her head bobbed as though it were too heavy to keep upright. 'God, this village. You're all so good at hiding things, aren't you?'

She stared at each of the people in the room in turn. 'Good at misdirection, too. You even had *me* thinking Billy was an abuser, someone to be fearful of. Even though I *felt* differently.' Tina banged her hand against her heart. 'I knew Billy wasn't capable of the terrible things you all accused him of. Deep down, I knew. But I allowed you all to persuade me otherwise. God, I even asked Pat to do a background search, check him out because you all thought there was something bad in him.' Tina stepped back and took hold of Pat's hand. 'You did so much to help me, Pat. You always went above and beyond and I'm grateful for that.'

'And Pat didn't find anything untoward, did he?' Lizzie said.

'Nothing. And that's when I began to pull back a little from the Mapledon Meetings, because I didn't want to be part of the baying wolves eager to attack Billy anymore. Billy and I had actually become close at one point – in secret, as I knew what the others would think – but I'd distanced myself again because of the things being said. The rumours. Once I realised they were unfounded, I tried to reconnect with him. Offer my support. But it seemed it was too late. And that's when my world collapsed.' Tina swiped at her cheeks, clearing the tears. 'I was distraught when Billy was accused of abducting Jonie. When Muriel told me Bella had witnessed her being taken into Billy's truck and driven away, I was furious at myself for being taken in, for believing Billy and not my friends or the villagers. I blamed myself for losing my daughter.'

A heavy silence hung in the room, and so did everyone's heads. In pity, in sadness or in shame.

'You shouldn't have blamed yourself, Tina. You were a good mum,' Anna said. Her voice sounded uncertain, and Lizzie wondered at the meaning behind the words.

Tina's gaze steadied on Anna. 'Oh, Anna. Little, naive Bella. I always welcomed you into my home; loved you coming over to play with Jonie. How could you have lied like that? *Why?*'

'She didn't lie, Tina. Leave her out of this,' Muriel said. Lizzie sensed she was about to launch into a rant, but she wouldn't allow Muriel to take control of the room.

'I've been in contact with Billy. My dad,' Lizzie said, before Muriel could continue.

'See! I knew it. You *are* both in on it.'

'Oh, shut up, Muriel,' Tina cut in. 'You've done enough damage. It's about time your daughter found out what you're capable of.'

Lizzie watched for a reaction from Anna. All she noted was shock. Did she really not know?

'Look, Lizzie – I get why you're doing this,' Rob said, taking the opportunity to step in. 'I know I upset you with what I told you the other day. But it's obvious to see this doesn't involve us directly.' Rob motioned from himself to his mum. 'You've got beef with the others; carry on without us. You don't need to drag my mother into this. She's done nothing wrong.'

'And I get why you're doing *this*, Rob,' Lizzie countered. 'You're one of them, an insider. And you protect your own. Especially when it's your own mother in the firing line. I understand. But it can't keep going on. This hideous lie has been allowed to fester for far too long. Maybe you don't know what really happened. It's possible you're as in the dark as I was.'

'You're delusional, love,' Nell said.

'No. I think you lot have the monopoly on that.' Anger and bitterness encased Lizzie's words. It was becoming harder to remain calm. These people were horrible, an abomination. 'I said when you arrived, you're ALL here for a reason, no one is leaving until we've heard the truth.'

'You can't keep us here, we're free to leave whenever we want.'

'Sure – I'm not taking you hostage, if that's what you think. But then, everyone here is already a hostage.'

No one disagreed. Everyone stayed in the room; their own

curiosity, guilt and stubbornness keeping them there. Even Rob.

'Carry on then, let's get this charade over with,' he said. His face belied his words. He knew where this was going, Lizzie realised. He was as defeated as the others, knowing whatever was coming would likely tear the fabric of the village's carefully constructed image apart.

'Tell me what made you realise you'd been right all along, Tina,' Lizzie asked.

'Billy did. He wrote to me while he was in prison. Told me everything.'

'How can you believe the man who murdered your daughter?'

'Stop now, Muriel. Stop,' Tina said. She gave a half-smile. 'Please drop the pretence. It's over. Don't you understand? You did what you felt you had to do to protect yourself and your family. Now you need to own up to your mistakes. I believed, and do believe, Billy. Because everything he said made sense. I stepped outside of myself, this village, and looked in from a different viewpoint. And like I said, it was obvious then.'

'What was?' Rob asked.

'Who was really responsible for Jonie's disappearance. Who'd carefully planned a scapegoat, who'd orchestrated the entire thing. Who had planted the fake evidence. Who had tidied up, covered up, and hidden the *real* evidence.'

'I'm guessing the answer is Muriel, then.' Rob sounded as though he was disappointed with Tina's reasoning.

'Muriel did all of those things, yes,' Tina said.

'This is ridiculous. I'm not listening to more of this garbage.' Muriel reached for the door, pulling it open, but Pat reached over the top of her, slamming it closed.

'But not alone.' Tina put her hand up to silence everyone. 'Muriel wasn't the one who did it all.'

'It was my dad,' Anna said. But her words were lost in the echo of the door banging.

'Say again, Anna?' Lizzie asked. She wanted Anna to say the words loud and clear.

'It was Eric, my dad, wasn't it?' Anna repeated more confidently. 'He was the one who broke in here and planted the necklace. It was mine, not Jonie's; we had identical ones.'

Chapter Ninety

2019

Eric

It was his day of reckoning.

Eric had known it would come one day. But knowing it didn't stop his guts from turning to liquid now. Didn't prevent the paralysis of his lungs, the gripping pain in his heart. Maybe he'd die right here, now. Save him from a fate far worse.

He couldn't really complain, though. He'd lived his life as he'd seen fit, enjoying years of freedom he didn't deserve. Years of over-indulgence: women, drink, food. He hadn't held back, never knowing how much time he had left.

Not long now, he guessed.

He turned, sensing someone behind him: the hairs on his neck bristled, standing erect in anticipation.

Was this it?

He clutched his chest; tried to catch his breath.

No one was there.

Not yet.

But there would be. Soon.

His time was running out.

Chapter Ninety-One

2019

Anna

She wasn't sure why she felt so shell-shocked. Before the text from Lizzie earlier, she'd been waiting for her mother to come clean – admit her father had been the one writing the letters, admit he'd planted the fake evidence to further implicate Billy. The Fishers had well and truly set the poor man up. Anna was responsible for the false witness testimony, her father responsible for the fake evidence; her mother was responsible for manipulating the entire heart-breaking episode so she could get her own way.

All to get Billy out of Mapledon because she thought him a risk to their tight-knit community – a risk to their kids. And it turned out he wasn't either of those things. He was merely someone who didn't 'fit' into her mother's ideals. Didn't measure up to her expectations, her standards. Muriel had made her mind up that Billy Cawley didn't belong and that was that.

But if Billy was innocent, who was really responsible for Jonie going missing?

'I'm not sure I'm understanding all of this,' Anna said. 'If we're to believe Billy's account, he was wrongly accused of abduction and murder – framed for it by my mother, and even my dad. But none of it brings us to a conclusion about what happened to Jonie. Where was she taken? By who?'

Muriel rushed forwards, embracing Anna in her wiry-thin arms. 'I'm sorry, love. I'm so sorry.'

Anna pushed away. 'Why?' She looked at the faces in the room. Her gaze settled on Tina's. 'Were you doing this thing with the dolls because my mum and dad planted the evidence?'

'Partly, yes,' Tina admitted.

'Partly?'

'And to point you in the right direction.' Tina said.

'So, the severed doll's limbs were for me, to get me to figure out my parents were involved in a crime?' Anna still felt confused.

'They *were* committing a crime – several in fact – and they made you complicit too. Something you seem to have conveniently forgotten.'

'I was a *child*, Tina.' Anna's face was hot, her skin prickly with an uncomfortable warmth.

'Yes, I get you were just a child yourself,' Tina said. 'I understand your memories were clouded, thwarted and then manipulated by Muriel.' Tina shot Muriel an icy glance. 'I'm not a mean person, Anna. Bitter, yes, angry too. From the beginning, when I believed your mother's lies, it was hard to forgive the fact you didn't go to the police station immediately. It ate away at me, knowing those lost hours had been vital – Jonie might've been found alive if only you'd acted straight away. It's the reason your mother and I grew apart. My inability to let it go, coupled with my resentment that it was my girl not hers that was taken, meant I had to step back from the friendship. But over the years – and by talking things through with Pat, and then Billy himself – I've come to realise I have to be gentle, almost, with you, at least. Allow you to come to the right conclusions slowly, in your own time. Well, with a little help.'

'Pretty big shove, I'd say,' Anna said. 'Torn-off doll's parts, cryptic clues, blood-filled bags on the doormat.'

'They weren't just for you, they were for Muriel too. To let her know.'

'Know what?'

'That I had learned the truth. I left the other clues too, so she was sure. Not only the notes but the necklace, the torn, bloody clothing . . .'

'What clothing? There wasn't any.' Anna frowned.

'No, I took that when you weren't looking,' Lizzie said. She'd been keeping quiet while Muriel, Anna and Tina had been talking.

'Oh. Why?'

'I thought it was significant to me. I thought it was *all* for me, seeing as it was my doll, Polly. And the material looked like a part of my dress, the one I had when I was eight. I thought if you saw it you'd never believe it wasn't Billy doing it.'

'Yes, Lizzie, it was yours. Or rather it was like it – just as the doll had been almost identical to the one you used to own,' Tina said. 'Your dad told me about how the dress had been found in his truck and seized as evidence. I searched for a close match on the internet, tore a piece from it and stained it with red food colouring. I remember Muriel telling the women at the Mapledon Meeting about it. She'd seen Eliza in it one day, noticed the bloodstains – jumped to her usual wrong conclusion. She'd no idea the blood was Billy's of course; she assumed it was Eliza's. And she wouldn't have known if it had been washed or thrown out in the time between Eliza being taken by social and Jonie being killed. But she'd remembered it and knew it would look bad for Billy – add to the public's perception he was an evil child killer once the news was out – so she found it and got one of the local boys to pop the lock on Billy's truck and stuff it inside before Bella gave the police her witness statement. Knowing they would search his truck first.'

'The local boy being?' Lizzie asked.

'I thought I was doing something good, for Eliza,' Rob said. 'That's why I agreed to do it.'

'Robert! Don't say another word,' Nell said.

'It's fine, Mum. You don't need to protect *me*,' he said. 'Muriel told me what Billy had done to Eliza, the abuse he'd inflicted on her and because of what had happened . . .' Rob's face flushed. 'Anyway, I knew Eliza had been hurt, so I wanted to help. Make sure Billy was punished. I didn't realise until years later I'd been lied to.'

'You don't even know how to break into a vehicle, Robert – don't be so stupid. You were only nine.' Nell's eyes were wide. Hadn't she known Muriel had asked for her son's help?

'Yep, and I'd been breaking in and out of the shop for months, Mother. Picking the locks was easy, so I didn't think the truck would be too hard. And as it was, it was unlocked anyway. But I didn't tell anyone that because I wanted to appear tough.'

'God, so you got everyone involved in this? How did you keep it all from Tina and Mark?' Anna looked straight at Muriel, but then jumped in again, answering her own question. 'Oh, hang on, don't tell me. Let me guess. *For the good of the community.* You told everyone who was complicit in the lies they had to stay quiet, close ranks, because Mapledon looks after their own. The real villagers, not the outsiders.'

'Something like that,' Muriel mumbled.

'Look, can we get back to the main point,' Rob said, his tone frustrated. 'Why would Eric plant evidence? It seems a pretty drastic thing to do to pin an abduction on Billy just to finally get rid of him from the village. Didn't Eric realise by doing that it allowed the *real* abductor to get away with it? There'd have been zero chance of Jonie being found alive – the police would've stopped looking once they had someone for it. How the hell could you have let that happen, Muriel?'

'Exactly, Rob. How could she?' Tina said.

343

'There was no abductor, was there, Muriel?' Lizzie said. 'There was no rush to find Jonie Hayes because she was dead from day one.'

All eyes were squarely on Muriel Fisher.

'Only one way she could know that, too,' Rob said.

'Yes. Because she knew who'd done it,' Lizzie said, glancing towards Anna.

'Fucking hell, Muriel,' Rob gasped. 'Knowing Jonie was already dead meant you weren't worried about the police not looking any further. You made Anna lie to them about what she'd seen to get what you wanted. Billy gone from the village.'

'But that wasn't the main reason,' Lizzie interrupted. 'Muriel ensured an innocent man got sent to prison in order to protect someone else.'

Anna felt her legs give way.

'It was Eric Fisher who murdered Jonie,' Lizzie said.

'No. No, you're wrong. My dad would never hurt anyone. Why would he?' Anna said.

'Almost everyone else in this village back then was complicit,' Muriel said, ignoring Anna's distress. 'Don't forget that when you're pointing the finger and judging me. If this gets out, me and Eric won't be the only ones to go down. You've heard of joint enterprise, aiding and abetting, accessory, perverting the course of justice and all that, I assume? We'll take you with us.'

'Jesus, Mum.' Anna's mouth gaped. 'I can't believe I'm hearing this.'

'I would say I'm sorry, Anna. But I'm not,' Tina said.

'Is this true, Mum?' Anna asked. 'Dad killed Jonie? I can't – I mean . . . it's impossible.'

Her mother said nothing. Anna wanted to launch at her, shake her until she gave answers. What reason would her father have to kill Jonie? 'Was it an accident, Mum? I assume it was an accident?'

'I'm sorry, love.'

Anna needed to know more. Every detail. But it seemed her mum had shut down for now. 'Where do we go from here, Tina? What exactly is it you want us to do?' Anna asked, all power in her voice gone.

'I just want to know where my little girl is.' Tina's face crumpled – the years of pain evident. 'I'm too tired to do anything; I'm not interested in going to the police. Billy's done his time. It's not like we can reduce the years he's lost inside a cell. But he's out now and deserves to at least know he's been vindicated, don't you think? And I deserve closure.'

'Well, Mum. You know where he is, don't you?' Anna butted in. 'Eric is the only one who can tell us where he took her. Unless, of course, you know?'

Muriel staggered backwards, her frail body hitting against the lounge wall. A few clumps of plaster dislodged and fell near her feet. 'Yes. I know where he is. No, I don't know where . . . where the body is.' She sounded dazed. Anna almost felt sorry for her. But it was brief. Her mother had lied, covered up a murder, framed an innocent man and helped the real killer get away. She understood Muriel had loved Eric, but to protect him to that level, above all else, was incomprehensible. If James had murdered a child and she knew about it, there'd be no way she'd be able to lie for him. Especially at the expense of her best friend. No wonder Tina hadn't spoken to Muriel for years. How had she waited until now to say anything?

Her mother was as evil as Eric.

'I'm so sorry, Tina,' Anna said. And she really was. Her family had inflicted so much on her. Even Anna had been involved – lying to the police about seeing Jonie get into Billy's truck. How could she have done that? She tried to remember she'd only been a child – doing as she was told. She hadn't meant for the lies to hurt people. Muriel would've made sure she'd drummed it into her – how she had to do right by her dad. Anna had loved him so much; she'd always been a daddy's girl. She knew

345

she would've done what she was asked if it meant keeping him safe. If only she'd known then that he'd up and leave her anyway.

'Yes. I'm sure you are, Bella.'

But Anna still had questions storming her mind. The important ones being: *how* and *why* had her father killed Jonie?

Chapter Ninety-Two

1989

A roadside in Mapledon

Wednesday 19th July – the day of

She was dead. There was no doubt – her pretty blue eyes were glazed, staring blindly up towards the mottled sky. A huge lump stuck out on her forehead, causing her petite face to look too big for her body. Deformed – fake, almost – like a broken doll. Panic set in, his breathing becoming fast, shallow – no oxygen was reaching his lungs.

Think, think.

There was no time for thought, only action. Someone would walk by, catch him if he weren't careful. He reached his trembling hands out, pushing them beneath her body. Her skin was cool to the touch.

Stupid, stupid man.

He frantically cast his eyes all around him. He couldn't see anyone. Would he get away with this? He lifted her – she was so light. Tears ran down his face; snot gathered on his top lip, slipping into his mouth.

What was he going to do now? Should he go to the village – own up? Say how it was an accident: she'd run out in front of his car; he didn't see her until it was too late. Tina and Mark would be distraught, but they couldn't blame him. The police couldn't blame him. Could they?

Would a post-mortem indicate otherwise?

More panic. His heart was galloping, his head swimming. He couldn't pass out now.

Come on, Eric. Sort yourself out.

What would Muriel say?

He laid Jonie Hayes' lifeless body inside the boot of his car.

Breathless, leaning against the driver's door, Eric took another good look around him. He felt certain no one had witnessed him doing it. Now all he had to do was dispose of the body.

He retched, doubling over, pain searing through his guts.

'Jesus Christ, forgive me.'

Chapter Ninety-Three

1989

Fisher residence

Wednesday 19th July – the day of, 10.15 p.m.

'It isn't how it should've been, granted. But it's happened now. You have to stay calm, Eric.'

'But what I've done . . .'

'Is done, Eric! It's okay.'

'How can you say that? How is this okay, Muriel? Are you bloody insane?'

'No. But *you're* acting like it. How can *you* turn on me? I'm protecting you. Now listen,' Muriel said. She held his hand, flipping it over and placing something on his palm. 'Take this.'

He shook his head, bemused.

'Seriously, Eric? Right – you have to go to Billy Cawley's place and get inside. Don't *break* in, or not obviously anyway. Wear gloves too – can't have your fingerprints anywhere.' Muriel's voice was harsh. 'Are you listening properly, Eric?'

'Yes, yes. Get inside, don't be seen, don't leave prints. But do leave this.'

He pointed at the necklace. 'But this is Bella's necklace, Muriel. I don't understand.'

'It's identical to Jonie's.'

'Why don't I just take Jonie's then.'

'Do you have it?' Muriel snapped.

Eric stared blankly about him for a moment. 'I thought I did . . .'

'If it turns up afterwards, this will come back to haunt us.' Muriel chewed her bottom lip. 'If Tina and Mark have it, or it's found at the scene . . . Shit, Eric. You should've been more thorough.'

'Sorry, *Muriel.* It wasn't as though I was thinking straight.'

'You weren't thinking at all.'

He bowed his head.

'For now, take Bella's and we'll search for Jonie's. Hopefully we'll find it before the police.'

'Talking of the police, what are we going to do about calling them?'

'I've got a plan that might work. I'll need some help, but I'm owed a few favours and the others will fall in when I tell them how this way we can be rid of Billy Cawley.'

'You think after they find out that they'll help us? You may be over-estimating people's belief in "the good of the community" on this one, Muriel.'

'Maybe. Maybe not. We have to try. I've already laid the groundwork, prior to *this* happening. It should work.'

'I don't think I can do this. Let me hand myself in to the police—'

'Over my dead body, Eric. Billy has had this coming to him – he's the perfect answer to our problem.'

'Don't you feel guilty?'

'I can't afford to.'

Chapter Ninety-Four

2019

Lizzie

Friday 19th July

It seemed to be going to plan. The truth was emerging as her dad had predicted. Almost in the order he'd predicted too. Lizzie gazed around in the dim light the mobile phones and two oil lamps offered. At each ashen face. She wondered what they'd look like in a minute.

'So, we've ascertained Billy Cawley is innocent of the crimes he was sentenced to, yes?' Lizzie said, her voice strong and clear. Heads nodded slowly, silently. Being in charge of this reveal gave her a bit of a kick, if she was honest. She imagined the headlines, the sensational story that would go with this scoop. *William Cawley exonerated in 30-year-old murder case. Mapledon villagers guilty of cover-up.* Lizzie slipped her hand in her jacket pocket, closing her fingers around the small, digital recorder. The last headline in her mind was one that might take more time. *Real killer discloses where he dumped 10-year-old Jonie Hayes' body.*

'Good.' Lizzie sucked in a deep breath before delivering her next line – the one she knew would get a big reaction. 'But I think you should tell Billy Cawley to his face,' Lizzie said.

Heads snapped up. Uneasy glances passed between those gathered.

The lounge door opened, and Billy walked in.

Lizzie sensed the tension in the room, noting the awkward shuffling of feet. Billy looked very different from the young man who'd left Mapledon. No longer scrawny-looking, straggly. He was stocky, muscly, hard-looking. If Lizzie didn't know better, she'd also assume he was someone to be afraid of: tough, with a ready-to-fight-anyone stance and intense, moody eyes.

'It's been a long time,' he said.

Chapter Ninety-Five

2019

Anna

All the air left her lungs.

The man she and her family had framed was standing among them. He didn't look as she'd imagined him; nothing about him resembled the images from her childhood. But she did sense the same fear she'd experienced when she'd played Knock, Knock, Ginger. She had that same urge to run away now. His solid form blocked the doorway, and even in the dim light she could see the intensity in his eyes. Was it hatred?

A queasiness swelled inside her. If Tina believed in him, though, then maybe he was all right. Perhaps he wasn't coming after them for revenge.

This thought didn't dispel the hundreds of butterflies currently loose in her stomach.

Her dad should be here. *He* was the one who should be facing Billy Cawley.

Anna kept her eyes downcast, afraid she'd catch his attention if she looked up.

Was she being a coward? It must run in the family.

His arrival had sucked the sound from the room – the silence following his opening line lingering for longer than was comfortable. Someone had to break it.

Tina was the first to speak. 'I think these people have something to say to you, Billy,' she said, going to his side and putting a tentative hand to his face. 'I'm sorry,' she whispered.

Anna wanted to say something but felt paralysed. Lizzie's dad had been given a thirty-year prison sentence for something *her* dad had done. A lot of years to waste for a crime he hadn't committed.

Eric Fisher was the murderer.

Anna couldn't get her head around that. How had her mother kept it from her? Self-preservation appeared to be the ongoing theme for the Fishers. Anna realised no one was looking in Billy's direction – she wasn't the only one hoping not to catch his eye. Although she'd sensed today would be 'the big one', being the anniversary of Jonie's disappearance, she had to admit, this wasn't what she'd imagined. This outcome wasn't one she'd even considered. But then, this couldn't be the final outcome – not the intended one, anyway. Because the real culprit, the one who'd done the deed, wasn't even in the room.

How could Billy exact revenge if the right people weren't there?

'What do you plan to do with us?' The voice sounded pathetic, weak. Nell, her head still lowered but her eyes looking up, was wringing her hands together as she spoke. Anna had a sudden disdain for the woman.

'To *do* with you?' Billy asked. He laughed. 'Have you not listened to any of what's been said?'

'Er – yes,' Nell said.

'Then you shouldn't have to ask.' Billy shrugged.

Nell seemed perplexed; the answer not good enough. 'I want to know,' she said.

'For Christ's sake, woman. I've had a lifetime – or what felt like it – to contemplate, to ruminate and to plan. If I were going to do anything in revenge, it wouldn't be to bring you all to my old bungalow, lock you in while torching it, and to watch it burn to the ground with you all screaming inside, would it?'

The horror on everyone's face at this suggestion was almost comical. Feet shuffled towards the door. Billy blocked it.

'Will you ever learn?' he mumbled. 'I want what Eliza . . . Lizzie . . . told you,' Billy said more loudly. 'For you to all admit what you did . . . and to apologise.'

'Because us saying sorry will make up for it? Yeah, right,' Rob said.

'It won't, no. But it'll give me some satisfaction.'

'Wouldn't punishing us be more satisfying?' Muriel said.

'I think you may have been doing that already.'

'It's unfinished, though, isn't it?' Rob said. 'I mean, you haven't even got the man behind it *here*. He's got away with it. Again.' His face held the expression of a sulking teenage boy.

Billy slowly nodded. 'There are two, actually.'

Anna noticed her mother sway. She rushed to her side, thinking she might faint.

'You feeling all right, Mum?'

'No. Maybe I need a doctor, I might . . . I might . . .'

'She's *fine!*' Billy snapped. 'Leave her. She stays. She's playing you, like she played you all.'

Anna swallowed hard. Obviously, more was to come. She wasn't sure she could take any further revelations.

'Get on with it,' Muriel said, seemingly having made a remarkable recovery.

'Well, *you* know, don't you, Muriel.' He gave Muriel a lopsided smile. 'One of them lost his mind long ago. The other will lose his life anyway – it doesn't need to be at my hand.'

'Why? What do you know?' Anna cut in, assuming it was her father Billy was referring to about losing his life.

'Eric's guilt runs deep. He's had each and every day to think about what he did, and he'll know I'm out of prison. I don't think he'll last long.'

'You're saying he's going to kill himself? Why would he now, just because you're free? You must've given him reason to think you're going to get your revenge – kill him,' Anna said.

'I've not given any reason for him to suspect that. But he'll *believe* it, because that's how he'd think if the roles were reversed. His mind will be working overtime. Because he's fully compos mentis and knows he deserves punishing. His mind's not addled, like the upstanding member of the community and man of God, Reverend Farnley.' Billy threw his arms up in the air, like he was presenting them to God.

'What's Reverend Farnley got to do with it?' Anna asked, the sudden shift catching her off-guard.

'Your dear mother was barking up the wrong tree with me, Bella.'

'It's Anna now.'

'Hmm. Okay, well, Anna – all the while Muriel had been sticking her nose into my business, trying to find something on me – a chink in my armour – her precious *Reverend* was the one abusing my daughter.'

'You have absolutely no proof of that,' Muriel shouted.

'You had no proof it was me, either, but that didn't stop you ensuring suspicion was thrown onto me. But you knew he was touching her; you knew *he* was the one Eliza was talking about when she used her doll to show you what he did to her, didn't you? You let him get away with it just so you could pin it on me. That's low, Muriel. Unforgivable. But because you then had something on the Reverend, you used him to get what you wanted. He was the one whose so-called evidence tipped the balance. It was the deciding statement that led social services to take Eliza from me.'

It was too much information in one go – the bloody *vicar* had been the one abusing Eliza? Anna looked over at Lizzie – her face was unreadable. How did Billy even know, though, when Lizzie herself had no memory of it? Anna's head ached trying to untangle the threads. It was nearing midnight and all she wanted was to get out of this dust-ball and shower, climb into bed and fall into a deep sleep so she could forget about what she'd learned. For a few hours at least. Everything Billy was saying came back to something Muriel did. Her mother had caused all of this.

'So, let me get this right. My *mother*—' Anna shot Muriel a piercing glance '—knew the vicar was the one abusing Eliza, yet did nothing apart from rope him in to help her blame Billy? Just to get what she wanted?' Anna glared at her mother. 'How bloody could you? You went on about keeping the kids of the village safe, then knowingly allowed a predator to remain in his position of trust—'

'No, no,' Muriel said, shaking her head. 'I didn't know for sure, and to begin with I thought his odd behaviour was because he was covering up for Billy – trying to play the good vicar who gave everyone a chance, not willing to rock the boat by making such an accusation. But then there were a few occasions when he caused me to question how *he* was with Eliza. For a long while I really did believe Billy was abusing Eliza. And when Robert had his incident in the bungalow, Nell thought Billy must've done something to him, too, and that added fuel to the flames. I put Reverend Farnley to the back of my mind for a little while.'

'Until you needed him, you mean? Then you approached him with your suspicions and gave him a get-out clause by blackmailing him to help you pin it on Billy, or you'd tell everyone what he was,' Anna said.

'Look, once Billy was in prison, I made sure Reverend Farnley left. I made it clear he wasn't welcome in Mapledon anymore. He was run out, rest assured.'

'Rest assured? Really? God, Mum. Great, so you made sure he left this village, but in doing so pushed him and his paedophilic tendencies onto another unsuspecting community? Good job.'

Muriel crossed her arms firmly. 'Actually, after everything that happened, he had a breakdown, became reclusive – he wouldn't have been a harm to any other children.' Muriel sounded almost triumphant. Anna felt sick to her stomach.

If she hadn't taken her mother's call on Friday, if she hadn't left Carrie and travelled to fucking Mapledon, she could've carried on not knowing. She'd lived without these truths for most of her life, she was sure she could've continued happily in her blissful ignorance.

But what about Jonie Hayes?

Didn't she deserve to be found? By denying the truth, Anna was denying her friend. Anna couldn't look at Muriel any longer. She turned her back and faced Billy.

'If you aren't back for revenge, why get Tina to play the stupid Knock, Knock game?' Anna asked.

'He didn't,' Tina said. 'I'd spoken to Billy about everything that had gone on. We'd had long discussions on the phone, written letters. I even visited a few times. I was very aware of the pain he'd gone through. Obviously I was in pain too. Have been since that day. It was *me* who felt the need for retribution. *I* wanted those who were involved to be punished in some way. I came up with the idea, and I convinced Billy to help by making sure I had the right "material". Lizzie had nothing at all to do with any of it, before you start too, Nell. She didn't come here for a story to sell to the papers. She came here for *her* story. To find out the truth about her childhood.

'I think we've all found out some truths now. But, Muriel?' Tina raised her chin in Muriel's direction. 'No matter the whys and wherefores, and with no other agenda apart from closure, I still have to know where my Jonie is. And you have to tell me.'

Chapter Ninety-Six

1989

Outskirts of Mapledon

Thursday 20th July – the day after, 2.30 a.m.

Eric had waited until the streetlights went out. Waited until he thought Mapledon's inhabitants would be sleeping soundly. All apart from one, anyway. He faced that man now and shuddered. Reverend Farnley stared at him, making him feel as though he were looking right inside his soul.

But he didn't, or couldn't, judge.

Muriel had assured Eric he could trust him to help. She'd told him *why* she was so sure. That this man was guilty of his own crimes.

Reverend Farnley got inside the car and Eric slowly drove out of Mapledon. He headed towards the vast moorland on the south side of the village. A great enough distance from the village to feel confident police resources wouldn't stretch that far. And in an even more remote area of the moors than those popular with walkers. Eric had heard about bodies being buried on moorland – bodies of people never found. Adults, children, lost to the earth. He had to hope this burial would also remain undetected. Forever.

It was a sight he couldn't have imagined in his worst nightmares. The limp body of a child being thrown into the ground by two men. A father and a Reverend. Eric looked to the heavens.

Shit. Please don't let there be a God. Don't let anyone know what I've done.

It had taken several hours to complete the task and it'd been achieved in virtual silence. The same as the drive back to Mapledon; Eric had nothing to say to Christopher Farnley. How could a man of God be inappropriate with a child? He wanted to say something. He desperately wanted to spit at him, tell him how vile he was. Hit him.

But how could he now? After all this?

He knew why Muriel had asked for his help. Eric couldn't have done it alone. No other villager – however much they supported Muriel and her cause – would've covered this up to the point of burying a child. Only someone as guilty as him.

Someone else who needed to keep secrets for their own survival.

God. The villagers had been afraid of what Billy Cawley might do to their kids, when all along it was their beloved vicar who'd been the one they should've feared.

And now, he could add himself to the list of people Mapledon should rid itself of. And he knew Muriel wouldn't stop until each on the list *was* gone, in one way or another.

As he stripped off his clothes and climbed into bed next to the warmth of his wife, Eric cried. He'd had secrets in the past – didn't everyone? But this was more than a secret. The implications of it were huge. To keep this quiet, stop the truth from coming out, he'd have to leave. There was no way he'd be able to face people every day knowing what he'd done.

How could he ever look his daughter in the eye again?

He pushed his body up close to Muriel's, sliding his hands over her waist, pulling her close.

360

'It's done,' he whispered in her ear.

She stirred. 'That part is. There's still a long way to go, Eric.'

He turned over, flicking the lamp switch. The light left the room.

Left him.

Chapter Ninety-Seven

2019

Lizzie

Friday 19th July

When Billy had mentioned Reverend Farnley, there'd been a moment when Lizzie thought the gathered group wouldn't believe it. Not a Reverend. Not the man who'd preached to his flock all about God. The man who'd seemed to care about his parishioners and had gone out of his way to encourage Billy to let his daughter attend Sunday school. Maybe his intention had always been to groom her – she was the perfect victim. Lizzie wondered if she'd been the only one. As much as she hoped it were the case, she had a bad feeling she wouldn't have been the first, or even the last, to suffer at the vicar's hands. Had the old man really lost his mind, or was that self-preservation too?

It'd come as a shock when Lizzie had been in the caravan with Billy and he'd told her about that, and how he suspected Muriel was covering for the Reverend *and* Eric. But Billy was convinced and his reasoning seemed sound. Having gone over and over the events, taking in what he remembered from the witness statements and reading the newspaper articles, together with Tina's and Pat's versions, it'd been the only logical explanation. With so much time to ruminate and go over every detail,

Billy had worked through a number of theories, but this one stuck, and it was the version of events that made the most sense to him: Eric was responsible for Jonie's death and Reverend Farnley had helped dispose of her body. Billy reckoned Muriel knew he'd been up to no good and used it as leverage – in effect blackmailing him to help her cover up what Eric had done. Billy remembered how Eliza had acted after every Sunday school session, and once Billy's ex-cell mate had fed back the information he'd found out about the Reverend's rapid exit from Mapledon and his subsequent breakdown, he'd been convinced the Reverend had been the one abusing Eliza, so would've been the perfect person for Muriel to go to.

Lizzie knew some of what she and Billy were telling the group of villagers was just supposition – a series of hypotheses her father had spent years formulating. But watching them all – their reactions – she had to concede he was probably right. No one seemed to be questioning it to the point she believed they would if none of it were true. There really was no planned revenge, though. As much as those standing nervously in the lounge clearly thought it was Billy's intention, they were wrong. Billy had said he wouldn't want them to ever be able to turn around and say, 'See, we were right about that weirdo Billy Cawley – did you hear how he exacted revenge on Muriel and Eric Fisher?'

No. He only wanted to hear them say they were wrong. They were sorry. And he wanted to help Tina – that's what he'd reiterated to Lizzie time and time again while they'd been sitting talking.

Lizzie had felt a surge of empathy for her birth father as she listened to how his sorry life had gone from bad to worse. How he'd been made the scapegoat for a horrendous crime. After a lifetime of thinking the worst of Billy Cawley, of believing the stories, gossip and half-truths, she found herself warming to this man, who by all accounts had sacrificed his freedom all the while knowing he'd been wronged along with Jonie Hayes. When

Billy spoke of Tina it was with such warmth. He'd told Lizzie how he'd always had feelings for Tina, even when he hadn't been able to communicate them effectively, and by the time he did it was too late – the awful events from Wednesday 19th July 1989 had overtaken them – and she'd shunned him.

He'd vowed to get out of prison in order to find the culprit, to prove to Tina once and for all it hadn't been him – so he'd completed all the offending behaviour rehabilitation courses, continuing to talk of his guilt despite his innocence – just so he would be able to get out. Now he was out, he'd told Lizzie he felt quite calm; his anger had dissipated somewhat. He'd learned a lot in his rehabilitation programmes that made him view things differently. Coming across as 'reformed' enabled the parole board to come to the decision he could be let out on life licence. As he put things together, though, he realised the justice he'd initially wanted wasn't as simple – and it wouldn't have the satisfactory outcome he craved. But he knew there was something he could do. An act of selflessness to try and limit further damage.

His aim now was to find Tina's daughter's body, and make sure she could finally have a real funeral for Jonie.

All they needed was for Muriel to tell them where to find Eric.

Chapter Ninety-Eight

2019

Eric

He'd called Muriel straight away – as soon as he'd been told about Billy Cawley's release. Warned her of what might come. What *would* come. Told her to keep a low profile. Just in case it did blow over. But he knew he couldn't be that lucky. Eric owed a debt to Billy. Not just any kind of debt either: he owed him his life. There was only one way he could repay that. And if he didn't offer to repay in full – then Billy would collect in person. He had no doubt of that. It had been almost a week since his release. There'd been two occasions in Eric's life where time had stretched – seemed infinite – when the moment of agony seemed never-ending. One was thirty years ago. The other was today – waiting for his punishment. He'd hoped it would be swift, over by now. Billy was dragging it out, making him suffer.

He couldn't blame him.

Billy – for all his faults, for all the bad things they'd attempted to pin on him – was an innocent man. Had been then, was now. For a second, he cursed Muriel. She'd started the ball rolling, and once it'd gathered speed there was no stopping it – it would knock down whoever got in its path. If she'd realised who it would damage, maybe, just maybe, she'd have had second thoughts. He liked to think so. She said she loved him, wanted to protect him. And to be fair, she had. She'd kept in contact with him even when he'd moved back down to Somerset. She'd been angry that he'd moved closer – only one county away. She'd liked him being in Scotland. The distance had made her feel more secure. But she'd come around, eventually. And she carried on updating him on his daughter's life, informing him when she'd married, when she'd made him a grandad . . .

A sob escaped his tight chest as he tried to imagine what his granddaughter looked like. He'd so desperately wanted Muriel to send photos of Carrie, but they knew it wasn't wise. Letters were risky enough. He wished Billy realised that he'd been punished too. He'd also lost out on seeing his daughter grow into a woman, missed all the major life events. The major one for Eric was how he'd missed the chance to be a grandad, to be involved in Carrie's life.

Muriel had called him a coward once. It'd cut through him – he'd literally dropped to the ground, his legs giving way. How could she say that? Because he'd gone – escaped as far away as possible? He hadn't just done that for himself. He'd done it for *her*. For *them*.

It had been an *accident*.

A tragic, awful accident. A moment he'd regret for a lifetime. For days, months and years afterwards, every other conceivable outcome had run through his mind. One that didn't involve the death of a ten-year-old girl. If he'd done something differently, might things have worked out for everyone?

Sitting at the window watching cars go by – waiting and wondering which would be for him – Eric contemplated whether he should go back.

Back to Mapledon to face the music.

He was dead whether he stayed in Somerset or went there.

366

He might as well do some good before the Reaper came for him.

Eric Fisher stuffed a holdall with some clothes. Then, with a creeping sense of doom, got in his car and set off for the place he'd once called home.

Chapter Ninety-Nine

2019

Anna

Once Billy seemed satisfied the truth had finally been spilled, after thirty years of Mapledon keeping it hidden, he opened the lounge door, standing aside to let people past him. Rob and Nell were quick to accept the invitation to leave, scuttling out rapidly, probably fearing he might change his mind. But Tina and Pat Vern hung back. And Anna did too, despite Muriel giving her a questioning glance as she herself edged closer to the door. To Anna, it all seemed unfinished, somehow. And she also felt the need for confirmation about what, exactly, was expected of her and Muriel next. Once Eric Fisher had been contacted.

Regardless of what Billy and Tina had said about not wanting to involve the police, Anna felt certain they'd come calling on the Fishers sometime soon. If Tina wanted Eric to tell her where he'd taken Jonie's body, they'd obviously want a proper burial – a full funeral. So, the police would become involved whether they wanted it or not.

Mapledon's secrets would become public knowledge. It was inevitable.

Unless Billy was planning on still taking the blame. If *he* was the one to disclose the whereabouts of Jonie's body, no one else would need to be implicated. Maybe he'd say it was his final confession. Surely, though, the opportunity to clear his name would override everything else. Anna's head throbbed. It was all too much to take in; too much to consider right now, past midnight in this derelict, ghostly bungalow. As the six of them, the remainers, stood looking uneasily at each other, Muriel began muttering.

'The fact is, you have no evidence . . . not really, it's all just hearsay and circumstantial.'

Anna laughed. A hysterical cackle she had no control of. Tears joined in, and before she knew it, she was sobbing.

How could her mother be so damned ironic? Could she not *hear* herself?

'Calm down, Anna,' Lizzie said, coming to her side. She placed an arm around Anna's shoulders. 'It's been a hell of a few hours, hasn't it?'

That was one way of putting it. Anna had lurched from one emotion to the next without warning. She was drained. Her thoughts chaotic. She took a few shuddering breaths in, enough to regain her composure without inhaling further dust particles.

'I can't calm down! We've just heard the same story, haven't we?' Anna gave Lizzie an incredulous look as she shook her arm off. 'When did you find all this out, Lizzie? Or did you come here already knowing the answers?'

'No, honestly; I was as in the dark as you were – until reaching Mapledon, anyway. Then there was a slow, creeping realisation that things weren't as they first appeared. Once I met Billy, and heard his side, some of the lies came to light. Then he told me stories that rocked the foundations I'd built, made me question what I thought I knew. It wasn't all from Billy, of course. Pat also helped fill in some gaps. As did Gwen, from Bulleigh Barton. I was surprised at her knowledge of the villagers, being she's a relative outsider – although I guess most of it *was* based on gossip. But those present here tonight have confirmed most to be true.'

369

'Get a roomful of people together – all of them trying to hide a secret – throw in one accusation and watch as the panic sets in,' Billy said. 'Doesn't take long for the first person to break – then the others to follow; the truth usually comes rolling out, each attempting to blame another. Self-preservation at its best.'

'Which is why I asked everyone to meet here. It was the quickest way to pull all the threads together – get to the heart of the matter,' Lizzie said.

'It's taken too long, but at least we have some answers now,' Tina said, her body encased in Pat's arms.

'You need to get Eric to talk now, Muriel,' Pat said.

Anna looked to her mother. She saw an old woman – one who appeared incapable of the actions she'd been accused of tonight. She now hoped that Muriel could give Tina what she was asking for. She'd protected Eric for too long already. She had to give him up now. 'I assume you've got a contact number for Eric, then?' Anna said.

'Your *dad*,' Muriel corrected.

'I don't think he deserves that status, do you?'

'Yes, love. He does.'

'After all *that*, you're still standing by him? He's a cold-blooded child killer, Mum.'

'Do you have a way of getting hold of him, Muriel?' Tina asked.

Muriel sighed, taking a long time to answer. 'Yes.'

'Once she speaks to him, what then? What if he refuses to tell us where Jonie is?' Anna said. It would be a huge setback now if Eric Fisher couldn't tell them. And what if Billy was right about it not being long before Eric took his life rather than face up to his crime? They'd never find out and all this would've been for nothing.

'When you talk to him, Muriel,' Billy said, slowly, 'you tell him I'm here. Waiting for his answer. And if he doesn't co-operate, his daughter will "disappear".'

'I thought you said you weren't interested in revenge?' Anna said, her voice high-pitched. Great that *she* was the bargaining chip.

'I'm not. Per se. It wasn't the reason for me returning to Mapledon. I was only here to visit my wife's grave, not to stir up trouble or disturb old ghosts,' Billy said. 'However, I met Eliza, and a need for her to know the truth overtook me. The situation now, tonight, has . . . altered things. And needs must.'

'Fine. I'll make sure she tells him that.' Anna wasn't sure she bought the "I was only here to visit my wife's grave" line. She knew in her gut there was an ulterior motive. She walked over to her mother and, taking her arm, guided her out of the lounge door, back through the hall and outside. She breathed in the clean air, deeply. Muriel was doing the same. Or she was hyper-ventilating, Anna wasn't entirely sure.

'We'll be waiting and watching,' Tina called out after them. 'Make that call tonight, Muriel!'

Anna and Muriel began the weary walk home. The progress was slow, neither of them seeming to have the energy to walk briskly.

'The why wasn't answered, though, was it?' Anna asked. 'I mean, *why* would Dad have killed Jonie?'

'I don't suppose we'll ever know that, Anna.'

'You *must* know. Didn't you ask him at the time? Won't you ask him now, when you speak to him again?'

'Can we leave it? For now. I'm done; I just want to be home.'

Anna, too, was drained. It seemed learning the truth was an exhausting experience. She wondered how the others were faring.

'As soon as we're home, though – you need to call him.'

It might be gone midnight, but their night wasn't over yet. While the task of contacting her father was a daunting prospect, there was no way she'd allow Muriel to put it off. Anna wouldn't sleep now until this was over.

Chapter One Hundred

2019

Lizzie

'Did that go how you'd planned?' Lizzie was sitting in her car, Billy in the passenger seat. The four of them who'd remained in the lounge after Muriel and Anna left, had carried on talking for a bit longer, thrashing out ideas of how to follow up on the demand for Muriel to contact Eric. Apart from Billy – he'd been quiet, not adding much to the conversation. It was as though he were holding something back. Not keen to share *his* plan of action. It made Lizzie nervous.

'Ah, sort of,' he said, his head cocked.

'Only sort of. What else had you hoped for?'

'Well, they didn't exactly *apologise* for causing me to spend almost my entire adult life behind bars, did they?'

'Not in so many words, no. But I think that some, at least, were very sorry. Even if those exact words weren't uttered. The expressions on their faces when the truth began emerging . . .' Lizzie widened her eyes. 'That must've given a degree of satisfaction?'

'I won't be satisfied until she's found, Lizzie.'

Hearing Billy say her name, rather than using Eliza, was like an electric shock pulsing through her body. Maybe she'd be able to forge some kind of father–daughter relationship with him now. Or would it be impossible after such a huge gap – after all that had gone on?

'Do you really believe Eric Fisher will confess? What if he doesn't *remember*?'

'Oh, he'll confess, all right. And trust me,' Billy said, his eyes burning, 'he remembers.'

Lizzie was uncertain how to respond to that, so instead shuffled in her seat, placing her hands on the steering wheel.

'Do you want me to drive you back to the farm? I could try and fit your bike in the boot.'

Billy shook his head. 'No, thanks. I haven't finished here yet.'

Chapter One Hundred and One

2019

Eric

The outside of the house hadn't altered.

Eric had parked two streets away and walked, ducking down the side entrance and knocking on the back window. Lights were on inside, but no one answered. He should've called before he set off. He checked his watch.

Midnight.

Where the hell was Muriel? There'd be no way she was out this late. There was a car in front of the garage belonging to Muriel's house. Not hers – he supposed it could be Anna's. If they were both here, was it because there was a problem?

His pulse hammered in his ears.

Billy's here.

The words flashed through his mind.

It was the only explanation. He strode up and down the garden, trying to release from his body the sudden surge of adrenaline. He wouldn't allow Billy to do it. Not after he'd spent the best part of thirty years away from his girls to keep them safe. He wasn't going to allow Billy to hurt them.

Chapter One Hundred and Two

2019

Anna

Anna got to the front door first, giving it a once-over – just in case. She gave a cursory glance to the camera as she entered. Muriel traipsed in after her.

'I think I'll head up right away, Anna. I'm so—'

'Er . . . no, Mum. Sorry. You need to call Dad.'

'Anna. It's ridiculously late. I'm not phoning at this time of night.'

'Seriously, I'm not able to calmly go up to bed and sleep after everything that's just been said. How the hell can you?' Anna's face was hot with anger at her mother's blasé attitude.

'Fine,' she said, wearily. 'I'll call, but there'll be no point because he'll be asleep.'

'I'd feel better if you at least tried, though, thank you,' Anna said, stepping aside to let Muriel go into the lounge ahead of her.

The time it took for her mother to find the mobile number and make the call felt unduly prolonged. Anna tapped her foot on the carpet as Muriel tapped out the number on the phone.

In the distance, Anna heard music.

'What's that?' She turned, walking into the kitchen. 'Mum?

Leave the phone ringing and come here.' Muriel did as Anna instructed and came and stood by her side. 'Listen.'

'He's here,' her mother said. She unlocked the back door. 'Come on in, Eric.'

Anna's mouth dried. Tears of sadness, anger and betrayal erupted as she came face-to-face with her father for the first time in thirty years.

'Hello, Anna,' Eric said. Bloodshot eyes, watery and sad, searched Anna's.

'Why?' She shook her head. 'Why did you do it?'

'It's not something I can easily explain,' he said, his voice thick. 'I'm so sorry.'

'Sorry? Oh, my God. I literally don't know what to say to you,' Anna said, turning her back and walking into the lounge.

She could hear whispered voices. Even now, she thought, they were keeping secrets. Hatching a plan. Trying to figure a way out of this mess without either of them ending up in prison. Anna wanted to scream, 'Whatever you're saying out there you can say to my face, you know.'

Her mother and father joined Anna in the lounge. It was a scene she'd never imagined could happen. And, in different circumstances, she might well have been pleased, taken it as an opportunity to get to know her dad again. But not now.

Anna's entire body was trembling. 'Where is she? Where did you take Jonie Hayes' body after you murdered her?'

Eric winced. 'Your mother's just told me Billy's here, in Mapledon.'

'Yes, but that's not answering the question,' Anna said, sharply.

'I will. I'll tell Billy where to find her.' His voice was weak, drenched in defeat.

'Well, that's big of you. Only taken thirty fucking years.' Anger spewed from her. It wasn't merely anger for him killing Jonie, but for leaving Anna when she needed him.

'I had to stay away, not have any contact with you. You understand that, don't you?'

'Yes, *Dad*. You had to stay away to ensure you weren't put in prison for your crime. You allowed an innocent man to be set up for murder, spend years in a cell, all so you could be free. I think I understand, yeah.'

'I've never been free, Anna,' he said.

'Tell that to Billy Cawley. Tell that to Tina. You're a coward, plain and simple.' Anna pushed past them.

'Where are you going?' Muriel shouted after her.

'To make a call,' Anna said as she left the house.

Anna walked to the end of the road, and once she had a few service bars, dialled Lizzie.

'Lizzie. He's here. Come to Muriel's . . . and bring Billy.'

Chapter One Hundred and Three

2019

Lizzie

Lizzie's heart leapt.

He's here. Bring Billy.

Anna's words echoed in her head.

'You'll never believe it,' she said, turning towards her dad.

Billy gave a small nasal laugh. 'Eric Fisher has come to Mapledon,' he said.

'Yes. Bloody hell. How did you know he'd come here?'

Billy had already convinced Lizzie to hang around after they'd locked the bungalow up. He'd asked her to drive towards Muriel's and park a street away.

They'd been sitting in the car talking when the call came.

'Gut feeling,' he said.

'Shall we walk from here, then?' she asked him.

Anna was standing at the open front door when Lizzie approached the house with Billy by her side.

'As much as he deserves it, don't hurt him,' Anna said as they walked into the hallway.

Lizzie could feel the tension in the house like an electric charge. She wanted to tell Anna not to worry; no one was going to hurt Eric. But she couldn't make that promise, because she didn't know. As an adult, she'd met Billy twice before tonight – she had no idea what he might be planning when he faced the man who should have served the sentence in his place. Just because he'd *told* Lizzie he wasn't there for revenge and wasn't going to hurt anyone didn't mean she one-hundred-per-cent believed him. She didn't exactly feel qualified to make that judgement.

Billy stared at Anna for what felt like minutes – it was as though someone had pressed a pause button. Lizzie reached out and touched his elbow, hoping to jolt him from his motionless state.

'I won't,' he said, finally.

The three of them entered the lounge. Lizzie's whole body was taut now as she looked at Eric Fisher and Muriel huddled on the sofa, their pale, fearful faces looking up as they saw her and Billy. Eric slowly got to his feet.

'Don't involve Muriel and Anna in this, please.' Eric's eyes pleaded with Billy. 'I'll tell you what you're here for, then you can do what you like with me. But don't hurt them.'

'Oh, Eric, Eric,' Billy said, moving closer to him. 'I've said already – I'm not here to hurt you, or them.'

A flash of confusion, or maybe it was disbelief, crossed Eric's face. 'You don't want revenge? You don't want me to suffer for getting away with it all these years?'

'My hatred for you and your family has lessened since I was first *framed*,' Billy said. 'I can't say I don't resent you, though. I still think "why me?" – that bothers me now as much as it did then. Although I think I've put all the pieces together, I'd still like to hear your side. Hear the reason why you and Muriel chose me. What I'd done that was *so* wrong you were happy to watch me go down for something I wasn't guilty of. But, as I have explained to your wife, daughter and the others – *I'm* not the bad one. Thirty years of self-reflection, deciding what was important and what wasn't, made me evaluate things differently. There's something to be said for being selfless, Eric. Isn't there?'

A look passed between them that Lizzie couldn't read. Eric's face flushed, and he became flustered.

'I'll take you to her,' Eric said, jumping to his feet. 'Do you want to do it now?'

'In a while,' Billy said.

Lizzie exchanged a worried look with Anna. It was clear that Billy had something more he wanted to say. Lizzie saw Anna lurch forwards.

'Look. I know what he did was absolutely heinous, and you suffered for that, Billy. But you said you weren't going to hurt anyone—'

'But I still have some unfinished business . . .' Billy said. His voice was soft, yet managed to sound menacing. Lizzie looked from him to Eric.

'Please, Billy, no.' Eric put his hands together, prayer-like. 'There's no need.'

'God, Billy. Wait!' Anna shouted. 'You can't hurt him, you promised.'

'I'm. Not. Going. To,' Billy said slowly, swinging around to face Anna. 'I know he was doing what he felt he had to do.'

'What do you mean?' Anna said, her brow creased.

'If I'd had the opportunity to fight for my daughter, I'd have done it in the blink of an eye,' Billy said. 'I understand why he did it, but I can't forgive him. Tina knows too. But we've made our peace with the lies.' He faced Eric. 'As long as you can give her what she wants – I'll give you what you want.'

Eric gave a nod of his head.

'What the *hell* are you talking about?' Anna said.

Eric gave a loud, juddering sigh. 'Sit down, Anna,' he said. 'Oh, dear God. This is something I never, *ever*, wanted to tell you.'

'No, no, no!' Muriel surged towards Eric; her fists held high.

Lizzie watched in astonishment as Muriel showered punches on Eric's chest.

'Enough! Mum, for Christ's sake,' Anna said, pulling at Muriel's arms, forcing them down to her sides. 'What is happening here?' Anna looked directly at Eric.

'You didn't mean to hurt her,' Eric said, his voice quivering as tears spilled over his cheeks.

Lizzie's mouth dropped. She shot Billy a questioning look. He obviously hadn't told her everything. Billy Cawley had held this last piece of the puzzle back from her – back from everyone who'd been gathered at the bungalow a few hours ago. He'd been waiting for Eric Fisher to slot it in.

Billy turned so he could see everyone's faces.

'*Anna* killed Jonie Hayes,' he said. 'And Eric took the blame for what little Bella Fisher did.'

Lizzie stood by helplessly as she watched Anna sink to the floor.

Chapter One Hundred and Four

1989

Bella

Wednesday 19th July – the day of

'Run, Bella, run!' Jonie screeched as she legged it down Blackstone Close.

Bella heard the cry as she watched Jonie disappear around the corner, leaving her trailing. With Creepy Cawley behind her, shouting and waving his arms. Jonie had left her. How could she do that? Bella dared to look over her shoulder as she attempted to run on shaking legs. He was going to catch her. Tears burned her eyes, her throat tightened. This was it. What her mother had warned her about. *'Don't annoy Billy Cawley'*, *'Never go to his place'*, *'It's not safe'*. All her mother's warnings now screamed inside her skull. As she felt a hand grab her hair, Bella knew her mum had been right all along.

'Think it's funny, do you?' Creepy Cawley bellowed in her ear. Bella felt warm liquid run down the insides of her thighs. Her head hurt where he had hold of her hair. He pulled at it, causing her body to turn around. Now she was looking directly at him. His breath was hot on her face; a strong, stale smell filled her nostrils.

'Please . . .' Bella cried. 'I'm sorry.'

'And you think that covers it, eh? Weeks and weeks of you little shits banging on my door, and all you can say is sorry?'

Bella couldn't move. Fear made all her muscles freeze. She was going to die. Creepy Cawley was going to kill her. Suddenly, her feet were moving. She wasn't doing it. He was dragging her. This was it. He was taking her back to his bungalow. She was never going to see her mum and dad again.

Something snapped. A burst of energy came from inside her and she pulled at his arms, freeing herself from his grip. She didn't stop to look over her shoulder this time, she just ran. As Bella rounded the corner, she noticed Jonie at the end of the road, slumped against a wall.

'Oh, there you are. You took your time – I was beginning to worry he'd got you,' Jonie said, before bursting into laughter.

A burning-hot sensation shot through Bella's body, making her face feel as though it were on fire. She clenched her fists tightly. 'I can't believe you left me,' she said, her teeth gritted.

'Well, what did you expect? You need to learn to run faster,' Jonie said. Then her gaze dropped. 'Oh, my God! You didn't!' Jonie pointed at Bella's legs. 'You peed yourself?' And she doubled over in laughter again.

'I *hate* you.' Bella pushed Jonie, hard. She heard air leave Jonie's mouth as she smacked into the wall. Bella didn't hang around. She ran down the cut-through, afraid Jonie would really hurt her in return. She wouldn't have liked being pushed.

'Get back here, you wimp!' Jonie's voice followed her.

Bella panicked. She realised the cut-through would eventually lead back to Creepy Cawley's, to the hedges that lined the end of his cul-de-sac; the ones they usually hid in before playing Knock, Knock, Ginger. Maybe if she hid there now, Jonie wouldn't find her; she wouldn't expect Bella to be brave enough to go near there right after he'd caught her.

Bella had only reached the grassy area, just short of the huge bushes, when Jonie came hurtling towards her, pushing her to the ground. They rolled around on the grass, Jonie yanking Bella's hair.

'How dare you push me!' Jonie yelled.

'You can't get away with leaving me like that, Jonie. You're mean and a bully.'

'Ahh, gonna go cry to Daddy, are you? You're such a baby,' Jonie said. She was sitting on Bella now, straddling her belly and pinning her arms down. Bella struggled beneath her weight, trying to wriggle free. But it was no good. Jonie was stronger.

'Get. Off. Me!' Bella thrashed as much as she could, managing to drag herself across the grass a few inches, but Jonie grabbed her again.

'What's your problem?' she shouted.

'You, Jonie. You are my problem. Always making me do stuff *you* want. You're selfish and I don't want to be your friend anymore.' Bella felt a relief saying the words out loud. The words she'd practised inside her head for months. She wanted to be free of Jonie Hayes.

'Tough. We're friends and that's that. Our mums are best friends so we have to be.'

'No, we don't!' Bella propelled her body once more, and finally broke free. She scrabbled on the grass, her feet slipping. She'd almost made it to the bushes, to the gap she could squeeze through, when Jonie's hand pulled at her ankle, and she collapsed on her tummy back on the grass. Anger flared. Bella reached her hand out in front of her, her fingers closing around a large stone. She flipped over on to her back, and as Jonie landed on her stomach, Bella swung her arm. The stone made a dull thudding noise as it hit Jonie's forehead.

For a moment, Jonie just looked stunned, but then she seemed to sway.

Bella watched in quiet horror as a huge lump swelled up on Jonie's head. It seemed to grow bigger and bigger while she stared. Was it going to pop?

Jonie sat back onto the grass. She slowly raised her hand, and as she touched the lump, her eyes grew wide.

Bella thought she saw hatred in them. She had to get away from Jonie. Now. Because it looked like she was about to go totally ape on Bella.

She quickly threw the stone into the bushes and got up, ready to make her escape.

'What have you done?' Jonie said, both hands now balled into fists.

She was going to attack again – Bella knew it. While Jonie was on the ground, she had to make sure she stayed there. Bella moved forwards, and when she was beside Jonie, she raised her foot, kicking her in her chest. Jonie again grabbed Bella's ankle, pulling it to make her fall over. But she didn't fall; she stayed upright.

'You're a bitch, Bella!' she yelled. 'And I never liked you, anyway.' She let go of Bella's foot. Which gave Bella the perfect opportunity to deliver another kick. Jonie fell back, her head slamming on the ground. Bella hesitated. The anger and frustration that had exploded from her came as a shock, but it was the first time she'd ever got the upper hand on her friend. She stood over Jonie, deciding in that moment she should make the most of it.

'Good,' Bella said. 'I never want to see you again.'

Jonie was making a strange gurgling noise. Bella bent down, close to her head. Over-reacting as usual, she thought, as she took hold of Jonie's locket necklace and pulled it. The chain broke. 'You won't be wanting this anymore, then,' she said, pocketing the necklace.

Jonie didn't answer.

'Hey! I said, you won't be needing *this* anymore.'

Jonie didn't move.

Bella gave her a nudge with her foot. Nothing.

'Jonie? Stop messing about.'

Bella grabbed Jonie's face with both hands, shaking it side to side.

Blood trickled from her ear. Jonie was silent.

What had she done? Bella staggered backwards, a sick feeling rising.

She looked around her. No one else was there. No one had seen what had happened.

Bella turned away from Jonie and pushed through the gap in the hedge. She should get help. She had to get an ambulance.

As she emerged from the other side of the bushes, into Blackstone Close, she hesitated. Maybe she should knock on Creepy Cawley's door. He'd be sure to come running out and then she could tell him to call for help. But as she came to the bungalow, she saw the truck had gone. He wasn't in.

She had to go home. Her dad would know what to do. She began running. With each pounding footstep, the words: *Bella killed Jonie, Bella killed Jonie*, chanted in her ears.

Chapter One Hundred and Five

2019

Anna

Friday 19th July

Muriel's concerned face was the first thing Anna saw hovering above her own when she came to.

'Anna, love. You gave me a scare, fainting like that.'

Anna sat up. Everyone's eyes were firmly on her. The last words she'd heard before blackness enveloped her repeated in her head: '*Anna* killed Jonie Hayes. And Eric took the blame for what little Bella Fisher did.'

'I – I don't understand,' she said. 'How. Why?' Anna stumbled over the words. For all those years, she'd believed Billy Cawley guilty of murdering Jonie. Moments ago, she'd discovered it was really her father, Eric, who was the child killer. Now, suddenly, they were passing that label on to her. None of it made sense. Even Lizzie, it seemed, was having trouble with this new information.

'Why didn't you tell me this before?' Lizzie's brow furrowed as she turned to look at Billy. 'When you were supposedly revealing the *whole* truth behind everything that went on. Why purposely leave out the fact the real killer was Anna?'

'I wasn't keeping it from you, as such.' Billy said. 'It just had to be revealed at the right time. Or what I thought was the right time. It's a bit of a bombshell to drop on anyone.'

Anna couldn't disagree there. But it was a bombshell she now didn't know how to handle. It was incomprehensible that she, as a ten-year-old girl, would have the capability to kill another child. Billy must be wrong.

But neither Eric, nor Muriel, challenged Billy's accusation.

So, it must be true.

'How come you're being so forgiving?' Lizzie asked.

Billy's face softened; his eyes closed as he took a long breath in, then released it slowly. 'I've had a long time to mull it all over – I've completed loads of rehabilitation programmes – and even though I wasn't the one who required it, or should've even been in prison, I found them helpful. I learned new skills to manage my emotions, and how to see things from different perspectives. I put myself in others' shoes and walked around a little,' Billy said. His eyes were focused on Eric. 'You protected your daughter, something I wish I'd been able to do for Eliza. I guess a part of me was jealous – and another part of me admired you.'

'But Billy – Dad – the Fisher family stitched you up! Made you the suspect and then, through their lies and help from the other hideous people of this village, ensured you were the one to go down for it. I don't get why you aren't going to do anything about it. You're armed with the truth now. Go tell the police!' Lizzie said.

'The truth will set you free,' Billy said, smiling.

'Exactly, so make sure everyone knows it wasn't you.'

'I am free, now. And the truth is out. Those who need to know, do.'

'Don't you want to see Eric behind bars. Anna, even?'

'Whoa, hold on,' Muriel interjected. 'You can't do that. Anna didn't even know, not really. She was just a child. It was an accident.'

'It's okay, Lizzie,' Billy said. He gave a weak smile, then laid a hand on her shoulder. 'You've only just learned about this, so it'll take a long while for it to sink in. Longer before you realise I'm right in letting sleeping dogs lie. They've suffered already, believe me. Years of being trapped in their lies. And in many ways, Eric has been a prisoner every bit as much as I was and he all but lost his daughter too. My prison term has ended. His won't. And Anna's is merely beginning. They don't need bars.'

'The right people should be punished – the person who committed the murder should lose their freedom.'

'I've done the time for it, Lizzie. I'm old now – I don't see the point of letting Anna go to prison – she's got a daughter of her own. I'm not going to be the one to rip the Fisher family apart. I'm not as bad as them.' Billy allowed his gaze to slowly move over Muriel, then Eric and Anna. 'And besides, I put the ultimate decision into Tina's hands—'

'Wait, Tina knew it was *me* all along? Why didn't she say anything earlier?' Anna said.

'Yes, she suspected even before I put my theory to her. Right from the off Tina had been angry with you and your mother for not going straight to the police when you'd supposedly witnessed Jonie getting into my truck. She didn't buy the shock story either. We talked at length, both during her visits to the prison and in letters, about how she felt, what she wanted to do.'

'So she devised this bizarre Knock, Knock game to let us know she knew, but that was it? That's enough, is it? Seems unlikely,' Muriel said.

'It might do to you. The important things to Tina were finding her daughter's body and ensuring those involved told, or were forced to tell, the truth. It's her who has decided to spare Anna. And Eric and Muriel too. She's the forgiving one; far more than me. I've got the opportunity to resume my life. I can, perhaps . . .' He looked to Lizzie. 'Well, I can maybe finally have some kind of relationship with my daughter, look after her. Tina doesn't have that. All I wanted was for her to be able to bury her child. And now Eric will come good, won't you, Eric?' He turned his attention back to her dad.

'Yes. I'm so sorry, Anna. You were never meant to find out – not like this.'

'But she already knew,' Lizzie said. 'Anna *knew* she was the one who killed Jonie. What do you mean, she was never meant to find out?'

'The shock of what happened somehow caused her to bury the memory of it,' Muriel said.

Anna lowered her head, hearing a subtle, dismissive huff from Billy's direction.

'How do you know that?' Lizzie said.

'Because she genuinely never appeared flustered when Jonie's death was spoken of. After she'd given her statement, it was as if she began to believe Billy was the one who'd done it, not her. I even began to believe it myself. I suppose the explanation I gave, the one reported, was easier for her. Better than thinking she took her friend's life.'

'*Did* you remember, Anna? I mean, wasn't there any recollection of the events that day?' Lizzie asked.

'Yes. Yes, there was. But Mum's right. I only really remembered what I'd been *told* happened. Those were the memories I carried forward. Once I became Anna, too, I think that helped. I was no longer Bella. Bella wasn't a part of me. I didn't want, or need her memories.'

'What about now? Now you know it was you, hasn't it dislodged any memory of it?'

Anna's mind conjured Jonie's face – the massive lump jutting from her forehead. She recalled her anger, the force behind her kick. The sound of Jonie's skull hitting the ground and seeing the blood leak from her ear.

'Not really, no,' she said. The lie came easily. She'd spent a lifetime constructing the narrative – she wasn't ready to let it go yet. She'd have to come to terms with this in her own time. She didn't owe Lizzie anything.

Even as she thought it, she knew she was wrong.

She owed these people everything. Her life. Carrie's life.

How would she ever be able to move forward from this?

'I think it's time, now.' Eric walked to Anna, giving her shoulder a squeeze. 'I'm so sorry, my girl. I'll be back to see you later.'

Eric kissed Muriel on the cheek and walked out of the door. Billy followed.

'What are you going to do now?' Anna asked Lizzie.

'I need to see my husband.'

'Do you think they've found her yet?'

It was three in the morning; the men had been gone for a little over an hour. Muriel, despite being ready to drop earlier and wanting her bed, had been sitting with Anna since everyone had left, her arm wrapped as far around Anna's body as it would reach.

'This doesn't feel real, Mum.'

'I know, love. I know.' Muriel stroked Anna's hair – the way she used to when she needed comforting.

'But, I've been so horrible to you. Said awful things about Dad. All along you'd been keeping quiet to protect me.'

'Yes. Some of the things you said were hurtful. The way you treat me sometimes is like a kick in the teeth. But it's my fault. It wouldn't have happened if it weren't for me. Things could've been so different if I hadn't started the ball rolling. My obsession with getting Billy Cawley out of Mapledon took over everything. I lost sight of all that truly mattered. Because of it all, I lost your father, then you. But it's your dad who took the brunt of it all, having to go and find her, then dispose of her body. He was broken. Broken because his darling little girl had done something so terrible, broken because he'd covered it up. He never could look you in the eye afterwards. He really did leave because he loved you. I didn't lie about that, Anna,' Muriel said, giving Anna's hand a squeeze.

'There was no other woman?'

'No. Never.'

'Is that why you never took off your wedding ring?'

Muriel looked down at her hands, turning the gold band. 'I hated what happened, hated the fact he had to leave us. After he left, it became a hideous nightmare – lies upon lies – in order to keep you from realising it'd been you who had killed Jonie Hayes. I spent hours with you, talking about Billy and how he'd abducted Jonie – trying to etch it into your mind, your memory. Nell, too. She'd always been loyal to me. She was the only one who knew it was you we were protecting.'

'How could she have wanted to help protect me after she found out it was me?'

'You didn't mean to kill Jonie – you told us about the fight. It was an accident. Your father and I knew it, and so did Nell. We all saw what Jonie was like. There were lots of things about her that didn't quite add up – she had a reputation, even at ten – for being nasty. Looking back, we thought she'd shown tendencies of a personality disorder. But Tina and Mark had ignored her behaviour. Nell did have reservations about trying to pin it on Billy. But she really was convinced he was guilty of abusing Eliza – the way Robert had acted after being in the bungalow that time had added to her belief, so she backed me. Always stuck by the story, never wavering. Even tonight.'

'Even after finding out about Reverend Farnley.'

'I know. And I'm aware of what you and the others think of me now. I really didn't just let him get away with it, though. I promise you. Once Billy was out of the picture I turned my attention to him. Your dad was still here then, so he helped to ensure Farnley moved on.'

'But other children, Mum – you could've prevented him from creating more victims if you'd reported him . . .'

'I may not have handed him over to the police, and by then I couldn't have done that without the whole story I'd weaved collapsing and your dad going to prison, but I did take what action I could to ensure his opportunity to continue any abuse was limited.'

'How?'

'I found out the parish he'd moved to, then anonymously tipped them off. I told them just enough information to give my accusation of paedophilia credence. His reputation was in tatters; no real evidence was needed in the end, and then he had a breakdown. The rest you know.'

'Seems no real evidence is required these days,' Anna said, shaking her head.

'In his case, it was deserved.'

'But not in Billy's case.'

'No. No. Although I can't say I wouldn't do it again if I had to,' Muriel said. 'If it meant protecting my family.'

Silence fell, then, while Anna struggled to take everything in. The layers of lies. So many things niggled at her, and no doubt over the coming days there'd be more. One of the things bothering her right now was how her mother had encouraged little Bella and Jonie to be friends if what she said was true. If they hadn't been pushed together all the time, none of this would've happened.

'If you thought Jonie was bad news, why did you let me play with her?'

Muriel gave a sigh and shrugged. 'Because I was best friends with Tina. I wanted you two to be good friends as well.' Muriel dropped her head. 'It made life easier; your father and I could spend more time at Tina and Mark's, or vice versa, if you two played together.'

'Right,' Anna said. She had a feeling many answers to her

questions would be 'it made life easier'. She wanted to ask *all* the questions at some point. Anna was so tired now, her eyelids felt like lead. She wasn't sure she could wait for her father to return with Billy. And Jonie's body.

She shivered. 'It does seem to keep coming back to you, Mum. Not that I can blame you for *my* actions.'

'Yes, it does. Don't worry, I blame me too. I was so shocked when you finally said you'd hurt Jonie, left her lying, not breathing on the grass near the hedge the other side of Billy's cul-de-sac. When Eric came back, ashen-faced, and told me how he'd found her, we weren't confident enough that we could get away with saying it was an accident. As awful as it is, I saw it as an opportunity to get Billy – they were right about that. And I'd much rather see him go down for murder than my daughter or husband.'

'Why didn't Billy get Nell here? Let her know he was aware of the full truth?'

'Because I suppose he knew I was behind it. Back then I was every bit as much of a bully as they considered Jonie to be. But I was an adult – I should've known better. Tina, Billy, they wanted me to be the one who paid the price. Not Nell. Not you.'

'How do I ever live with the knowledge I killed her; that I'm the child murderer, not Creepy Cawley?'

'I can't answer that, love. But until last week, you'd been living a good life, doing good things. Continue doing that. Only time will tell how you will deal with it. I'm sorry it came out, I really am.'

Epilogue

2019

Mapledon Church

Thursday 2nd August

The coffin was white. Tiny.

Tina Hayes walked beside Pat, her head bowed, as he carried Jonie's remains down the aisle.

She'd waited for thirty years to put her daughter to rest – to finally fill the empty grave she'd tended to during that time. The tears spilling down her face now were ones of relief. She'd spent all the tears for grief over the years. Finally, she was able to say goodbye.

Only a handful of people joined Tina and Pat to pay their respects, sitting quietly and very still, in the first pew. Tina had let her thoughts be known prior to the service: the villagers of Mapledon were *not* welcome. It was family and honest friends only. Billy Cawley wasn't there either. As much as Tina would've liked him to be, she knew he wouldn't be allowed within ten miles.

She'd spoken to him several times after he'd found Jonie's bones. He took the blame, as he said he would. After Eric had shown him the site where he and Reverend Farnley had buried her, Billy had contacted the police. Told them since he'd been released he'd been determined to remember where the body of little Jonie Hayes was, telling them he'd visited the area and recalled the location and wanted to do the right thing.

He'd known there'd be refreshed media interest, but Lizzie had helped out there – she'd arranged an exclusive interview with the 'man who'd murdered Jonie Hayes', making sure she only revealed what was necessary and rounding off the article with how William Cawley had been released on parole from his thirty-year prison sentence having proven he was capable of change; his risk to the public had been reduced by successfully completing the required rehabilitation programmes. She'd reiterated he'd remain on parole until his death and that he was now attempting to rebuild what life he had left.

Lizzie had been surprised that Billy had refused to apply to the high court to gain a new identity, preferring to stay as William Cawley despite the possible repercussions. He was, however, keeping a low profile, remaining in the caravan on the farmer's land. Lizzie had the *real* story, the one recorded on her phone that night; she'd kept it just in case. There were two separate audio files: the one from the bungalow, and then the one she'd instinctively began recording when she'd stepped into the Fishers' house later the same evening. It was *that* one she'd copied to a USB.

Billy'd left a note for Tina. Given her an open invitation to visit him sometime if she wanted. Tina knew she'd take him up on it. It was the least he deserved. He'd performed a selfless act for which Tina would never be able to fully repay him. Certainly one the Fishers couldn't.

Even though Billy couldn't attend, Lizzie had. She and Dom had travelled down especially and were staying at Bulleigh Barton B&B again.

'Thank you for coming,' Tina said as they walked to the grave in the churchyard, to Jonie's final resting place.

Lizzie smiled. 'Thank you for asking us.'

After the coffin was lowered and handfuls of earth were scattered over the shiny white lid, they began walking back to the gate.

'It's lovely to see you and Dom looking so happy,' Tina said. 'I'm glad some good came from this.'

'So are we. It's been a long journey. I'm relieved it's over,' Lizzie said. 'Sorry,' she said quickly, 'I didn't mean . . . that was so insensitive.'

'It's fine, Lizzie. Please don't. No need to walk on eggshells. This is closure for me.' She smiled, patting Lizzie's arm. But Lizzie caught the slight twitch of Tina's mouth as she uttered those words, saw the flicker in her eyes. Was this closure really enough?

'Thank you. We're actually talking about starting a family.' Lizzie looked up to Dom.

'Oh, that's fantastic!' Tina said.

'It is, isn't it?' Dom beamed.

'And what about you and Billy? Are you going to keep in contact?' Tina said.

'Yes, that's the plan. I want to keep an eye on him, check in regularly to make sure he's coping with life on the outside,' Lizzie said. She didn't add how she also wanted to make sure he didn't do anything that could land him back in prison. They'd had a heart-to-heart about Reverend Farnley after the revelations he'd been the one to abuse her as a child – and Lizzie got the distinct impression Billy didn't think the man had suffered enough.

They reached the gate, and for a moment they stood in silence.

'Come back and see us sometime?' Tina said. Her eyes glistened with tears.

'Of course.'

They hugged, and Lizzie took the opportunity to slip the small USB stick inside Tina's pocket before they each went their separate ways.

The church bells had stopped ringing.

'It's over,' Muriel said.

'Is it?' Anna drained the last of the coffee from her mug and placed it into the sink.

397

'Thank you for coming here today, Anna. I couldn't bear to be alone, knowing what was going on just up the road.'

'No, it's not the easiest of days, is it?' Anna said. 'But it's closure. For some, anyway.'

Muriel nodded, then said brightly: 'Your dad sends his love, by the way. He was here yesterday, popped in before he left for home.'

'Where is home for him now?'

'Some place in Somerset. He's been living there for years.'

'I thought you said he'd gone to Scotland?'

'He did. Back when all this first happened. But he couldn't stick the weather. Played havoc with his arthritis.'

'Oh, right. He's not going to come back here now? Seeing as the truth is out, surely he could?'

'No. Too much water under the bridge for that, love.'

Anna made a move towards the door. She wanted to head back home. Carrie had been beside herself worrying she'd be gone for longer than the promised day. Not surprisingly, she didn't trust Anna after she'd left her for almost two weeks in July. Since leaving Mapledon after the evening when it was revealed she'd killed Jonie, Anna was taking time to adjust to her newly acquired knowledge. Bit by bit she'd remembered that awful Wednesday afternoon, snippets of it coming to her in slow motion, like action scenes from a film.

She hoped one day she could forgive herself, but she didn't hold out much hope of that. The most she could manage was to live a good life now; be a good mum. She owed that to her dad. Eric had done what he did because he thought it was the only way to protect her. The only way he could ensure she lived a happy life. Whether she'd deserved that opportunity instead of Billy Cawley was a question she asked herself daily.

'Come back with me, Mum. Leave Mapledon – live with me and Carrie,' she said as she reached the front door.

'I'd never survive outside of this tiny village, Anna. It's my home. Where I belong.' Muriel opened the door, and Anna noted her quick, sideways glance to check there was nothing hammered to it. 'Mapledon looks after its own, love,' she said.

'Does it?' Anna said, kissing her mum on the cheek. 'Do you think Tina would echo that sentiment?'

Anna didn't wait for a response. She knew there wasn't one.

Driving up the hill, Anna looked in her rear-view mirror, watching her mother waving on the doorstep until she dropped out of sight. As she drove past a parked car, it pulled abruptly away from the kerb. She squinted, checking the mirror to see who the driver was. It appeared to be a woman, but she couldn't make out who. Anna didn't think much of it as the car followed a short distance behind her.

She turned onto the main road leading out of Mapledon.

Leaving the village and hopefully its ghosts behind her.

ACKNOWLEDGEMENTS

My thanks to my amazing agent, Anne – you are truly the best, and to Kate Hordern, Rosie and Jessica Buckman for your hard work and continued support. I'm so proud to be with KHLA.

Huge thanks to my fabulous editor, Katie – you go above and beyond and I'm very grateful for your enthusiasm and excellent editing skills. You are an absolute joy to work with. My thanks also to the rest of the dynamic 'Team Avon' – I thoroughly enjoy working with you all and thank you for continuing to publish my books.

As ever, I'm thankful for the unwavering support from my family and friends. Thank you to Doug, Danika, Louis and Nathaniel for being my inspiration and strength. My thanks also to Josh – you're all I could hope for in a son-in-law (well, you might be in about ten years…) and I am so thrilled you and Danika made me a Grammy! Isaac is utterly gorgeous, and I cannot wait to read him stories (not mine, obviously). And to Emily – thanks for making Louis happy and for being super supportive by reading *all* my books. My thanks, as ever, to my sister Celia, Pete and my wider family for their continued support and for coming to my talks and book signings – you are all fabulous. There'll always be two special people missing from these events and celebrations: my wonderful Mum and Dad – I miss you both. But I know you'd have been proud of your 'clever' daughter.

I loved writing *I Dare You* – I felt it stretched me as a writer and there were some interesting challenges along the way. Massive thanks to my talented friend Lydia Devadason who helped iron out the first draft with her fabulous eye for detail. My thanks also to San and J, Tracey, Tara, Libby, Carolyn and Caroline – it means a lot to know I have good friends who I can turn to when things get tough.

Special thanks to Jon Meek from Waterstones, Newton Abbot, for his amazing support and for championing my books at my local store. I'm so grateful for your enthusiasm and for all your help with arranging signings and launches!

Thank you to those who help spread the book love – bloggers and reviewers do an awesome job and are always happy to support writers. I've been lucky enough to have lots of top bloggers shout about my books – I appreciate your hard work.

There are many other people who are important to me and during the writing of this book will have helped in some way. If I haven't named you, it doesn't mean you don't matter. If I'm also important to you, you'll know how thankful I am anyway.

Ultimately, getting my books into the hands of readers is the goal, and every time a reader tells me they've read and enjoyed one of my books I know it's all been worthwhile.

This is for my readers – I hope you enjoy my twisted offering . . . *I Dare You.*

Your daughter is in danger.

But can you trust her?

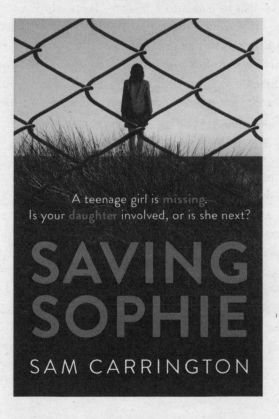

Available now in paperback and ebook.

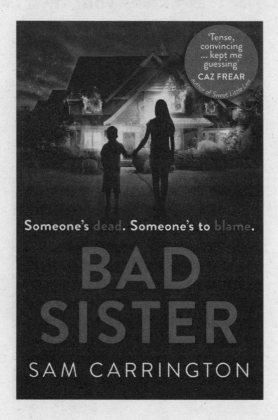

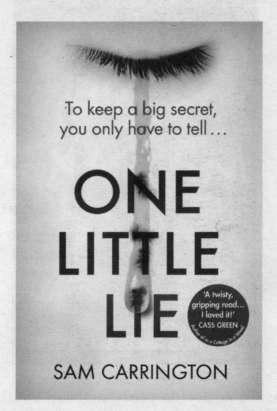

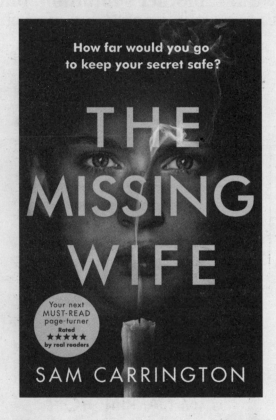